GETTING BACK

WILLIAM DIETRICH

GETTING BACK

William Dietrich

WARNER BOOKS

A Time Warner Company

WARNER BOOKS EDITION

Copyright © 2000 by William Dietrich

Cover illustration and design by Tony Greco

Warner Books, Inc.
1271 Avenue of the Americas
New York, NY 10020

Visit our Web site at
www.twbookmark.com

 A Time Warner Company

Printed in the United States of America

Originally published in hardcover by Warner Books
First Paperback Printing: March 2001

10 9 8 7 6 5 4 3 2 1

To June and Gordon

Acknowledgments

WRITING IS a solitary art but a book is a collaboration. I'd like to thank my agent, Kris Dahl, for encouraging the development of this idea, and my editor, Rick Horgan, for his enthusiastic insight, suggestions, and support. Interviews with several environmentalists—particularly Dave Foreman, one of the founders of Earth First!—contributed to the notion of creating a wilderness big enough to be lost in. (Though not through the means described in this novel!) The philosophical debates in *Getting Back* are inspired by real ones I encountered as an environmental journalist for the *Seattle Times*. My wife, Holly, made an indispensable contribution as research collaborator, Outback companion, and soul mate. Finally, I'd also like to thank the people of Australia. Their enthusiastic sharing of the continent was a vital contribution to this book.

GETTING BACK

PROLOGUE

Everything he knew was useless now.

There was a cold clarity to that realization, a crystallization of hopelessness that in its own odd way was bracing. It was the first coherent thought to penetrate Ethan Flint's panic in some time. He acknowledged, with an acceptance that was calming, that he was probably doomed.

The cries of pursuit were growing closer. The heave of Ethan's chest and pounding of his heart had quieted enough to hear the sound drifting across the desert, its harsh rasping reminding him of the caw of crows. He'd grown up with the urban birds, watching them multiply on songbird eggs until they flew across the endless rooftops like plumes of smoke, and they spoke in a language hard and aggrieved. It was a relative of that sound the fugitive heard now: human calls that were shrill, excited, and without remorse. It was a yipping designed to induce fear and at first Flint's brain had screamed the need to think so urgently that it drowned out every other thought. Now his peril was being more rationally—more grimly—absorbed. He was being hunted, but why? By whom?

The day had climaxed into an oven of punishing heat, the air so dry that Ethan seemed hardly to sweat. He understood this was an illusion. He was parched and rapidly dehydrating, despite his knowledge of how dangerous such a condition could be. There was so much he'd memorized before coming to the desert: the proper salt balance, his necessary caloric intake, the dimensions of a solar still, or how to splint a bone or identify an edible plant or make fire with a lens. He'd sought to be an aboriginal engineer, a wilderness technician. A lot of good it was doing him now! The plane crashed, his friends dead, his carefully chosen gear a growing deadweight. And now this unexpected pursuit. When running for your life you don't have much time to index-search the precepts of *Wilderness Comfort* on disk, he observed wryly. His peril would be funny if it wasn't so frightening.

Perhaps it was a bad dream. Certainly Australia seemed unreal. The sand was too red, the sky too blue, the desert brush a vivid, improbable green. Like a children's coloring book. The landscape shimmered and danced, its insubstantiality matching his sense of being trapped in a nightmare. But the pain was real. His head ached and every attempt to rest gave the flies a chance to find him again. Their buzz was as tireless as the sun.

The impossibility of his situation seemed so enormous that he had difficulty processing its logic. He was a sheeter, slang for a computer engineer who matrixed corporate spreadsheets into four-dimensional game theory, and his whole life was built on mathematics. He was an *artist* of the rational, his boss had praised him. A wizard, a master, a lord of the logarithms. Ethan had swaggered through code like Daniel-fucking-Boone. It was all worth squat right now, a fact that seemed cruelly unfair. Shouldn't all his work, all his education, and all his technological expertise give him *some* kind of edge? No. Of course not. Cops, credentials, résumés, diplomas: thousands of miles away. And he'd *asked* for this! Paid a small *fortune* to do it! Enormously funny, really. A tremendous joke on him. Clearly something had gone monstrously wrong—so nonsensically and outrageously wrong that he thirsted for not just water but retribution. Oh, what rank *incompetence* this confirmed among the bastards who'd sent him here! What *lies* they'd told by not telling him enough! If he got home he'd . . .

What?

Somebody would listen, wouldn't they?

If he got home.

Ethan glanced back. His glimpse of his pursuers produced an instinctive shock of fear. There was an animal wildness about them, a shedding of restraint, that was as unbound and tangled as their hair. He was so disoriented! Drugged for the flight, awakened in wreckage, the harried pilot who unstrapped him displaying none of the cool aplomb he'd come to expect. The aviator had punched out, parachuted down, and moved in anxious jerks, desperate to get away from the wreckage that smoked like a beacon. The plane had broken into two parts, the forward section with his dead friends skidding to the far side of a low rise. Ethan had wanted to go there but the pilot refused. "You don't want to see your friends."

Instead the rattled aviator had unscrewed a tail panel and unbolted an orange-colored electronic box, cursing as he struggled with the tools. Then he brusquely jammed the added weight into Ethan's already-stuffed pack. "This is what's going to keep us from having to walk to the beach," the man had explained gruffly. "If I can get the rest. Wait here." Ethan waited as the pilot trotted toward the nose, and when he'd become bored sitting in the heat and sand and finally trudged up the rise, thinking he was hallucinating a curious murmur of voices, he'd seen a swarm of scavengers who looked like urban groundlings. They'd pinned the pilot against the blackened fuselage like a trapped rabbit, their movements quick, their tone mocking, and their skin brown and hard as bark. "Get *back!*" they'd howled at the pilot. So Flint had run before he'd fully realized he was running, confused by the impression of faded synthetics and wooden spears, wire decorations and ragged hair, a melding of Stone Age and Information Age: twenty-first-century Huns.

Now he could hear their crowing. Getting closer. Drawing near.

Ethan was so tired. His feet felt made of concrete and he glanced down to check if the sensation was literally true. No, made of clay. The designer swirls of his Orion Supra boots had disappeared beneath a sheath of red dust, the laces ragged already. My, they'd been striking shoes! The urban boutique had been designed to look like one of the lost canyons of the Colorado, its walls sprayed with gunite and its light mimicking the desert sky, painting the rock with a day's rotation every hour. The boots had rested in a cleft beneath reproduced Indian petroglyphs, their sinuous curves caressed by a red beam of laser light emanating from the eye of a robotic eagle. The effect was as artful as a museum display and despite their ludicrous price he'd bought them instantly. The damn things still hurt, however, and they left gridded prints that mimicked the Manhattan street system, a conceit he'd thought cleverly ironic at the time. Now his tracks seemed as obvious as a sidewalk. He had to get out of the dirt and onto bare sandstone, in the approaching hills.

The thought of shedding the boots did not occur to him.

He did sling off his pack in a regretful acknowledgment that he was carrying too much, grunting in relief as it thumped down into the dust. Its colors had gone red as well. Time to lighten.

The task was painful. He'd spent months assembling this gear, web-scanning outdoor advice, downloading lists, and even shopping in *person* instead of electronically to signal his seriousness. This wasn't a wuss weekend of a guided trek in Patagonia or Nepal, dammit, this was *real*. The last wilderness! The toughest test left on the face of a fast-shrinking earth! The weeks of preparation had given his life an edge he'd never experienced before. Wilderness! He'd demanded the bottom-line best because it was his friggin' *life* that was on the line out here, by God, and he paid top dollar for it. Beautiful stuff, virtual jewelry of the outdoors, scratch-resistant, waterproof, shining. Now he had to leave it? Oh, the *outrage* he'd express if he got home!

He threw the computerized Global Positioning System out first. A week's wages, and so far it had delivered nothing but static. Baffling.

The laser range finder worked well enough but it only depressed him to learn how far away the distant hills really were. He abandoned that too. Both were left in open view: maybe such expensive toys would slow his pursuers down.

After two hundred yards he stopped and considered again.

The palmtop solar computer went next, its dietary calculations confirming what he already knew—that he was hungry—and its Library of Congress memory cache still entirely untapped. With greater regret he threw out the Symphony-Pod and headphones, the cellular receiver for satellite news, the foil solar oven, and the coffee grinder with wind-out antenna and stamp-sized TV. Pricey, precious stuff, designed to give his challenging trek a fringe of fun. Now it was metallic junk he'd trade for a liter of water. He sipped the last he had—a half swallow—and heaved on the pack again. Noticeably lighter, he thought bitterly, and none too soon: the faint whoops were drawing closer. He set out again at a half trot, climbing toward the cracked, polished rocks of ancient hills. They shone like cooked meat.

Despite his anxiety Ethan was slowing, the heat leaching his Health-Plus conditioning. Water was the problem, his throat thick, head light. A burst of effort, a long drink. After that, maybe, he could hide.

Figures flickered through the scrub below, his discarded gear eliciting caws of triumph. Ethan didn't know if his hunters wanted the gadgets or regarded his droppings as a kind of bleeding. They loped like wolves, burdened with nothing, and he conceded he was still carrying too much. But what more could he afford to lose?

At a rock overhang he heaved off his pack again. There was little choice but to jettison necessary items and circle back for them later. The tent, the Spider-Fiber hammock, the sleeping bag, the Duraflex cookware, the fuel cannisters, the battery packs. He yanked them out with furious jerks of his arm, angry at the waste. A change of underwear, his camp shoes, his digital recorder. All abandoned, just to get away. How he wished for a gun! But that was against the rules, wasn't it? Everything was against the rules.

He pulled out the orange-painted metal box the pilot had insisted he carry. Heavy as a shot put, dense as stone. This would get them back? He was a gadget freak but the instrument was unrecognizable. A switch, a button, a few socket ports. He flicked the switch back and forth, punching the button. Nothing. Well, the pilot said it wouldn't work by itself. Ethan hesitated only a moment and then heaved, watching the box kick up a spurt of dust before it tumbled into a ravine. Good riddance.

Then he started upward again, studying the surrounding hills. All he had to do was outrun them, hide, and come back. He was smarter than they were, right? He'd always been smarter than almost anyone he knew. So what insanity had brought him here in the first place? What was he trying to prove?

That he could survive, he reminded himself. That he could go into the wilderness by himself, face life at its most fundamental and formidable, and prevail. It would validate his existence as something more than a cog in a global machine.

Had he been seduced? Drawn into this place by a commercial come-on full of bland reassurances, peppy encouragement, and appeals to his own vanity? Or had he deliberately surrendered his head to his heart in order to break free of the logical prison his career had become, essentially making the decision to come here long before he'd heard of this place? He'd run to a continent that promised respite from contemporary anxieties and monotonous routine, a refuge from the tangled demons of his id. Maybe fear had brought him here. Or some pathetic dream of freedom. Another joke: he wasn't sure himself.

Ethan realized dimly that he was bleeding. The scrub was thorny and the grass pricked as he pushed through it, like a stuttering stab of electricity. Everything seemed hard and angular here: the rocks, the bushes, the light. As rough-edged as the city but in an entirely different way. Even the dirt was unwelcoming. Alive with ants.

He'd give anything for a drink of water.

He sensed more than saw the flicker of movement at the periphery of his vision. It was on the ridge above and disappeared as soon as he registered its presence. Ethan glanced wildly about. The calls had stopped, he realized: was it because his pursuers had fallen back? Or because their net was drawing tighter? He began to trot faster, his breath a saw against his throat.

There it was again! A silhouette on the crest of the ridge above, running easily, checking his location and then disappearing. Christ, the pursuers were even with his own position! They hadn't slowed to pick over his things at all!

He had to throw away the last of his old world.

He staggered as he let the pack slip off his shoulders a final time. It represented everything that was to have kept him alive. Now he swung it in an arc like an Olympic hammer thrower, grunting. The pack lofted out over a canyon and fell, thudding onto a steep dirt slope and skidding into scrub. He took a deep breath. While the loss of his pack left him floating with release, it also made him feel feeble. His armor had been stripped.

He set off at a dead run.

Ethan cut downhill, picking up some speed. Running to water! His pores were so dry that his skin stung. Puffs of dust shot up with each heavy thud of his boots, ankles twisting as he fought for balance on loose rocks.

Another darting blur at the edge of his vision, this time downslope. He frantically cranked his neck to either side. More shapes, pacing him, and he heard the pound of footfalls behind. What did they want, now that he'd shed everything he brought?

He cut to the left, following a broad ledge. The cliff shielded him from the view of any pursuers above and the drop to his right prevented those below from easily following. If he could just lose the ones behind . . .

The urbanite accelerated, his heart pounding, his vision dim. A shrill cry went up, high and warbling, and adrenaline jolted him like an electric prod. They were close! Too close! Faster, faster . . .

Ethan was in the air before he realized the ledge had ended. His legs chugged at nothing, his arms flailed. Like a silly cartoon character, he thought morosely as his panic gave way to a black, fundamental regret. Then he fell.

He hit a slope and tumbled, wondering dimly which bones would snap first. The calm clarity of it, the sober acknowledgment of miscalculation, surprised him. His fear had been replaced with stupid sorrow. What an ass he'd been for coming here!

Then he hit something hard, spun, and blacked out.

PART ONE

PART ONE

CHAPTER ONE

The city filled its vast central basin like a reservoir fills its impoundment, chains of linked town houses lapping at a litter-encrusted shoreline of brown, scabby hills. The hills had been set aside as park a hundred years ago and had slowly strangled into wasteland: neglected, junk-filled, eroded, dangerous. Eruptive urban growth had long since spilled past them and flooded the valleys beyond to bury farmland, swallow rural communities, and engulf remnant woods. This overflow of the urban grid had no final boundary: its horizons were lost in haze, its edges smeared by cancerous growth. The sky was stagnant white, the city gray, and the occasional splashes of architectural color only emphasized the monotony they were painted on. In this dense human colony land was like gold, space currency, and square footage the source of rivalry and aspiration. Houses were bonded like Siamese twins, or stacked like the comb of a hive. Each looked like its neighbor: cramped, clay-colored, straining for a scrap of view. Their yards were patios, scabby greenery enclosed in pots. On the worst days, when the light was flat and the wafer of sun melted at its edges like a seltzer tablet, the city was a hard, ugly place.

Yet the beast retained the seductive throb of human life. At night its arterials were ribbons of light and its tiled plain of asphalt and plastic roofs was broken by archipelagos of soaring skyscrapers and corporate pyramids. Malls were emporiums of bright commerce and cafés spilled onto sidewalks. Winking hovercraft darted like fireflies and info-lasers stabbed skyward toward satellites. Corporate names crested buildings like proud coxcombs, crowing with a glow of marketed pride. The beacons intended warmth, like the remembered reassurance of the lamp or tavern sign, but—bloated to football field dimensions—they instead drenched their neighborhoods with commercial glare. The sign war extended to the sky, where searchlights cast logos on nighttime haze, lasers flickered to announce openings or bankruptcies, and blimps drifted with holographic tidings. The city's signs were a galaxy of rival artificial suns and the pictures they cast were of an idealized, desired, half-remembered, and romanticized world: glistening beaches, convivial families, green meadows, detached houses. "In the world of United Corporations," read one, *"everyone can win, all the time."*

In Quadrant 43, between the St. Francis and Reagan Expressways, a twenty-first-century pyramid rose from its walled enclosure of plasti-marble plazas, boxed gardens, and black reflecting pools: a glass and metal pointed office building one hundred stories high. Its colored panels and opaque windows shimmered as they chemically changed mood with the time of day: the smoky blue of morning giving way to noon's perky silver, mellowing to a burnished copper as the day waned, and finally darkening to a swallowing black. The windows looked out, but no one could see in. Utility tubes popped from the ground and fed the pyramid's base like placental cords. Inside, Microcore's headquarters had its own shops, its own restaurants, its own banks, its own hydrogen pumps, and its own kiosks. It was a world within a world.

The chairman sat in her office at the pyramid's summit like an insect queen. Level and location on each of the one hundred floors below were allocated on the basis of rank. At each floor, supervisors occupied offices on the outer rim in a cordon. Within was a maze of cubicles that penned their subordinates, the partitions low enough to ensure that heads could be observed bowed in work.

This laboring center was a ghostly group. Even dark complexions looked pale from the flush of light that crept out from the edges of the opti-glasses that had replaced computer screens. The workers typed, murmured commands, clicked. The results created flickers of light that played across their temples like an echo of thought. There was little noise above the hum of Muzak, the beep of terminal signals, and the drone of ventilation. It was unseemly to yell, startling to laugh, and easier to communicate electronically. People had become extensions of the wires they were hooked to.

The chairman rode up and down the inner face of the pyramid in an elevator of smoked glass, hung from an angled track. The privacy enabled her to see the employees of each floor without being seen, the box whispering like a gray ghost. Everyone wondered, of course, what the chairman did when she rode up and down past her thousands of minions. Did she calculate profits, note empty cubicles, play a head-vid, point out a suggested promotion? No one knew. Few below the upper floors had ever seen her. Everyone strove for graduation to those upper floors.

At each level, an electronic ribbon of scenic vistas and encouraging slogans circled the central cubicles, giving a border of color. "Microcore," read one. "Where *win-win* is a way of life."

On Level 31, Cubicle 17, Daniel Dyson ignored the encouragement of the videograms and set his opti-glasses aside. He was preoccupied with a more personal goal: the quest for female attention. Specifically, Daniel had calculated that the walls of what he called the rodent corral— beige cubicle dividers, to match the beige carpet and beige desks and beige terminals and beige walls of Level 31—were high enough to allow him to secretly prepare, and yet low enough to launch, his latest experiment in physics and flirtation. Mona Pietri, Cubicle 46, was the latest woman of his dreams: dark-haired, doe-eyed, and curvaceous as a sine wave. Daniel suspected genetic and surgical supplementation had enhanced what nature had initially bestowed but was willing to embrace this commitment to self-improvement as a sign of inner beauty. God, she was stacked! She, in turn, was utterly oblivious to his existence. Which made her, of course, all the more desirable. Unable to concoct a corporate excuse to work with her, Daniel had decided to send an invitation to share the latest beverage craze (a Mongolian fermented mare's milk cappuccino, the latest morale booster of the corporate cafeteria) the old-fashioned way: launching it by catapult. Fate and physics would determine the arc of romance.

Daniel had constructed the miniature war machine out

of office supplies that had outlasted every promise of office automation in A.D. 2048: pencils for beams, thumbtacks and paper clips to drill and fasten, rubber bands for bracing and to provide torque for the catapult's lever arm. He attached the helmet of a Star-Trooper action doll to the arm with a combination of chewing gum and Bond-It adhesive. Within the helmet nestled his missile: a raspberry chocolate wrapped in a ribbon of paper. On the paper he had printed:

> *Mona*
> *I'm gonna*
> *Getta Mongo*
> *Will you gongo*
> *With me?*
> *Cubicle 17 (Daniel)*

Poetry was not one of the skills listed on his corporate performance appraisal. Still, he calculated its attempt was potentially more rewarding—or at least more interesting—than working on the software Meeting Minder, which was what he was supposed to be doing. A military history major in college ("And what are you going to do with *that* in a world of no armies?" his father had protested in futility), Daniel had an academic's understanding of how a catapult was supposed to work. Calculating its trajectory was a matter of trial and error, however, and Daniel figured he had only one chance at launching his bid for amour before supervisors put an end to his experiment. He'd done a few test firings across the width of his desk. Now he wound the torsion rubber band tighter to achieve the calculated distance and sighted toward Ms. Pietri's pretty head, as remote and alabaster as the moon. "One small step toward sexual chemistry," he whispered, hoping she liked chocolate.

"Fire!" A few neighboring heads snapped up. No one thought for a moment that a cubicle was in flames. It was just Dyson, who had a reputation for keeping things interesting.

The chocolate shot ceiling-ward, the ribbon of its message unexpectedly unreeling. That tail was enough to spoil his calculations. The projectile went awry and dropped like a meteor into the lair of Harriet Lundeen, the Level 31 floor manager. Its whap was a note of doom. The poem bore his return address.

"Uh-oh."

"If you're declaring war, Dyson, you'll lose," his colleague Sanford predicted from the cubicle next door. "The gorgon has never been beaten."

Meanwhile, desirable Mona hadn't even looked up.

Daniel waited a full minute for a reaction, time enough to hope his missile had fallen undetected or that Ms. Lundeen had elected to ignore his misfire for the price of a chocolate. Maybe she was hoping *she* could meet him for a Mongo, the old bat. He covered his catapult with waste paper in the desk basket.

But no, here she came with the countenance and body of a Wagnerian Valkyrie, lacking only breastplate and horned helmet. The ribbon poem was held out like a piece of decaying meat.

"Is this *yours*, Mr. Dyson?"

"You looked hungry," he tried.

"My name is not Mona."

"That's true. Actually, I was routing that to Ms. Pietri."

"I see." She sighted toward the goddess of Cubicle 46.

"And 'gongo'? What does that mean? Is it lewd, or are you merely witless?"

Dyson smiled with as little sincerity as he could muster. "I'm trying to be creative, Ms. Lundeen. It's asking if she'll go with me. I think it makes sense, in the context of the poem. Like *Jabberwocky*."

Sanford snickered.

"Jabber what?"

"It's another poem."

Lundeen considered whether he was putting her on. "Your literary taste is as bad as your aim," she finally decided. Then she glanced sourly around his cubicle. "And your discipline." Every other employee on Level 31 had adhered to the request to maintain an "orderly and respectful desktop decor" in line with corporate atmospheric guidelines. Dyson's, however, was a pocket of cluttered individuality: pictures of climbers on Everest and camels in the Sahara, bearded revolutionaries of the nineteenth and twentieth centuries, two tattered pinups discreetly draped with Microcore calendars, a meditatively chewed plastic stegosaurus, several holo-movie figurines, parts from a magic kit, food wrappers, stained cups, and a Cuddle Doll with a noose around its neck.

"I was just straightening up."

Her stare was not amused. "Cultivate conformity, Mr. Dyson."

He tried to look solemn. "We all aspire to be like *you*, Ms. Lundeen."

She held up the chocolate. "You could do worse." She put it into her mouth and repeated a habitual warning as she chewed. "If you can't adapt to Microcore, you may end up in a place even less to your liking."

It was an empty threat, he knew. Employees were like

barnacles: you could hardly pry them loose with a stick of dynamite. "That's hard to imagine," he said.

"So is your promotion." Daniel's poem fluttered into the wastebasket.

Sanford came around the cubicle wall to fish it out. "Will you 'gongo'?" he read.

Daniel shrugged. "I needed a rhyme."

His colleague shook his head. "You're never going to bongo Mona Pietri with lame stuff like 'gongo,' Che." The nickname was taken from one of Daniel's revolutionary pictures. "Why don't you try being normal instead?"

"Because I'm not," Daniel replied.

He went for a Mongo by himself. Lights brightened and then dimmed in what was marketed as an "architectural warmth cocoon" as he walked down the pyramid's corridors, the bubble of light making him feel on stage instead of cozy. A soft female voice activated in the walls as he strode, reminding him of corporate philosophy. "You are your group," she murmured seductively as he passed the copier room.

"Profit makes possibility," she reminded near the Telecom pod.

Daniel took the stairs instead of the elevator. "Work for a good retirement," she whispered as he trotted down the steps.

Her voice followed him to the hallway, the rest room, the cafeteria line.

"Share the enthusiasm."

"Change is risky."

"Believe in belonging."

The voice was as unheard, and omnipresent, as the

shadow-Muzak it interrupted. It cajoled, nagged, promised.

The cafeteria chatter was of web celebrities, game scores, designer drugs, faddish restaurants, and clone-organ operations. An accountant's bray of laughter was so obnoxious that Daniel thought the donkey should clone himself a new head. Then he sat alone, sipping his sour drink and imagining improvements to his catapult. "I hear you're seducing harridan Lundeen," someone called from across the room.

Daniel ignored the comment, stacking sugar tablets into a castle wall. Someday he wanted to defend a real castle.

Sanford came through the line and slid into a seat opposite. "The gorgon won again," he judged.

"I don't care what that old biddy thinks." Dyson sipped his Mongo, wincing at its taste. They said it was an acquired habit.

"It ain't what she *thinks,* it's what she can *do.* She called maintenance to do some midday cleaning."

"So?"

"Your wastebasket is empty now."

The catapult! "Shit. I thought she hadn't noticed it."

"When are you going to learn, Dyson? Go along to get along."

"I *try* to get along. It's not my fault everyone but me is crazy." He sipped again. It was possible he was the only real human being on earth, he'd theorized, and everyone else was a participant in an elaborate hoax to fool him, for unknown but no doubt evil and nefarious reasons. This could explain why everyone else seemed to tolerate a bureaucracy that drove him crazy. "The catapult actually worked rather well, I thought. The problem was the payload."

Sanford resisted any temptation to congratulate his engineering. "Sanity is the most democratic of definitions, my friend," his workmate counseled. "The majority gets to decide what's normal. Odd man out is the one who gets labeled insane."

Dyson pointed to his brain. "Maybe I'm just ahead of my time. The mark of genius."

Sanford laughed. "I'll put that on your urn registry. 'He was right after all.' I'm sure it will be a great comfort when you're dead."

"Or behind. Maybe I was born two hundred years too late."

"Judging from your office political skills, I'd say you were born yesterday."

Daniel's smile was rueful. "Mona, I'm gonna," he promised softly.

"You still have a chance. I just saw her in Telecom. No doubt word has gotten around and given you an excuse to talk to her. 'I built an engine of destruction and crossed the horrible Harriet Lundeen just for you.' What woman could resist?"

Daniel sighed. "Just about every female I've met since third grade." He stood. "Still, ours is not to wonder why, right old chap?"

"Aye! Ours is but to mate and die!"

"Remember the Alamo!"

"Don't fire until she rolls her eyes!"

"Into the breach, my friends!"

"Hey. Don't talk dirty."

*　　*　　*

Mona Pietri was struggling with the Telecom console. New features had been added that theoretically doubled its speed and realistically multiplied the ways in which it could possibly malfunction by a factor of five. The snarl of error messages gave Dyson a chance to introduce himself and demonstrate male prowess, though in truth he didn't know much more about the console than Mona did. Still, he bluffed his way through to a "ready" promise on the view screen by hammering on the machine's buttons. She granted him a look of approval, giving no hint she knew she'd been the target of romantic bombardment less than an hour before.

"I don't know why it has to be so complicated," she pouted. Instantly, he was in love.

"Microcore's purchasing agents make three times as much money as we do buying this junk and then depend on us to document the need to upgrade it," he explained. "If we ever mastered our equipment, their usefulness would be over. It's *designed* to torment."

She looked uncertain. "I don't think the corporation really intends that."

"Oh, but they do. Microcore is a pyramid built on a program of ever-increasing complication. 'We make things hard so you can take it easy,' but of course it never gets easier at all. Microcore snarls, so it can cut its own Gordian knot."

"Its what?"

Maybe he could impress her with trivia. "Gordium was an ancient city. The chariot of its founder was tied to a post by a knot so complex that legend promised it could only be untied by the future conqueror of Asia. Alexander the Great came to the place, considered a moment, and then cut the knot with his sword."

She nodded hesitantly.

"He fulfilled the prophecy, you see. Just like Microcore fulfills the promise on its box that *this* software will cut the knot created by its last box. Of course our sword ties a new knot to replace the old to ensure a market for next year's release. It's the way of the modern world."

"It's your job."

"Our job. 'Microcore, where reinventing the need for our existence is a way of life.'" He grinned. "It's vapid, but it feeds us."

Mona looked uncomfortable. "I don't think you should be so negative," she decided. "I don't think it helps the group."

Miscalculation! "I'm not negative. Just honest. Candid."

"I don't think you believe in what we're doing."

"Look." He considered what to say. "I'm just trying to analyze our market role clearly and find some humor from poking fun. I don't really object. I just look for opportunities to show . . . initiative."

She brightened at that. "Initiate consensus!" she recited approvingly, remembering the corporate slogan. "Plan time for spontaneity! Discipline toward freedom!"

He looked at her with disappointment. "You've been listening to the walls, I see."

She nodded. "I've memorized them all. Maybe you should too, Daniel. I think you'd be happier if you better understood why we're all here."

CHAPTER TWO

Alone again. That evening, Daniel lay back in the viewing chair of his cramped studio apartment and cruised his video wall. He'd been putting off an upgrade and the chips that drove it were a little cheesy—he hated the planned obsolescence that forced him to keep up—but it still managed to generate convincing three-dimensional imagery in colors brighter than real life. Sound rippled around the corners of his small room like a brook around a boulder, splashing him. "Welcome, Daniel," a female voice greeted in a whisper. "Have *you* invested in *your* future today?"

He began to net-surf, skimming across a downloaded rush of tropical beaches, mist-shrouded mountain peaks, and adrenaline-jolting thrill rides. A dinosaur roared, an elephant trumpeted, and Napoleonic cavalry thundered into a smoky valley, his chair rocking slightly with the drum of the hooves. Women more impossibly beautiful than any he'd ever actually seen beckoned alluringly. "At Turner-Murdoch-Disney," an avatar-guide purred, "we promise the *best* in fantasy entertainment! Experience utter danger without the risk of real injury, exquisite sex without commitment or disease! Any time, any place, for any reason: as always, your securi-lock keeps your fantasies as private as your own mind! So come dream with us, with the aid of the finest actors and writers and technicians in the world . . ."

Yet nothing caught his fancy. He clicked restlessly, the usual vividness seeming flat and artificial. "Click 1-800-Companion," a program tempted, "because friendship *can* be bought . . ."

That one mocked him. Mona, I'm gonna . . . call 1-800? Pretty pathetic, Dyson, he lectured himself. My life spent in video half-lives more interesting than my own. Click, click, click, flick, flick, flick. Reality, then! The news was of rare, remote disaster that confirmed his own safety. The market twitched to tremors too faint to feel. Commentators excitedly recorded the linkages and breakups of celebrities he could never hope to meet. Economic indicators were up—*everyone can win, all the time*—but then they were always up under United Corporations. Or about to *go* up, or taking a breather after a sprint of upness. He skimmed like a skipping rock over the bloated bandwidth, numb from the predictability of it. Newer, better, faster. The more insistent the promise, the more his own world seemed to remain unchanged. There were fads, of course: quick, insistent, and forgotten until economically recycled by nostalgia and irony. His closets were filled with the detritus of fads. All closets were. All fads were global now.

He clicked and tapped, following the links his hacker pal Fitzroy had taught him. The web had grown so vast it was fundamentally unexplorable, unpoliced. Its sites outnumbered the population of the planet. It had become a gargantuan network of electronic rooms, corridors, passageways, and barriers: endless, tangled, secretive, and dreamlike. As deep and unknowable now as the human mind, a haunt of inner fantasy and murky rebellion. A descent to its cyber underground was like falling down a rabbit hole.

Had he found them or had they found him?

They'd come to him first, he remembered, but probably only after being alerted to his discontent by his e-mail whinings or his grousing to some co-worker who already belonged. It was hip to not take United Corporations seriously. So popping up on his wall out of nowhere one evening had come a single word that intrigued him:

Disbelieve.

Then an Internet address into a laborious maze with just enough irreverence to be tantalizing. There was a shadow net under the official net, he knew, a Hades of the skeptical and the unhappy. Its coding was breakable, to be sure, but it took the authorities time to find and break. The illicit nature of it was thrilling. But finally he'd come to some electronic doors that barred further descent.

Keep Out.

He cracked some code, made some end runs, guessed some riddles, and received a few half-baked conspiracy theories for his trouble. He was still too straight, bogged in the cyber underground's tar: the corporate drone, the hacker who couldn't quite hack it.

Frustrated, he called Fitzroy.

"What the hell do you want that garbage for?" the ex-cop had growled from his video wall. Fitzroy hacked code for a living now, making three times the money he'd earned policing it. He'd found Daniel floundering on the web once, offered some free advice, and then regularly milked him of money for one insistent need or another. "It's just a bunch of loonies. Rumors as news. Losers."

"They're different."

"So is a rehab ward for the morally impaired. You want to spend a month there?"

"Come on, Fitzroy, can you get me in or not?"

"I can get you started. Then you have to play along with their paranoia while they suck on your bank account. It's a scam, Dyson."

"I'm bored. I've heard rumors about these guys. They *question* things."

"Ask 'em how many answers they've got." But he sold Daniel enough passwords and puzzle solutions to get him in.

Daniel found himself in a gothic mansion of paranoia, an odd net-world of conspiracy theories, web-porn, unproven sex scandals, dark fantasy, irreverent satire, pseudo-science, alien abductions, and rambling political discourse. Garbage, Fitzroy had predicted. People who preferred to believe the bizarre over the mundane no matter how improbable. Links were constantly disrupted by authorities trying to police the net of trash and new cells opened up as fast as old ones evaporated. Postings were made by characters calling themselves Swamp Fox and Robin Hood. It was a game.

So Daniel surfed after his failure with Mona Pietri because he was more thrilled at being there—at being *in*—than with any information he was finding. *"If everyone wins, how do we feel what it means to lose?"* pleaded a posting this evening. *"If this is heaven, where is hell?"*

"Level 31," Daniel offered lightly, typing. "A Microcore help menu."

"Who is Satan?"

"Harriet Lundeen." Maybe someone would pick up the name and she'd flicker through a hundred conspiracy theories. The gorgon, unmasked. He laughed to himself.

"What if you could really fight evil, Daniel?"

He stopped at that. Who was this cowled figure looming on his screen who knew his name? You never used your real name in the cyber underground. He explored under the sobriquet Gordo, taken from an action toy he kept on his desk. Gordo Firecracker, nemesis of evil.

"How do you know my name?"

"I am a would-be friend."

Daniel paused. He was suspicious of would-be friends. He knew there were informants, spies, and censors who cruised the web, occasionally making an embarrassing arrest. Still, he was curious.

"Who are you?"

"I am Spartacus. I am Robespierre. I am Thomas Paine and Vladimir Lenin and Vercingetorix and Crazy Horse. We exist, Daniel. We oppose. The cyber underground is more than a toy. The world has gone into a coma and we want to wake it up."

He hesitated at that. There was an unspoken line between satire and treason, and this kind of stuff was subversive. Illegal. But kind of cool too. That's what he wanted to do, wake up. How secure was the encryption on this site?

"Are you brave enough to help?"

Yeah, you chicken, Dyson?

"Are you intelligent enough to care?"

Care about what? That was the problem, wasn't it, that no one cared about anything anymore. "Help with what?" he typed.

"Do you know what a truth cookie is?"

Ah. Software vandalism. "I've heard of them." A prank virus or a sophomoric Trojan Horse. Saboteurs slipped them into web products sometimes, like Microcore's. You ran the application and some illicit message popped up. Dumb stuff, mostly. Jokes, digs at the rich and famous, or kooky theories of oppression and malfeasance. Water cooler talk. But they worked like a kind of underground newspaper, the opposition's version of reality. The whole practice was more annoying than threatening to United Corporations. There were electronic screens to weed the junk out, and employees suspected of inserting a truth cookie or reading too many of them sometimes wound up being given an "opportunities transfer" to a lower level. Dangerous as hell, really, to play with this stuff. And fun to sneak looks at it.

"We need your help, Daniel. The world needs a truth cookie in your product. The world needs to wake up. We can make it safe, very safe. All of this is encrypted. Your electronic tracks erased. It's risk-free, if you trust us."

Trust who? Daniel felt a flush of tension. "I don't have the expertise." How could he slip a cookie into something like the Meeting Minder? It had to be impossible.

"We'll teach you."

"I don't have the truth."

"We'll show you the truth. Look at this. It needs to be known."

Some code flashed on his screen. It was a series of encryption keys, a path into some company's database. An address within it. They wanted him to look at some file.

"I don't know you," he protested, typing. I don't trust you, he thought. A faceless cowl, a challenge out of nowhere. Who was this guy?

But Spartacus was already gone.

The code hung on his screen like the grin of the Cheshire cat, taunting him. You chicken, Dyson?

He got up from his chair a moment and moved restlessly around his dim apartment, a cat prowling its cage. This was real, wasn't it? Not a vid fantasy but real people, doing real resistance, provoking the establishment. Questioning, challenging, free-thinking. But for what? What difference would it make? There were power struggles on the United Corporations board, yes, but the world was too comfortable to tolerate real change. People rose and fell, but the consortium of corporations that ran the world prevailed. No one *wanted* truth cookies. Not really. Except that everyone read them. Repeated them in whispers. Added them to the nagging doubts and list of jokes. And now he was being asked to be a part of it.

How had they found him?

But then he'd found them, hadn't he?

Daniel sat back down and began going through the gift of code. As he'd suspected, it was for a company. Something called GeneChem. Another bioengineering firm, it seemed, one of thousands. The numbers took him past its electronic doors, into its vaults, and then into its cabinet drawers. Stealthily, slyly, like a thief in the night. It was slick, easy, unbelievable. A true insider had delivered this code. Like grease through a goose. He snatched, downloaded, and as fast as he was able, he was out and off the net. Damn!

He let out a breath. He'd been sweating.

The file was a memo, he saw. Scientific gobbledygook, most of it. He skimmed it once and then went back to read carefully. Once, twice, three times before he really understood it. More gene-splicing, playing with

DNA. Nothing new there. This time it was for cereal grains, he gathered, and the variation . . .

Would spread disease. To insects. Wiping out some pest species entirely.

So?

But after Australia, wasn't that illegal?

Truth cookie. Could he do it? Did he want to do it? And if he did do it, would it make him some kind of outlaw in the Sherwood Forest of the cyber underground?

Cultivate conformity, Harriet Lundeen had advised.

But she didn't have a secret, did she?

He'd sleep on it.

CHAPTER THREE

In the mornings he ran to run free. His favorite time was the stillness of predawn, when the city lights were fading and the sky was luminescent pearl before being bleached by full morning. The air was still stale from urban inversion but had always cooled by night's end, and the rhythmic pounding of his feet down the urban canyons put him in a trancelike state that lifted him out of his surroundings and into a different, imagined world: empty, clean, uncomplicated. It was the same fantasy world he chased in his hasty vacations and urgent weekends. He ran because he was calmed by the thump of his own pulse. He ran because exhaustion replenished him. He ran because sweat made him clean. He dreamed of running so far that someday he would reach an edge, an ending, and a new beginning, but he never did. The city just went on and on and at the end of the longest runs—when he was bent, heaving, his droplets of perspiration striking to make stars on the pavement—he was always where he had begun: in the grid, the community, the perfect inescapable world of

United Corporations. Breathless, wrung out, trapped, alone.

Then three mornings after his challenge from the cyber underground, she ran by him.

She wore her dark hair under a cap that day so that in the dimness he thought she was a man at first, given her easy lope and tall confidence. Women usually stuck to the security of the clubs to avoid unfiltered air and urban grit and the sullen stares of the drug-dazed groundlings who lay listless in the shadows. This woman did not. At first Daniel used her passing simply as an incentive to quicken his own pace, keeping up but hanging back fifty feet. Only slowly did the details of the runner's gait and figure make him realize he was following a female. He was intrigued but concerned. She was not just outside, but alone—and thus courting risk that couldn't be calculated, danger that couldn't be calibrated. In a world of ever-improving safety, longer lives, and cradle-to-grave security, what rare dangers remained created in ordinary people an ever-rising anxiety. Life had become a series of guarantees, and to abandon actuarial certainty for the sake of an outside run seemed brazen. Because of that he was intrigued. Who would take such a risk? He followed her, the beat of their footsteps making a synchronous echo against the enclosing steel and glass, studying the nape of her neck and willing her to turn around. She ignored him.

The woman took a bridge across the concrete chute of a dry river and on past the rust of decaying freight yards. Daniel had never come this way. Weeds had rooted in the cinders of the tracks and he noticed white and yellow blossoms on their stalks, a sign of life's tenacity. She darted across a spray of broken glass, ducked through a gap in the fence, and jogged by the rust-reddened wall of a warehouse. She trespassed where whim took her, as if boundaries were something to be ignored. She ran across an overpass, through a wilted square of park, and down an avenue of gray and chipped apartment blocks. Then she abruptly stopped.

"Why are you following me?"

Daniel pulled up panting. She hardly seemed winded. Her face was slightly flushed and the exercise had put a sheen to it, he saw, her skin caramel, her eyes large, luminous, and dark. Her figure was formless beneath loose clothing but her face was quite arresting: not just pretty but intelligent, with a stamp of character, or at least self-assurance. High cheekbones, a sensuous mouth. A knockout, really. She looked at him curiously, wary, watchful. He swallowed, using his forearm to wipe his brow of sweat.

"I was worried," he tried to explain, not really certain what the explanation was himself.

"Worried?"

"About you."

"Do I know you?"

"No . . . No, of course not. I just rarely see other runners, and a woman . . ."

"So?"

"Just that you might meet someone . . ."

"The only other person out here is *you*."

He raised his hands to show they were empty. "I just . . ."

"Are you some kind of pervert?"

"No! No. But you should be careful . . ."

"Do you think I can't take care of myself?"

He smiled at that. "I get the feeling you can."

She seemed slightly mollified. "You shouldn't follow people. Not women. It's frightening." Her look flickered away a moment, distracted by a thought, and then came back boldly. She didn't seem very frightened.

They were silent, eyeing each other.

"Look, I apologize if I made you uncomfortable. My name is Daniel. I saw you and I was intrigued. Women don't run alone at this time. It might be dangerous to be outside."

"It's mentally dangerous to stay inside."

He paused. Daniel felt the same way, but he hadn't met a woman who shared the sense of being caged. The ones he knew seemed to enjoy their security. "The streets can be a maze. I run a lot. I thought maybe I could help you find your way."

"I'm trying to lose my way."

He stopped again, uncertain how to respond. Tiny beads of sweat had appeared on her forehead and she took off her cap, shaking her hair. It was thick and jet black, lustrous. Who was this woman?

"What's *your* name?" he asked.

She considered. "Is that important?"

He thought a moment. She was expecting an intelligent reply. "Some cultures named people for what they were, like Smith or Baker," he said. "Some thought you became your name. Some were named for things observed at birth."

She shrugged. "It's Raven."

"Raven . . . ?"

Her caution was understandable. "That's all you need to know."

"Okay. Named for your hair?"

She smiled. "If I was named for what I looked like at

birth my name would be Prune. Raven was a creature of legend. Smart, elusive."

"Like you?"

"Maybe. You said we become our names."

He nodded. "And what do you do?"

"I think a better question is *why* do you do."

"Why?"

"Think about it." She turned to begin running again.

"Wait!"

She glanced over her shoulder. "Yes?"

"I want to see you again."

"So run. Maybe we'll meet."

"No, see you where we can talk."

She turned to face him. "Are you asking me on a date?"

The question was so challenging he thought she was about to say no. "There's a good new restaurant . . ."

"Date restaurants are overpriced and pretentious."

Jesus. This was a hard one. "Well, I know a club . . ."

"I don't like clubs. It's too loud to hear, and when the music stops there's nothing worth hearing."

He took a breath. "What *do* you like?"

She looked at him, judging in a way he didn't entirely like, and for a moment something in her eyes passed like a shadow. "I like cyberspace," she finally said. "People have time to think before they communicate, and they have the anonymity to be themselves."

"I have to talk to you by e-mail?"

She laughed. "I like exploring."

"I do too. The cyber underground."

"The what?"

"Free thinkers on the net. They question things. Lead

you to new places." His offer was implicit: I can show you.

"Ah." She nodded but seemed unimpressed. "I've heard of that, I think. Unhappy people."

"Independent people."

She studied him again, his clothes stained with sweat, his manner betraying an underlying frustration, and came to a decision. "How about a different underground?"

"What do you mean?"

"Do you know the Pitney Tube stop?"

"Yes . . ."

"Meet me there tonight at nine."

"Tonight?"

"Yes." She smiled encouragingly. "Come hungry. Bring a light."

"A light? For what?"

But she was already sprinting for a corner before he had a chance to consider or change his mind. "Bring a sense of adventure!"

A sense of adventure. Daniel slipped off his opti-glasses, rocked back in his cubicle chair, and stared up at the acoustical cones which jutted like stubby beige stalactites from the ceiling of Level 31. When had he lost his? When he realized the planet was so thoroughly mapped that a palmtop and satellite could pinpoint your location to within a few feet of every rock and tree? When he was cut from enough teams that he went from playing sports to watching them? When he was bruised in enough relationships that he went from looking for commitment to avoiding it?

Adventure happened to other people. He'd realized by age fourteen that he was never going to be an astronaut or mineral aquanaut. Those anointed were special, their talent and selection by means mysterious and exclusive. How had their lives taken such turns? He was repeatedly urged to be ordinary, to fit in, to join groups. So he'd earned grades that were good but not special, made friends who were fun but not close, bought toys that were expensive but not meaningful. Taught that the universe was trillions of miles across and billions of years old, he came to the private conclusion that it probably really didn't matter then whether he, Daniel Dyson, dust mote of Creation, turned left or right. He went to school because you were supposed to, and got a job because you were supposed to do that: it was not that he wouldn't consider an alternative but simply that he had trouble conceiving of one. Everyone did what he did, and took more pleasure than he could in dressing to the latest fashion, embracing the latest fad, and being hip to the latest stars, food experiments, and electronic gadgets. In a mammoth world of migratory careers and anonymous neighborhoods, conformity was the route to community: it was how one *belonged*. All this left him feeling detached instead of included: the crowd would cheer when he would have preferred to observe in contemplative silence. Daniel had learned he could frighten himself with a thrill ride, excite himself with erotica, dare himself with adventure vacations, and exhaust himself in a gymnasium workout. But life? That, it seemed, eluded him. He was living his life waiting for life to show up.

His parents didn't sympathize with this dissatisfaction. "Life?" his father had responded scornfully to his complaints of aimlessness. *"Life?* Real life is getting kicked in the goddamned teeth. Life—for most of that goddamned history you study without seeming to learn a goddamned thing—was beating your brains out without reward: coming home so damned tired you can hardly sleep because of the way your body ached, and then getting up the next day to do it all over again. Life was getting sore and sick and old and passed over, or dying young. That was what real *life* was about. Life was *losing.* So now we have a system where you don't have to lose, where people are comfortable, where things don't blow up or break down or go off in unpredictable directions—and you're complaining you're *missing* something? What you're *missing* is sorrow. What you're *missing* is despair." When his father proclaimed this, repeating something scripted, his habitual quiet desperation would give way to the kind of choleric excitement that eventually killed him. Life? Who needs it? And then his father had dropped dead.

Daniel stood up from his desk, stretching his back. The room was dim, the flickering of his colleagues' optiglasses illuminating it like the cold firelight of an old television. There was the ambient hum of the hive. The head of a supervisor, round and featureless behind the smoked glass of one of the periphery offices, rose briefly in curiosity at his movement and then went down again, as placid as a grazing cow. Balloons floated above one cubicle, marking a birthday for Cynthia Eaton. Life's passages. On a table by the water cooler was a half-eaten cake.

What was *missing,* Daniel should have answered, was purpose. He'd succeeded in every task scheduled for him—school, a job, a home—except deciding for himself what success *was.* His father claimed to have suffered no such misgiving, accepting his corporation's goals. He'd lived anxious, died young, and seemingly been proud of the whole sorry progression of it. At least he'd defended typical existence with exasperated doggedness, believing it the path to the least pain. In actuality, Daniel *envied* his father's sense of belonging. But he didn't share that sense. He'd been excited by his first days at Microcore like any new employee, relieved that the trauma of job interviewing was over and anxious to get on with the business of finding an apartment, acquiring possessions, and maybe even hunting for a wife. Yet it seemed to him that the more the company spoke about opportunity, the less it offered, and the more it preached unity and profit goals, the more he felt alienated by its desire to absorb him and all his energies—to suck *his* life, whatever it should be, into the greater life of its pyramid.

Maybe he was too selfish. Maybe the others saw something he couldn't perceive. Perhaps that explained their enthusiasm. He didn't know.

Like many people, Daniel was a voyeur of lives that seemed more interesting than his own. He enjoyed cyber videos, movies, books, and music. He'd been bored by any practical course of study at university and so indulged himself with a pursuit of history: what his father called "the irrelevant weight of the past." There he could go back to a time when the world was still unmapped, and wit and skill were requirements for advancement. It seemed to him that choices were simpler then: to bend sail onto spars, blaze a trail, fight a battle. Life was more romantic, with a clearer trajectory of youthful ambition and mature accomplishment. At Microcore, things were backward. The young were promoted over the old. Enthusiasm was valued more than experience, provided loyalty was sufficiently demonstrated. The key to success was unity toward corporate goals and social cultivation.

Daniel resented these requirements because he wasn't any good at them. He mocked the system because of his own lack of confidence at ever being able to succeed in it. He constantly betrayed himself.

For a break from the monotony of code debugging, he walked to the supply room. He didn't need any supplies but he liked the smells of paper and glue in the room, a musty contrast to the antiseptic plastics of Microcore's corridors. He felt comforted by the accumulation of bulk products, like sheaves of arrows kept in a castle armory against attack by an enemy. Reams of colored paper were aligned like the ranks of Napoleonic soldiers, a bright and proud symmetry made glorious by the certainty it would be shattered—not by battle, he conceded, but rather by the more mundane sacrifice of memo and brochure. Glory! That's what life lacks, Daniel thought. The chance of sacrifice for a doomed ideal, or to run to a new world to create ideals for yourself. There was no *room* for glory in the modern world, he thought. No room for catapults.

Raven had said to bring a light, and he liked that. How often in the city did you have to provide your own illumination? Or heat? It was so bright you could never see the stars. He liked the serendipity of their encounter, a chance meeting that was now to lead to a rendezvous in a subway station. "Bring a sense of adventure!" He'd thought it wasn't needed. Maybe tonight, with this intriguing new woman, it would be.

CHAPTER FOUR

She was prompt, which Daniel had learned not to expect from women. *She* was waiting for *him*.

"Where are we going in the subway?" he asked.

"Not where you'd expect."

Daniel didn't really care. Her habit of answering obliquely amused him for the moment, and he frankly evaluated her at the entrance to the tube station as she'd evaluated him. Raven had not dressed in anything really feminine, but her cover-suit of synthetics stretched enough to show her to good advantage, slim but with some shape to her. Enough to make him curious to see her in something else. Her hair cascaded down her shoulders and subtle jewelry sparkled. Her choice was the understatement of a woman who understood her effect on men. Daniel had dressed casually but with thought as well, the walking shoes and durable denim shirt trying to suggest a kind of vigorous energy he calculated she might look for in a man. If so, she gave no sign she noticed.

"You look nice," he offered.

She smiled politely and dipped a shoulder to slip off a small backpack. "I carried this from home so now it's your turn for a while. It's dinner."

"When I suggested eating out, I didn't mean to be so literal."

"We're going to be far out. Did you bring a light?"

"I didn't know what you meant. I've got a flashlight, an antique cigarette lighter, and a matchbook. I would have brought a table lamp but it was awkward under my arm."

She laughed at that. "Good! It's best to be prepared." Then she skipped ahead of him and down the stairs into the tube station. He followed.

Commuters were still streaming upward to go home, trudging in a sluggish gray river of the rumpled and tired. None smiled. Whisper-signs tried to cheer them. "In the world of United Corporations," murmured one, "security assures happiness."

Daniel got out his fare card and prepared to breast the current but Raven tugged his arm.

"This way."

She ducked into a shadowy side corridor past posted signs that limited entry to authorized transit employees only. Did she work for the tube? They came to a locked door. A tapping of her fingers at the keycard panel and they were in, the heavy metal clicking behind them. They were in a maintenance storeroom, Daniel saw, filled with janitorial supplies. "You're a sanitation engineer?"

"I got the combination from a friend. He works here part-time."

"Ah." Was she looking for a mop and cleanser tryst? "Come here often?" he asked lightly, glancing around at the shelves of chemicals. "We could've just gone to my place."

She was at the back of the room, working at something on the wall, and didn't even bother to glance back at him. "Don't kid yourself." There was a clank and she lifted a vent grate to one side. "Come on."

There was a sign above the vent opening: ENTRY FORBIDDEN.

"Can't you read?" he joked.

She was already backing into a concrete chute, her legs dropping down out of sight. "Can't you think for yourself?"

He followed her to the back of the room and ducked his head through the opening. A concrete tube with rungs led into darkness below. Raven had already swung onto the ladder and was rapidly climbing downward, a light at her belt illuminating the next rungs. Daniel followed, mystified, his feet fumbling in the gloom.

When he reached the bottom thirty feet below he switched on his own light. Three tunnels branched out, bulbs glimmering distantly down two of them. There was the wet, dusty smell of concrete. "Are we supposed to be down here?" he asked.

"Who are you asking, Daniel? Me? Them?" She pointed toward the surface. "Or yourself?" She waited a moment for his answer, watching his face.

He looked around, then grinned at her. "Lead on."

She took the central tunnel and they emerged in a wider underground corridor, this one brightly lit by lamps every thirty feet. It stretched to a vanishing point in each direction, branching tunnels marked by ovals of shadow. There was a low hum of ventilation fans and a current of air. The concrete tube walls were lined with pipes, two of them a meter wide and others stepping down in size to an electrical conduit the width of a garden hose. Signs dangled with numbers and arrows. Dyson felt as if he was in a labyrinth. "Where are you taking me? To the minotaur?"

She glanced at him appreciatively. "A classical reference. Are you a scholar?"

"A history major. Damned useless, my father called it."

"Did he? What does your father do?"

"He died in marketing, a profession so futuristic in its outlook that he had a heart attack trying to stay trendy. He didn't regard history as merely irrelevant, he saw it as a threat to all he worked for. Which guaranteed I'd gravitate to it."

"He sounds like a man of strong opinions."

"Loud opinions, anyway. He believed in the kind of progressive change that keeps things exactly the way they are. I think he liked what the world became. Organized."

"And you don't?"

"It's dull."

"Do you really think so?" She looked at him with interest.

"I feel squeezed, sometimes."

"Yes." She nodded as if he'd given a correct answer. "And what about your mother?"

"She learned not to have opinions, which I guess made her minor in feminist literature useless as well. All theory, no practice. She used to say I inherited some of her waffle genes."

"And did you agree?"

"I didn't agree with much of anything after age twelve.

But like most kids I didn't prevail, I merely escaped. A history degree was my best revenge."

"You sound about as close to your parents as I am to mine."

"Too strict?"

"Too . . . absent. I was adopted." She didn't seem inclined to elaborate.

"When she was widowed my mother announced she was turning over a newly independent leaf," Daniel said. "Three months later she married a clone of my father and retired with him to Costa Rica on the insurance. I haven't seen her for two years."

"And you feel guilty?"

"Relieved."

She watched for some sign of how this estrangement affected him, but his mask was indifferent. "Well. My theory is that no one knows what's needed or useless until they're dead. Maybe not even then."

"So how do you choose?"

"You follow your heart."

"Even into the pit of the minotaur?"

"The mythical monsters have been sponged from our world, Daniel. We're not in a labyrinth, we're in the Utiligrid, the utility network that feeds the city. These tunnels go for miles—miles and miles. They lead to reservoirs, power rooms, sewers, waste masticators. It's amazing, really."

"And we're not supposed to be here."

"*I'm* supposed to be here."

"Why?"

"Because it makes me feel alive!" She lifted her head and shouted. *"Alive!"* The call echoed down the corridor.

"Jesus! You'll get us caught!"

She laughed. "Maybe. Are you frightened of that?"

"No." He glanced over his shoulder. "Just nervous, okay?"

"There's nothing down here but utility robots, with brain chips about as smart as the potato variety. And we're not hurting a thing by exploring. Come on, I can take the pack for a while. We'll go to our picnic spot."

"No, I've got it."

She teased him. "Gallant as well. A man of the past."

"Sometimes I think I'm in the wrong century."

"Do you?" Again, she seemed to be appraising him. It reminded him of the joke about a first date being a job interview that goes on all evening. She didn't offer agreement.

Walking the Utiligrid was indeed like exploring a labyrinth but Raven seemed to know where she was going. "I've learned to read the signs," she explained. Occasionally the ground would tremble from the passage of a tube train overhead, or they would hear the rumble of pumps from behind steel doors, but mostly there was a humming stillness, their steps echoing on concrete.

"It's eerie down here," Daniel said. "Empty, like a catacomb."

"Don't you like it empty? Everywhere else is full."

"I like to get away."

"Down here is an away that gets to the heart of things."

Suddenly a dot of red danced across them and there was a warning beep. A detection laser. They turned and saw the lights of a maintenance-bot growing in intensity as it sped down the tunnel toward them, its orange crown flashing. "Uh-oh," Daniel said. The machine could summon the police. "Run!"

He yanked her arm and they sprinted down a side tunnel, Raven actually laughing as they fled. There was a bang as the janitorial vehicle took the corner too hard and bounced off the concrete. Then it was wheeling their way, beeping madly, its dim circuitry probably assuming they were some kind of giant rat in need of fumigation. He turned into one tunnel and another, utterly lost, and then Raven sprinted ahead of him to lead, twisting this way and that in the maze like a deer as the alarm shrilled behind them. Daniel followed her as he had on the run, noticing the swell of her hips and rhythm of her bottom as she ran. You sexually hopeless lunatic, he scolded himself. Then she pointed above at a dark hole in the ceiling and sprang, grasping a pipe. She looped her feet to catch the overhead piping with her heels and then boosted herself up into blackness. Daniel jumped, pulled, and kicked his legs to follow. They were in a tube that led upward but his climb ended when he banged into a steel cover. There was just enough room under its lid to squeeze together above the pipes.

She was breathing hard, grinning at him as the robot cart went honking by underneath in what seemed to be a machine imitation of frustration.

"What if it calls for help?"

"I don't think the cops like to come down here."

He realized that they were pressed against each other to wedge in place and he could feel the softness of her hair. Her smell had the sweetness of slight perfume and the tang of sweat. He was considering whether to try to kiss her when she turned and kissed him, quickly and hard. "That was fun!" she whispered.

"You're going to get us detained."

"No. The robots are stupid."

He leaned forward to kiss her again but she pushed him back. "We can't stay here, though, in case they search this quadrant." She dropped down through the pipes to land lightly on the floor.

"I thought you said the cops don't come," he called down to her.

"I've never seen them, but . . . Come on, before it comes back."

"Great." He dropped to follow her jogging form through the corridors.

She turned this way and that with determined purpose, glancing upward at the dangling signs periodically for reference. The frantic beeping of the robot quickly receded and they began to relax, slowing to a brisk walk. As Daniel got his breath back he noticed a background murmur that rose in volume until it became the roar of falling water. She led him into a side passageway and down a flight of wet steps, his curiosity growing as the noise grew. Then out onto a balcony grating.

"The water comes from the mountains," Raven said. "Someday I want to see its source."

They were overlooking an underground reservoir, lit by only a few lights. A vaulted ceiling receded back into darkness. Water was pouring in from an unseen pipe, creating a pattern of ripples that sparkled in the artificial light. The water glowed blue, emphasizing the cistern's clarity.

"This is my private spot," she said. They sat.

"How'd you find this place?"

"I've been coming down here for two years."

"And you never got lost or caught?"

"No one ever challenged me. I started drawing maps, deciphering signs, and slowly figured it out. It's been like exploring an underground world. When I found this reservoir it was like I'd discovered my own private lake."

"Less pretentious than a restaurant, quieter than a club."

She smiled. "Exactly. You should like me, Daniel. I'm a cheap date."

She opened the pack and took out their dinner. Ordinary stuff: farmed-salmon sandwiches, wedges of genetically enhanced vegetables, vacu-packed brownies. "What did you bring us to drink?" she asked mischievously.

He opened his mouth in surprise. He'd supposed they would buy something.

"No matter." She pulled out a small pail that was tied to a string and lowered it over the railing to the pool below. When it filled, she lifted it up and sipped. Then she held it out to him with two hands like an offering.

"Is it safe?"

She laughed again, that delicious laugh. "It's the same water in your apartment except it hasn't flowed through the grub of city pipes yet. This way I don't have to carry a canteen. Water's heavy."

He took the pail and drank, watching her over the rim. It seemed sweeter and colder than the water at home. "I'll bet this is against the rules."

"Everything is against the rules, isn't it?"

"Everything that's good."

They ate quietly a moment, Daniel unsure whether he liked her or was merely intrigued by someone so eccentric. It would be interesting to get her in the same room with harridan Lundeen.

Yet despite the kiss and her trespassing boldness she also seemed somewhat shy, he judged. Or at least reserved. Guarded. Her enigmatic replies deflected as much as they revealed, and she volunteered little. Why had she brought him here?

"This isn't exactly the great outdoors," he finally ventured, trying to feel her out.

"Don't you like it?"

"It's weird. Interesting. Not a typical choice."

"I'm betting you're not a typical man."

"And you're not a typical woman?"

"No."

He made a guess. "A loner?"

"I'm not alone with you."

Daniel took a bite of brownie, watching her. Pretty. Smart. A bit full of herself, maybe. Self-absorbed, certainly. But interesting too. He leaned forward slightly and watched her unconsciously lean away. Standoffish: she liked to control relationships. Her assertion of leadership kept her safe.

"Why did you bring me here?" he asked.

She smiled mischievously again. "You're cute. Handsome, even."

He rolled his eyes.

"No, that's not it," she corrected.

"Thanks, Raven."

"It's more that you're curious. That you think. That you question. That you explore."

"Like you."

"Maybe like me." She sipped from the pail, setting it down. "So. Have you decided why you do?"

He sat back. "I don't understand what you mean by that."

"Well . . . what do you do?"

"I work on software at Microcore. Dumb stuff. I hate it."

"Why?"

"Because it's pointless. Right now they've got me on a project called a Meeting Minder. It tracks your schedule and analyzes its patterns, prescheduling based on your past activity. The goal is to make the next year as close to the last one as possible, for maximum efficiency. They're expecting a best-seller."

"I know it's *dumb*. I meant, why do you work on it?"

He looked at her in surprise. "Because it's my job. Everyone has a job."

"Why?"

"'United Corporations has the right job, in the right place, for everyone,'" he quoted.

"No, *why?*" She looked impatient, as if he were slow.

He felt irritated. "What do *you* do?"

"I'm an investigator."

"Investigating what?"

She waved her hand. "Here. This. Now. Me. And you."

"Not exactly the wilderness."

"Something that's been explored by others can still be a wilderness to you, if it's your first time."

He looked around. "Well, you've got *me* lost."

"Do you like being lost?"

"I don't know." Was this a conversation or an interrogation? "It's not a question that occurred to me."

"Sorry. I ask a lot of things, don't I? I'm curious too."

"I'm not mindless like that janitor robot, Raven."

"I didn't say you were."

"You imply it by acting superior with your 'whys.' I think, I read, I have hobbies. I just built a catapult. I'm on a career track but I'm also my own man and I have adventures in my own way. Right now I'm trying to hack into Microcore's expense database. I want to put my bosses' obscene work charges on the corporate intraweb."

She looked interested at that. "Why?"

"Why, why," he mimicked. "You're like a two-year-old. Why? To elevate the gossip. To show I can."

"What's the point?"

"The point is that there is no point."

She began to nod, then shook her head. "I understand your point about pointlessness. But hacking into expense accounts is kind of juvenile, don't you think?"

"It's just a different kind of investigation, no different than this tunnel. I'm also in touch with the cyber underground."

"You mentioned that before. A bunch of people pretending, right? Rebels without a cause?"

"It's people who think for themselves. I think you'd be intrigued, if you tried it."

"Perhaps," she conceded. "But what's there to see, really?"

"You learn what's truly going on, without the United Corporations spin." He wanted to impress her. "You can use it to wake up."

"But do you really believe that stuff? I mean, I heard it was . . . crackpot."

"They put me inside another company, Raven. They let me download its secret."

Now she looked intrigued. She sat up straighter, tucking her legs beneath her. "What secret?" As conspiratorial as a schoolgirl.

"Well, I don't know . . ."

She leaned back, disappointed. "Rumors, right?"

"No, this was real." Could he trust her? Here was a soul mate, he hoped. Someone who felt like he did. "A file. Genetic plans by this company to modify cereal grains to transmit disease to insects."

She took another sip of water, watching him. "Bugs? What's wrong with that?"

What *was* wrong with it? It seemed less sinister when he tried to describe it. Was this really worthy of a truth cookie? Suddenly he was less certain. "It might wipe out whole species. It messes with the environment."

"Oh." She thought. "There's been a reform law, hasn't there? It's probably okay if all these scientists are working on it, don't you think? What company?"

He was discouraged at her reaction but didn't want to back down. "GeneChem."

"Never heard of them. But to play devil's advocate, they're not in business to screw up, right? They're not in business to break the law. We modify crops all the time. Have to, in a world with twelve billion people."

"So we unleash disease?"

"On insects, sure."

"What about Australia, Raven?"

"We learned from it, I hope." She glanced away a moment and then back, as if trying to decide whether to tell him something. "Look, I'm not endorsing this GeneChem. I'm just asking how are we—you and me—to know? We're not scientists. We're not management. There's a difference between poking fun and challenging expert opinion."

She was watching him again and he didn't know if this was what she really felt or if she was testing him somehow. Dammit, he couldn't figure her out. "What if this mutates?" he asked.

"What if grasshoppers eat all the wheat and the world starves? Daniel, civilization has been modifying crops for ten thousand years. Now this underground of yours gives you one file and suddenly you have a monopoly on truth? Maybe there's more to the story."

"You sound like United Corporations. 'Trust us. You don't see the big picture.' Their patronizing attitude drives me crazy."

"I'm not patronizing you."

"Then kiss me again."

She looked suddenly uncertain, and turned away. "No." She wanted to, he was sure of it.

"You kissed me before."

"I . . . I was in the moment."

"What about this moment?"

She turned back, taking a breath. "I don't have to kiss you just because we came down here, or just because I did it once, or just because you're hacking corporate secrets, or just because I'm playing devil's advocate."

He slumped back. "Okay. All right already."

"I *want* to kiss you, except . . ." She paused, uncertain, looking at him curiously as if he baffled her as much as she baffled him. There was something she wasn't saying. "This electronic snooping is . . . in the establishment's arena, you know? Their game. I brought you down here because it seems outside that world. I thought you might feel the water, the magic of this place. I don't think you did."

"How do you know what I feel?"

"I know."

"I don't think you even know how *you* feel, Miss Why. Or *why* you do. One minute you're breaking into utility tunnels and the next defending their witch doctory."

She looked down at that. She was thin-skinned, he thought, and there was a moment's satisfaction at pricking her. But the arguing was silly.

"Raven, I think we need to reboot." It was slang that had come from the early days of computers.

"Yes, I don't want to quarrel. I was just debating a point."

"About corrupting the ecosystem?"

"About feeding the world."

"So I should ignore this kind of GeneChem stuff? Ignore the truth?"

"You can't know the truth. None of us can."

"I know the sloganeering of United Corporations isn't the truth."

"But don't you accept it? Conform? Compromise?"

"I'm tired of compromising. I'm tired of being the odd man out at work."

Again she looked interested. "Why?"

He groaned. "Why am I tired?"

"Why are you always the odd man out?"

"My colleagues say I don't believe in anything, that I have no faith in what we're doing." He stopped, as if to consider the truth of that opinion for the first time. "I don't know. I just look at everything sideways and it comes out funny."

"What if the sideways view is the right one, Daniel? What if you're right?"

"What if they're right?" He shook his head. "Now

you've got me talking like you, going in circles. Waffle genes." He looked at her in discouragement. "I don't even know what side you're on."

"No. You don't know which side *you're* on. That's all I've been getting at."

He stood, suddenly tired of this. "Look, I'm sorry I disappointed you."

She stood too. "You didn't. It's for the best, I think."

"Am I going to see you again?"

She shook her head. "I don't think so."

"Okay. Fine."

"It's not for the reason you think."

"Sure." He glanced around. "Maybe you could show me the way out of here?"

"Listen," Raven said, reaching out to grip his arm. He started at her touch. "If we live in their world we make a thousand compromises, right? We take their pay, eat their bioengineered food. It's inescapable, correct?"

He looked at her gloomily.

"Unless we truly escape," she went on.

"But we can't, except to cyberspace," he said with exasperation. "That's my whole point. That's why the cyber underground is important. The world's one big company now, or at least a consortium of them. One country, one culture, one bottom line."

"What if it wasn't, Daniel? What if there was an alternative?"

"Escape? Where, down here?" He glanced up at the concrete ceiling. "No thanks."

"No, someplace else. Do something that takes courage to do."

"What do you mean?"

She took a breath. "I might go away. That's what I meant about not seeing you. Not kissing you."

He was puzzled at this. "Away?"

"There's an adventure company."

"Oh." Adventure travel was commonplace. Daniel had climbed, rafted, paraglided. "I've done that. It makes a good vacation."

"No. This one is different."

He frowned. They weren't different. They shepherded their clients, showed them some dirt and flowers with a down-home twang, and at the end held them upside down until all the credit cards fell out of their pockets. It was an industry like any other: its thrills and corny jokes and well-worn trails and easy lectures as ritualized as Japanese theater. "How is it different?"

"Sometimes you don't come back."

"The trek is dangerous?" There were always release forms because some of the climbs and treks and dives were genuinely risky. It was danger that gave it the thrill.

"It's in Australia."

"What?"

"It's a new company called Outback Adventure. Immersion in a total wilderness. It's up to you to find your own way out."

"Raven, that's crazy."

"It's the ultimate challenge, Daniel. The toughest thing left."

"But Australia is quarantined. The plague . . ."

"Is over, according to this new company."

"But that's why this whole thing about GeneChem could be important! The fiasco in Australia . . ."

"Has been learned from."

"You can't be serious about going there."

"I want to experience true wilderness."

"In the Rockies, not there! It's got to be a scam."

She shook her head. "I don't think so. United Corporations has kept it quiet for a reason. For the few who seek them out it's seen as an . . . outlet. A test. An opportunity. It's kind of exciting, actually. To be chosen, I mean. They don't take just anyone, Daniel."

He looked at her in disbelief. Australia! The place was a planetary nightmare, a scientific embarrassment. Even if the travel ban had been lifted, it was like proposing to honeymoon in Hiroshima, or take the waters in Chernobyl. It didn't make sense. "Raven, the place was a hell hole."

"During the Dying. Now it's pristine." She looked away. "That's what they say."

He swallowed. "And you're going?"

"Maybe."

"Alone?"

Slowly, she nodded. "I'm better alone, I think."

He managed a pained grin. "Thank you for sharing that."

She cast her eyes downward. "I didn't mean that quite the way it sounded. I might go with the right person, if I could find them, but so far I haven't. It has to be somebody ready to change their life. Somebody who can't stand their life here. Somebody Outback Adventure would take." She waited.

So that was it. This had been some kind of audition. Had all her friends already turned her down? "Why haven't I heard about this Outback Adventure?" he stalled.

"It's a secret, a secret you have to keep. They have to

control public knowledge to make it work. A secret like your GeneChem."

"And you think I should go too?"

"I'm not sure you're ready, Daniel."

"You don't know that."

"It's you who doesn't know."

CHAPTER FIVE

S till smarting from Raven's doubt, Daniel was called into the office of section supervisor Luther Cox four days later. Harriet Lundeen issued the invitation to enter what the office serfs called the glass cages. An employee of Dyson's rank was hired in the supervisory offices, fired (or "given an opportunities transfer") in the supervisory offices, and otherwise had little reason to be there except to receive bad news. If Microcore had glad tidings to extend they would be announced out in the cubicles, where other employees could either take heart at group reward or redouble their competitive efforts to match the good fortune of a colleague. Public display of reprimands and demotions, in contrast, was considered to be bad form—and unnecessary, since news of what went on behind the closed door usually swept through Level 31 like wildfire anyway.

"Sit down, Mr. Dyson."

Daniel sat in a couch that faced his supervisor. The sofa was so soft that he sank almost to his haunches, an awkward position that left him unable to see the top of the man's desk. Cox loomed above him, his balding head like an egg against milky sky visible through the tinted glass of his window. Daniel assumed the choice of furniture was deliberate.

"You wished to discuss the Meeting Minder, sir?" he preempted, hoping to steer the conversation in a neutral direction.

Cox looked surprised, and slightly confused. "No." It was apparent he had little idea what his employee was working on. "This concerns your extracurricular activities, Mr. Dyson."

"Extracurricular?"

Cox picked up a folder and pretended to read. "I've received a report of employee intrusion into corporate-secure computer files. Specifically, Microcore expense report recordings by its senior employees—though the target hardly matters, given the serious breach of the company's ethical guidelines."

He started. "Who said this about me, sir?"

"It hardly matters, does it? We've had our experts look into the matter and your electronic fingerprints are all over the system."

Daniel shifted uneasily. He was better than *that*, wasn't he?

"This isn't the first report I've had of a problem with your attitude. We have logs of cyber chats with a lot of unproductive people. Postings from the net's underground. Search engines for the unsavory. You seem to spend more time whining than working."

"My electronic communications are supposed to be private," he objected.

"You're sarcastic in company meetings." His boss was now reading from the folder. "You mock or ignore group dynamic interaction exercises. Your absences for alleged illness are excessive. Your pace of promotion lags behind target timetables. You display little concern for your future: your saving, retirement, and insurance allowances are nowhere close to suggested goals. You procrastinate on assignments you don't like, finish those you do in half the time, and then play games with the remainder. Your desk is a pigsty, decorated with objects calculated to offend the political sensitivities of just about every demographic group. Your cultural attunement is appalling."

"Attunement?"

"Now Ms. Lundeen has had to begin confiscating your toys." Cox bent to a box and put something on the edge of his desk. It was the catapult, of course. "Model making isn't in your job description, Mr. Dyson. What if you'd put someone's eye out with this thing?"

"It was designed to lob more than throw. And the payload was only a piece of—"

"Enough!" Cox brought his fist down on the catapult and its pencil-arms blew apart with a crack. Fragments went flying across the room.

There was dead silence for a moment.

"What if that had put *my* eye out?"

His boss's look was thunderous. "Then we could believe in poetic justice."

Daniel was silent. Cox could make his existence an unhappy one.

His supervisor sat back and sighed theatrically, having given this lecture before. "This company and section is run on the principle of hierarchy and harmony, Mr. Dyson. On group cooperation. On a common belief in our goals, processes, and schedules. Increasingly, you don't seem to share that."

The quiet was so intense that the ventilators seemed to roar as Daniel fought to maintain the composure that had been drilled into him all his life. Of *course* he didn't share it. He never had. You went to school so you could work so you could retire so you could die? It was absurd! No one had ever wanted to pay him for exploration of subjects he found interesting, and yet his employers seemed equally bored with what they *did* assign. Life was numbing, dammit. Friendship had given way to "relationships." Marriage was fragile. Entertainment was isolating, a retreat into private fantasy. Art had become a slavish recycling of what had sold before. Scientific discovery had become so technical that it spoke only to specialists. He felt like a cog in an accelerating machine that had forgotten its own purpose. Process had *become* the goal. The schedule had *become* the measure of success. He didn't share this? Of course not!

And yet there was no alternative. You endured, or were reassigned to a worse endurance. The world had become homogenized. You compromised and conformed and measured any rebellion into tiny, permissible packets of individuality. Until you were brought up short, like now.

None of this could be voiced, of course. There was no graver sin than pointing out the obvious. "Look, Mr. Cox," he said carefully. "I'm not trying to be disrespectful or cause trouble. I just get a little bored sometimes. My group calls our project the 'Mindless Minder.' Maybe if I could get a promotion out of your section to a higher, more challenging level . . ."

"Deserved, no doubt, for your sterling leadership skills."

"Maybe if I had a chance to demonstrate them . . ."

"Demonstrate to who, Mr. Dyson? Who would follow

you? Before you can lead, you must learn to follow. Before anyone believes in your direction, you must believe in yourself. Everything I've just recited predicts the classic pattern of workplace failure. A person who chooses not to fit in, who is unfit for group cooperation, and thus individual advancement. A malcontent."

"I'm trying to *stay* content, by having fun."

"By snooping, gossiping, building toys."

"By trying to bring some life to this place. Come on, Mr. Cox, you know what it's like here. No wonder they built the damn headquarters like a pyramid. Everyone inside it acts like they're dead."

"Speak for yourself."

"We call it the velvet coffin! It's so comfortable it's confining. We've got the health plan, the vacation plan, the Christmas plan, the retirement plan, the job development plan, the mortgage plan, the partnership plan. Next we'll have the sex plan! My life is set before I've even lived it. Employees here joke we're like vampires. We only come alive at night."

"The world is organized that way for a purpose, Mr. Dyson. From purpose comes reward. That's what is lacking."

"My reward?"

"I don't find your flippancy funny. You mock our system here, but it's built on the first economic model to enjoy true global success. If you don't believe that, read your history books—I know what you studied in college—and compare the past to the present. Unemployment? It's gone: the United Corporations of which we and every other multinational are a part has the right job, in the right place, for everyone. War? Gone from a world in which the multinationals have merged with government to eliminate such gross inefficiency. Crime? Largely gone with guaranteed rehabilitation. The morally impaired are given new lives. Poverty? It's gone except for the voluntary poor: in the United Corporations world, success is the product of group achievement, while failure can only be the result of individual inadequacy. In today's society, *everyone* becomes a winner—*if* they belong."

Daniel sat without expression. He'd heard this a thousand times.

"And why this success? Because United Corporations has allowed market forces to achieve their potential. Yes, there are a lot of rules, but in a planet still gaining a hundred million new inhabitants every year, those rules allow all of us to live in enlightened harmony under the Singapore Model. You can't argue with that kind of contentment."

"It's so perfect it's boring."

"That's what you don't understand, Mr. Dyson. *That's* why you feel unchallenged. It's not perfect! Perfection is an ever-receding goal! Our lives can never be boring because we're always in pursuit of unobtainable perfection! Sustained challenge! Under United Corporations, things are *always* getting better, all the time—but always can get better *still.*"

"Do you really believe that, sir?"

"Believe in belief, Dyson. That's the key." His look softened. "I'm not deaf to your pleas for a challenge, you know. I want to channel your ambition. I want my employees to be where they belong. So I want you to think seriously about your future. I want you to be alert to new opportunities. There may be a way to tap your energies, who knows? But *first* you have to prove you can meet the expectations of our work environment here."

"And if I can't?"

"United Corporations has the right job, in the right place, for everyone." The threat was clear. "It's time to grow up."

The reprimand gnawed at Daniel the rest of the day. It confirmed what he already knew, that his career was going nowhere. Grow up? He felt sometimes that he was the only grown-up in a pyramid of obedient children. Yet he'd trapped himself in a pointless strategy of mild rebellion that accomplished nothing except to keep him from rising above Level 31. There was a very real chance Cox could choose to send him down for insubordination and poor performance, at which time he'd become a pariah to whatever level had to take him in. The Mona Pietris of this world would regard him as toxic waste.

Worse than this gloomy review of his prospects was his suspicion of betrayal by Raven. Had she tattled on his hacking boast? If not, the timing of his section leader's lecture was remarkably coincidental. If so, why? Because he hadn't jumped at the chance to vacation in a continent once ravaged by plague? Ridiculous. Yet doubt built on doubt. Was it mere coincidence that he'd met a lone, pretty woman out running in the dimness of predawn, so incongruous and enigmatic? Everything about her seemed so different from other women he had known: challenging, independent, mysterious, like a . . . rebel. A priestess. A spy.

To spy on what? Daniel Dyson, low-level key clicker in one of a million ant nests of capitalism? The man on a path to nowhere? It was absurd. Spies are supposed to seduce their victims, not dismiss them in an underground tunnel. Computer files had been erased to the electronic waste bin with more ceremony than he'd been dumped by Raven. She'd probably already forgotten his existence.

He'd not forgotten her, however. She was a misfit and argumentative, but then so was he. Accordingly, he was intrigued by her. No other woman he'd met questioned so much. He'd believed for a moment that they felt the same things, shared the same longings. The fact she'd seemed to conclude otherwise had left him all the more determined to prove it to her.

He'd once thought he had all the time and all the women in the world. Not that he was particularly successful at romantic conquest, but rather that romantic possibility seemed theoretically inexhaustible. There were six billion women! He looked for flaws because he was naive enough to expect perfection. And so when he fell in love with a woman named Katrina who'd subsequently proven challenging in her eccentricities, he'd let her go. He'd been too proud to risk failure by trying to win her over. Too arrogant to accept her faults.

She'd haunted him for the next three years.

Now he had that same sense of puzzled excitement again. As if he *knew* Raven. One sojourn in a glorified sewer pipe and she'd brought back that same rush of unstable desire. An echo of pained longing. And now the reprimand had linked them again, right?

You idiot, he kept repeating to himself. Leave her alone.

The admonition did no good. He walked after work to clear his head of her and yet the city seemed vacuous. The incessant pop songs of the cafés and arcades seemed annoyingly repetitious. The iridescent avenues, ablaze from shows and pleasure palaces, seemed like a deliberate distraction from whatever he was truly straining to see. He couldn't decide what to eat from the food court choices, where ever more inventive spicing had so exhausted his palate that he could taste nothing at all. He finally retreated to his apartment and scanned eight minutes of entertainment listings, finding nothing that engaged either his mind or his emotions. He had nowhere to go, nothing to do, no one he wanted to see. Except her. Had she betrayed him?

He sat on his terrace and watched the artificial suns of advertisers rise into the dark sky once more as he chewed on a Ready-Meal. Life was easy if you simply went along, he conceded. Work was usually an undemanding set of rote motions, his pay was adequate for all but the silliest luxuries, and entertainment could be as all-consuming as one wished. Other people lived for baseball or theater or console games and seemed content. Why couldn't he? *Why* did he do?

Damn her. It was necessary to find her for his own peace of mind. He'd put it to her plainly: did you rat on me? She'd deny it. He'd ask for a meeting to clear the air. If she showed, it would be excuse enough to . . .

He didn't even know her last name. Yeah, you know what you were thinking with.

He went to his terminal and sat for a moment, drumming his fingers in frustration. What was the name of her vacation company? Outback Adventure? He ran computer searches for it and found nothing, which was strange. Had it all been a lie?

He ran searches under her name. *Raven.* He turned up ornithology texts and Native American legends, but no address or link. Good grief. And he was contemplating mucking about with truth cookies? He was a humbled hacker, his electronic trail at Microcore embarrassingly plain. An amateur in an age when privacy consultants made millions.

So it was decision time. How serious was he? Did he really care?

Of course he did. It was a challenge now. It wasn't boring, like Microcore. He called Fitzroy. The one-time cop had the pals, the codes, and an e-vault full of passwords. But it would cost Daniel a thousand dollars, a day's wages, to get a lead on a woman who had rejected him. Foolish, he knew.

Dammit though, he wanted to confront her. He wanted to *know*.

"Yeah?" Fitzroy's grizzled head, swollen to giant dimension on Daniel's vid-wall, popped into view. Christ, the man was ugly at that resolution. Bagged, rheumy eyes, sallow skin, veined nose. Nobody had to be homely anymore: why didn't the guy get a laser-lift? Because he lived in his machine, not the world: a cyber hermit. It was the one place he had power, his own personal heaven.

"I need something."

"Hold on." The screen fuzzed, came back. Fitzroy had switched on his scrambler. "Yeah?"

"A woman."

"What a surprise. Geez, I've never heard that one before."

"I've got a first name and some tourist outfit she says she might sign on with, but that's all. I need their numbers. Can you get it?"

The private detective snorted. "That's it?"

"If it's easy, maybe you can give me a discount."

"Fuck that. Give me what you got."

"Her name's Raven."

"Raven? What the hell kind of astral handle is that? She a fucking Indian or something?"

"No. Maybe. I don't know, what does it matter?"

"You couldn't get her last name?"

"It didn't come up."

"Gotcha. Well, what's her company? Where does she live?"

"I don't know. I first ran into her in Calabria and met her later at Pitney Tube."

"Geez. Either the shortest relationship in history or you move quicker, with less talk, than anybody I've heard of. You don't know *anything* about her?"

"If I knew anything I wouldn't need you. Look, I may be getting jacked around here—I'm suspicious of her—so's there's a company I want you to check out. Called GeneChem. Heard of it?"

"Spell it. There's only about fifty million fucking gene-soft-micro-tech bullshit companies out there by now, all of them farting vaporware and DNA that doesn't work. I wish they'd go back to vanity names you can remember. Like Chrysler. Or Kellogg. What was wrong with that? Mine is Fitzroy Investigations. Simple. Honest. None of this net-web-splice-tel crap, you know?"

"Right." Daniel spelled it. "Now, this Raven says she's going on a trip with a company whose name you'll like. Simple. Honest. Outback Adventure."

"Outdoor Adventure? This is, what, swing sets? Pickle ball?"

"Outback, not outdoor. Adventure travel."

"Oh yeah, right. Bugs and dirt. Jesus, people are stupid. That's another five hundred."

"Why can't I ever get a discount, Fitzroy?"

"Because I have to eat." He clicked off.

Daniel paced, straightening up. He was as neat at home as he was untidy at the office. The company shrink would have a field day with that one. After an hour there was a chime and the detective was back on his screen.

"I don't see the transfer in my account yet."

"I wanted to make sure you could get the stuff. That was a thousand?"

"Fifteen hundred, Einstein."

"Whatever." He clicked some commands. "It should be there."

He saw Fitzroy glance away, then back. "Nobody wants to pay their fucking bills."

"What you got?"

"The only thing in our favor is the unusual first name. There's just a few of them so I could eliminate by age, location, occupation, no possible interest in outdoor adventure—that kind of thing."

"And?"

"And this is some broad you're stalking, if I got the right one. Fancy name, fancy address. She even looks good on her ident-screen. This the one?"

Raven even took a good license picture. "That's her. The last name?"

"DeCarlo. Lah-de-dah-dah. De-Carrrr-lo. My, my. I don't think you can afford this one, newbie."

"She's actually a cheap date."

"Cost you fifteen hundred this night, Romeo. Listen, I got her number. And her address. You want that?"

"Of course."

Fitzroy blanked out and the screen flickered with the information. Daniel printed it out and destroyed the file and transmission record. He was in enough hot water for privacy violations already. Paper you could burn, eat, shred. Bytes were forever.

The detective came into view again. "And the adventure company?" Daniel asked him.

"That one's odd. No open-door web address, no ad, no listed number. Pretty tough to buy from."

"So I get a refund?"

"You gotta be kidding. I found 'em—through an industrial link to export firms. They've got a keyworded web entry, encryption, a bunch of other bullshit."

"Export firm? What does that mean?"

"A kink in your romance?"

"You can't kink what you don't have. But maybe this woman is being conned; she thinks it's a vacation outfit. You sure you got the right company?"

Fitzroy laughed. "If you got the right name. Maybe they put airholes in their shipping containers!"

"Can I get in?"

The detective shook his head. "The site is invitation only. You need the password, the encrypted entry code, and it's all proprietary. Maybe this broad knows it." His grin was a leer. "For fifteen hundred bucks, she'd better know something."

CHAPTER SIX

You found me."

There was no surprise in Raven's voice, no delight, no disapproval. It was rather a flat statement over the vidphone, her face on the monitor displaying a cool perusal of his own. It was as if she'd expected to hear from him again.

"I need to see you."

"Are you sure that's wise?"

"We need to talk."

"Why?"

He could accuse her of getting him into trouble at Microcore, but suspected she'd simply hang up. "It's about this company you said you might go with. Outback Adventure. There's something funny about it."

Her look was wary. "What do you mean?"

"It's not even a regular company, I think."

"You've talked to them?"

"No. But I asked about it and it's not listed in any regular—"

"There's a reason for that."

"What reason?"

"You have to ask them."

"I can't even figure out how to reach them."

"You need a code."

He was puzzled. "But that doesn't make sense for a company trying to attract customers."

"That's not what they're trying to do."

"They don't need customers?"

"Their customers need them."

What the hell did that mean? "Listen, Raven, what do you really know about this outfit?"

"It changes lives, Daniel."

"How?"

She said nothing.

"Please see me," he asked again. "I don't want you to get hurt by signing on with the wrong group."

"I told you I could take care of myself."

"Please. I need to talk with you."

"About what?"

"About . . ." *us,* he wanted to say. "About the Outback."

She looked at him gravely, evaluating again. "If you're sure. I thought you didn't like the idea of Australia."

"You told me I didn't know what I liked."

"I tried to make you think. Now you've found me. It's happening as it's supposed to. So I'll talk to you again about it, if you insist. But it's your idea, not mine."

"I've got your address, I could—"

"No." She shook her head decisively. "I'll meet you . . . I'll meet you at Cordoba Mall. A coffee place, Anthony's. I want to explain the situation so you don't make a mistake. Okay?"

It was something. "Tomorrow at eight?"

"Tomorrow at eight. Bring a sense of adventure."

He half expected her not to show up. Instead she came and was prettier than ever. Raven was wearing a dark dress with a floral print and gold jewelry set off against her black hair, and the dress caressed her in a way to confirm his speculation about her figure. The effect was a quiet elegance completely at odds with the jumpsuit she'd worn for underground exploring. She was like a woman who'd gone from camping to cocktails. She ordered black coffee, declining his invitation for a light dinner or dessert, and eyed him speculatively. She was subdued, as if undecided about something. Him, he supposed. Her smile was completely false.

"Thanks for coming," he said politely.

"You must have made an effort to find me," she observed as the waitress left. "I didn't leave you much to go on. I didn't think you'd want to see me again and I wanted to give you an excuse not to."

"Why didn't you think I would want to see you again?"

"I wasn't at my best in the tunnels. I get moody sometimes. I don't blame people if they're put off by it. It's just the way I am. A loner."

"I wasn't put off. I thought you were interesting. I just wasn't sure you liked me."

She was saved from having to answer immediately by the arrival of their coffee. She spooned some sugar into hers, stirring it thoughtfully, and then looked up at him. "I like you, Daniel," she finally allowed. "But it makes me uncomfortable, frankly, that I like you. I don't like everyone I meet."

"Oh." He was uncertain how to respond to this. "But then I got in trouble at work," he finally continued. "About some of the things I told you about."

She shrugged. If she'd betrayed his confidence she didn't want to admit it.

"It got me thinking," he went on, watching her. "I'm not really happy at my job. They're not happy with me. Maybe I need a break. So I got curious about this Australian thing you mentioned, this Outback Adventure. I've never heard anything about treks like that. I wonder if it's even true. So I tried to find them and couldn't. They're not easy to find."

"I know." She looked at him speculatively. "I mentioned it because I thought you might be interested, but then as we talked I changed my mind. I doubt it's for you."

"But it is for you?"

"Not necessarily. They probably wouldn't pick me, either."

"Pick you?"

She avoided his eyes again, playing with her coffee spoon. "I told you it's not like the usual adventure company. It's limited entry, a privilege. You have to find them, and apply, and then they don't take everyone. It's very exclusive."

"But how do people find them?"

She shrugged. "Through an acquaintance." She was careful not to say "friend," he noticed. "Sometimes people just stumble across it, the ones looking for something. Sometimes the company finds you. It pops up on your screen."

"That's weird, isn't it?"

She took a sip. "Is it? They seem to find the right people to go."

"Outback Adventure is listed as an export company, not a tourism outfit."

She shrugged.

"How do you know they're even legitimate?"

"I've talked with them."

"And?"

"It's exciting, Daniel. Life-changing. They just have to keep a lid on information about the situation in Australia. That secret part adds a thrill."

"But not for me."

She sighed. "That's for you to decide, isn't it? I'm just trying to . . . not waste your time." Raven glanced out at the mall for a moment, then returned her gaze to him.

"Why wouldn't I fit?"

"Because you're confused. Because you have to be absolutely certain you belong there. It's a very rugged experience. Maybe you're better at adjusting to the city than you think, even if you don't realize it right now. My advice is not to give up on Microcore. It's a good company. They know what they're doing."

"But I'm *not* adjusted. It's always the sideways view, like we talked about."

She glanced out the café again. Did she have some boyfriend waiting out there? Her distraction irritated him. "Then call them up if you want."

"I can't. It's encrypted."

"I know. There's a password. Or words."

"Can I get them?"

She shifted restlessly. "I'm only hesitating because I don't want to mislead you. It's dangerous, difficult."

"Which you can take and I can't."

"I didn't say that."

"Give me the password, Raven."

"I warned you, right?"

"You've done everything but let me judge."

"All right." She conceded the point. "You can log in with 'Erehwon.'" She spelled it.

"What does that mean?"

"It's just code. And the passwords are 'Getting Back.'"

"Getting back? To what, nature?"

"It means whatever you want it to mean, I suppose."

"But why an export company?"

"To deter the casually curious, I think. To discourage mere tourists. After you listen to them it will make more sense."

"What if we looked into it together?"

She took another sip. "I don't think so."

"As friends. We could even go together. Friends."

"I'm not your friend, Daniel. I'm just this strange woman you met who's revealed a potential opportunity and decided it's better for us each to go our own way." She stood abruptly. "Look, this discussion is hard for me but I can't really explain why. Maybe you should just forget it. Forget me. Get on with your life."

"I don't have a life."

"Don't look for it from me."

"I'm looking for something to shake up my life. Maybe this Outback Adventure is it."

"Maybe. But you have to decide without me." Then she walked quickly away.

The code gave him access to a web site with an opening picture of a red-sand desert, dotted with bright green trees. Australia, he assumed. Projected onto his apartment video wall, the scene had a brilliant vividness. Daniel felt like he was standing on a dune, heat on his back. The immediacy was arresting. "Welcome to Outback Adventure," a female voice intoned. "To begin your adventure, please enter the passwords."

Dyson remained puzzled. Why would any company make it an obstacle to hear about its product? Surely that violated some profit commandment. Maybe it was a kind of reverse psychology.

He cleared his throat. "Getting Back." There was a pause and then two tiny figures appeared at the edge of his screen, confirmation that the site had been activated. The two began angling up the dune toward Daniel.

A teaser scrolled across the bottom of the screen. "For people who ask not *what* they do, but *why* they do." Then the picture froze.

So Raven DeCarlo was a parrot of slogans. Not that different from Mona Pietri, perhaps.

"Show more," he ordered.

The couple advanced again, coming side by side near the top of the dune and closing to almost fill the screen, wind blowing through their hair. Daniel almost laughed. They were both striking and bizarre. The woman had flame-colored hair and sapphire-blue eyes (Daniel suspected imagery augmentation) and was a model of barbarian chic: her fur and leather garb was cut to show a flat midriff and a muscled thigh. She wore armbands of bone and leather and was holding a staff. The man, dark and chiseled, was in skintight Ninja black from neck to boots, a bandolier with silver throwing knives cinched taut across his chest. The pair looked like they belonged in a B-grade fantasy. He knew they were actors in front of a blue screen, projected onto a distant Australia. What kept Daniel from surfing on in dismissal was the look in their eyes as they gazed out over the desert. Whether acted or real, they seemed to have found what they were looking for. It was a look of triumph, of fulfillment, of satisfied destiny.

No one in the city looked that way.

"Welcome to the Outback, Daniel Dyson," a voice boomed, its amplification like a growl of thunder.

Hello God, he thought wryly in reply.

"Can *you* meet the challenge of Outback Adventure?"

Daniel was surprised at the speed with which his identity had been confirmed by the company. Corporate identification of those logging on to web sites and the greeting of electronic customers was routine, but this time it happened so fast it was almost as if they'd been expecting him. Raven again? Or just good demographic sifting?

"I've never heard of your company," Daniel challenged.

The redhead turned to look and smile. Her teeth were perfect, her skin glowing, her breathing . . . fetching. "Would you like to know more?"

"Yes," he replied, his curiosity only one of the things aroused.

Now Mr. Bandolier turned to him. "Virtual reality, Daniel. Odd term, isn't it? As if an imitation of life is worth spending your life on. Are you tired of pretend peril and artificial ecstasy?"

"I do things."

The desert dweller smiled. "And is what you do what you think life should be? Or does it feel like some distant imitation of it? Like touching skin through a mitten. Peering through fog."

Daniel was quiet. Sometimes life did feel like that.

"What if you had a chance to feel life raw? A chance to explore a new world and in doing so, explore yourself? A chance to start fresh?"

"On a vacation trek." Daniel was dubious.

Mr. Bandolier shook his head. "Outback Adventure is no vacation, my friend. No walk in the park. It's the toughest outdoor experience you could ever encounter. It's only for people willing to risk their life so they can finally truly live it. *That's* the test. That's the price." His eyes were challenging.

"And why would I do that?"

"Do you ever long for a place with no rules except the discipline you establish for yourself? A place without clocks, commutes, or committees? A place of self-reliance where you gather your own food, find your own way, and learn the challenges and satisfaction of simple survival? Are you ready to face true wilderness? That's Outback Adventure, a truly once-in-a-lifetime experience!"

Daniel was baffled. There was no shortage of adventure travel companies in the world. They'd take clients anywhere they dreamed: pampering them in the Amazon, perching them on camels in Mongolia, or pitching tents on an Arctic ice floe. All supplied food, however—except this one, apparently. And the location! "Outback is a word associated with Australia," he objected. "I thought entry to the continent was banned."

The man smiled and nodded, sharing the secret. "For ordinary people it is, Daniel. For the select few who find our company, who identify themselves through their own initiative, and who want a chance at something different, United Corporations has designated Australia a clean slate, an empty continent, a disease-free place for men and women to test themselves in a new beginning. There hasn't been an opportunity like this for hundreds of years."

Daniel was intrigued. He'd enjoyed vacation expeditions but also felt they'd been choreographed. To wander on your own . . . "So what, exactly, *is* Outback Adventure?"

The woman smiled and leaned toward him, revealing more cleavage, eyes dancing with flirtatious amusement. "What *is* it?" she repeated in mock surprise, as if she'd never heard of such a question. Then she threw out her arms to embrace the country she was in. "It's life stripped of artifice, Daniel. It's nature that hasn't been smothered by man. It's clean air, sweet rain, rainbows, and thunderstorms. It's more stars than you thought possible to fit into the sky. It's open country without a track or a trail. Most people find that scary. Do you?"

He frowned. "I don't know." They hadn't really answered his question.

The man nodded. "Of course you don't. None of us did until we met with our Outback Adventure counselor. That's where everything becomes clear. And not everyone who contacts us can be invited to make this journey. They have to be special. Independent. Adventurous. Would you be willing to take our survey to see if *you* qualify for a personal interview?"

Daniel paused at that. This exclusiveness again. They wanted his money but required some kind of test before they'd take it? While the premise was intriguing, this was commercial confidence bordering on arrogance.

"I'm not much for surveys."

"I think you have what it takes, Daniel," the woman encouraged.

Dammit, they'd made him curious. "What the hell."

The pair nodded approvingly. The Australia scene dissolved and he was looking at a walnut-paneled office with leather-bound books, overstuffed furniture, and lighting so soft and indirect it made him squint. It was a 3-D cliché of a psychiatric den: authoritative, dark, and calming enough to persuade an entrant to have his head shrunk. He almost laughed again, and yet the predictability of it did put him somewhat at ease. Electronic surveys like this were ubiquitous, he knew, as companies probed both job applicants and customers. A somewhat older, handsome woman was sitting in a maroon chair wearing pearls, pumps, and a business suit of classic and modest cut: stylish, professional, reassuring. "Hello, Daniel," she said in a low, warm voice. "I'm Dr. Cynthia Chen, Outback Adventure's preliminary screening consultant. Experience has taught us that while some people are suited to life on their own in the wild, most don't really belong there. If you don't mind, I'm going to ask you a few simple questions. This is strictly confidential and is just to give us a better idea of who you are so we can help you decide if Outback Adventure is best for *you*." Her tone was kind.

"I don't really like questionnaires."

"It doesn't hurt." She smiled as if they shared agreement about the absurdity of it all. "It's kind of fun, actually."

"I'm not sure I want you to know who *I* am. I want to know who *you* are."

"These questions are your gateway to learning that.

Believe me, it's for the good of both of us. We don't want to waste your time—or ours."

He remembered vocational tests in school. One suggested that half his class become farmers, when there'd been almost no vocational opportunities in farming for fifty years. The kids had hooted in derision. Now here Daniel was again, trying to fit some shrink's personality grid. He sighed. "Fire away."

There were no preliminary questions about his age, weight, health, family, hobbies, or skills. He'd been a net-entry since birth, and a punch of buttons could deliver to anyone who cared an avalanche of files groaning with information about his buying habits, subscriptions, employment records, and memberships. Privacy laws had broken down under the continual assault of hackers, lawyers, web solicitors, journalists, and snoops, and targeting businesses often knew more about their consumers in a statistical sense than the consumer himself. Instead, Dr. Chen's queries focused on Daniel's self-analysis, ranging from the trivial to the fundamental:

"Do you sometimes wake just to see a sunrise?" she asked.

"I get up early to run." He shrugged. "Sunrise is one of the reasons. It's hard to see in the city."

"Do you like to try new things?"

"It's hard to find new things. That's the problem, isn't it?"

"What kind of watch do you own?"

"Jesus, I don't know." He looked at his wrist in puzzlement. "It's just a watch. Ganymede, I think. Does it matter?"

"What would you order for your last meal?"

He pondered. "I've never been convinced I'd have much of an appetite."

She laughed approvingly.

It was a bullshit test, Daniel decided, another part of an elaborate psychological come-on. He'd been enlisted in the effort to recruit himself. Accordingly, some of his answers were serious but others were flippant. She made no objection to the latter, going down her list calmly. The doctor is a holo-recording, he reminded himself. You can't provoke a true reaction.

"Are you a leader?"

He hesitated, then admitted his supervisor was right. "No."

"Are you a follower?"

That was easier. "No."

"Are you brave?"

"I've never had to find out."

"Are you smart?"

"Taking this test, I'm beginning to wonder."

"Do you like people?"

What was the right answer on that one? Were they looking for hermits or class presidents? "Depends on the person, doesn't it?"

"What do you live for, Daniel?"

"Myself, I guess." Might as well be honest.

"And is that enough?"

"Sometimes." He paused. "No. But I don't have anything else. Anyone." He certainly wasn't making much progress with Raven. Or Mona Pietri, for that matter.

"Are you happy?"

He sighed. "Sometimes. Not really. I don't like the way things are."

"Would you eat grubs to keep yourself alive?"

"Grubs? What the hell is a grub?"

"A larval insect."

He laughed. "If I would, does that mean I'm happy? Or simply crazy enough to go on your outdoor outing?"

Dr. Chen smiled. "Congratulations, Daniel. You've passed the first test of Outback Adventure."

"That's it? I'm insane enough to go?"

"You've been accepted as a *candidate* for the experience of a lifetime. To pursue this possibility further you must make an appointment to meet your Outback Adventure counselor."

"Good grief. You don't make taking my money easy, do you?"

"At our corporate offices we'll explain the program and schedule you for excitement if you decide to participate."

"Schedule for excitement?" He rolled his eyes.

"We choose our words carefully, believe me."

He looked at her skeptically. "And how much will this once-in-a-lifetime experience cost me?"

"One year's salary." She didn't even blink.

"What!"

"The fee is to test the seriousness of your commitment."

"It sure as hell does! I can't afford that!"

"Yes you can." Her look remained serene.

"I'm sorry. I'm not going to pay that."

"Yes you will." Her confidence was infuriating. "It's a small price to come alive."

CHAPTER SEVEN

The address in Daniel's city was in the tower of an anonymous skyscraper cluster forty minutes away by tube. Discreet lettering in the lobby announced the firm's presence on the thirty-third floor. The elevator opened to reveal a number of nondescript small offices: a title company, a financial newsletter, a laser-lift skin clinic. The tour agency door was solid wood, plain, and locked. OUTBACK ADVENTURE, a tiny sign read in letters slipped into the kind of bracket that could accommodate a rapid turnover of tenants. He glanced at the ceiling. A vid-snake was watching him.

Daniel hesitated, then knocked.

Silence.

He looked at his watch: on time. He tried the knob but it didn't budge. He knocked again. Nothing.

Dammit, it wasn't lunch, but there was no sound from the other side. He eyed the keypad lock and punched some numbers at random without effect, quickly becoming bored. "Hello?" Finally he retreated across the hallway and slid down the wall, sitting expectantly on the floor. He'd wait for the bastards.

With that there was a buzz, a click, and the door swung quietly open. He stood awkwardly and walked over, poking his head through. The inside revealed a small waiting area with ugly plastic molded chairs, a desk, and a pretty receptionist. She smiled. "Close the door behind you."

He stepped through and the door clicked shut.

"Your appointment?"

"To see Mr. Coyle," he said grumpily. "My name is Daniel Dyson."

"Please have a seat, Mr. Dyson." She gestured at the plastic chairs. "I'll inform Mr. Coyle."

"You didn't answer my knock."

"Yes we did. Eventually." She regarded him with quiet amusement.

"You don't want clients to come in?"

"Eight percent of our applicants are turned away by that door and that's for their own good. They wouldn't do well with Outback Adventure, would they?"

He sat while she announced his arrival. The chairs were as uncomfortable as they looked. The brochures on the table featured the same wilderness couple he'd seen on his video wall. There were pictures of empty desert, red-rocked gorges, and bounding kangaroos. The text was spare. "Like primitive life itself, this is a journey with no schedule, no itinerary, and no set destination— except self-realization."

A Zen thing, maybe.

There was a buzz and she looked up at him again, smiling. "Your counselor will see you now." He went through another solid wooden door.

The man who met Daniel reminded him a bit of the

brochure Ninja, but without the knives. Elliott Coyle was dark-haired, tanned, and dressed in a charcoal sport coat over a black silk crew shirt and dark pants. He wore black Dura-Flex slippers. A silver pin on his lapel was the only bright point to catch the eye. It showed a kangaroo. That would be something, Daniel thought, to see a wild kangaroo.

"There are thousands of them—hundreds of thousands—where you're going." Coyle had followed Daniel's eye.

"How do you know I'm going?"

"I've read your profile, Daniel. You belong there."

"You have a profile?"

"The screening questionnaire, a background check. We don't send just anyone on Outback Adventure. It's too expensive for both of us. So we try to guess—an educated guess, but a guess nonetheless—who truly belongs there. The information we have on you is very promising."

"I'll bet it includes my annual salary, if that's my fee."

Coyle smiled. "Touché."

"Secret passwords, locked doors. Your company doesn't make sense."

He nodded. "You want to know more, of course, which is why I'm here." He stuck out his hand. "Elliott Coyle." The handshake was firm and brisk. "I'm your assigned counselor, the man whose job it is to convince you the experience is worthwhile, to help decide if we should give each other a try, and then guide you through preparation if we come to agreement. I feel it's safe to say that what I'm offering—what *we're* offering—will change your life."

"Who is 'we,' exactly?"

"Outback Adventure is a travel consultant that contracts with the umbrella governing arm of United Corporations. We have exclusive excursion rights to offer wilderness experiences in Australia."

"And Australia is quarantined. Off-limits. Dangerous, last I heard."

"It was. To keep management of the continent controllable, we haven't advertised its change in status. Instead we screen candidates to find the few who can realistically take advantage of what we have to offer. You're in a select group, Daniel."

"So how did you find me?"

"You found us, remember? That's the first requirement. Friends tend to tell like-minded friends. We keep a low profile to discourage the casually curious. We register as an export company. If we didn't take such steps, the screening would become unwieldy. The idea would intrigue more people than you might think."

"So how do I fit?"

"You're also the right age, the right fitness, the right . . . temperament. We think. The only one who can really answer that is you."

Daniel wanted to digest this for a moment. "If I go, do I get Cave Girl?" he deflected. He solemnly held up a brochure.

Coyle laughed again. "I wouldn't mind time in the Outback with her myself! Alas, she's an actress, Daniel. We're offering wilderness, not Club Pleasure. You'll have to find your own companionship, if you want it." He winked.

"You've got to make a better pitch than that, Mr. Coyle. Especially for a year's goddamned salary. Anyone who would pay that *is* crazy enough to go."

Coyle nodded. "Absolutely right. So why don't you sit back and let me give you the spiel? Then you make up your own mind. No pressure, no sweat. I think you'll be intrigued, at the very least."

The chairs were far more comfortable than the plastic ones of the waiting room. Daniel sank in one and donned headgear for the presentation, adjusting the fit and sound. A desert panorama opened up again, gloriously empty. The sky was a brilliant blue, dried clear of haze. The sand was a vibrant red. Coyle walked into view. Daniel knew he was simply giving his pitch in front of a blank screen and was being projected onto the head-vid presentation, but the combination was effective. It was as if the two were together in Australia.

"Every schoolchild knows the tragic story of the Australian continent," Coyle began. The scene changed to rangeland being eaten to stubble by hundreds of browsing rabbits. "A virus concocted to control the nation's feral browsers unfortunately mutated and jumped to humans. While Australia was effectively quarantined before the infection could spread, both the targeted animals and most of the continent's human inhabitants, except for a handful of refugees, were wiped out. This was a key factor in passage of the Genetic Engineering Reform Act, of course. Meanwhile, this catastrophe was considered so threatening to the world population at large that the continent was quarantined. The refugees were interned on the Seychelles Islands. Australia was permanently blockaded to prevent salvage companies or treasure hunters from landing and running the risk of contracting and spreading the disease. To further discourage such illegal access, all detailed maps, coordinates, and geographic information detailing the continent were purged from world databases. To the extent possible, Australia was put out of sight, out of mind, as an emergency measure of public safety. Until now! Because United Corporations turns problems into solutions. Because United Corporations believes that *everyone* can win, all the time." Daniel saw a picture of smiling backpackers winding down a palm-shaded desert canyon. The water pool next to them was turquoise.

"The solution Australia represented was an answer to the problem of wilderness," Coyle went on, now seeming to lean against a palm tree. "The public's desire for natural preserves had first been accommodated during the population explosion of the twentieth century. Scenic areas of valuable land were deliberately set aside in countries such as the United States and Canada to satisfy the demands of individualists who wanted to experience the outdoors." The head-vid panned a group of dirty, happy hikers eating lunch along a mountain trail. Then the view lifted to show an alpine meadow and cascading glaciers. The scenery was breathtaking.

"Despite such political generosity on the part of the national forerunners to United Corporations, none of these land seizures truly replicated wilderness. All were relatively small, quickly became crowded, and were crisscrossed with trails. They were surveyed, mapped, and offered rescue if something went wrong." There were scenes of horrid overcrowding at the rim of the Grand Canyon, in a Yosemite parking lot, at a Yellowstone geyser. Long chains of recreationists wound along trails that had been trampled into trenches or mud bogs. Scraps of litter blew across an eroded clearing. A mountain lake was shown posted for pollution.

"The environmental extremists of the late twentieth

century" (there was old tape footage of demonstrating greens) "demanded more. They proposed gigantic new wildernesses" (a map showed green stains growing like amoebae on western and northern North America) "so vast that people could literally get lost in them. But there was no *room* for more. Humanity needed resources to achieve our quality of life." Daniel was transported to a shopping mall, where happy families strolled with packages under their arms. He grinned sardonically. He'd never seen a family that happy.

"Until, that is, Virus 03.1 struck Australia. Unfortunate tragedy has presented the world with an island as big as the United States but emptier of people than Antarctica. How dangerous would Australia remain? United Corporations' board members" (there was a picture of familiar faces meeting at the U.C. board table, the men and women looking handsome and wise) "turned to science for more answers." Daniel saw hazard-suited investigators fanning out across the landscape like cautious moonwalkers. "These experts concluded Australia no longer has plague." The scientists had gathered back by their aircraft and were pushing their hoods back to grin in relief. The scene dissolved to one in a laboratory, zeroing in on a white-coated scientist perched on a stool and looking like a favorite grandfather. "Virus 03.1 died with its human carriers," the scientist assured Daniel with a smile. "It's as extinct as smallpox and AIDS." Then Coyle was back, posed now in front of the New York headquarters of United Corporations. "It was then that U.C. saw a *win-win* solution."

The scene changed once more to abandoned, derelict cities, empty mine pits, and drought-stunted grazing land. "Australia had always been underpopulated, dry, thin.

The first European explorers, the Dutch, didn't even want it. Asian traders visited only to obtain dried sea slugs sold in China as an aphrodisiac. Even after the English came, they found mostly desert and arid savanna. Meanwhile, environmental extremists continued to raise objections to some of the world's most promising and necessary development projects. Accordingly, United Corporations saw opportunity where everyone else saw disaster. Our leaders quietly proposed a compromise. We will preserve in its wilderness state this entire *continent,* they offered, in return for environmental compromise on other key issues. Greens will get a natural preserve of unprecedented size so long as they abstain from unreasonable obstructionism elsewhere. And to show our good faith, the most vociferous, vocal, skeptical, and committed environmentalists are invited to be the first to test themselves against the challenge of Outback Adventure!" Daniel saw a group of young, ruddy-looking adventurers waving goodbye from an aircraft. He thought he recognized a couple of the faces from news shows. The agreement must have worked, he realized, because environmental protest had indeed become muted.

"This achievement was deliberately unpublicized, the news organizations of United Corporations recognizing that controversy is worthwhile only when it is the servant of consensus. Publicity would only invite tragedy. Australia would continue to be reported as unsafe to discourage thrill-seekers, looters, or relatives of the dead wanting to make reckless pilgrimages. The naval and satellite patrol of Australia's coastal waters would be maintained.

"The board deliberately decided to maintain the continent in permanent, purposeful decay. The panic and rioting that broke out during the plague had already damaged Australia's urban areas, and since then rot and rust have done much more. The continent's cities are deteriorating ruins and its roads are crumbled and drifted over. More importantly, most of Australia's interior was empty of people even before the plague, and today little sign can be found that humans ever ventured there. The island has reverted to a wilderness of sand, broken concrete, and scrap metal, a wilderness so absolute in its isolation that its like is found nowhere else on earth. Electronic databases, books, maps, films, tapes, and television shows on Australia have been systematically pruned. This fosters the decay not just of the nation's physical infrastructure but its informational infrastructure as well. True wilderness is not just the absence of the human footprint, it is the absence of human knowledge. To the degree possible, United Corporations has achieved both." Coyle had a look of solemn satisfaction.

"Today, then, Australia is a place of purposeful mystery, a deliberate step back in time, a mythic place, an Eden. And now the licensed consulting firm of Outback Adventure has been hired to screen a chosen few to experience the challenge of true wilderness exploration and personal self-discovery." Background music began to swell as the couple of the brochures walked into the glory of a desert sunset, hand in hand. "These are people who are not satisfied with the everyday, people who have advanced beyond mere recreation, people who feel compelled to challenge the unknown. Those who graduate from Outback Adventure form the most select fraternity in the world!" As the head-vid reached its climax, Australia dissolved to show Mr. Bandolier transformed into a ruggedly handsome captain of industry who walked like a lord across his factory floor, his industrial robots bowing like nodding oil pumps. His female companion was shown as the bride in a costly cathedral wedding and then as an executive moving into a high-rise corner office with a stunning view of the city. "These are today's hardened heroes . . ." There was a final picture of green mountains climbing to snowy peaks, and then a dissolve.

Daniel removed his headgear, somewhat dazzled from the images of Australia's vastness. He was also visibly skeptical.

"So. What did you think?"

"A bit heavy-handed at the end there, Elliott."

His counselor, who was now sitting across from him, shrugged disarmingly. "You found the script a little corny? So do I. But there's truth in that corn, Daniel."

"I don't understand why I haven't heard more about this before. I mean, an entire continent? For wilderness recreation? And then you don't tell anyone about it?"

"To publicize it is to spoil it. We don't want the refugee community lobbying to go back; they have new lives now. We don't want pilgrims or mourners or looters. And United Corporations didn't set this up to make big money, or post big numbers. We did it to satisfy the craving for adventure among a select few, some of them frankly troubled, with the idea that this might help both them *and* society. Win-win! That *this* was the very best way to use the new Australia."

Daniel shifted uncomfortably. "How so?"

"Be honest with yourself, Daniel. Are you fulfilling your full potential at Microcore? Are you doing everything you could for United Corporations? Our superiors look at people like yourself and they wonder. He's bright. He thinks for himself. But he also has trouble fitting in.

So. We can leave him at a Level 31 job and let him stop growing, becoming deadwood. Or we might find something that pushes him to the limit, that tests just what he *is* capable of, and thus which grooms him for future leadership in U.C. society. Outback Adventure is meant to be a transforming experience. Those allowed to go are an elite."

"But keeping it a secret . . ."

"To publicize the opportunity is to cheapen it. The next thing you know there'd be cyber underground guidebooks, secret maps, and so much speculation that the journey would contain as much surprise as Planet Disney. We live in a world of twelve billion people, and a continent's preservation as complete wilderness is both bold and somewhat artificial. The board's choice would be economically controversial, to say the least. As a result, continued concerns about plague serve our purposes. So does quiet. We can't really keep you from telling a few war stories to close friends, of course, but you'll sign confidentiality agreements if you go. And believe me, they are *enforced*. No books, no speeches. No fame. Key people will know what you accomplished, but only them. We're not going to sacrifice the unique experience of future adventurers to satisfy the ego gratification of their predecessors. You're being offered a chance to qualify for the fraternity that really runs things on this planet of ours. There's a lot of competition to get in, and admittance is tough. You have to prove yourself. This is one way. It works."

Daniel nodded slowly, intrigued despite his doubts. "So who can go?"

"Ah. You're beginning to realize how rare this offer is. The answer to your question, of course, is the fit. The smart. The committed. The daring. And the dissatisfied. The ones to whom ordinary life is for some reason not enough. The oddballs, the misfits. Do you recognize yourself yet?"

Daniel said nothing.

"You go only with what you can carry on your back. Maps are prohibited. So is any weapon beyond a knife. You can take electronic devices, but only receivers: take your solar-cell TV, if you must, but leave your satellite phone at home. Our promise is that if you go, you won't know exactly where on the continent you are. Or precisely where you're going. Or how long it will take. You'll be as blind as Columbus, as bold as Magellan. No other adventure company offers such realistic challenge. We guarantee it!"

"A year's salary for that?"

"Listen to me. Everest is old, routine. You know that. The Sahara has become a holiday junket. Both Poles have resort hotels. Every river has been rafted and every reef has been dived. There's only one place of mystery left on earth: Outback Adventure's Australia. That's what the money is for, Daniel: the ultimate challenge of the ultimate wilderness. You bet it costs dearly! You have to want it so bad you can *taste* it! Because that's the only kind of person who can make it there."

He took a breath. He *could* taste it. "How does it work?"

"We have a meeting where you'll meet your fellow adventurers. Many decide to go in groups, something we recommend to both enhance your own survival chances and lower our transportation costs. We give you training. We have experts on the continent and books or tapes you can review on its ecology and geology. You'll go prepared.

We'll give you a list of suggested equipment but it's up to you to prepare and equip yourself. You'll survive on your brain and your back. You make your preparations, train for six weeks, wait, and then we call without warning to inform you it's time to come to the Departure Port. Ready or not, here you go: we feel that edge adds to the experience, and weeds out the last few with secret doubts. You quietly quit your job in advance—don't worry, come back and you'll be wanted for something special—and fly to Departure. All volunteers are drugged to sleep for shipping."

"Like export cargo."

"Exactly. We transport you at night to a point somewhere in the continent's interior and set you down to awaken at dawn. Your goal is to trek to Australia's east coast and find its exit port, Exodus. Then you return to United Corporations' world, renewed and toughened. An eighteenth-century man of action in a twenty-first-century world! Survive this and you can kick corporate butt anywhere you go. But you have to survive it. There's no hospital, no rescue, no emergency food or water. We don't come get you. You're on your own."

"Jesus." He drummed his fingers, a nervous habit. "What's the risk?"

Coyle pushed a button of the chair-file under his cushion. Liability forms slid out of a desk chute and he plunked them in front of Dyson with a thump. "Some people don't make it. A lot of people, actually." He nodded as Daniel's brows lifted. "The risk is higher than high-altitude climbing. Sky diving. Hang gliding. Free diving. You name it. This is the riskiest thing on earth. And yet competition to participate is fierce. Only *risking* life, after all, makes you feel truly *alive*."

"Worse than climbing?"

"Worse than many wars."

He took a breath. "All right, Elliott. Have *you* done this?"

Coyle looked at Daniel a long time without expression. "Yes. Once."

"And survived."

Coyle smiled thinly. "Living proof."

"And were you transformed?"

The counselor had a faraway look in his eyes. "Oh yes."

"And now?"

"I became a believer, Daniel. A convert. An apostle. So now I'm employed explaining all this to people like you. That's what I wanted to do when I got back. It was what I was put on earth to do, I'm sure of it."

"And you recommend it?"

"No. Never. It's so hard that I just give you a choice. You have to choose yourself. It's the choice that determines whether you're ready to go."

"How many choose not to? Don't they spill your secret?"

He smiled. "Frankly, few who learn this much turn us down. We're careful what we reveal, to who. Those who do say no recognize the need for discretion. We explain it to them."

"So I can walk out of here right now?"

"Absolutely. And I'd understand perfectly. *I* wouldn't go now. I've got a wife, kids. I'm too old now, too soft, too content. I like *this* world. That's what *I* learned in the Outback. So I'll shake your hand and pat you on the back if you want to quit right now." He waited.

"Quite the salesman, aren't you?" Dyson picked up the liability forms and examined them. Leave his job? Give up his savings? Go wander in the desert and maybe die out there? Was he that crazy? That unhappy? That unfulfilled?

"Don't go unless you're absolutely sure, Daniel. Don't go unless you need to find something you can't find here."

He thought of Raven. "Like why do I do?"

"Yes. Like that."

He took a breath. "Got a pen?"

Coyle handed him one.

Daniel looked at it, rotating in his fingers. Are you brave? Dr. Chen had asked. *I've never had to find out.*

He bent to sign his name.

"I want to test myself."

CHAPTER EIGHT

You've given notice?" Sanford asked, mystified.

"Quitting," Daniel confirmed to his workmate. "You have to keep quiet about it until after I'm gone."

"They're just letting you go?"

Indeed they were, Daniel thought. Luther Cox had expressed neither surprise nor interest at the news: *I hope it's for the best,* he'd said remotely. *We'll fill in for you whenever they call.* "Didn't even feign regret, I'm afraid."

"But why?"

Why do you do? Daniel thought to himself. Because it committed himself. Because it cut his ties. Go, go, go. "I'm going away," he replied.

"An opportunities transfer?"

"I'm going to the wilderness, Sanford. Taking a break from the routine."

"You're quitting your job to go on vacation?"

"It's sort of open-ended. Unclear when I'll get back. It's not really a vacation, it's . . . a kind of lifestyle change. I want to do something different."

Sanford thought about this. "When do we fight over your scanner and disk repository?" he asked, ever practical, scanning Daniel's desk for other valuables.

"I'm on staff until the expedition starts. Then it's yours."

"So when's that?"

"I don't know. We're not allowed to know."

"What?"

"The surprise departure is part of the wilderness experience. You prepare, wait, they call, bang. You're off."

"That's weird. Off where?"

"To the desert."

"Really?" Sanford had a fondness for Nevada.

"To a wilderness desert, not a casino desert."

"Oh. Which one?"

"I can't say. I'm not allowed to say. I don't really know, actually. It's all set up by an adventure company. Some new outfit you've never heard of. Neither had I."

"Jesus, Dyson, this is pretty offbeat. For what?"

"To explore."

"Explore what?"

"I don't know. Nobody does. That's the whole point."

"*What's* the whole point?"

"To have an adventure. To go do something risky where the end isn't preordained. To trade security for excitement, comfort for experience, entertainment for self-exploration."

"You sound like a commercial. Or somebody who's been brain-scrubbed. Let me get this straight. You're leaving Microcore to go on some expedition that starts who knows when, going to who knows where, for who knows how long, for who knows what reason?"

Daniel shrugged. "It's not for everyone."

"It's not for *anyone* with common sense. Have you totally lost your mind? You're going to give up a good job . . ."

"Oh, please . . ." He looked amused.

". . . to go to some desert you can't even identify? And pay *money* to do it? Why, because you don't like the looks of Harriet Lundeen? Because you can't make it with Mona Pietri?"

"Because I'm being buried here, Sanford. Buried alive. You are too."

"Better than being buried *dead* out in some desert."

"You paid to go down the Mekong . . ."

"That was different."

"How was that different?"

"I didn't quit my job. They set up camp, set down camp chairs, and set out the booze. We had an itinerary, not to mention sonic-guard to keep out the insects. Women came along. It was fun, dammit. *That's* what was different."

"Different? Or predictable?"

"Here's a news flash for you, Dyson. I like things predictable. Most people do."

"Such as this job?"

Sanford glanced around the monotony of Level 31 and nodded solemnly. "Such as my pay. Predictable as clockwork."

"There's got to be more."

"There isn't any more. That's what you don't get, or won't admit. You're a romantic and life isn't. Life is just . . . life. You want green, go to the park. You want animals, go to the zoo. You want sunstroke and snakes, go to the desert."

"No. I'm going to find more. I'm going to find it, and bring it back, and show you. Shove it in your face."

"A rattlesnake?"

"Freedom. Self-discovery."

His workmate rocked back in his seat. "You'll discover things all right. Discover that hunger and fear don't make you free."

"Maybe *that's* the point."

"Suffering?"

"To overcome it."

Sanford laughed and threw up his hands. "Go! Wander in the desert. Have visions. Bring back a prophecy; my last fortune cookie was a bore."

"I'm just tired of being safe."

"Well, I predict you'll get tired of being *unsafe* in about fifteen minutes." He shook his head, looking at Daniel speculatively. "There's some other reason, isn't there? Something that pushed you into this. What? Some kind of trouble? A woman?"

"There's no woman."

"Some muscle-thighed rock spider with breasts the size of coconuts?"

"There's no woman. It's just me. For me. I mean, don't you ever get tired of the routine here, Sanford?"

"Of course I do. Everybody does." He stood up and gazed across the top of the cubicles. "And I'll tell you the one thing you'll get for your money. It will make Level 31 look pretty damn good."

That night he called her again. Not because this was about Raven, of course, but because . . . because he wanted her to know. That he'd signed up. That they'd taken the man she thought they wouldn't take. So there.

On the sixth ring the circuit transferred and a voice came on line but the video picture was grayed out. "Hello?" A man's voice. Damn.

"Is Raven there?"

"Who's calling?"

"A friend."

"Your name?" He could hear clicks on the line.

"I'm just a friend. Look, could you put her on, please?"

"I need your name."

More funny sounds. Were they recording? "My name is none of your damn business. Let me speak to Raven."

There was a long pause. Then, "Miss DeCarlo is no longer here."

"What?"

"Miss DeCarlo is not here."

"This isn't her number?"

"She's left the city for an outdoor excursion."

He stopped at that. Had Raven gone too? "Do you know when she'll be back?"

"No. Do you wish to leave a message?"

Well there wasn't much point in that—if she was off on an Outback Adventure. Had he triggered her like she triggered him? "Who is this?"

"Do you wish to leave a message?"

More clicks. Was this guy a boyfriend, or something else? A mechanical monitor? "I want to talk to her before she goes."

"That's impossible."

To talk? Or was she already gone? "I want a forwarding number."

"Do you wish to leave a message?"

"There's no number?"

"Do you wish to leave a message?"

He drummed his fingers, considering. "Yeah, I want to leave a message. Tell her I called."

"We'll do that."

The connection went dead.

Daniel stared at the phone a long time. They hadn't asked his name.

Room upon room, level upon level, link upon link. A descent into an underworld in which the passwords and riddles and locks were always changing, identities shifting, allegiances unclear. Not just cyberspace, but a cyber pit of mysteries. He clicked and probed, searching for himself: could he find any reference to Outback Adventure? His search engines revealed no matches. Information on Australia had been wiped, except for rumor and uncertain memory. Coyle was right. It was ignorance that made wilderness.

Disbelieve.

Spartacus again, like an electronic nag. *Have you decided, Daniel?*

"I'm going away."

Away? Where?

"To the wilderness."

There is no more wilderness. Except here.

"I'm going to a special place."

Your place is here. With us.

"I can't do your truth cookie. I don't know how and besides, they've made me. I'm dangerous to you now. They found out about my hacking and they watch me. So . . . I'm going."

There was no response.

"I'm sorry. I know this GeneChem stuff is—"

There's nothing in the wilderness. That's why it's called wilderness.

"I think I can find something there."

What?

What indeed? Raven? "My reason for being."

Your reason for being is here.

"Goodbye. I have to go now."

The truth is inside, not outside . . .

CHAPTER NINE

I'm crazy, but not a fool."

The phrase became Daniel's mantra as he started his preparations. You make your own luck, he told himself. He would research, he would train, he would purchase, and because of that he would survive. When he awakened in the Australian desert he would be self-contained and self-sufficient, a twenty-first-century primitive, ready to live as prehistoric man must have lived but with the added edge of modern technology. The challenge was daunting, but also energizing. Once equipped, he would need no one and nothing, except the fruits of the earth. He would enjoy total freedom.

Because of the peculiarities of its challenge—the emphasis on self-survival, unaided and undirected—the training and guidance from Outback Adventure was alternately generous and guarded. The mix put him off-balance. From earliest memory Daniel's life had been crammed with advice: recited by parents, drilled by teachers, whispered to him from office walls, pounded at him in commercials, nagged by machines due for a tune-up, or scolded by corporate officials conducting performance appraisals. Everyone, it seemed, knew exactly what he should do next. Until now. He could learn quite a bit about generic survival tactics, and very little about the place he would use them. Survival could be taught. Australia must remain mysterious.

What Daniel was presented with were catalogs. There were endless lists of available equipment. Inventories of Australian plants and animals. Data on the temperature (hot), rainfall (erratic), and elevation (low). Survival manuals so general that they included advice on building igloos, drying fish, and distilling sea water. The descriptions of the country he was to be deposited in, however, were spare.

"That would defeat the whole purpose, wouldn't it?" said Elliott Coyle.

"It's just odd, and difficult, preparing for a place that's been turned into a deliberate secret. There're no maps and no journals by previous adventurers."

"How did Columbus prepare? Cabot? Boone?" Coyle tapped his head and heart. "In *here,* not out there. They knew little of where they were going, but an immense amount about seamanship or forest travel. They succeeded on common sense. If *you* succeed it will be because of you, not because of us."

That's what he wanted. That's what he feared.

The shopping was initially exhilarating. Suddenly, money seemed to have no meaning. Departing on something as timeless and ill-defined as Outback Adventure was liberating. He felt like a kid in a candy store who could buy to fulfill a fantasy: Second-Skin to don for cold desert nights. A solar blanket squeezed into the size of a matchbox. Chem-candles to start fires. Torso webbing to hold clip-ons. Freeze-dried Stroganoff, couscous, strawberry shortcake, and Szechwan chicken. A water purifier, a solar battery recharge wafer, vitamin drops, a solar-lithium flashlight, a hydrogen pellet stove, Spider-Line, Supra-Boots, and a bush hat with band pockets for fish hooks, spare buttons, a barometer, and data wafers for his palmtop computer.

He spread it across the floor of his apartment and regarded its titanium glitter with initial glee. The paraphernalia of survival! Yet as he toyed with his acquisitions, weighing them individually while toting up his load, he began to feel misgivings. How much of this world did he really want to saddle onto his back? Every step would be a reminder of where he'd come from. Would that be reassuring, or oppressive? He sat on his couch and looked at his purchases, receipts curled like party streamers and box lids gaping like hungry mouths. He put on the bush hat and regarded himself in the reflection of a computer screen.

"G'day, mate."

He frowned.

"You look bloody ridiculous."

Suddenly the gear seemed a miniaturized replication of the United Corporations world, as cumbersome as a space suit. Out of curiosity he bundled the instruction booklets and weighed them. A pound right there.

He sat down again and began to think.

How could he carry enough on his back to keep alive for the months it would likely take to hike to the Australian coast and find Exodus Port? Even with the new food concentrates it suddenly seemed impossible. To be put down in the middle of nowhere, to find your own way to an unclear destination . . . was he insane? But then that was the nature of exploring, wasn't it? "Because of you, not because of us," Coyle had said. Damn right it would be a way to explore himself.

Raven carried no water underground because she knew where to get a drink. "Water's heavy," she'd said.

He moved to his window and watched the pigeons fluttering across Silicon Square. They carried nothing at all, and neither had primitive man. If you knew what to eat, the wilderness was a garden. He needed to carry less on his shoulders and more in his head.

He went to a hardware store and bought a dowel and block of wood. Then he came back, sat down, and began drawing up a new list of what he thought he truly needed. Next to it he wrote a goal: "45 pounds." He scratched some items out and added others. How light could he travel? How fast could he move? He considered, then wrote again: "35 pounds?" He flipped through the books. How good a garden was Australia? He'd been taught all his life that information was the tool of success, and now information was frustratingly vague. He underlined a passage. "Your environment is neither friendly nor hostile, but rather the product of preparation and the discipline of your mind."

He took the wood block and with a pocketknife whittled a small depression in it, then roughly sharpened one end of the dowel so it rested in the new hole. The wood shavings he carefully hoarded. Then he began to experiment with ways to pivot the dowel in the hole.

Four hours later, the building superintendent was pounding on his door. "Dyson! Hey, open the door if you're in there!"

Daniel opened it a crack. He looked tired.

"Christ, the stink!" the super greeted. "The goddamned fire alarm sounded! You okay? You burn something?"

His tenant held up a blackened piece of wood with a look of grim satisfaction. "I started a fire, Mr. Landau. With this."

The superintendent looked at the charcoal in bewilderment. "With what?"

"Friction. I made fire from my hands."

Landau paused. Thank goodness this loopy kid had already given notice. "You're a friggin' nut case, you know that?"

Daniel nodded.

"Listen, Dyson, you can't start fires here. You know that. It's against the rules."

"Everything is against the rules." He set down his wood and put up his hand to close the door. "I'm done now, don't worry. My arm is sore." He jerked his head in the direction of his carpet, littered with packages as if at Christmas. "I just have to take some things back to the store."

If information on Australian geography was meager, information on survival tactics was not. Daniel became a repository of trivia. Rommel's troops drank two and a half gallons of water a day in the desert, he read. Workers at Hoover Dam consumed an average of *six* and a half. African natives had used pierced and blown-out ostrich eggs as canteens. Rubbing oneself with chewed tobacco warded off insects.

"Too bad it's a controlled substance," he muttered.

Physical training became an obsession. Now his miles were timed. Alternate days were spent with weight and tension machines. He logged endless crunches, sprints, and even began a martial arts class. Daniel wasn't especially quick or coordinated, but he decided the discipline and drills of Asian combat couldn't hurt. He also sought out advice on practical, gut-level street fighting—more to give himself self-confidence than because he expected to have to use the knowledge.

One of the trainers, an ex-cop, looked at him doubtfully. "Hit first and give it everything you've got, Coogan," he said, wryly using the name of a current action hero. "It will all be over in fifteen seconds, one way or another." He looked Daniel up and down. "It wouldn't hurt to know how to run, either."

Daniel loaded his pack, weighed it, and then went over his list again. He filled it with rocks equal to twice the weight and climbed the stairs of his building. Then again, and again, and again. He spent a night on the roof in a bedroll with ground cover, kept awake by the lights and the heat. His back was stiff by morning.

He stalked, and butchered, a possum he spied prowling through garbage, comparing its internal architecture with the manuals he was reading. He practiced until he could hit crows with rocks. He ran in a downpour, drank water sluicing off an awning, and measured how much he could catch in his hat.

People ignored his eccentricity. Everyone moved in a bubble of anonymity.

The exception to this was an orientation and final screening session for regional participants, the first of several weekend seminars for the next class of Outback Adventurers. "We thought you'd like to see who you might rub elbows with in the bush," Elliott Coyle told a gathering of two dozen in a windowless rented conference room in the basement of Outback Adventure's office tower. "Just so you know you're not alone in your desire for wilderness challenge."

"Or our insanity," someone quipped. The group laughed nervously.

Daniel glanced around. Most of the participants looked to be in their twenties and thirties, a third of them women. A few had the whippet leanness of endurance athletes but the majority looked reassuringly ordinary, and uncertain about whether they were in the right place. They glanced at each other shyly.

"Some of you will insist on traversing the Outback on your own, we know, but most of our participants choose to form a small group," Coyle said. "I encourage you to consider it. For ourselves, it simplifies problems of delivery. For you, it enhances the chance of survival. Not to mention the possibility of forming friendships that will last the rest of your lives." He paused to let them consider that.

They looked at each other uncertainly. Who would they get along with? Who could they trust?

"We're also going to subject you to a physical, some inoculations, and a final psychological screening to make sure you're *really* Outback Adventure material. While some of this may seem intrusive, it's the kind of thing that could save your life in the end. So please, bear with us and accept our judgment."

The group looked surprised. They'd already made their decision and paid a deposit. Now there were last-minute hurdles?

A hand went up. "Did I miss something here?" the person who'd made the earlier quip now caustically asked.

Coyle looked at the short, wiry, thin-faced young man

raising the question. "Ah yes, Mr. Washington. Ico, isn't it?"

"It is, Elliott." He stood. "So glad you remember me. Now, if I remember correctly, *we're* paying *you*. And we have to go through more bullshit tests? Come on! We're ready to go or we wouldn't be here."

Coyle looked at him calmly. "If you're ready, Ico, you won't have any problem with our tests. And if you don't like the Outback Adventure program, then obviously you *aren't* ready and can expect a full refund." He let his stern gaze pass across the room. "This is your life at stake here. We're not going to put you out there if you don't belong."

Washington sat down. "Corporate nonsense," he fumed. A couple of candidates snickered and a few others looked uncomfortable. Coyle ignored the rustle and called a couple of names to begin the screening.

The man sitting next to Daniel smiled. "That boy *needs* to get into the bush," he whispered. "I just *want* to."

Daniel studied his companion. The man was big, dark, and powerful, so long and solid that Daniel thought he looked like a folded tree.

"Everyone in this room has been tested up the kazoo since birth," Daniel whispered back. "Who wants any more?"

"You do what you have to do to get where you want to go," the man replied. He held out a hand. Like shaking a baseball mitt, Daniel thought. "Tucker Freidel. I was an Alaskan trapper in a previous life. And a Zulu warrior in the life before that." His brown eyes smiled.

"Daniel Dyson," came the reply as his arm was pumped. "And in this life, Tucker?"

The man grinned good-naturedly. "A failed computer

salesman. My theory is, I can't do worse in the wilderness."

"At least you're honest."

"And as fed up as that little guy there. I'm willing for a last poke in the butt if it gets me out of here and into God's country."

"We're going to find God out there?"

"I sure as hell am going to look. I figure I might need Him."

"But not a computer."

Tucker laughed. "I sure as hell ain't packing one!"

"You know what Captain Cook said about the aborigines?"

"Captain who?"

"One of the discoverers of Australia. He said, 'They may appear to be the most wretched people upon earth, but in reality they are far happier than we Europeans. Being wholly unacquainted not only with the superfluous but the necessary conveniences so much sought after in Europe, they are happy in not knowing the use of them.' " Daniel winked. *"Happy in not knowing the use of them. Like computers."*

"And how do you know shit like that? You with Captain Cook in a previous life?"

"No, just a history major in this one. A walking repository of trivia. Though I guess you *could* call college a previous life. Or a hallucination."

Tucker laughed again. "Or a damn waste of time. But then, so was my marriage and most of my career."

"So now you're here."

"So now I'm trying to get *there*. Listen, do you know why I'm really going?"

"Why?"

"Because it's the one thing a computer would never do. There's no logic to it. I'm going because it's *there*, like that Everest guy said. Because it *feels* right. I like the *pointlessness* of it. The one time in my life when I'm not doing what I'm *supposed* to do. Can you understand that?"

Daniel nodded. He liked this guy. He seemed unpretentious, down-to-earth, self-aware.

"How'd you hear about it?"

"Tipped by a correspondent on the web. Pen pal fellow failure. I'd heard rumors, floating in the cyber underground, but never knew it was real."

"So what did you think about Coyle advising us to team up? Are you game for that? Maybe we could be partners."

Tucker eyed him speculatively. "Maybe. What do you do when you aren't quoting history?"

"I thought it was supposed to be *why* do you do. The what is a software writer."

"Sheeit."

"The why is . . . I don't know why. I haven't thought it through as clearly as you, perhaps. That's what I'm looking for out there: why."

"That's what unites this bunch, I'll bet. We're all looking." Tucker glanced around at the other chatting adventurers. "Listen, I wouldn't mind teaming up but I've already got someone else who wanted to tag along." He pointed. "That cute little girl over there. The one with the short black hair. Name's Chiu." He caught her eye and waved to her. "Amaya! Help me check this guy out!"

A young, pleasant-looking woman with a ready smile came over. She wasn't really little, but shorter and slighter than either Tucker or Daniel. Her round face was open and cheerful and her dark eyes danced as she looked up at each in turn.

"This is Daniel. He wants to come with us. He can quote Captain Cook."

She cocked her head. "How useful. And his field of expertise?"

"He says he's a software writer. I think that means he can type." Tucker laughed.

"*And* a military engineer." Daniel said it lightly. "I build catapults."

"Why Tucker!" she exclaimed. "*Exactly* what we need!"

"What do *you* do, Ms. Chiu?"

"Partly stand in Tucker's shadow," she teased, stepping slightly behind his powerful form. "He's the brawn and I'm the brains, right, Freidel?"

"I ain't doing *all* the lifting."

"I'm also an executive suck-up by profession, and amateur naturalist and closet romantic by inclination."

"Executive suck-up?"

"Assistant, associate, deputy, and lieutenant, rising horizontally from one middle-management post to another. A gofer who finally answered to one idiot too many and decided to really go. I love adventure stories, so I've decided to live one. And I'm fascinated by nature."

Like Tucker, without pretense. "We all seem to have a lot in common."

"And two strong males! You two can break trail. I'll point the way."

"Lewis and Clark and Sacajawea," Daniel said.

"Except a hundred eighty degrees in the opposite direction. We want to go east, gentlemen, not west. I'm already contributing, you see, by making that clear."

Tucker scratched his head in mock befuddlement. "And doesn't the sun set backward Down Under?"

Amaya rolled her eyes. "I never did have a proper taste in men. So do you really build catapults, Mr. . . ."

"Dyson. Daniel Dyson. A little one, once. It got me into trouble."

"War machines usually do."

Daniel liked her banter. This could be fun.

"I saw you talking to the hand-raiser," Tucker said to her. "What's he like?"

"Smart. As in mouth, ass. But quick too. Maybe we should enlist him."

Daniel was doubtful. "That guy?"

"He's interesting. He'll talk your ear off. Come over and meet him."

Ico Washington wasted no time in presenting them with his worldview. He had curly hair and olive skin and a restless manner, his eyes flicking around the room as he talked. He fizzed like a shaken bottle.

"I don't take these Outback guys seriously," he explained. "I don't take anyone connected with United Corporations seriously. I haven't heard an honest word since the delivery doctor slapped my butt and extended condolences, just happy-talk bullshit my whole life and an unending list of rules and come-ons. I mean, a year's salary to dump me in some desert? It's *gotta* be a scam. And when an oily snake like Elliott Coyle says gee, not all of you may get to go, I *know* I'm being taken."

Tucker frowned. "So why are you here?"

Ico laughed with self-deprecation. "Because this is my peek behind the curtain, man. This is my chance to look from outside the box. I figure that out in the bush there's no wall whispers, no head-vid, no committee-meetings-from-hell. For once I get away from the ambient noise, you know? So I can think. So I can consider. So I can plan."

"Plan what?"

"Permanent escape." He nodded, as if confiding a great secret. "I don't want a temporary furlough, I want *release* from this bullshit corporate world. I want to experience real freedom. So I go along with their little mind games, even while I let them know I see through them. Because this isn't a vacation for me, this is a turning point. Once I'm down on that Outback ground, I'm not the same guy coming back. I'm going to imagine a better life. I think they're betting a taste of dirt and bugs will teach me the benefits of the United Corporations world, but I'm going to be finding my own world. We're Pandora's box, man, and they've no clue what can happen when you open the lid."

Daniel frowned, recognizing a bit of himself. "So what is it that *you* do, Ico?"

He looked at them smugly. "I see things clearly."

CHAPTER TEN

By design, there was no one to see them off.

There were thirteen pages of rules to replicate wilderness experience: "Condition 27: You will not write or speak about this experience. Condition 63: You will have completed and filed with Outback Adventure a last will and testament. Condition 81: You will have been screened and found free of communicable diseases."

Condition 17 specified an unpredictable departure time. No goodbyes to family or loved ones. No hugs. No weeping. No notice. They came, you went, like a furtive kidnapping. Daniel's call buzzed through at the trailing edge of night. "I'm in the lobby, Daniel," Coyle's voice calmly announced. "It's time for adventure."

He groaned. "Jesus, what time is it?"

"Just before dawn. The favored time for surprise attack."

"All right," he said groggily. "I've just got to pull my stuff together."

"Five minutes."

"Elliott . . ."

"Five minutes. We told you it would be like this. Cold plunge. The time for second thoughts is over."

Daniel knew the opposite was true. He could still quit, even now. The urgent, disorienting departure was a final test. "I'll be down. Everything's here. Just a couple items I've been debating to take."

"If in doubt, leave it out."

He swung out of bed, dressed without a shower, and grabbed his gear. His last pained decision had been to leave his sleeping bag behind in favor of a lighter, slimmer, tougher bedroll. He needed to *move* to survive. After another minute's indecision he pocketed the toy action trooper next to his computer. Gordo Firecracker, tough guy amulet. Then he glanced around a last time.

The apartment was already bare. He'd made arrangements for the last of his belongings to be packed and moved into storage. The video wall was a dim gray, his computer cabinet lightless. Now he threw his Microcore identity badge into the trash. "Mona, I'm gonna," he recited. Goodbye to the goddess, goodbye to the gorgon, goodbye to all that. "Raven, I'm . . . cravin'." Craving what? Sand in his cereal? Blisters on his heels? "Cravin' to find out *why*."

Coyle saw him into a cab and gave him tickets for a shuttle. A red-eye flight to a coast city, leaving in forty-five minutes. "You'll meet the others for final departure there." The door slammed.

Daniel keyed down the window. "Aren't you going to wish me good luck?"

His counselor was silent a moment. "Luck is just preparation plus opportunity," he finally recited. In the darkness of predawn, Coyle's expression couldn't be seen.

There was a two-hour flight to the final departure point, the two dozen other adventurers scattered at random through the plane, a few sleeping and most just quiet, lost in their own thoughts. At the airport an unmarked bus met them for transport to an industrial airfield. More than a hundred people had assembled there for flights that would scatter them like shot across the continent of Australia. They checked into musty dormitories.

"Barracks," Ico corrected. "Crap left over from the army or something. Unloaded on these guys, or picked up for a song. You'd think for a year's salary they'd give us a last night in a hotel room."

"My guess is it's a last reality check," Daniel said, sitting on a bunk. It creaked, its wire web apparent under the thin mattress. "So we're clear what we're getting into."

"And my guess is that they're a bunch of cheap bastards who know if we're already dumb enough to sign on for 'adventure' that we'll tolerate any fleabag they check us into."

"A small price to come alive," Amaya teased him.

"Yeah, what difference does it make?" Tucker said. "Tomorrow we wake up on the sand."

"It matters if someone snores. You snore, Freidel?"

"I dunno. If I do, I sleep through it like a rock."

"*That's* a question that would've been useful on the questionnaires," Ico said. " 'Do you snore?' But oh, no, they gotta know what my favorite damn color is."

"What'd you say?"

"Green. The light that says go."

Told they'd leave before dawn again the next day, the four companions decided on a final party in a nearby restaurant, their evening celebration wired with the adrenaline of excitement, a magnum of champagne, and tabs of EcSotica drug. They laughed so hard they finally cried about snarled commutes, dead-end jobs, blank-brained bosses, mortgages on units they hated, and insurance on lives they'd felt were hardly worth keeping. Now it was all going to be gone, poof, and they'd wake up to find themselves in the Outback, life reduced to a hunt for food to eat and water to drink. Simple. Stark. Scary.

"Did you *see* that guy?" Ico snorted excitedly, spitting a bit of champagne across their table as they talked of hopes and fears. "Came out of their phony last-minute screening positively mystified that he didn't get in. 'Gee, I met all the criteria. Golly, I don't know what the problem was. But at least they turned me on to an executive opportunity at DisneySoft I'm sure is just as exciting . . .' What crap. They tried to get me to back out too with their song and dance about a good job elsewhere. I didn't fall for the ploy. It's a test, man, a trap. These guys are Machiavellian."

"How can they make any money if they keep turning people away?" Tucker drunkenly wondered.

"By making it hard to get in! Christ, try to keep people out of a nightclub and they'll line up around the block. This idiot will tell his friends he washed out and half of them will sign up to replace him. They're playing us, man. They're reeling us in."

"So aren't you upset at being netted?" Daniel asked.

"Nope." Ico poured another glass. "Because I'm riding the fishing boat to a better place, my man. Because all their bullshit is just a taxi for my mind."

They barely got two hours' sleep before being awakened at three A.M. and electro-bused to the waiting transports. The night was chilly and dark, and a light fog drifted off the harbor. Daniel could see that their craft was marked by a nondescript OA on its fuselage. This jet would take them to some transfer point and then smaller hovers would disperse individuals and small groups, they'd been told. Sleepy and hungover, they shivered gloomily. The freight decks of the aging terminal were shut.

"Damn, I'm tired," Tucker said.

"We'll sleep on the plane," Daniel assured him.

They got a breakfast of stale donuts and instant coffee while they waited for the jet to be readied. "They spare no expense," Ico observed.

"We're getting to see a place few people have ever visited," Amaya replied, as if to justify the unceremonious send-off.

"What, Australia? Or this dump?"

Daniel wondered if Raven had come through here. He found himself thinking about her with almost irritating frequency, like a worry he couldn't put behind him. Had she gone to the Outback? Was there a chance they'd meet there? What would she think of him if they did?

"Okay, form up! Bring your gear!" It was time. The ramp personnel waving them through were in red jumpsuits.

"Is this where we return?" Tucker asked one of them.

The man shook his head.

"Where then?"

"Beats me, buddy. I'd lobby to come back through Hawaii."

Their gear was searched, and a probe found data wafers in Daniel's bush hat. They went into a computer for scanning, and any mentioning Australia were deleted.

"It's just history!" he protested. "Background!"

"It might contain geographic detail. You were told that was cheating, Dyson."

"You didn't even read it!"

"Didn't have to. Besides, you don't need history where you're going."

Ico lost a compass that had a comm-phone slyly built in. "It's a compass, dammit!"

"With a radio. Looks like you're going to tell direction by the sun, sport."

"I want a receipt for that!"

The worker set the instrument on a metal counter, picked up a hammer, and swung. There was an expensive crack. "Don't need one. You can have it back. Next!"

"Fucking storm troopers."

"Next!"

Tucker and Amaya were clean.

They shuffled out onto the dark tarmac, bent under their gear. A line formed as the leading adventurers shrugged off their packs and disappeared aboard. As he waited for his turn, Daniel glanced idly around one more time and saw an electro-bus with no lights hum up to another freight dock. A line of men shuffled off it, heads bowed, shoulders stooped, barely visible in the dark. They wore the same jumpsuits as the ramp workers, he saw, but their scalps were shaved and there was the glint of something silver on their necks. Were the jumpsuits red or . . .

"Ico, look. I think those might be convicts."

His companion glanced that way. "Bullshit."

"No, really. Look at their necks. Those might be stun collars. I read about them. It's designed to jolt if they try to run away. I thought that crude stuff had been rendered obsolete by treatment, but there they are." Daniel had never seen a convicted criminal outside of video and holographic shows. He was fascinated.

"Hmm." Ico considered. "If those are moral-impaireds, why aren't they in a clinic? What are they doing here?"

"Getting a ride to rehab, I'd guess. They must have just been convicted."

Ico looked from the convicts to the men in jumpsuits who were processing the departure of the Outback Adventurers. "Look at our own goons," he nodded. "For all we know, the guys frisking us are rehabs. More nickel shaving by Outback Adventure. No wonder the food is swill."

"You might remember the cuisine more fondly after days surviving on ant balls," Amaya reminded.

"Whose balls?"

"Balls of ants, collected on a stick."

He laughed. "You can tell me about it, Chiu. I brought Solar Chow."

"Looks like you got enough to feed us all." She eyed the massive pack Ico was bent under. "How are you going to carry all that?"

"On my back, sweetheart."

"How heavy is it?"

"Seventy-five well-chosen pounds to keep me not just alive but comfortable. Don't worry, I'll *still* leave you in the dust."

"Really? Okay, wise guy: first one to camp. I win, you cook me your chow. You win—"

"It ain't a bet, sweetheart. This food's for me."

"Hey, who are *those* guys?" Daniel asked one of the

red jumpsuits. The man looked at the distant shuffling line of convicts he was pointing toward.

"Them? Just the morally impaired."

"Criminals? What are they doing here?"

"Our company has a lot of transport contracts." He laughed. "Be careful you don't get on the wrong one!"

"Hell," another joked, "I think these fools are *already* on the wrong one."

"A few days in the wilderness and they'll want back on *any* transport," a third added.

"Enough," their supervisor snapped.

Nervous laughter rippled through the passengers waiting on the tarmac. "Boy, they really know how to put us in the mood, don't they?" said Tucker.

The supervisor suddenly eyed him. "You can still back out."

Tucker thrust out his chin. "No way."

The jumpsuit nodded.

On board the airplane, Ico pushed his way forward. "I want to be up front."

"What does it matter?" Daniel said. "We're going to be put to sleep."

"It matters."

They followed Ico to the front and Daniel lay down in his berth, watching as a med-op strapped him to his bunk. The man tugged hard and the straps went tight. "Preparing me for a lobotomy?" Daniel tried to joke. His heart was beating faster and he realized his nervousness was about to turn to fright. Was he doing the right thing?

"The straps keep you safer in turbulent air." There was a prick as a tube was inserted. "And this dope feels a hell of a lot better than getting a lobe cut out." He felt a warm flush begin in his arm and flood his body. This was it. Next stop, the Outback.

The med-op's face loomed over him, blurry and indistinct. "You okay?"

"Yeah. I can feel it." Daniel felt himself begin to relax.

"What are you hoping to find out in the wilderness, sport?"

He smiled at himself, drifting down into warm fuzz. "I'm chasing a question, I guess."

"A question?"

"Yeah. 'Why?' " He felt himself start to float. "Or a woman."

The attendant chuckled. "There're easier ways to get a date . . ."

PART TWO

CHAPTER ELEVEN

Daniel swam up out of a well of drugs and into an instinctively familiar music. The sound was uneven and yet strangely rhythmic, sweet and welcoming. It was birdsong, he dimly realized, a dawn chattering that he'd never heard from his soundproofed apartment in the city. This is what morning is *supposed* to sound like. He blinked and propped himself up on his elbows, looking fuzzily around. The landscape was alive with birds, flitting from tree to tree. Black ones, green ones. He recognized some from his reading: thornbills, honeyeaters, fairy wrens, crested pigeons. Green mulga parrots, iridescent in their plumage, were as startling in the tropic desert as ice. Even more improbable were the pink cockatoos with a crest of feathers that strutted across the grassy clearing like a troop of chefs on parade.

He'd made it. He was in Australia.

The sun was just rising and the light was a wonder. There were white-trunked trees at the border of the clearing—river or ghost gums, he guessed—and they glowed in this dawning perpendicular light like fluorescent tubes, as if lit from within by a life that answered the solar rays. Their dark shadows made an arabesque along the ground. Beyond was a crumbled ridge of red rock, its broken parapets studded with trees and bushes of a strange electric green. The rock was on fire with light, its red an echo of the new sun, and the sky at the crest of the ridge was a deep, well-water blue that framed the dazzle below. All the colors seemed exaggerated, as in a dream, and it occurred to him suddenly that he could still be dreaming, drifting in a drug-induced haze of anticipation. Only the others could confirm reality. He sat up, wincing at his stiffness, and looked for them. Amaya and Tucker still lay as if they were dead. Ico, however, was already sitting up with his back against his pack, looking at Daniel with amusement. He put his fingers to his lips so as not to break the moment and then nodded. The meaning was clear: isn't this great?

The ground sloped away to some water, shallow pools glimmering in a broad pan of sand. Reeds grew on the fringe of them like a brilliant slash of lime. More birds flitted among the rushes, calling out cries of joy.

He'd done it. He'd found Eden.

Slowly Daniel stood and rotated around in dazed confirmation. There was not a house or a vehicle or a contrail in the sky. There was *nothing*, except the birds and the trees and the smell of sweet water. It was the emptiest, fullest place he'd ever been in, and the realization was both exhilarating and disquieting. There was a peculiar clarity to the air, and it took a while for him to analyze what it was. Not just the lack of haze. No, it was the absence of machine noise. No hum, no drone, no grumble, no tick. No clockwork regularity. Sound instead was uneven, the sharp staccato clicks and rustlings of insects and small reptiles and flitting birds seeming jazzlike in its evolved disharmony: a riff, an improvisation. There was a welcome to such discordance but also a somewhat disturbing anarchy to it, an irregularity he wasn't yet accustomed to. He realized suddenly how the aboriginal drumming and chanting that he'd always found dull must have seemed utterly revolutionary to early man: chants and songs that were repetitive, mathematical, predictable, reassuring: an answer to the drumbeat of their own hearts. Order, to combat the dissidence of unruly nature.

As the sun climbed and the light grew flatter and more intense, the other two began to stir. While he waited, Daniel took his bearings. The clearing was a logical drop point, he observed: open, and close to water. He wondered if Outback Adventure had used it before. The area seemed so untouched that it felt like they were the first humans to ever be here, that Australia's long human history had never existed. Perhaps they *were* the first, since the plague. Coyle had explained that adventurers were set down in widely dispersed places, since the company had an entire continent to choose from. The idea was exhilarating. In the city, every place he stepped had been trod a thousand times before. Here his footfall might be primary. He was Adam! Deliberately isolated so that each group achieved the independence and self-reliance it was seeking. There could be no second thoughts about waiting here at the drop-off point for a ride back home. The transport wouldn't return no matter what happened. The time to back out was gone.

The finality of it was delicious, but so daunting he momentarily felt he was looking over a precipice into a chasm too deep to see bottom.

Amaya stirred, small and pretty in her sleepiness, and

slowly sat up, looking around with dawning delight. "It's beautiful!" she cried, rubbing her eyes. "I feel like my brain's made of cotton from those sedatives but my God, the light! It's like a painting! Better than I dreamed!"

Tucker groaned and began to move as well. His eyelids fluttered. For a moment a look of fear crossed his face, and then he relaxed. He remembered.

Ico stretched, stood, and glanced around more appraisingly. "We're out of the cage," he pronounced.

"I still feel hungover from those chemicals," Daniel told him. "How about you?"

He looked sly. "I'm sleepy, but not from any damn witches' brew cooked up by Outback Adventure. I stayed awake and listened to some of the cockpit chatter."

"Stayed awake?"

"I told you I don't trust the bastards. I've got some friends in what you might call 'the medicinal trade.' There are things you can get that counter the normal sedative cocktail. I took some before we boarded and it fought the drugs. It was a little hairy—my heart raced for a time while I was trying to play possum—but it worked. I kept listening for hours until I got so damned tired and bored I just fell asleep naturally."

Tucker shook his head. "You're one paranoid dude, you know that?"

"I just wanted to make sure I knew what I was getting into, so I could scream bloody hell if I didn't end up liking it."

"And do you like it?"

Ico looked around. "So far."

"Where are we, master spy?" Daniel asked.

He looked sheepish. "Australia." There was a long pause. "I didn't pick up any coordinates. It was kind of hard to follow the airline bullshit. They seemed to have code words."

"Great. Did you learn *anything?*"

He winked. "The co-pilot is screwing an attendant. They talked about that for a while."

The others laughed. "Good job, Sherlock," Tucker said.

The eavesdropper grinned. "At least I tried. We hairless apes need information to survive. Right?"

"Which we don't have," Daniel said.

"Well," Ico added, "I know where we aren't."

"Kansas?" asked Tucker.

"No, where we're supposed to be." He enjoyed their mystification. "Since I was awake anyway, I had a little fun at the transfer point. They tied tags to us like corpses to sort us out. I had a minute to shift them while we waited on gurneys in the dark. We've been put where one quartet was supposed to be and they've been put in our place. Funny, no?"

"You switched our destination?" Amaya asked. "Why?"

"We don't know where we are. But now they don't either." He bent back his head to shout to the sky. "You lost your luggage, you arrogant bastards!" Some of the birds flew up in alarm.

Daniel shook his head. "You're crazy, you know that?"

"Damn right I'm crazy. Why else would I be here?"

There was some befuddled silence as the others digested what Ico had done. It shouldn't matter, should it? "So," Daniel said, "we don't know where we are or exactly where we have to go. Should we talk some strategy?"

"Australia generally gets wetter the farther east you

go," Amaya recited, remembering the geography they'd been briefed on. "The desert looks pretty dry beyond the trees of this oasis. Judging from that, I'd say we have a long ways to go."

"That's good," Tucker said. "I came for a long ways."

"Let's be pessimistic," Daniel said. "Say a thousand straight-line miles to the coast, and we average fifteen a day."

"But only ten in a straight line," Amaya amended.

"Yeah, okay. So that's a hundred days. A bit over three months. We can do that, right?"

"I don't know if we can move even that fast," Tucker cautioned. "Eventually we have to look for food, water. Finding our way . . ."

"We should allow for injuries and rest," Amaya said. "And some R&R."

"We should allow for the possibility they set us down ten miles from the west coast and we have to walk across the whole bloody continent, which is as big as the United States," said Ico.

"Which is exactly the puzzle we asked for, right?" added Tucker.

"We know the most important thing," Daniel said. "We have to walk toward that rising sun. Exodus Port is on the east coast."

"And maybe we *do* know more," Ico added.

Tucker grinned. "Uh-oh, here it comes. He heard something after all."

"No. But I wasn't content with being spoon-fed by Outback Adventure, either. As far as I was concerned, they were the *first* challenge, with their 'we'll tell you this but not that' bullshit. So I did a little research outside the envelope."

"And?" Amaya asked.

"I bought a map."

"What! How?"

"You can get all kinds of stuff on the black market."

"They didn't confiscate it?"

"Not unless they unsewed my sleeping bag." He bent to his pack. "I put it in my lining."

Tucker was shaking his head. "You're something else, you know that, Washington? What you did *is* against the rules. What you did *does* defeat the purpose."

Ico was using a penknife to cut a small slit in his sleeping bag. "It defeats *their* purpose, which is to have us wandering around the desert like morons. My purpose is to prove I can beat the system and think for myself." He brought out a folded paper. "We're at war, people. With nature, with Outback Adventure, and with time. I intend to win." He unfolded the map. "Ta-da!"

"It doesn't matter," Daniel dismissed.

"Here, see?" Ico held it up proudly.

"It's useless, Ico."

He looked irritated. "What do you mean?"

"Show me on that map where we are."

"We're going to figure out where we are. With landmarks."

"Show me where we're going."

"Give me time, Dyson."

"Even if we had a clue where we are on your map, we don't know if it's fake or real. It could lead us astray as easily as take us where we need to go. It's a complete waste of time and money." He didn't like the fact that Ico had brought a map without telling them. Or eavesdropped. Or switched their drop-off point. It was an arrogant little stunt.

"Daniel . . ." Amaya mediated.

"Maybe," Ico said. "*Or* it just may save your ass." He was defiant. "I checked my supplier out. I believe this is real. And I'm trying to play the game by *my* rules."

"No you're not. You're trying to cheat. I want to beat them fairly, by finding our own way."

"You want to jump through their hoops. Good doggie."

"I think you should have stayed home if you need a damn road atlas . . ."

"Boys! Please!" Amaya looked like an exasperated schoolteacher. "Is this some kind of testosterone thing, or what?"

"It's a philosophical discussion," Daniel said.

"About ends and means," Ico added.

"Well, *this* boy thinks we ought to stop talking and start walking," Tucker said. "You two can argue along the way. About a hundred paces behind Amaya and me, please."

Ico sighed and shrugged. "Okay, I'll tuck the map away for now. You'll be asking for it later. In the meantime, which way, Mister Let's-Do-It-The-Hard-Way?"

Daniel pointed toward the rising sun. "That way."

Before they set out they filtered and drank water from the pools until they were satiated, trying to flush the last of the sleep chemicals from their systems. Then they filled all the water containers they had. With several weeks of food on their backs, they agreed, water posed their biggest challenge. They had to find it every two to three days, at most. Then, that goal established, they started east, following the base of a rocky ridge that led roughly in that direction. The walking was neither particularly difficult nor easy. There was little soil, the ground instead dominated by sand, clay, rocks, and a dry, clumpy grass that pricked at them when they brushed it, forcing a meandering course between its tufts. "Spinifex," Amaya identified. It was necessary to watch constantly where one stepped, but the route was fairly level and it was not hard to make progress in an easterly direction and keep oriented.

As delighted as they were to finally be in Australia, Daniel thought, it was satisfying to begin making progress across it. Ahead was their simple new goal, behind a confirmation of how far they'd come. Progress! A mile already. He knew he shouldn't be counting steps, but the habit of setting a schedule, measuring miles, and listing goals was impossible to break. They were not accustomed to wander.

The air had the same astonishing clarity of the videos they'd seen, with no atmospheric haze to soften what seemed a hard, angular land. The few clouds that had been present at dawn disappeared, leaving a blank blue sky of steadily increasing heat. As the sun rose and the shadows shrank, every grain of sand and waxy leaf seemed picked out in detail. In this light there was no mystery about the kind of place they had come to. It was brittle, thin, challenging.

"This is real in-your-face kind of country," Tucker called it.

As if to make his description literal, the flies came as the morning warmed, swarming in numbers beyond the experience of any in the quartet. The insects didn't bite but they orbited the adventurers' heads with a persistence that soon grew annoying. They buzzed into ears, eyes, nose, and mouth, seeking human fluids, and were kept at bay only with a tiresome flapping of the arm.

"Lord Almighty," Tucker complained. "I don't remember being told about these."

"I read about them," Amaya said. "The joke is that your waving arm was the Australian salute. Some claim the Europeans brought them. They're a curse, for despoiling the land."

"I just got here. They should go curse someone else."

A hot breeze kept the bugs at bay for a while but any stillness brought them back. "A thousand miles with these guys?" Ico panted.

"There's about thirty that have landed on that house you're carrying on your back," Tucker said. "Not that you'd feel the difference."

"It's your lunch, Freidel. Buzzing wilderness protein."

"Seriously, man. How can you expect to carry all that?"

"Flies?"

"No. Half an outdoor store."

"This pack is going to keep me not only alive, my good Tucker, but comfortable. It's a hell of a long walk to the beach and I'm not going to be miserable the whole time."

"You just need to keep up, that's all."

"I am keeping up, big guy. In fact, if I don't run *you* into the ground, I'll give you my coffeemaker." He nodded. "To carry."

The intensity of the southern sun soon became apparent. Much of Australia was as close to the equator as Mexico, and the solar radiation was more powerful than what the four were accustomed to. They stopped frequently to make adjustments. With the coolness of dawn swiftly evaporating, jackets came off and sunscreen came on. They donned wide-brimmed hats and sunglasses. Ico dug into his pack and brought out a fine mesh bag stuffed with food. He emptied the containers into other pockets in his pack and slipped the bag over his hat and head, pulling the drawstring around his throat. "Voilà!" he announced. "No flies!"

"But you can't see what we came for," Amaya objected.

"I can see a hell of a lot better through this mesh than with flies in my eyes."

Tucker grinned. "Wait until he needs a drink of water."

Sure enough, when Ico loosened the net to drink, flies found their way inside the opening and began feasting on his sweat. He swatted angrily but the insects couldn't find their way back out. "Damn!" Finally he furiously pulled the bag and hat off his head and shook them to rid himself of the bugs. More insects whined around his head. "I don't believe this!" The others laughed.

He glared, then looked thoughtfully at the invention balled in his hand. "Don't worry, I've got a tube in this hardware store on my back. Next time I'll use it as a straw. I'll get it right." He jerked the net back on.

"Isn't that hot?" Amaya asked.

"It's shady."

By lunchtime the heat pressed down with the weight of an iron and the morning excitement had given way to a dull dizziness. The flies were so persistent that the others began to envy Ico's head net. Finally Daniel spotted a shadow on the ridge and suggested they take a break. The shadow was made by a rock overhang, its shade dropping the temperature a good ten degrees. They collapsed in its gloom and noticed with relief that the flies didn't like to follow them into the cooler dark. Weary, they slowly unfastened pack pockets to nibble lightly on their food and sip water. Then they lay back.

"So, are we having fun yet?" Ico asked.

"It's a little bleak," Tucker admitted. "Still, it beats working for a living."

"I've worked up a good sweat."

"You know what I mean. This is different. We're doing what we *want* to do."

"I read that primitive tribes had to work as little as two hours a day to feed themselves," Amaya said. "The rest was leisure."

"To do what? Swat flies?"

"You don't like it, Ico?" Tucker asked.

"No, I do, I do. I think. The Big Nothing. It's what I came for. Different perspective, right? But I'm not going to pretend it's paradise, either."

"It's hotter than I expected," Daniel admitted. "And this is the Australian fall?"

"They don't really have an autumn," Amaya said. "I mean where leaves come off. But it should keep getting cooler. Our summer is their winter."

"This is fall? What the devil is summer like?" Tucker wondered.

"We should reach the coast and get back long before we have to find out," Amaya said.

"And if not?" asked Ico.

"We'll be acclimated, I hope. If we're stuck eight months and see their summer solstice, on December twenty-first, the sun should be directly above the Tropic of Capricorn at noon. We can measure its angle above us and try to calculate our north–south position from the Tropic. Get a better sense of where we are."

"Oh good. Let's stay and fry our brains. Much easier than trying to read my map."

"We'll also look at the stars tonight and find the Southern Cross. You can tell position by the distance of constellations above the horizon. The difficulty is determining our position east and west. That's what gave navigators fits for centuries."

"And that, of course, is what we need to know."

"Isn't the whole point *not* to know?" Daniel interrupted. "I'm not here to argue against maps, Ico, but didn't we come here to live in the moment without all these numbers fixing us in space and time? I caught myself guessing distance. But really, who cares where we are? For the first time in my life I'm just walking. I don't know how far we've come. I don't know how far we have to go. I don't know what time it is. My mind isn't three days ahead and two days behind and anticipating fifteen appointments and worrying about my retirement and my headstone. Suddenly my stomach is all I need to keep track of mealtimes and the sun is my alarm clock. I'm here, taking in the now."

They considered that.

"I agree," Ico said. "It's why I felt it didn't hurt to switch our drop-off point. Let's live in the moment. But at some point we have to get back." He glanced at his wrist. "It's one-seventeen, by the way, if I'm in the right time zone."

"It's when you throw that watch away that you'll be in the right zone."

"Touché." But he kept the watch on.

They looked out at the desert from their rock shelter. A slope of sandstone gave way to a plain as flat and featureless as the face of a calm ocean. Stunted trees and shrubs, gray-green, studded the pan of sand out to a horizon where the ground evaporated into a shimmering mirage of blue water, bleeding into an equally blue sky. Nothing moved, except a hawk wheeling on the thermals.

"Get back?" Tucker said suddenly. "Hell, I just got here."

As the afternoon progressed the desert became more beautiful. What had seemed to be crabbed trees cowering under the hammer of the sun at noon now lengthened with their afternoon shadows, trunks of white and gray taking on sinuous grace. Colors grew richer as the sun dropped, sand making snaking dunes of an eerie red. They crossed two sandy watercourses with no visible water. Amaya pointed out that the tiny ants that marched everywhere on the riverbanks seemed absent on the dry streambeds. "We should camp on the sand," she observed. "Less bugs." It was prettier on the empty rivers as well. The white eucalyptus grew taller and more beautiful than the desert bush, and seemed in its serene majesty as timeless and still as the rocks.

At a third riverbed they found a pool of standing water and stopped, the sky on fire behind them, a deepening blue ahead. "Honey, I'm home!" Ico called, heaving off his pack in relief. They guessed they'd come ten miles.

Daniel was the only one who hadn't brought a tent, deciding to rely on a light tarp instead. Bright fabric mushrooms puffed up from the other three to form an instant village, the thin nylon a comfortable shield against the emptiness of this great outside. There was a bit of awkward unfamiliarity as they set up their stoves and prepared their first real meal, sharing dishes, but also good humor at the fact they were succeeding on their own with these simple tasks. Tucker dragged in some wood and lit a fire with a match. Its purpose was more psychological than to heat or cook. "Man is here!" Tucker shouted to the desert. "He will prevail!" The noise drifted away across the sand.

"And woman." Amaya had erected her tent first.

"There's only one of you," Ico noted.

"She'll prevail anyway," Daniel predicted. "Smarter, saner, and more centered than any of us."

She grinned at him. "Centered, or self-centered?"

"The center of our universe," Ico crooned.

As the light disappeared, so did the flies. Stars began to pop out, first like isolated beacons and then faster and faster, like a growing storm of snow. The night shone with starlight, the silken ribbon of the Milky Way a familiar streak but the constellations strange. Amaya pointed to a cluster of stars to the south. "The Southern Cross," she said. "We'll keep it on our right as we travel."

Sparks climbed skyward and seemed to join the stars. Daniel got a laugh with his story of how he'd started a tiny blaze in his apartment.

"I'll pay fifty bucks to see you do that again," offered Ico.

"You brought *money?*"

"Just what I had. In case we got held up somewhere." He shrugged. "I'll probably keep it though, for emergencies, and pay you at home."

"That's crazier than rubbing sticks, you know that?"

"Come on, I want to see you do it."

"No, I'm too tired. Last time it took me hours. Besides, you'll get to see me do it for free once we run out of matches."

"Civilization starting to look better then?" He held up a match.

"Not good enough that I'd want to be carrying seventy-five pounds, like you're doing."

Ico grinned. "It gets lighter with every match."

The light and food and rest relaxed them, erasing memories of the heat of the day. They laughed at Ico's espresso maker with its solar battery chip, but they each had a cup.

"See, what I'm looking for is *balance*," he explained. "I know this shit is silly, but why not take the best of both worlds and enjoy ourselves out here? It's society I don't like, not technology. Bureaucracy, not gadgets. My goal is to find out what's really necessary, what's really important, and then plan permanent escape. I take the essentials into a wild pocket of the world—maybe even sneak back here—and live *my* life, not theirs. Even Robinson Crusoe had a lot of shipwreck gear to salvage. I'd want that too."

"You don't happen to have an ice cream maker stuffed away, do you, Crusoe?" Tucker asked. "I'm craving strawberry ripple."

"Nah. But maybe there's still wild cows in Australia. If you catch one, Freidel, I'll make you a latte."

Despite his weariness from the day's walk, Daniel was too restless to immediately sleep. He strolled up the riverbed, the gray sand shimmering under the stars and the night strangely comforting in its glow. This was not a scary place at all, he decided. He also liked the smell of Australia. There was none of the odor of moist soil and decay like some wet northern forests he had hiked in, but rather a scent of dry wood and plant oils that strangely reminded him of dusty furniture. The aridity seemed clean.

He could hear animals scuttling away in the night and he wondered who the group's neighbors were. There were no large predators in Australia, he knew. Eventually they might run into wild domestics—dogs, camels, cows, pigs—but for the moment nature seemed unfamiliar, harmless, and discreet.

He sat on a log, looked up into the night sky, and shivered. The glorious immensity! Not just of the universe, but this strange red desert. It was intimidating to think of being so far from help, but liberating too. He could go anywhere, do anything. *Be* anything. All the restraints were off except the ones remaining in his head. This could be heaven, he thought: roaming endlessly with his house on his back and exploring the uncharted terrain of his own spirit. He could do it forever with the right person. Daniel wondered if Raven was out there somewhere, and if so whether she was walking with a man other than himself. He wondered if he'd ever see her again.

There was a rustle and he turned. It was Amaya.

"Can I join you?"

He beckoned and she sat down on the log next to him. "It's nicest at night," she said. "No wonder that's when most of the desert creatures move about."

"I think we're going to have to change our habits. Move early and late, hole up at midday. We're prisoners of that sun."

"Prisoners? I thought we came here for freedom, Daniel."

"Oops."

"We just need to get in rhythm."

"That's what I meant. But it was an interesting slip. I've heard that when you're jailed long enough you never really get free. You become a prisoner in your own mind.

Everything looks like a wall. And you learn to like your jailers."

"You're worried that's you."

"Of course."

"We do have to be realistic about what we can achieve out here," she said. "Animals aren't really free. They spend their lives bound by the weather, the seasons, and hunting or being hunted. We shouldn't romanticize them or their existence or pretend we can find a life without limitations. But I liked what you said today about getting away from numbers and schedules and maps. I think we're here to break bad habits, or at least recognize and examine them."

He looked at her face, pale in the starlight. Amaya was actually quite pretty, he decided—not beautiful in the conventional sense of a model but rather kind, good, with bright, intelligent eyes, a wide smile, and a grounded sensibility he found reassuring. Her appeal snuck up on you. It was interesting she'd sought him out. "I think the voice of reason so far has been you," he said. "Us boys can get kind of silly sometimes. We enjoy the arguing. It's like a game."

"I know."

They sat for a while, staring up at the sky.

"I never knew there could be so many stars," Daniel said. "We never see them at home. The light they cast is amazing."

"Maybe someday those stars will be our new wilderness, do you think? A wilderness to explore that goes on to infinity. But not yet. We've barely put our toe into space, so for now this is as far out as people like you and I can get."

"Did you ever want to be an astronaut?"

She shivered. "No. Space seemed too cold."

"So now you're a bush ranger instead."

"I'm just a woman who wants to fall in love with this world as it is, or rather was. I don't need the planets. I want to feel at home *here*."

"And do you?"

"After one day? It's too early to tell. But I'm glad I came."

"I was right about you being centered. You seem the most balanced of any of us. You recognize what we're seeing, you don't complain, and your gear seems well organized. You're so normal I'm wondering what you're doing here."

She laughed. "Looking, like everyone else."

"Looking for what? A place?"

"No, a person. That's what women look for."

"A boyfriend? You've sort of cut down the number of possibilities, haven't you? Three losers?"

"Daniel, you're not fair to yourself. But no, not a boyfriend. I want a companion in a place that gets rid of all the modern complications that get in the way of friendship—and I may have found three such companions already. But that's not the person I mean."

"Someone to love, then."

"Someday. But another, first."

"Who?"

"Me."

He waited for her to explain.

"It's true I haven't found love yet," she said. "But what I realized back home is that first I have to find myself."

CHAPTER TWELVE

They rose at dawn again, as enchanted as ever by the ethereal light, and ate and packed quickly. Despite the lack of schedule they couldn't break the habit of disciplined briskness, readying quickly so they could put more miles behind them. Daniel, who had brought no tent and no sleeping bag and no stove, was ready first. His pack was lightest because the others were carrying more food as well.

His supply was mostly power rations and staples, like rice. The others carried more elaborate freeze-dried meals.

"I've got enough for a month if I stretch it," Daniel told them when Ico asked. "What I really need to do, and want to do, is live off the land. Otherwise I'm just a tourist."

"More power to you," said Ico carefully, "but I mean no offense when I say we should each eat what we carry. I'm packing twice the rations but I didn't bring all this food to feed anyone else. I just don't want any expectations down the line, okay?"

"No one expects you to feed us. If I lived off you, Ico, I

wouldn't have achieved a thing by coming here. I don't want the fish. I want to learn how to fish. And if I catch one, I'll share it."

"No, Dyson," Tucker said. "Then you teach *us* how to fish."

"I'll be impressed if you just find enough water to fish in," Amaya said.

"We'll find everything we need once we learn how to look." Daniel took the hunting knife he had brought and cut a staff of tolerable straightness from a gray-leafed, spiny bush, sharpening one end. "Voilà," he announced. "Walking stick, javelin, water probe, and ridgepole for my ground cover in case it rains. Free, portable, disposable, and replaceable. The perfect product. Patent number 8765321."

"Yeah, but can you swat flies with it?" Ico asked.

They set out, their boots striking up little puffs of dust as they walked, the pink powder settling on their ankles and shoes like fine talcum. The heat rose again, the insects came back, and this time there was no convenient overhang for a midday refuge. They rested in the shade of what Amaya identified as a mulga tree, their thirst enormous. Even though the air was too dry for them to visibly sweat, their thickening throats were warning enough of how the desert baked out liquids. They drank freely to replenish themselves. The horizon was a shimmer of heat haze and the range of hills they'd been following was flattening out. Ahead was a flat plain of scrubby emptiness, with no visible landmarks. It looked as featureless as an ocean. All they could do was follow compass, sun, and the stars to the east.

Conversation lagged as the weight of their packs bit deeper and the insects became more annoying. At one point Ico got out his map, studied it, and then shrugged and put it back without comment. The desert was so featureless that there was nothing to establish their position with, even if the chart was real.

Still, the freedom to choose their way was liberating, Daniel thought. They saw no kangaroos but did spy a dingo, a dog first brought by the aborigines and now wild as the wind. It loped into the brush ahead of them like a furtive coyote. There were birds, flies, ants. On a dare, Amaya tasted one of the green ants that the aborigines ate and said it tasted bitter, but mostly like nothing at all. She was the one who stopped most frequently to mentally catalog shrubs and grasses. Hawks and kites orbited in the sky.

Daniel periodically threw his makeshift spear at a rock or twisted dead tree trunk, his accuracy inconsistent but slowly improving until he began to tire. Ico, working to keep up under his heavy pack as the hours went by, shook his head in amusement. "Look at that, he's better than a dog. He throws his own stick."

"Just aiming at the flies, Ico," Daniel replied. "I plan to spear them all."

Tucker called a halt at mid-afternoon. "Blisters," he announced.

The others took the opportunity to examine their carefully padded feet, readjusting protection and massaging red spots. "I'm so swollen it looks like I'm walking on melons!" Amaya wailed.

"I thought I was in shape but I'm finding muscles the gym didn't know I had," Daniel confessed.

"I'm finding pain my muscles didn't know they had," Ico sighed, leaning back against his massive pack. The others raised their eyebrows. "I know, I know, it's too big. Hey, I'm eating my way through it."

Their hope of camping in a riverbed was dashed when none appeared the second evening. The initial exhilaration was gone and they felt not only tired but dirty. Ico sneaked a glance at his watch. He was waiting for the sun to go down. There was no fresh water and they realized they had to ration what was left.

"How can we walk without water?" Tucker asked worriedly as the night's eventual chill lured them tighter to their fire.

"It looked like the land falls off a bit ahead," Amaya replied. "We look in the depression for a riverbed and search seriously for water. We can't push farther until we find it."

"But that's not very far," Ico objected. "We need to make our mileage."

"No we don't. We need to drink."

The stark truth of her statement sobered them for a minute.

Tucker shivered. "And it's cold tonight. Colder than it was last night. Roast during the day, freeze at night."

"That's the desert for you," Daniel said. "We should have caught that dingo."

"To eat?"

"No, to cuddle with. Aborigines used their dogs for warmth. A cold evening was a three- or four-dog night."

"Awooooo," Tucker called. "Maybe I can lure one."

"With that call they'll try to mate," Ico said. "That'll warm you up. Of course there's another alternative." He smiled sweetly at Amaya.

"In your dreams, Washington."

"I'm just inventorying our resources."

"Use your gadgets to keep yourself warm."

* * * *

They found another sandy riverbed at noon the next day, but even after following it upstream for several miles they found no water. "Doesn't this country have any *wet stuff* in its rivers?" Tucker asked rhetorically. "This is weird." Lunch was quiet, the flies so persistent that the travelers had mostly given up trying to swat at them, though Ico still wore his head net. They were down to a quart of water each.

"If we don't find more water we might have to hike back," Daniel said gloomily. "We can't go on without it."

Amaya looked thoughtfully at the sand. "I've got an idea," she said. "Let's go back to that bend we passed a mile or so ago."

"I don't want to go backward," Ico groused. "In fact I don't want to do anything right now. I'm exhausted. Let's nap."

"I told you that you were carrying too much," Tucker lectured.

"I'm keeping up. I just don't want to go into reverse."

"What's your idea?" Daniel asked Amaya.

"There's probably water under the sand here. Deserts swallow it after a rain, but it doesn't disappear. We just have to dig in the right place."

"So what's the right place?"

"I'll show you. Come on, Ico, it's not far."

"Aw, Mom."

They trudged back. It was strange to encounter their own footprints; it was the first sign of humans they'd seen in this place. At the bend of the dry river there was a sandy bluff the water had eaten into, and a hollow in the sand beneath it. "The dynamics of the surface water digs out pools at places like this," she explained. "I'm betting there might be another pool beneath us, in the sand." She dropped her pack, got a stick, and began to dig. "Come on."

The men joined her, each taking a turn. It was blisteringly hot. "If you're wrong, we're going to melt right here," Tucker warned.

"Yes. This is our first real test."

Two feet down the sand darkened, then grew moist. "Widen the hole," she directed. The sand flew more furiously and then they stopped, exhausted.

Dirty water drained into it. "It's just mud," Daniel objected.

Amaya scooped out the muddy water and cast it aside on the sand. "That's just from our disturbance. Now we wait. The trick in the wild is patience."

They retreated to the shade of some gum trees and sat, weary. The sun was dipping lower and they allowed themselves sips of their last water. "I thought it would be easier to drink out here," Daniel admitted. "If Outback Adventure drops people in at random like that, I mean. The company didn't emphasize water-finding skills and the desert is pretty green. I assumed we'd find some water each day."

"Maybe *that* was our first test," Ico replied. "Our assumptions."

"The good news is, it's a test we're passing," Tucker said optimistically. "We found water anyway, right?"

Time crawled on. Daniel lay back to study the branches of the trees, watching the flitting birds. Wanting something to do, he began to try to identify them. Ico had taken out a book on disk. Tucker dozed, and Amaya sat as if meditating. The group was nervous but no one wanted to articulate it. They could die out here, and no one was coming to their rescue.

As the shadows lengthened a bird fluttered down and hopped to the lip and then into the trench. It gave a call and flew out. Amaya came out of her trance and crawled forward, lying on the lip of the hole as if mesmerized. Then she turned to grin. "Daniel! Bring a cup!"

They camped in the riverbed that night, first drinking their fill from the slowly filling hole and then carefully refilling their water bottles. As Amaya had predicted, cleaner water had flowed into the hole, filtered by the sand. They drank and drank, and then collected more water to wash, a reminder of civility that helped revive their spirits. The success of the well restored their confidence. With patience, they could prevail.

A new moon rose and Daniel decided to go hunting. Taking his spear, he climbed out of the riverbank and into the surrounding bush, moving slowly and taking his bearings frequently so he wouldn't get lost. Twice he saw furtive movement and once he threw at it, hitting nothing. Still, his ability to negotiate the wilderness in the dark encouraged him. It was another step toward being at home here.

They broke camp before dawn to set out east again, having filled every possible container with water. The sun was fixing their schedule: a hard morning's hike, a siesta, another spurt toward likely water and camp. As they moved out some large forms bounded away in front of them.

"Kangaroos," Daniel breathed.

Even Ico, bent under his heavy pack, brightened. "Cool!"

"When are you going to hit one of those, Daniel?" Tucker asked.

"When they agree to stand still."

The sky was as shiny as blue porcelain, the desert as red as Mars. They wound eastward through shrubby trees spaced like slalom poles. Amaya spotted some sap on another mulga tree, collected some bits on a stick, and ate it. "It's sweet, like candy," she said. Dubious, the men tried it.

"Well, better than ant balls," Ico said.

"How do you know?" she teased him. "I haven't made one of those for you yet."

They found water again that night, this time in a series of pools on the surface, and Amaya found some wild passion fruit in the creek bed, splitting the orange rind and sucking out the seeds. Their sense of familiarity was growing. They built a fire again, and as its coals burned down Daniel slipped off to hunt once more, his confidence growing at his ability to navigate in the dark. He began to move slowly, walking a short distance and then stopping to stand perfectly still, his eyes searching the monochromatic moonscape for movement. After an hour, his effort was rewarded: a shape in the darkness moved, then hopped toward him. A kangaroo. He sucked in his breath and waited. It hopped closer. He raised his makeshift javelin, and as he did so his own movement alerted the animal and it bolted. By the time Daniel threw, it was a shadow bounding into the dark. He trotted to pick up his spear. Next time he'd have to stalk with his arm already upraised. Still, he felt satisfied he'd found big game. He spent a few minutes simply throwing: rocks, sticks, his spear. He was training unfamiliar muscles in a skill that dated back a million years.

As he slowly worked his way down the riverbed back to camp he heard some gentle splashing and stopped again, alert. Something was in a pool of the riverbed.

Slowly he crept ahead, his spear upraised, his head down. He pushed his head through some bushes and then stopped, sucking in his breath. It was Amaya, bathing. She was naked, standing in water to her thighs, her slim body luminous under the glow of the night sky. She was scooping up water and letting it pour onto her face, and then run down her small breasts and smooth belly. The drops glittered as they bounced off her, falling into a mirror of stars. She washed with the same unconscious grace of a wild animal, and Daniel was jarred by the natural beauty of it, entranced by her form's pearl luminescence under the night sky.

He didn't know whether it was best to try to retreat, possibly startling and embarrassing her with his noise, or to step into view as warning, intruding on her respite. Finally he decided to do and say nothing. She dipped to her shoulders in the cold water with a gasp and then sprang upward, the water spraying as she shook herself, her arms flung out. It was erotic to watch the water stream down her but also innocent, primeval. There was an abstraction to the scene. Her features were indistinct and so there was only the sculpture of her limbs and torso, bent this way and that. Daniel was transfixed. Finally she finished and waded to the shore to slip into her underwear and walk back to camp. She paused a minute and looked across the pool as if staring directly at him, then slipped away into the dark. He waited ten more minutes and then followed. She'd retired into her tent. He slipped into his own bedroll, looking up into a night sky that seemed like a pool of dark water itself.

The next day was long and hot, and the following evening they were on a scrub plain and couldn't find even a likely place to dig. They nursed what water they had carefully, sprawled on the red earth. After a few minutes Tucker sprang up again. "Ants! I'm on a damn nest!" He moved to a new spot, searching the ground carefully. "Some campground," he grumbled.

"All we can do is sleep as best we can and push on," Daniel said.

The dryness was beginning to be discouraging. He felt sunburned, insect-bitten, and grimy, and had yet to get close enough to an animal to successfully kill it. He knew he hadn't been patient enough but didn't want to hold up the group to take the time necessary to learn how to hunt. At some point, though, they would need the food—even Ico. Daniel mused about making a bow and arrow, but it sounded difficult and he knew the aborigines hadn't bothered even when shown them by visiting tribes; their spears and throwing sticks and rocks had been adequate to bring down game. All he was lacking was skill.

"We'd better walk tomorrow until we find water," Ico said. "Walk and pray for rain."

They hiked on the next day through the midday sun, conversation trailing off into numbed silence under the pounding heat. Red dust puffed up from their footfalls. The morning's birds disappeared and the desert was as still and radiantly hot as an emptied parking lot. Nothing moved except the flies, no breeze blew, and there was no sound except the creak of their gear, the trudge of feet, and the relentless buzz of the insects. They joked halfheartedly about missing beer, or air conditioning, or a winter blizzard, but after a while the jokes seemed lame. The liberation from noise and humanity was beginning to seem oppressive. It seemed like they'd been walking forever and had encountered only a vast nothing; that they were no closer to finding whatever it was they were looking for than they had been in the city. It was becoming harder and harder to pretend their outing was a good time.

It was sunset when they finally came to another riverbed, this one broad and shallow in a valley so imperceptibly sloped that they hadn't realized they were in one. There were no standing pools, no likely bends, and a test dig yielded nothing but dry sand. They slumped around the hole wearily.

"We're exhausted," Amaya said. "We'll have to ration what we have and search more carefully in the morning. We'll find a place for a well like last time."

"What if we don't?" Tucker asked.

She brushed her hair back from a dirty cheek, tired. "We will. If it was going to be easy, there would be no point in coming here."

Daniel nodded at her. He'd found himself looking and thinking about her differently since seeing her at the pool, and even though he hadn't said anything about it, he thought she noticed. She turned her head away shyly.

"This is fucked, you know that?"

Ico's complaint was ignored. What could they do?

He persisted. "I mean, dying of thirst was not a part of the brochure that I remember."

"Ico, stuff it, okay?" Daniel said with irritation, turning to unstrap his bedroll. He was tiring of the little man's attitude. "We're all hot and tired and thirsty."

"Maybe we're doing something wrong. Maybe we're going in the wrong direction."

"You want to walk *away* from Exodus Port?"

"I just want a drink, man. Doesn't it ever rain?"

"It does up there." Tucker pointed. To the north, lightning flickered in the dusk. They heard the distant growl of thunder. "Maybe we'll get a storm down here."

Ico stood and looked to the north hopefully. "Hey! Rain! Come this way!" He waved his arms. "Yoo-hoo!" He turned to the others. "We just need to think as well as walk, that's all I'm saying."

"So think, don't complain."

Ico watched the luminous horizon, rumbling like an artillery barrage. "If rain comes, we should put out some containers to catch it. And a ground sheet."

"Now you're an optimist again."

He grinned. "In this godforsaken place? I'm not stupid, Tucker. Just desperate." He bent to his pack. "Just in case we get lucky, though, I'm going to put out every dish I have."

CHAPTER THIRTEEN

Daniel's exhausted dreams were so turbulent that at first Tucker's warning cry seemed to come from the miasma of his nightmare.

In his sleep he was lost on a vast white plain. It was as flat as a piece of paper and crisscrossed with his own tracks. His footprints led off confusingly in all directions and he was uncertain if the whiteness at his feet was sand or snow. There was an ominous rumbling in the distance. Daniel was overwhelmed by a feeling of sad uncertainty, of having made a fatal wrong turn, and the resulting dread was threatening to paralyze him. Before he could decide what to do, however, Tucker's cries became more insistent. Finally they blew the vividness of his dream into the shards of dark reality and he opened his eyes. It was night in Australia, black and confused.

"Get up!" Tucker was roaring. "Get up, get up! It's flooding!"

The big man was dragging something uphill. It was Amaya's tent, Daniel realized, and the woman was yelling inside it. Then the horizon flashed and in the lightning's lurid blast he saw trees shaking wildly and the glint of something wet pouring toward him like a chocolate slurry. It was as if the land had risen and was being shaken toward him in undulating waves.

Flash flood!

Daniel's bedroll had the grace of being zipperless, and he was out of it and scrambling for higher ground in an instant, instinctively dragging his bedding with him. A breaking wave of muddy water was pouring down the dry river bottom to devour their camp. As he surmounted the bank and grasped the trunk of a tree, lightning flashed again and he saw the water strike something angular and carry it off. There was a muffled shout. Ico's tent! In numbed fascination, Daniel watched one of the containers that had been put out to catch some raindrops being swept away in the current.

The wall of water had appeared out of nowhere and now it roared by with a furious gush of rolling stones, pitching logs, and jabbing branches, devouring everything in its path with the noise and clumsy power of a medieval army. The sound was overwhelming and the night had turned pitch black, Daniel's blindness relieved only by strobes of lightning. The flashes were dry—there was not a drop of rain—and yet even as he registered the weirdness of this the storm opened and a cloudburst sluiced down, adding to the din. Daniel felt he'd been clubbed, so heavy was the water. It pushed him to his knees.

"Ico! Daniel!" It was Tucker, shouting from the dark trees farther from the river. Daniel groped in that direction. There was a flash of lightning and he saw the tall man leaning against a tree with rainwater streaming down his face. A stunned, wet Amaya was crawling from her tangled, muddied tent, her eyes wide, and she clutched a moment at Tucker's leg as if to seek reassurance. Daniel stumbled up to them.

"You all right?" They said it simultaneously.

"Ico," Daniel gasped. "I saw the river take him. We have to go hunt downstream."

Amaya stood unsteadily, the rain lashing at them, and then gripped them both with a look of grim determination. "We might need a rope!" she shouted. "I'll get the clothesline we rigged! You two start down and I'll follow!"

"Are you going to be all right?" Daniel shouted back.

"Yes, yes, go on!"

Tucker pulled at him and the two men moved off clumsily in the dark, following the edge of the flood but keeping a wary distance as sections of sandy bank collapsed. The water bucked and pitched, eating at the shore with greedy menace, and both men feared their companion was already gone.

There was a flash and a following crack of thunder so close upon it that they staggered as if an artillery shell had gone off nearby. Sparks flew in the night and there was a crash of something falling in the trees. Daniel wanted desperately to crouch and hide and wait until the storm was over, but forced himself to keep going. He tripped, sprawled, and got up again as Tucker hauled on his arm. "I heard a yell!" the big man shouted.

They felt their way to the river's edge, rain beating on them like hail. Lightning stabbed again and they saw a tree had toppled into the current, something synthetic caught in its branches and fluttering in the current like a flag. Ico's tent! There was another yell and they saw a dark shape in the branches that could be someone's head.

"Ico!" Tucker roared. "We see you! Work yourself this way!"

Their companion was obviously trying, but any loosening of his grip threatened to release him into the current. "I'm going after him," Tucker growled. He leaped in, dropping to his waist on the upstream end of his log, and immediately his feet were jerked out from under him and he went under the tree, saving himself only by grabbing the bark and hauling himself back upward on the downstream side. With difficulty, he heaved himself back onto shore, spitting dirty water. "Damn!"

Daniel studied the tree trunk shuddering in the flood, its roots not yet fully pried out of the ground. "I'm lighter!" he shouted above the rain. "I'll climb out to him and you follow. When I get to him, hold my ankles and don't let go!"

The tree was slick and shook more violently the farther he inched out along it, the flood sucking at the wood. In perspective he felt like a bug swirling toward a drain, his face just inches from the water. "Ico!" he screamed into the storm. "Work this way!" An arm flailed as their companion struggled to do so, grasping a new branch and letting go of the old and then being jerked furiously by the current, his body like a rag snapped by the wind. Ico's strength had to be ebbing.

Daniel felt Tucker's huge hands grasp his ankles like a reassuring vise and the clamp was enough to give him the courage to stretch farther toward the third man, as if on a rack. Lightning lit the river and they glimpsed each other's terrified face. Ico reached, touched blindly, grabbed, slipped, and then snared Daniel's wrist with his other hand as he was being pulled away by the current. The fumbling was enough to pull Daniel from the tree as well and they pivoted, Daniel's legs in Tucker's grasp. Then with a frustrated grunt the third man was levered off the tree too and the trio was in the flood waters, swirling downstream in a confused tangle.

They went under, Ico clawing in terror at the other two. Everything seemed stronger than Daniel: Tucker, the frantic Ico, the kick and butt of the river. They struck something hard and it was enough to ricochet them to the surface, sucking in breaths that were half water and half air. They were in a mad pirouette, totally disoriented.

"Tuckerrrr!" Amaya was somewhere on the bank, sprinting ahead of them, and they thrashed in unison toward the sound of her voice. A bolt of lightning illuminated the uncoiling arc of a hurled line. Tucker's arm went up and he caught the rope just as Amaya was taking a desperate turn around a tree. The line tightened and so did the muscles on the big man's arm as he gripped with all his might. Now the river worked in their favor, pivoting them into the bank. They banged against roots, scrabbled, and clung, gasping for breath in the water-filled air. Daniel got an arm around Ico's chest and hauled and finally they were up, their knees on sand. He felt Amaya's small hands trying to drag them and slowly they worked away from the flood's grip. Ico was coughing and cursing.

The men lay as if dead for a moment, the woman crouched over them like shelter from the storm. Only slowly did the group realize that the rain had stopped as suddenly as it had begun. The cloudburst had moved south, the electricity of its fury glinting there. The river was still full, but its roar had become less angry. The crest of the flood had passed them.

"You okay, Washington?" It was Tucker, his chest still heaving as he gasped in deep breaths.

"Hell no." Ico groaned. "I almost drowned." He was soaked and coated with sand, looking as thin and forlorn as a wet cat. "I had to get out of my bag and then out of my tent . . . damn, I was scared! Where did that water come from?"

"You prayed for it, if I remember correctly," Amaya said.

"Flash flood," Daniel explained. "The desert doesn't absorb water, so a storm upstream sends all the rain down . . . I should have remembered that. We're lucky we all didn't drown. We were stupid to camp in the riverbed when we saw that storm."

"It came and went so fast," Amaya said.

The stars were popping out again, illuminating the churning water with dim light. "Now we know why the ants don't nest in the riverbed," Tucker said.

By morning the river was gone again, leaving only periodic pools. For breakfast they ate some peanuts Amaya had brought into her tent. The rest of their food had been carried downstream and they'd have to look for it. "At least we have water," Daniel tried to joke.

"Even that will be gone again in a few days, I'll bet," Amaya replied.

Tucker shook his head. "When they said 'adventure,' they weren't kidding."

"They should have warned us about the possibility of floods." Ico was glum. "This isn't right. There's something about this whole thing that's not right. We could have *died* in our beds. Shouldn't they have warned us?"

"You said that before," Tucker chided. "Notice how hard it is to file a complaint?"

"Oh, I'm going to complain all right. I'm going to raise bloody hell."

"Come on," Daniel argued as much to himself as the others. "This is what we paid for. We're alive, and we're learning. That's the whole point, isn't it?"

"Learning what damn fools we are," Ico said.

They fanned out downstream and began retrieving gear, some of it half buried and much of it dented or torn. It was hot, dispiriting work because so much had been lost. They brought what they salvaged to an assembly point under a red river gum tree on the sandy bank and went through it, hanging food bags out of the reach of ants. Slowly, a meager inventory began to emerge.

"We have three of the four packs," Daniel summarized. Amaya's had not been found. "One tent. Tucker's is lost, and Ico's is in rags, but his sleeping bag is salvageable. We can cut it in two for the men to use as blankets, and use Ico's tent fabric to repair Amaya's. My bedroll was saved too. The best news is our boots."

The others nodded. They'd gotten in the habit of propping them upside down on branches to keep out snakes or insects, and the bushes they'd used had been high enough on the bank to be out of reach of the river. They could still walk.

"But some of the clothes and utensils are gone," Daniel went on. "We'll have to share. And the food . . ."

"Half was either lost or spoiled," Amaya said gloomily. "We should have hung it up like the shoes. It would keep it from animals as well."

"Next time. We're learning, okay?"

"So what are we going to eat?" Ico asked.

"What we always intended to, the food of the land. We just have to learn how to do it a bit quicker, that's all."

"Daniel, let's face it. We're screwed." It was Tucker. "All that gear . . ."

"Lightens our load. Look, now we can move lighter and faster. The aborigines didn't need that crap and neither do we. Ico was about to sink into the sand with all that gear."

"No I wasn't."

"We've still got one compass, some matches, a stove." Daniel felt in his pocket and pulled out a small figurine. "And this. Good luck charm."

"What the devil is that?" Ico asked.

"Gordo Firecracker. Righter of wrongs, nemesis of evil."

"And the worst-performing charm I've ever seen. Haven't you heard of St. Christopher?"

"We're alive, aren't we? And light-years ahead of our primitive ancestors still. And all we have to do is walk out. Walk to the coast and go home."

"A thousand miles."

"Maybe. We don't know that. Maybe less. Maybe even farther. But we can *do* it. We're a bit bruised, a bit wiser, a bit tougher. I hope. This is what the adventure is all about."

"The riskiest thing on earth." Ico was quoting Elliott Coyle. No one needed to reply.

"Well, we lost some canteens," Tucker said. "That's serious, for sure."

"It's time to find some gourds. Some of the aborigines made water bags from kangaroo skin. And maybe we'll travel by night instead of day to conserve how fast we use water."

"And we've got to hunt," Tucker added.

"You and I are going to do that right now. Seriously. We need to learn in a hurry. Amaya and Ico can check out the plants around here. We've got to supplement the pack food we have left, starting immediately."

"Who put you in charge, Dyson?" It was Ico, looking tired.

"The weather."

They spent two days at the site of the flood. Relieved from having to cover distance, they began to notice more details of the country they were in. The desert seemed most alive at dusk and dawn, when day and night shifts of animals converged and the coolness encouraged browsing. The rain had brought an instant riot of new growth, and the nearby grassy plain was blooming with wildflowers that shimmered like a rainbow sea. Amaya found gourds to hold water and urged the others to look for brightly colored fruits that would indicate ripeness. They found wild orange, wild fig, bush tomato, and plum. The fruits were smaller and less sweet than what the adventurers were accustomed to, but edible. They ate them cautiously, nonetheless, so as not to cramp their stomachs.

Hunting success was slow. Twice more Daniel encountered kangaroos in the evening but was no more successful in getting close than before. He had more luck with the Outback's huge lizards, some three and four feet long, which could be found dozing in the sun. With a patient stalk, a sprint, and hard throw, he managed to spear two, clubbing the stunned animals before they could scuttle off. He gutted them with his knife, the blood staining the sand, and then swaggered back to camp, swinging his kill by their tails.

"Well I'll be," Ico greeted. "Dyson killed some dinosaurs."

"It's a start," Daniel said.

"You won't mind if I observe they look about as appetizing as toad shit."

"You won't mind that I don't give you a share."

"Ah." Ico looked at the reptiles more closely. "They do have a certain beauty, I now see."

"Goddamned gorgeous if you're hungry enough."

"Conceded."

They built a fire and sampled the meat.

"A year's salary to eat lizard," Daniel joked, secretly pleased at his success. Great white hunter.

"Ain't bad," Tucker judged. "Like chicken."

"Everything tastes like chicken," Ico reminded.

"Not this, I'll bet." It was Amaya, slyly holding something up.

The men recoiled. "What in the hell is *that?*"

She was holding up what looked like a white, writhing worm, or a huge naked caterpillar. It was longer and thicker than a man's thumb. "It's a witchetty grub. I read about them. You dig at the base of a witchetty bush where the ground is cracked . . ."

"A what?"

"Those gray, ugly shrubs. The grubs live in the roots. You crack the root to get at them. I tried it. It's hard work."

Ico laughed. "You've got to be kidding. That's a big bug, right? It's got segments, spots . . ."

"It's supposed to be rich in protein and vitamins and very filling."

"Filling enough that I'll bet no one ever eats two," Daniel said.

"I'll bet she won't even eat one," Ico said. He reached in his pocket and pulled something out. "Here, I had this on me when the flood hit." He slapped down a wrinkled hundred-dollar note. "This says there's no way anybody is going to eat that."

"The aborigines did."

"I want to see *you* do it."

She held up its writhing form. "I'll share it with you, Ico."

"I'd rather starve."

"You haven't even been hungry yet." Suddenly she tilted her head back, closed her eyes, and dropped the grub into her mouth, swallowing with an audible gulp without biting.

"Oh my God!" Tucker cried.

Ico was awed. "More astonishing than Ursula Uvula on Sex-Net."

Amaya looked straight ahead, fighting to keep it down. "The trick," she breathed tightly, "is to swallow it head first so it can't crawl back out." She shivered, then smiled. "It's really not too bad. I can't feel it moving." She snatched up the hundred dollars. "I want more when I make an ant ball," she said fiercely.

"It was worth a hundred bucks to see you do that," said Ico. "My God, Amaya, you are some woman. I'll have some fantasies about that one."

She threw some sand at him.

"No, really," he persisted. "That was better than fishing us out of the drink."

The foraging had restored some confidence and they set out east again. The loneliness of Australia was its pre-eminent characteristic: in the week since they'd arrived they'd seen no other human, encountered no other track, and discovered no road or evidence of past habitation. It was as if they were the last, or first, people on earth. The spangled night sky emphasized their feeling of smallness and Daniel realized what a distorted sense of reality it had been to spend most of his life in enclosed rooms.

Rooms were accomplishment enough to make their human builders feel important and small enough to make their occupants feel big. A room represented not just interior space but boundaries, enclosure, fortification, territory. The desert felt just the opposite. The flatness was so monotonous that there was little feeling of getting anywhere, and the sky so huge that Daniel felt like a microbe under the eye of the sun. Instead of being depressed by this perception, however, he decided to be encouraged by it. If he was not dominating his environment then he was becoming a part of it, woven into its web. It didn't make him smaller, it joined him to something bigger. Since he was made from chemicals first forged in exploding stars, he reasoned, he shouldn't be intimidated by the vastness of the sky but feel at home with it. Sister stars! For the first time in his life he didn't have to get out of his apartment, or workplace, or city, to get somewhere. There was no there, everything was *here*. He was always—no matter where he slept—home.

"So, are you finding what you were looking for?"

It was Amaya, dropping back to walk beside him.

"In part. I was just thinking I like the immensity of the place. It makes you feel less significant and more so at the same time, and somehow that feels right."

"Really? I'm a little frightened by it. It's bigger than I imagined. That flood, the suddenness of it, scared me."

"You didn't seem very scared. That was quick thinking to get the rope."

"I wasn't thinking, I was reacting. What if you three had drowned?"

He glanced at her. "It would have left the most resourceful of the four."

"No. I would have died, very lonely and very afraid and very quickly. I know that. It's beautiful here but I don't have that feeling of rightness yet. I think women need something more."

"People, I think you said."

"A person." Her look was both challenging and questioning.

Daniel was quiet, trying to decide how he wanted to respond. He liked this woman.

"You said you've found only part of what you're looking for," she finally went on. "What part are you still seeking?"

He took a breath. "A person."

"Oh." She watched him, his face tan, his clothes red from dust. There was a new hardness to him, she realized. Less of the boy and more of the man. Now he was looking straight ahead, avoiding her implied question. "We have that in common, I guess."

He stopped then and turned to her. She stopped too. "I joined Outback Adventure because I met a woman who told me about it," he explained. "I think she might have come here before me. I'm not really looking for her, but I wonder if she's out here somewhere. I wonder how she's doing. It wouldn't be honest not to tell you that."

Amaya nodded, trying not to betray emotion. "I understand."

"I like you, Amaya. You're like her, in a way."

Her smile was pained. "Daniel, that's great. I hope you find her."

"I just didn't want to mislead you or anything." He felt awkward, and suddenly resentful that she'd made him talk about it. He hadn't been thinking about Raven and now he had to.

"I appreciate the honesty."

"I mean she doesn't even like me, as near as I can tell. I just need . . . to be sure."

"That's fine. I was just curious. I'm sorry."

He squinted at her. "It must be hard for you being the only woman. I hadn't thought much about that."

"You're all behaving yourselves." She looked away. "I wouldn't mind finding your friend, though. Finding another woman. I think it would be less frightening."

"Sometimes I think she's out here, nearby. Like I can feel it."

"That sounds nice."

"No. It's distracting."

They were quiet for a while. Finally he reached out, his fingertips touching her hand. "Amaya, you'll find what you're looking for. Not just yourself, but someone else. I know it."

"I'm sure I will," she said lightly, looking around at the desert to avoid his eyes. "Sometimes the trick is discovering what you've already found."

CHAPTER FOURTEEN

The landscape became increasingly monotonous as they walked eastward. The terrain was flat, watercourses had disappeared, and the vegetation was shrublike and gray. Distance was beginning to take a toll. Pant legs were becoming frayed from the constant friction of stabbing grass and brush, and the flood had stolen replacement clothing. Daniel gave up a pair of shorts to be shared as a source of patches. They'd salvaged two hand-sewing kits that were proving invaluable, but had already consumed most of their thread. "We can unravel more from a pant leg," Amaya suggested.

Their feet were increasingly sore from the pounding, and their collective weariness seemed to be cumulative. Each night did not provide enough rest to make up for the exertion of the previous day. Yet instead of slowing they pushed harder, trying now to get to wetter, better country. Discouragingly, the terrain grew drier and hotter. They were walking on an ancient seabed on what is geologically the world's oldest continent, its mountains worn to nubs and its valleys filled with sediment by unimaginable time. It was so unchanging it seemed as if they were walking in place.

Their anxious progress gave them little time to hunt or forage, and their remaining food supply was falling rapidly. The strategy was to replenish it in kinder country, if they could find it, but meanwhile they looked when they could. Daniel still made his dusk circuits from camp, and managed to bring in two crested pigeons, a rock wallaby (a small, agile relative of the kangaroo), and a monitor lizard. Just for amusement he caught and carried back a thorny devil, a small squat lizard defended by conelike spines. It looked like a bizarre monster out of a lurid movie.

"You finally found something that looks worse than the food in junior high," Ico assessed.

One evening Daniel came back with a troubled look.

"No luck?" Amaya asked.

"No, I saw something," he said slowly.

"But didn't spear it," Tucker observed.

"Didn't even get close. I was too startled. It moved . . . like a man."

"What?"

"It was one of those things you see out of the corner of your eye. I turned, and it was gone. I shouted, but there was no answer. I couldn't find any trace of him. Or her."

"Another adventurer?" Amaya wondered.

"Another mirage," said Ico. "So far I've seen two ice cream stands, an Olympic-sized pool, a phantom beer truck, and a Tahitian topless troupe."

They laughed.

"Seriously," said Daniel, "could someone be following us?"

"If they are, they're more idiotic than we are," Ico said. "I think we're completely lost." He dug out his map again and studied it. "It may be stupid to simply strike due east if there's wetter terrain to the north or south. Maybe we can find a real river to follow, or at least mountains that would catch and funnel more rain."

"You want more rain?" Tucker asked. "After that flood?"

"I want normal rain. Sensible rain. Useful rain."

Tucker bent to look over his shoulder. "So where are we?"

"That's the damn problem. I don't know." He turned the map sideways. "This doesn't show rivers anyway."

"Ico, you got taken, you dumb paranoid."

"No, this is real, I'm convinced of it. If I can just get oriented."

"Well, it's stupid to go off north or south if we don't know what's in that direction," Daniel said. "They told us it gets greener to the east. We just have to keep going."

"What if they were lying?" Ico asked.

"Why would they do that?"

"Maybe that's the game. To catch them in their lies. It's getting browner, not greener."

"Ico, *that's* paranoid."

"That's the observable truth and we better start talking frankly about what we're doing. They said we'll live by our wits and what's on our backs. Well, we've lost half what we had on our backs. We need to think."

"Think, not panic."

"If we don't find water, it doesn't matter," Amaya said.

Tucker nodded. "Two days back to the last water hole and none tonight, either. I'm almost dry."

"So," Daniel reasoned, "the riverbeds we've encountered have run mostly north and south. Going east should be the best bet to cross one."

"What if we don't?" Amaya said. "This plain may be waterless. Maybe we should retreat and try following one of the dry beds we've already found."

They sat, considering that. Finally Tucker shook his head. "And get nowhere. Daniel's right. We can't start walking in aimless circles looking for water. All we can do is put on the miles until we hit the next source and then decide what to do."

"What if we don't agree?" Ico asked.

"We vote."

"We split up," said Ico. "I'm not betting my life on majority stupidity."

"No!" Amaya cried.

"We're not splitting up," Daniel said wearily. "We'll agree as a group or we'll end up dying as individuals. But first we have to walk to water so we can think straight. East looks as promising as north or south. Let's stick to it."

There were no answers. Ico reluctantly put his map away.

They built a fire and slept uneasily. Daniel was restless, waking sometimes with the feeling of being watched. But there was no one out there.

He roused Tucker in the chill of predawn. "Come on. We need to hunt."

The big man groaned. "Can't we wait for a well?"

"I'm thinking an animal might lead us to one."

They crept out of camp under the fading stars, the sky beginning to blush to the east. They heard the call of a few waking birds, but otherwise the desert seemed empty. Except for the scuttle trails of a few crawling insects, there was no sign of game. After half an hour they sat down.

"This is more discouraging than selling computers."

"You really couldn't sell any?"

"I really didn't *want* to sell any. I didn't care. All my life nothing I've done has quite jelled. I just want to succeed at something, but first I have to decide what I want to succeed at. Now it looks like I might succeed at dying of thirst."

"We just have to hang in there. Do you know what happened to Burke and Wills?"

"Who?"

"The first white men to cross Australia, south to north. They left most of their party at a creek, pushed on, almost reached the sea, and came back. They were starving. When they got back to the creek their help was gone. Their companions had given up the wait that morning. They died."

"Geez, there's some luck." Tucker looked out over the desert. "You were a history major, right?"

"Military history."

"And why that? All that killing?"

"I liked the courage. Courage I doubted I had. Like the Spartans."

"I heard of them. Kick-ass guys, right?"

"A Spartan who came home heroically dead from battle was a joy to his mother, but one who died with a wound on his back was a humiliation. They were awesome. Three hundred of them took on a Persian army of tens of thousands, and almost won. They blocked a pass."

"Almost?"

"They were betrayed and the Persians got around

them. But until then they were invincible. They gave the rest of Greece time to prepare."

"So what happened to them?"

"They died. It was a sacrifice."

"And like their moms, you think that's good."

"No, I think it admirable. What's life for? For them it was to train, and die like heroes, and save Western civilization. They found their why."

"And for us?"

"We just have to prove we can stick it out, Tucker, until we find our own why. Prove that people still belong to a place, instead of the place belonging to them."

"I hope I belong here. It's not as easy as I thought."

"I won't disagree with that."

"It's not the dying I would mind. I just want to count for something, you know? In today's world there's too many of us, so nobody matters."

"Out here you matter."

They sat for a while, the lack of a sign giving them little inducement to look farther. Then something big flicked out of sight.

"Kangaroo!" Tucker breathed.

"No," said Daniel, suddenly uneasy and sitting straighter. "It didn't jump like that." He peered hard at the shadowy brush but couldn't see any movement. "It was that guy again. Come on!" They trotted to where they'd seen the figure and separated, looking for tracks.

"Uh-oh," Tucker called. "Oh boy. You were right."

Daniel came over. As the eastern sky glowed a brighter pink, he saw what his companion was hypnotized by. It was a human boot print, but not one of their own. The waffle soles of a hiking boot. He looked closer. The tread design was peculiar. The grid looked like a street map.

"We got company," Tucker said. "Is that good?"

Daniel glanced around. "It must be another Outback Adventurer. Why'd he run?"

"Maybe he's a loner."

"Maybe he knows the way to water."

They followed the tracks, winding circuitously through the brush. The course seemed deliberately confusing. "He's trying to lose us," Daniel said. "Or get us lost."

"So where *is* camp?"

"We'll see the breakfast smoke when Ico and Amaya wake up. He must have seen our fire last night."

"So why doesn't he just say hello? This is weird."

As the sun broke the horizon they saw another flicker of movement at a low ridge crest. As soon as they saw it, the stranger was gone.

"Goddamnit." Tucker bolted ahead, moving agilely for such a big man. He bounded up the lower sand slopes of the ridge and scrabbled toward the steeper rocks.

"Tucker! Wait up!" Daniel trotted after him with his spear.

Tucker was up on the ridge now, hoisting himself through the boulders in hopes of getting a glimpse of the elusive fugitive. He climbed heedless of caution, half leaping from one hold to another. Daniel stopped to map a more prudent route.

Then Tucker screamed, springing backward from the rocks as if he had been fired from a cannon. He made a twisting loop, roaring and flinging his right arm, launching something long and rubbery into space. Then he crashed into the dirt at the base of the rocks and rolled downward, Daniel following through Tucker's cloud of dust.

"Snake!" Tucker shouted, curling into a ball and holding his arm. "Snake, snake, snake! Oh-my-God-it-hurts!"

"Tucker, stop! Where's the snake?" Daniel pulled at him wildly, fearfully looking for the reptile before realizing that it must have been flung away. The big man no doubt put his hand into a nest in his anxious scramble upward. Now Daniel grabbed his bitten hand and saw fang marks plain in the flesh in back of the thumb, the skin beginning to swell. He paled. Australia had some of the most venomous snakes in the world.

"It hurts so bad," Tucker moaned. "I *hate* snakes!"

"Then you should have gone to the Arctic." It was a lame attempt at levity. Daniel yanked at the man's shirtsleeve, ripping it from the shoulder. He wound the material around the forearm and pulled tight to make a tourniquet. A pocketknife made a quick, bloody incision and he squeezed the flesh, hoping he was squeezing some venom out. His friend howled as he did it, blood spraying to spatter gray leaves.

"Jesus, what a mess!" How poisonous was it?

Tucker was sweating despite the dawn cool, his chest heaving frantically. Daniel was frightened he was going to die. "Okay, lay back, I'm going to get some help," he told his friend with more reassurance than he felt. Their antivenin kit had been lost in the flood. "You're going to be all right, understand?"

Tucker nodded, pale with fear. "Where's the snake? I'm afraid of the snake."

"The snake? You must have put it in orbit. Don't worry about snakes, your thrashing has just about scared the shit out of everything in Australia, with legs or without."

"That's good." He gave a grimaced smile. "Man, I'm hurt from the fall too. What a screw-up mess."

"I'll be right back, okay? Just wait."

He groaned. "Like I'm going to go anywhere."

Daniel could hear the confused calls of the others and shouted back, jogging off in that direction. They were only a few hundred yards away. He stumbled into camp.

"Where's Tucker?"

"Snakebite," he gasped.

The other two looked stricken.

"And I was right, someone else is sneaking around here."

They looked about wildly.

"Look, I think the stranger's gone, but Tucker's in bad shape. We'll have to carry him into camp."

"We can't carry Tucker!" Ico protested. "He weighs a ton!"

"I think we have to."

They hurried back to the weakening man. He was delirious when they got to him, curled again and shaking, looking like a ghost from the coating of dust. "Holy shit," Ico breathed. "He looks like he's dying."

"What kind of snake?" Amaya asked.

"How do I know? It's not like it matters now."

"How can we move him?"

It was Ico who had the idea to build a triangular travois like the Plains Indians and drag their big companion. They cut branches and vines to fasten a crude frame, rolled Tucker onto it despite his roar of protest, tied him down, and gave a tentative heave. The poles dragged along the ground with less friction than his full body. "Okay, this will work," Daniel said. "Here we go. One, two, three, pull!" A jerk and they were off, dust spurting from the ends of the two poles. Weaving this way and that, they pulled him back between the mulga trees and got to camp at mid-morning.

When they returned, all their food—except the sack Amaya had hung from a bush—was gone. Their campsite was spotted with the strange maplike grid of a waffle-soled boot.

A trail of boot prints led east and so they went that way too. The four of them had one gallon of water left to share and the temperature was arcing with the sun. Tucker had slipped into uneasy sleep on his travois, his bandaged arm grotesquely swollen. Flies crawled across his sweating face.

They managed half a mile per hour and collapsed by noon. The sled was exhausting.

"Look, we have to leave him," Ico croaked.

"No way!" protested Amaya.

"Just until we find water. Then we come back and get him."

"Ico, he could die!"

"We'll all die if we don't get some water."

She shook her head. "You two go ahead then. I'll wait with him."

Daniel vetoed that. "I'm not leaving you alone with this crazy guy wandering around. And I don't want just one of us scouting for water, either. We have to stay together."

"Dyson . . ."

"Come on. This guy, or guys, must be heading to water too. We follow them as a group. It's the safest way."

By mid-afternoon, though, the growing impossibility was obvious. Their water was gone. The desert shimmered, its heat climaxing near one hundred degrees.

The trio was exhausted from their turns pulling the travois. Tucker seemed to be slipping into permanent unconsciousness. And the landscape was unchanged.

They dropped into the shade of a stunted tree, a parade of ants marching up its twisted trunk. A kite wheeled in the cloudless sky. They felt absolutely demoralized and exhausted.

"We're done," Ico said.

"Don't say that," Amaya pleaded.

"Even if we find water we've lost too much gear. We don't have much food, we don't have tools . . . what did we last, a week and a half? They'd laugh, if they ever knew."

"We've just had bad luck. That guy robbed us. That's like trying to murder us."

"Ten to one he's succeeded within twenty-four hours."

"But why?"

"Maybe he got hungry himself. So he preys on the newcomers. Dog eat dog. There's a survival lesson for you."

"Then why not just slit our throats? He could have, last night."

"Maybe he's fastidious."

Daniel looked up at the desert sky. Not a cloud, not a plane, not a hope. He hadn't known it was possible to feel so alone. "Okay, Ico, you go on ahead," he conceded. "It's our only chance. Take the water containers and we'll wait with Tucker. I don't want to leave Amaya alone."

Ico nodded. The decision was inevitable. "I'll need the last food."

"No."

"Dyson, I have to eat to hike. I'll push faster with it than without it."

"No. I want you to come back."

"Jesus!"

"The last food stays here. You're the one who talked about splitting up."

Ico sullenly gathered up the remaining canteens as Tucker groaned restlessly. Amaya dug in her pack and gave him some of their last emergency ration bars. "Daniel didn't really mean that," she whispered.

"Yes he did." Ico left without looking back.

They watched the sun set with their hopes. Daniel had seldom been truly thirsty before, but now his throat was closing, his tongue swelling, and the need for water was intruding on all other thoughts. Soon it would hurt to talk.

The flies left, the stars came, and a chill crept into the air. He looked at Amaya, sitting small and forlorn next to Tucker. "Amaya," he croaked. "Come here." She crawled to him and he put an arm around her. "Help me stay warm."

"I'm scared, Daniel," she confessed. "I want to go back."

He hugged her, kissing the top of her hair with his dry, cracked lips. "Me too. But we can't, not yet."

She cuddled, relaxing in his embrace, and they listened to the sounds of the night creatures. The heat of her body felt good. A spark of life. "I'm glad I'm not alone," she said.

He nodded. "Me too. Can I make a confession?"

"A deathbed one?"

"Don't say that."

"I'm sorry, I'm just trying to joke. Go on. Confess."

He hesitated. "I saw you a few nights ago. In the river."

"In the river?"

"Bathing."

"Oh." She was quiet. "How did I look?"

"Beautiful. The stars, the water . . ."

"You were just horny. Or thirsty."

"No. It was nice. You were nice. I just wanted to say that."

"A compliment?"

"That's what I meant."

"All right. Good. Now, can I make a confession?"

"Of course."

She looked at him mischievously. "I saw you too. Watching, I mean."

"Oh."

"I liked it."

"Good." He lowered his face to brush against her cheek and she turned and kissed him then, their lips dry but the touch a quiet comfort. "I wonder what would have happened if we'd had more time?" he asked.

"I'm glad we had this time."

He lay there, holding her, wondering what the morning would bring. Maybe there'd be a miracle. Maybe it would rain again.

Eventually, they slept.

Daniel was prodded awake at dawn. Silhouetted against the light of the rising sun was a stranger, dark and dirty, with hair down around his ears. He was tanned a tobacco brown and wore faded synthetics patched with animal leathers, with a bone necklace that rattled when he moved. His boots, Daniel sleepily realized, left the same gridded print they'd spotted at their camp. Like a street map. He was holding a skin of water. They could smell it.

"Want some?"

The two untangled themselves and sat up. They noticed Ico a short distance behind, like a trailing schoolboy. Uncertainly, they nodded.

The man uncapped the water skin and drank himself, rivulets running down into the stubble of his beard. Then he held it out to them. "I wasn't going to come back for you, you know."

Daniel stretched his arm out and took the water skin. The warm dusty water was the sweetest he'd ever tasted. He swallowed a mouthful and gave it to Amaya.

"Careful!" the man told her. "Sip, or you'll throw up!"

She complied.

"Then why did you?" Daniel croaked.

"He came up on me when I nodded off," Ico spoke up. "I didn't have time to run. I think we'd better throw in with them."

"It wasn't *him* who brought me back," the stranger said.

Daniel looked up at him, puzzled.

He jerked his head backward. "It was her."

Now Daniel noticed there was a third figure in the shadows, slim and erect, looking at them with surprise. "So it *is* you," she said, stepping forward.

He jerked in recognition himself.

It was Raven.

CHAPTER FIFTEEN

You're not supposed to be in this sector," Raven said to Daniel, her eyes flickering from him to the young woman at his side.

He stared back in amazement, taking in the familiar features. Her dark hair had been pulled into a ponytail, accentuating high cheekbones turned bronze by the sun. Her eyes revealed puzzlement. Unlike his huddled posture of defeat, she carried herself with familiar athletic quickness and grace, like a poised deer. He was confused by her confusion: he thought she'd be surprised he'd come to Australia at all, not that he was in any particular spot.

"You told me you didn't think you'd come here," he countered, his voice a croak. "Then I called and you were gone."

"Yes." She looked at the three newcomers as if trying to decide something. "My situation changed."

Daniel sipped more water and sat up straighter, the liquid tingling as it circulated, relieving the ache in his brain. "Your timing is good. We were in bad shape."

"You're very lucky."

Amaya was looking at Raven with a mixture of bewilderment and mistrust. Raven glanced at her, considering. "This is a surprise for both of us, as you can see," she said to the other woman. "We knew each other before."

Amaya absorbed this.

Daniel pointed at the man accompanying Raven. "He stole some of our food," he accused.

"No I didn't," the man said. "I saved it from a dingo. If I hadn't taken it, it would be gone."

"We ran to save Tucker," Amaya explained meekly.

"And left your means of survival to the dogs. I went to find Raven so we could decide what to do. I wasn't sure you could, or should, survive. You're in a hard world now and we weren't planning to meet anyone out here. Then we found this little guy—"

"Ethan, enough," Raven interrupted. "After talking with Ico there, we decided you needed rescue." It was clear the decision had been hers. "He told us about you."

"Why did you run from us?" Daniel asked Ethan.

"Because our business is private." He looked at Raven with the dubious expression of a follower still questioning the decision of his leader.

"And this complicates everything," Raven added. She looked out across the desert as she thought. It was almost as if she was sorry she'd found Daniel. Was she involved with this other man?

"We could just point them toward the compound," Ethan said.

"And get the Warden suspicious at the news of us? I don't want him coming out here. Besides, this group is in no condition to drag the big man that far." She pointed at the groaning Tucker. "What kind of snake? Did you see?"

"No idea."

"Well, if it was a taipan he'd probably be dead by now. Maybe just a death adder; he's too big a mouthful for that kind despite the name."

"So Tucker will live?" Amaya asked.

She shrugged. "He'll die, or get better."

There was a moment of silence at this appraisal. "She sounds like my doctor," Ico finally quipped.

Raven for the first time allowed a half smile. "You start to appreciate their wisdom out here." She looked at Daniel and Amaya. "Can you walk?"

They nodded uncertainly. "I'm feeling better," Daniel said. It was not just the water, it was this encounter with a Raven who seemed to know what she was doing. Confidence was as infectious as panic.

"Their sled might work to drag him as far as Car Camp," she said to the man called Ethan. "They can rest there while we search."

"And then what?" he asked in exasperation. "Who is this guy, anyway?"

"A friend." It was the first time she'd said it. "And *then* we decide what to do next."

Daniel was filled with questions. Who was Ethan? Search for what? "How did you first spot us?"

"Your fires," Raven said. "We thought you might be someone else."

"This Warden?" Amaya guessed.

"Yes. We needed to know who you were."

Amaya leaned close to Daniel, her eyes on Raven. "Is this the person you were talking about?" she asked softly.

He knew what she meant. "Yes."

Amaya looked dismayed. Raven was taller, prettier, stronger, Daniel saw through her eyes. More assertive. No, he wanted to say, it's not like that. But before he could think of what to say to the two women that would work, Raven spoke up.

"We knew each other," she said. "That's all."

Daniel didn't like that, either.

"Knew how?" Ico asked impatiently.

"She's the one who told me about Outback Adventure," Daniel explained stiffly. "She gave me the passwords. But she didn't tell me she was going."

"I didn't know then. I came in part because of you."

"Ah," Ico said, as if he understood everything. "And who's this guy?"

"Ethan Flint," the man said.

"Another trekker?"

"That was the plan."

"What happened?"

"My transport crashed."

"Oh, dear," Amaya said. "But you're here on vacation, like us?"

He laughed sardonically. "It's probably more accurate to say you're here in prison, like me."

"Prison? What the hell does that mean?" Daniel asked.

"That you can't get back unless—"

"Ethan!" Raven's voice was a warning.

"I knew it," Ico groaned. "I knew this was somehow fucked. Outback Adventure has screwed us, right? What, we have to pay more now to get out? Is that the scam?"

Ethan shook his head. "I wish it were that easy."

"Don't pay any attention to him," Raven said. "He doesn't know what he thinks he knows."

"I know enough to know—"

"I'll explain what I can soon enough," she went on quickly, firmly. "First we need to get to more water before the sun gets too high." Clearly she wouldn't tolerate too many questions yet. "Come on, we'll take turns pulling your . . . sled."

"Travois," Ico corrected. "But what the hell is your companion talking about?"

Raven said nothing. Ethan looked away.

Ico bent to pull the travois with Daniel. "There's something weird here, Dyson," he whispered like a conspirator. "When this pair found me, that woman of yours recognized my name."

With Raven and Ethan adding their energy to pulling the travois, progress became steady. They turned more north than east, Raven usually pointing the way but consulting occasionally with Ethan. When Flint took a break from the travois, walking silently as if lost in thought, Ico moved up beside him.

"Who the hell *are* you, really?" he asked.

Ethan glanced at the shorter man. "I'm you, three months ago. Hapless. Clueless."

"Gee, thanks."

"My equipment lost. My clothes still in tolerable shape. My fat reserves still intact and my self-confidence gone. Dropped into Australia like a virgin of fraud."

"And now you're an old pro who saved us."

"Not me. The deal was to take your chances in the desert." He nodded up toward Raven. "She's your Good Samaritan."

"Why?"

"Your buddy, obviously. I think it's foolish, letting you tag along."

"Who is she?"

"One of us, she says. Outback Adventurer."

"You don't believe her?"

"I don't disbelieve her. She just knows a little too much. For example, how does she know you?"

"She doesn't," Ico said, "unless Dyson mentioned me somehow. And if he did, why would he even remember?"

"Why indeed?" Ethan looked ahead.

"Unless word of my charm gets around."

Flint laughed at that.

"Listen, what in hell is going on?" Ico persisted. "There's something wrong with this whole deal, right?"

Ethan smiled faintly. "Let's just say you have more company out here than you expected."

By mid-morning the six of them had consumed Ethan and Raven's remaining water supply, and Daniel was worried they'd soon be in the plight they were in before. It was hot again, the weight of the sick man oppressive. They seemed to march in a cloud of flies. The land was featureless, intimidating in its monotony, and Raven seemed distant, as if still trying to decide something, glancing occasionally back at Daniel. Then shortly before noon Ethan led them into a crack in the earth that had been invisible until they came to its lip. It widened to a curious ravine enclosing a kind of oasis. A few gum and palm trees huddled in the geologic wrinkle, hiding from the worst of the sun. They dragged Tucker down into its shade and collapsed with relief.

"Where did this hole come from?" Daniel asked.

"I'm guessing a collapsed cave," Raven said, "but I don't really know. There's a spring at one end but it's too mineralized to drink from."

Ico's nose wrinkled. "It stinks like rotten eggs."

"Sulfur," Amaya guessed.

Raven looked at her with curiosity. "You're a geologist?"

"Just an amateur naturalist. I never liked the jobs I had so I studied for ones I hadn't. I wish I'd been a scientist on one of those old sailing ships, finding hundreds of new species at every landfall. Australia is so unfamiliar it's almost like that."

"She's found us plants and stuff," Ico said. "Things to eat. But not enough to drink. And if we don't find water, I don't know how much farther we can drag Tucker. He's just too big."

"If we don't get some fluids into him he's going to get too small," Daniel worried. "He'll dry up like a raisin." He turned to Raven. "I thought you were taking us to water."

She looked at him with smug amusement. "I have. Like the tunnels."

They looked around. "Do we have to dig?" Amaya asked.

Ethan laughed. "In this heat? Outback adventure! Outback murder is more like it."

"You've got water right under your nose," Raven said. "Or above it."

"Where?" Amaya said, frustrated. "I don't see it."

"Didn't you notice the rain the other night?" Raven asked.

"Notice it? We almost drowned in it," Ico said. "But

the water's long gone. All I see are sand and bugs." He was watching a line of ants march up a tree.

"Exactly. The desert holds its floods in all kinds of places. Haven't you ever wondered why those silly ants spend their time parading up and down a tree?"

They all looked at the insects now. "Foraging for food, I suppose," said Daniel.

"And water." Raven stood. "First lesson: think like an animal. Like any animal, no matter how small the brain, because they need the same things we do. Birds need water, so a zebra finch can lead you to it. Trees need water, so you can cut into the roots of a bloodwood tree to drink. Ants need water, so they'll climb halfway to heaven to find it . . ." She sprang up, grasping the smooth trunk, and shinnied, grasping a branch to haul herself clear of the ants. Above was a dark opening in the wood. "Some of these trees have hollows," she called down, "and the cavities are a good place to look for a drink. The rain funnels into them and takes a long time to evaporate out." She snapped off a twig and cautiously probed, then lifted it out to show the end moistened like a dipstick. "Ethan! Throw up a cup and water skin!"

They spent an hour resting and drinking in the shade. Amaya foraged and found some bush plum. Life began to seem bearable again. They didn't ask how their guide had learned so much about the desert.

Raven looked at the fruit with approval. "Very impressive. I hope you can find other things that are useful."

"Like an oasis that doesn't stink so much," Ico said.

"Actually, sulfur's useful," Amaya said. "For a million things. Old medicines, pigments, dyes, food preservation, gunpowder . . ."

"Gunpowder!" Ethan exclaimed.

"The old black powder. Sulfur is one of the basic ingredients. The ancients used to call it brimstone."

"I knew we were in hell," Ico said.

Raven looked thoughtful. "Maybe you should collect some of your sulfur."

"What for?"

"We're in a world of scarce resources. Something like that could be useful."

Amaya shrugged. "I could. We don't have much else left to carry except Tucker." She got up to gather some.

"I'll help," Raven said, standing to brush herself off. "Knowledge like yours is vital. It's the only edge we have."

"Yes. It's just when the facts get ahead of wisdom that we get into trouble."

Raven nodded. "So are you finding it?"

"Wisdom? More than I bargained for, I think."

Her new companion smiled. "It's nice to have another woman along."

Amaya looked surprised at that. "Is it?"

"You can talk to men only up to a certain point."

She winked. "Then you think of other things to do with them." Jaunty now, glowing from Raven's appreciation of her abilities, she led the way to scrape some sulfur.

Daniel watched quietly, going over his previous encounters with Raven in his mind and wondering at her coincidental appearance. What exactly had she said to him? Why wouldn't she say more now? Who was she, really?

The women came back with the mineral. "The prospectors of hell," Ico greeted.

"Fruit of the land," Amaya replied.

As they gathered their things to move on, she drifted to Daniel. "Your friend Raven seems adept," she murmured to him.

"Yes. The only problem is, I'm not sure she's really my friend."

Before they set out again, Raven opened a packet of dried leaves and distributed a small pile on each of their cupped fingers. "Chew this," she instructed. "It will make the last few miles before camp go faster."

"What is it?" Ico asked dubiously.

"Rock pituri. The aborigines used it as a stimulant. It gives you energy and relieves thirst."

Ico stuffed some between gum and cheek as instructed. "Like cardboard," he said thickly. "What happens if I swallow?"

"Don't. It's a stimulant, not a food. You can also put the juice on cuts and stings to relieve the pain and promote healing." She spat, businesslike, and rubbed a gob on Tucker's bitten hand. He jerked at the touch and then relaxed again. "It helps fight any poisons."

The drug worked as promised. The travelers felt a flush of energy like a jolt of caffeine that helped get them through the afternoon heat. Tucker groaned in delirious dreams, his face and body spotted with flies, but some of his normal color seemed to be returning. Indeed, it looked like he might live.

The country they were trudging through was parched, however, the plain beginning to break toward low hills, the vegetation gray and dead-looking. Part of it had been burned black by fire. To the exhausted Daniel, Australia seemed an ugly place getting uglier, a sand and rock waste that led nowhere. A prison, Ethan had called it. What did that mean?

He planned to confront Raven that night.

Meanwhile step followed step, the puffs of dust rising, the horizon shimmering in its heat haze, the flies not as bad here but still present, a solitary hawk orbiting like a sentinel of doom. It was like his dream, he thought. He was lost on a blank plain.

Suddenly something glinted in the sun ahead, a familiar kind of flash that instantly caused him to become alert to the geography again. It was a reflection in the lowering sun. "What's that?" he asked Ethan, the two of them bent forward as they dragged the travois.

"Trash. Civilization."

It was broken glass, Daniel realized. The newcomers stopped, strangely dazzled by this sudden apparition of a shard of old technology. They'd come to a dirt track through the scrub desert, he saw, overgrown and decayed. Gullies cut across it and brush sprouted in its middle. On its shoulders were pieces of glass from bottles thrown by bush motorists long dead. Amber, green, clear. The party put down the travois and poked around at the fragments like bent birds, as intent as archaeologists. It was a reminder that another world still existed.

"Where does the road go?" Daniel asked, suddenly imagining it merging into pavement, freeways, ruined cities, and abandoned ports. Leading toward home.

"Nowhere," Ethan said. "It's an old station track that washes out, the station long gone. Nothing goes anywhere anymore, because there's nowhere in Australia to go to." He watched Ico fingering the dirt with amusement. "Your friend never see litter before?"

"Not here. It's startling, after so much nothing."

"There's leftovers from the Dying all around, if you know where to look. We'll camp by an old wreck tonight. We call it Car Camp."

"Don't you want to follow the road?"

"I said roads don't go anywhere. They're just lines on the earth with no purpose. The only place around here has no road in and no road out, because there's no place to go to or come from."

"And what place is that?"

"Erehwon. End of the line."

Daniel squinted, remembering. "That was one of the code words to Outback Adventure."

"Was it? The Warden just thinks it's a joke."

"You keep mentioning this Warden. There's one here?"

"You'll meet him. He runs the place."

"The prison keeper."

"It's another joke. Except it's not, really."

"You say there's no place to go to and yet you're out here, going someplace."

"That's different. That's her idea." He jerked his head toward Raven. "She thinks she can find something and asked me to help her look for it. The first hope I've had in a long time."

"You two are . . . ?"

"Allies. Nothing more."

"And what does Erehwon mean?"

"I've already figured that one out," said Ico, who was listening. "It's an old name, from utopian literature. 'Nowhere,' spelled backward."

They followed the track for a quarter mile eastward before leaving it and striking north across the desert again. The stops were brief, but Raven's sense of purpose had given Daniel's group new energy. They marched without complaint except for Ico's periodic habitual wisecracks, and even he seemed happy now that they had direction.

"Are we there yet?" he jokingly called once, mimicking a tired child.

"Maybe here is there," Daniel replied. "Each place is the right place."

"Oh, please."

Raven looked back at them with interest.

As they trudged along, Daniel realized that meeting Raven and Ethan had given rise to a new emotional confusion. There were other people in Australia! He'd known that, of course—known about other Outback Adventure clients, at least—but actually meeting some changed the virginity of the place. So did the old track. Australia was still wilderness, of course, but suddenly a wilderness that at once seemed more familiar, more menacing, and more haunted. A populated wilderness. A wilderness with ghosts. His journey had changed in a subtle way.

The feeling of disorientation increased when they came that evening to a rusting light truck that was half buried in the sand of another dry riverbed. There was no road or track that he could see and so he assumed the old station vehicle had somehow been carried downstream by past floods. Its windows and upholstery were gone and its paint blasted away by sun and sand. The remains were the same color as the rusty hills, slowly melting back into the earth. And yet it was a human artifact, a reminder that people had long lived in this so-called wilderness: for fifty thousand years or more, anthropologists said. He was trekking in their shadow.

There was a rock cairn marking a well and they drank again. Tucker had come drowsily awake and was alert enough to begin rehydrating his body. As he drank he began to revive, croaking some puzzled questions. His dreams had confused him, but now he watched their new companions curiously. Dusk fell and Raven built a fire. Ethan disappeared for a while and then reappeared with a dead and gutted kangaroo slung over his shoulder. Clearly Daniel could learn something from their aloof companion's hunting skills. Ico was drowsing against the metal body of the old truck, seeming to take comfort from the flaking metal. Daniel got up to watch Ethan skin and butcher the animal.

The kangaroo was gamy, stringy, and good: as solid a meal as Daniel's group had had in several days. Tucker ate some, woozy but stabilizing. "Just a little on this stomach of mine," he said.

Ethan allowed a grin at how much the other three consumed. "Tomorrow I'll spear an elephant."

The stars came out, a familiar and comfortable ceiling now. Daniel felt an immense tiredness steal over him, as if he could sleep for days, but first he needed some questions answered. Where were they going? What was this Erehwon?

"Outback Adventure lied to us, didn't they?" he finally asked to begin things.

Raven's face was like an abstract painting, the fire flickering to illuminate first this plane, then that one, causing her to shift shape with each tongue of flame. She didn't reply, just looked at him with sadness.

"They didn't tell you everything," Ethan said.

"You don't know everything," Raven warned.

"I know the most important thing."

"Which is?" Ico asked.

"You're not supposed to get back."

CHAPTER SIXTEEN

It was suddenly cold despite the fire. Ethan had voiced a suspicion that had been nagging ever since Ico Washington's paranoid theorizing.

"The adventure is supposed to be permanent," Ethan said. "United Corporations thinks we'll be happier down here."

They looked at him with a combination of fear and disbelief.

"Some get back," Raven said.

Ethan glanced at her. "Maybe."

There was quiet as the newcomers absorbed this revelation. Elliott Coyle had said he'd gotten back, Daniel remembered. Elliott Coyle had promised an Exodus Port. "I thought the whole point was to find the way home," he said to Raven.

"The point is to let you realize *this* is your home."

"You knew this and you came down here? You knew this and you didn't tell me?"

She was silent.

"We didn't know any more than you," Ethan said. "The convicts told us."

"*What* convicts?"

"The morally impaired who can't be rehabilitated are exiled to Australia. They're ruled by one of their own."

"This Warden is a criminal?"

"*You're* a criminal, Daniel. A voluntary one."

"This makes not a bit of sense," Ico said. "Except that we saw some shave-headed goons being herded onto a transport when we departed."

"There you go."

"It's supposed to be for everyone's good," Raven explained. "A new colony, like the British made in Australia. To give people like yourselves—ourselves—an outlet for our energies. In the old days there was a frontier, or a war. Now, there's . . . this."

"We didn't volunteer to be pioneers," Ico said.

"But you did, in a way."

"No," Amaya said. "It's just an adventure trek. A vacation, though an unusual one. We hike to Exodus—"

"There is no Exodus, is there?" Daniel said heavily.

Her voice was flat. "No. Not exactly." There was something more she wasn't saying.

"You knew this and you came here?" Ico was incredulous.

"The people who come here *don't* know it, obviously," she replied.

"She hasn't told you half of it," Ethan added bitterly. "You thought you were going to a kind of wilderness heaven, right? In actuality, they duped you into volunteering for hell."

You may end up in a place even less to your liking, Harriet Lundeen had said to Daniel once. Could the gorgon have known? Heard dark rumors? Or only wished what others had made true? "I still don't understand," he said thickly, even though he felt with a growing sense of dread that he did.

"It's so obvious it's comic," Ethan said. "They maroon us by giving us what we want."

"What we want is to get back home," Amaya said.

"That's the joke. You *are* home. There *is* no getting back. Or rather, you've already gotten back. You *wanted* to come here."

Tucker shook his head slowly.

"Look," Ethan said. "Did you really think they were going to give a whole continent to a handful of urbanites to work out our angst? Come on! Don't you know the history of Australia? It began as a penal colony, right? It was settled by British convicts. This continent was a safety valve to relieve the pressure of inequities in the motherland. The hard-core murderers went to the gallows but the petty thieves, the political rebels, and the urban poor came here. What could be more logical, after the plague, than to use an empty Australia as a penal colony again?"

"But we're not convicts," Amaya objected.

Ethan laughed at her. "You're dissatisfied. That's become a secret crime."

"But *we* approached *them*," Daniel said. "I couldn't even *find* Outback Adventure without help. How would they know . . ."

"Right. *You* approached *them*. Proof of guilt."

"And things like your reprimand," Raven added. "Your troubles at work."

"But how would they know about that?"

"Daniel, don't be naive." She sounded impatient, as if she was having to explain something to someone particularly slow. "They know everything. They *listen* to everything. They talk to people like Luther Cox and Luther talks to them. Once they got everyone onto the Internet, nothing was private anymore. Your life wasn't locked in your head and your desk drawer, it was spewed in electronic bytes across a global network. They told you it was encrypted but spying became child's play. You spied to find me, right? They know us better than we know ourselves, from our electronic droppings. Why was the government so enthusiastic about the Information Highway? It was another way to watch and control."

He stared into the campfire, not liking being played the fool.

Amaya was looking from Raven to Daniel, considering all this carefully. "Yet the person who told Daniel about Outback Adventure was . . . you."

Raven shrugged with dismissal. "That happens all the time, I think. People like us seek each other out, inform each other of the possibility, and even sign up together. We betray each other. They count on it."

"Who is this 'they'?" Ico asked.

"United Corporations. They ensure stability by putting potential troublemakers down here."

"Troublemakers?"

"Unhappy people. Misfits. Malcontents. Independent thinkers."

"That's a crime?"

"Not by statute, but the system works on . . . conformity. You know that. I think they try to get everyone on the same track. The young adults they don't succeed with go . . . here. You all selected yourselves. You all had a dozen chances to back out."

"Our punishment is getting the life we asked for,"

Ethan added. "The irony, the humor of it, is quite sublime."

"Yeah, I'm really laughing." Tucker's look was grim. "So you two are what? Fleeing from these moral-impaireds?"

"Not exactly," Raven said. "We think we may have a chance—an outside chance—to really get back." She looked at Ethan for confirmation.

"Raven says the transport that crashed when I arrived should have been equipped with some kind of transponder, or transmitter. Something to signal for help. We came out from the Warden's little colony to look for it. Now, I guess, you're going to look too. I didn't think we needed you, but she wasn't willing to let you . . ."

"How did you know about this transmitter?" Amaya asked slowly.

"I worked in aviation for a while," Raven said. "It's a guess. A hope. But it's worth pursuing if I ever want to get home."

"Avionics?"

"Yes . . . electronics, communications, that kind of thing. After stumbling onto Erehwon I met Ethan and he told me about his crash. It got me thinking."

"We're near the wreck?" Daniel asked.

"Pretty close. We'll try to find it tomorrow. So I think we should stop talking about this until then. Believe me, I know how confusing this is. Let's deal with it when you have some hope."

He felt dazed. He'd found her, and might even be marooned with her. Or not. He stood and moved off toward his bedroll in the darkness to think.

Amaya quietly approached Raven as the group broke up. "You don't seem as bitter as Ethan," she observed.

"I just admit that I chose to come here."

"You don't seem to be as shocked as us."

Raven looked at her evenly. "I've had more time to think about it."

"Think about our betrayal."

"I'm just a person who takes life as it comes. So should you." Then she moved away.

The next morning the group split in two. Amaya, remote and lost in thought, elected to stay at Car Camp to nurse Tucker. Daniel and Ico, however, decided to accompany Raven and Ethan to find the remains of the transport.

"We're nuts if we let that bitch move out of our sight," Ico muttered to Daniel as they set off. "There's something more she isn't telling us. You're so pussy-blind you can't see it, but I don't trust that siren to tell night from day."

"I hardly even know her, Ico."

"Yeah, right. She seems to know you down to the color of your shorts."

They walked northwestward, Ethan leading the way and happy to be free of the burden of pulling Tucker. He was back on their primary mission but still treated the newcomers as if they were unwanted, or as if there was some unspoken rivalry. He kept an emotional distance.

The pair had fled eastward from Erehwon, Raven explained as they walked, and the community would assume they were trying to cross the desert to get to the coast on their own. Members of the Warden's group deserted periodically, despite warnings of the trip's futility. Once out of sight of the compound, however, Raven and Ethan had circled back west toward Flint's crash site, stumbling on Daniel's party in the process. She seemed troubled by that coincidence.

"So what exactly are we looking for out here?" Ico tried to clarify.

"An emergency beacon," Raven said. "Something on the transport to call for help. All aircraft have one."

"Why wasn't it triggered in the crash?"

"We don't know," Ethan said. "The Warden took some kind of transmitter but it doesn't work. Nothing electronic seems to work here."

"So we're looking for something that does," she said.

"Why would *it* work?"

"That's technical."

He looked at her with dissatisfaction. "Then what?"

"We call for help."

"It would still operate after all this time?" Daniel asked.

"If it's standard, the batteries should last for a year."

"You never told me you worked in aviation."

"I never told me a lot of things."

They walked on in silence. Finally Daniel addressed Ethan. "What exactly happened to you?"

"I was coming here for the typical wilderness experience," he explained. "My transport crashed. I woke up still strapped to the bunk, half the plane gone, and everyone but the pilot dead. He unbuckled me, told me to wait, and went to the forward part of the wreckage I couldn't even see to get something. Then these strange people showed up—it was the Warden's convicts—and I ran. I fell, blacked out, came to. The pilot was missing. I think he told them they could get back if they caught me, but they couldn't. They let me live afterward because it was clear I didn't know a damn thing—or that if I did, I couldn't let it slip if I was dead. So the Warden took me back to Erehwon. There's a mix of convicts and refugee trekkers there, all of us confused. I thought I was stuck here forever until Raven came along."

Daniel glanced at the woman who had intrigued him. She seemed to have discovered a way out of this exile when everyone else had failed. Interesting.

With Ethan recognizing the country with increasing confidence, they found the transport by noon. It was in two pieces. There was the intact tail where Ethan had survived, its metal frame glinting in the heat. Then a stretch of unmarked desert where the nose section had skipped ahead over a rise, followed by a sand furrow still seeded with debris. At its end was the burned-out hulk of the forward section of the aircraft, the fuselage ripped open to the sky.

Ethan hung back. "Some of my friends might still be in there."

"Yuck," Ico whispered.

It wasn't the possibility of bodies that made Daniel reluctant to approach the forward fuselage. Rather, the derelict machine made clear just how completely cut off from civilization they now were. Somewhere in the sky above, satellites orbited. Somewhere across the heat-glazed horizon the sea broke, and out there ships ran and jets flew toward populated shores. But all that was across a gulf as impassable as the abyss between the stars, and instead of reassuring him of the reality of civilization, this burnt husk confirmed how far he was from it.

"It's not a sight to inspire confidence," he said.

"Where one transport came, another might follow," Raven countered. "Come on, this is the way home."

The group went cautiously forward. Despite Ethan's

uneasiness, whatever corpses the transport had contained were long gone, disposed by scavengers and decay. One cockpit seat had disappeared where the pilot had ejected. The other remained, the instrument panel stained dark with what might have been the co-pilot's blood. It was the panel itself that interested Raven.

"See the empty place that held an instrument?" she said. "That must be what the pilot came back for: a transmitter."

"Which the Warden took and which doesn't work," Daniel summarized.

"Yes. So now we look at the tail."

It was a pillaged stub, some of its metal panels stripped for salvage and its seats uprooted. The absence of fire had saved Ethan's life and made that part of the wreckage valuable for salvage. Raven crawled into the rearmost recess and hunted, then backed out. "The other instrument I'm looking for is gone too," she reported. "There's a hole where it's been removed."

"Great," said Ico.

"No, that's good. It fits my guess. I think the pilot gave it to Ethan."

"How do you know that?"

"The pilot gave me *something* for safekeeping before we separated," Ethan said. "I was pretty groggy, but I knew he was anxious to get some other component and leave. He told me that what he was stuffing in my pack would keep us from having to walk to the beach, but I didn't understand what he meant."

"So what happened?"

"He left and the convicts came, drawn by the smoke I suppose," Ethan said. "And he was screaming, and I was running for my life and trying to lighten my load . . ."

"You threw it away."

"I didn't know what it was. I resented having to carry it."

"He threw the damn thing away," Ico repeated to Daniel. "Unbelievable."

"You'd better hope so," Ethan said with irritation, "or the Warden would already have taken the only way out of here."

Daniel looked out the oval opening of the sheared-off tail at the desert. "What if we can't find it?"

"That's not an option," Ethan said.

They came back out. "I'm looking for a box smaller than a shoe box," Raven told them.

"Oh good," Ico said, glancing around. "That will stick out."

Ethan pointed to some sandstone hills on the horizon. "I ran that way and threw things into a ravine. We'll have to search there."

As they hiked toward the hills, Flint's memory of the place began to come back to him. Here he'd left a GPS and range finder, he pointed, both long since pirated and scrapped by the Erehwon group to make metal tools. Farther on . . . yes, he'd come this way, he thought. The ravine looked familiar, as did the crest of the ridge. The convicts had found and looted his pack near here. But the useless box which he'd never mentioned to the Warden . . . it could have been dropped anywhere.

"All right, we'll spread out and search the ravine," Raven said. "Meet by that pink rock by dusk. Ethan, where did you fall from?"

"That way," he pointed.

"I'm going to look up there. The rest of you try here." The men slid down loose scree into the brushy gully.

It was stifling hot. Flies found Daniel, there was no water, and he searched in a fog of depression so thick that it was difficult to even function. This is what his life had come down to: searching a hot desert for a metal box to get back to a place he'd been desperate to flee from just two weeks before. What would he do if he *did* get back? He could no longer imagine a future.

Hours went by with no sign of a human artifact. He drifted down the ravine from the other two men, looking as much for shade as for an electronic black box. He suspected that Ico, skeptical of the whole story, was already napping.

Then, while sitting despondently beneath a gum tree and studying a sandy bottom raked by intermittent water as artfully as a Japanese garden, he realized their mistake. The floods! In the months since Ethan's crash there must have been enough rain to carry things downhill. Or downstream. It was the hunt for their supplies all over again! The box was heavy, no doubt, more like a rock than a log. Still, streams had the power to move entire boulders when running high. Think like an animal, Raven had told him. Now he had to think like a rock. How far could a flood push it? Where in the stream course would it come to rest?

He quickly walked a mile down the ravine bottom, seeing nothing, and then turned to return upstream more slowly and carefully, probing the center of the sandy basins where the heaviest debris would collect. He found rocks all right, and even at one point some dampness signaling water close to the surface. But a transmitter? He worried its weight would have carried it beneath a covering layer of sand.

What saved him in the end was that the box was orange, its battered surface flecked with scratches revealing a black undercoating like a speckled egg. The beacon was jammed under a larger boulder, sand sucked away from it by the current. Could such a thing still work?

The metal was hot to the touch so he wrapped it in his shirt like a baby, carrying it upstream. Ethan and Ico were waiting at the pink rock, looking hot, sticky, and depressed, and so he shielded it behind his back until he came up to them. Then he held it out.

"Here it is," he announced. "Phone home."

Ethan looked at it warily. "That's it?"

"I'm asking you."

He looked at it dubiously. "I can hardly remember." He peered closer, inspecting the switch and socket ports. The memory of it was coming back to him now—his familiar world of electronics seemed an eternity away!—but how much did he want his new companions to know? "I guess so."

"Good grief," Ico said. "Well, let's go find Raven. She must be upstream."

There was no stream of course, just the sandy bed and a bottom of heat. It ended in a cul-de-sac of cliffs with a litter of boulders at their base. Raven was in the shade of one, looking drained.

"We found it," Ethan called. "Maybe."

She didn't look up.

"You don't seem very excited," Ico observed.

She looked up at him morosely, clearly disturbed. "I found *him*."

Ico walked past her into a cluster of boulders, the others following. The rocks formed a kind of nest with an open-roofed room in their middle.

"Ouch," Ico breathed.

A cross hung on the rocks, except a moment's inspection revealed the cross was really a man, or had been a man, arms outstretched where he'd been pinioned, and now almost black and desiccated by the sun. Dried flesh pulled back from screaming teeth. Eyes gone. Stained strips of clothes and leathered flesh.

There was a glint on one finger. Daniel stepped forward. "Academy ring."

"So we've found your pilot," Ico said.

Ethan was looking at the figure in dismay. "I didn't know the Warden did this. They told me the pilot was missing and . . . I didn't ask. My God, the man could have helped us! It's insane."

"This Warden of yours must have really been pissed off."

Raven had come in behind them, looking upward. The rocks radiated heat like an oven. She looked not so much horrified as depressed.

"I guess we want to steer clear of the morally impaired, right?" Ico said to her. "Good thing we're getting out of here."

She looked at him sadly. "There's something I haven't told you."

CHAPTER SEVENTEEN

They buried the pilot in the sand, Raven taking care to first remove his ring and the molar filling of identification micro-data that had replaced the dog tag for employees on remote and risky missions. Then the group filed back to Car Camp as the sun sank, walking the last few miles under the stars. They were exhausted, but they were also impatient to learn what Raven had to tell them. She simply suggested she save it until Amaya and the recovering Tucker could hear too. She walked ahead of them as if rehearsing what she would say.

Upon returning they built up the fire.

"What I haven't told you is that we have to go back to Erehwon," Raven began without preamble. "We have to go see the Warden."

"What!" Ethan cried. Clearly, she hadn't told him this.

She nodded, acknowledging his surprise. "You already know ordinary communications don't work in Australia. You know the Warden took a transmitter from the plane—from the pilot—and it didn't work."

"So?" Daniel said. "That's why we found this one."

"Yes. Because the continent must be jammed." She glanced around, gauging their reaction. "Outback Adventure—United Corporations—doesn't want its clients calling out. You need a special instrument."

"The Cone!" Ico said.

"Hmm?"

He looked excited. "I stayed awake when they shipped us out here and heard the pilot talking about some damned Cone. I thought it was a password, slang, for the continent. But what if it's this zone of jamming?"

"You stayed awake?" Raven asked.

"Damn right I did. My trust only goes so far, and a good thing too. So they fly us into this zone made from . . . what? A satellite?"

She nodded, watching him. "The question is whether they could do that over an entire continent."

"Strongly enough to confound weak consumer electronics, I'll bet. Maybe strongly enough to defeat ordinary rescue beacons. They used narrow-focus satellite jamming beams in the Taiwanese War."

"That explains why my GPS didn't work," Ethan remembered.

"My stuff too," Ico said. "I thought it was just on the fritz."

Raven nodded. "When I came here and recognized there was no normal exit point, I began to think about alternative ways to signal for help," she explained. "Then I talked to Ethan and he told me about his crash. My theory is that no pilot would fly into this place unless they could expect rescue in the event of disaster, but that United Corporations would want to make sure it wasn't sending rescue craft in after the wrong people, risking a hijack by the morally impaired. The survivor who was signaling had to be someone knowledgeable enough to do *something* to activate the rescue beacon: a bona fide pilot, in other words. When I heard that the transmitter the convicts had brought back from the crash didn't work, I at first thought they simply must have taken the wrong one. But that made no sense—if they'd stumbled on the *right* one, U.C. would be sending its rescue crew into the lion's den. There *couldn't* be a right one. So then I reasoned the transmitter must require another component to penetrate this jamming—an idea I remembered from my aviation work. The beacon only works if a pilot puts two halves together: the transmitter itself, and the activator we just found. I think the body we discovered confirms this idea."

"How so?" Ethan asked.

"My guess is that the pilot tried to bargain for his life by promising he could signal for help if they could catch you, because you were unwittingly carrying the crucial component—the activator to penetrate this jamming. But when they found you unconscious, you didn't have it. It wasn't even in your pack. Maybe the pilot remained evasive in hopes of finding the activator by himself, later. And the Warden, in an impatient rage, killed him."

"So now we have to go to this psycho and ask him for the other half?" Ico asked. "This is the plan you didn't tell us about?"

"Ask. Take. Bargain. Whatever it requires to get back."

"Great. Whoopee."

Amaya was looking at Raven skeptically, glancing

from her to Daniel. "You figured this out all by yourself?"

"I'm not promising it will work. It's a chance, that's all."

"Nobody's that smart, Raven."

"It's common sense, Amaya."

"You said you knew avionics. Tell me what a neural-rod stabilizer is."

Raven looked at her with irritation.

"Tell me what a wing pulse-circuit is."

"That wasn't my area."

"You don't know a thing about avionics, do you?"

"I don't have to prove myself to you! You're just jealous of my relationship with Daniel!"

He looked up at that, curious. What relationship?

"You don't know a thing about aviation," Amaya persisted. "But you *do* know a lot about Outback Adventure. You're lying to us, aren't you? Just like you lied to Daniel."

"I'm trying to help you!"

"Why were you so surprised to find him here? You were the one who told him about Australia."

"It's a big continent!"

"Why did you save us at all?"

"I'm beginning to wonder that too! Go back out into the damn desert if you don't like my help!"

"Who *are* you, Raven?"

She was angry. The two women glared at each other.

"Who is Luther Cox?" It was Daniel, interrupting softly.

Raven turned to him impatiently. "You know who he is. Your supervisor back home."

"Sure, *I* know. But how did *you* know last night? I never mentioned him to you."

"You must have." Her eyes flickered away.

"No I didn't."

"You just don't remember."

"Amaya's right. You know too much. When we were dying of thirst and you found us, you knew who Ico was, and his relationship to me—even though we haven't talked since I met him. You've always known too much. You recruited me, didn't you, Raven?"

She stared back at him, her expression flat. "You recruited yourself."

"What are you talking about?" It was Tucker, sitting up against his propped travois.

"She works for them," Daniel said, watching her. "She came on to me and talked wilderness but she was working for them all the time. It's the only thing that makes sense. She's some kind of agent. She found me, and got me interested, and gave me the passwords to get in, even while pretending she didn't want to. It was a seduction, a seduction without sex. She worked with my employer to do it. And now she's still working for them, but doing what? Picking up junk from the Outback?"

They were all watching her now.

"Burying their dead," Ico guessed.

"Why, Raven?" Daniel asked softly.

She took a breath. "It's for your own good."

"Being abandoned out here?"

"For society's good."

"For *your* own damn good, I'll bet," Ico charged. "How much are they paying you? My God, she's from the kind who put us here! If she's their agent, she deserves to be hung up on the rocks like that pilot!"

"*You* put you here!" she retorted. "Think! Weren't you told the dangers? Didn't you have chance after chance to back out? *You* were the ones who were convinced you could survive here!"

"Until we found an exit. Not forever. Not with a bunch of damned convicts."

"You'll *be* here forever if you string me up. Yes, I work for them. And yes, you may despise me. But I'm your only ticket out of here. This rendezvous wasn't planned, but you help me and I'll help you." She glared at him. "I've already saved your miserable little life once. I didn't have to do that. I could have just left you in the sand."

Ico scowled at her. "You've got the miserable part right."

"Why?" Daniel repeated, sorrow in his voice. Whys filling his mind like the whys she had challenged him with in the tunnels.

Raven glanced around at all their faces, their confusion and mistrust and looks of betrayal, and sighed. "United Corporations doesn't despise you people," she explained wearily. "They admire you, in a way. But they can't *afford* you. They're *afraid* of you. In the old days, society might have had a use: explorers, soldiers, entrepreneurs. But the world's full. Twelve billion people now. You live in the wealthy part and you don't realize how fragile everything is. How on the edge the planet is. If the system fails, if the economy and ecology collapse, billions will die—billions! Survival requires conformity. And because of that, the sideways view isn't an inspiration. It's a threat."

"That's crazy," Tucker said. "What about new ideas?"

"They don't *want* new ideas. Modifications, updates, yes, but nothing truly revolutionary. Don't you understand? The population has aged. The world has become conservative. The twentieth century was a nightmare of new ideas and it led to war, genocide, terror, and depression. Nobody wants to go back to that. We can't afford to go back to that."

"Like ancient China," Daniel recalled. "Fossilized. It sent out the greatest fleet of discovery in history in the Middle Ages, circumnavigated the Indian Ocean, found nothing superior to the goods back home, and disbanded the ships. It didn't want new ideas either."

"Which meant it was ultimately exploited by Europeans," Ico said.

"Except there are no more Europeans," Raven explained. "No upstarts, I mean. Everyone on the planet is the same. Same products, same restaurants, same songs, same stories, same ethics. People still cling to the rituals of old traditions, to promote tourism if nothing else, but really it's just one big country now. Or one big company. There are no foreigners anymore. No barbarians. And China lasted longer than anybody: that's the lesson United Corporations takes from history. China endured. United Corporations has to endure. My God, the entire system is built on stability over time: the stocks, the bonds, the revenue streams, the retirement plans. The greatest good for the greatest number."

"You believe this?" Daniel asked her.

"I *know* it. I *lived* it. I'm an ethnic Balkan, Daniel—a Gypsy, in part, by heritage—and in my early world things weren't quite so tidy and constipated and boring as in yours. In the early years of this century we had revolution every thirty minutes, and a new ideology every hour. We had to check each morning to see what our money was worth. My family lost everything—everything! And my father lost his *life*, dying in the riots. So when U.C. finally began to buy things out, to stabilize the currency, to put an end to the irrational nationalism and ethnic strife that had caused so much destruction—when United Corporations put the poor back to work—I had hope for the first time in my life. Hope! From the stability you think is dull."

"Yes, but . . . this?"

"To protect the greater good they stand for. Sure, I work for them. I *believe* in them. And now you'd better believe in me."

"But what are you *doing* here?"

"Cleaning up after Ethan's crash. United Corporations doesn't like to leave anti-jamming devices loose. And the pilot was the son of a prominent family. They wanted to know his fate."

"Are you going to tell them?" Ico asked.

She looked down. "No. He'll have died instantly. Heroically."

"They sent you all the way down here to mop up?"

"For that and for . . . reeducation."

"For what?"

"A reminder to me of what we're about. What the alternative to a United Corporations world, to a civilized world, is. What kind of people are put down here. They thought I might be having doubts about my job. That I might be going soft."

"Why?"

She looked at him. "Because . . ." She stopped.

Amaya watched her and Daniel sadly from across the

campfire. She knew exactly why Raven DeCarlo had struggled with doubts about her job. She knew exactly why she had decided to save four people she would have been better off leaving for dead. Because of the restless, questioning, kind, and in his own way strong young man she was speaking to. Because her betrayals had finally become personal.

"I just can't believe they put you in the same sector!" Raven finally exclaimed. "They told me I wouldn't see you!"

"That was a mistake," Amaya said quietly. "Ico switched the destination tags. They don't know we're here."

They rested two days at Car Camp, giving Tucker more time to heal. As the venom wore off the big man was gaining back his customary animation and habitual good cheer, and he began hobbling stiffly around the place. "I died and came back, children," he told them. "I had such weird dreams that this place is starting to look downright normal. I came back for a reason, I know it. I came back because there's something I have to do."

Everyone else was wary. The hope represented by the battered box of flaking orange paint had been doused by their distrust of Raven, who remained subdued but not contrite.

"How did you know enough to quiz her on avionics?" Tucker privately asked Amaya.

"I didn't. I just made stuff up. She could have bluffed me."

"You outfoxed her, Amaya."

"Or she wanted to tell."

Only Ico seemed capable of thinking ahead. He showed Raven his stained and battered map, asking her if it was accurate (she said she knew no more about the geography of Australia than he did), and he speculated excitedly about what might happen if they got the beacon to work and a rescue craft came. Would the surprised pilots simply take them back? Or would they have to hijack the aircraft and fly to a refuge?

"The one thing for sure is I'm not staying on the ground here," he promised.

Raven's smile was wan. "Let's see if we can get it to work, first." Somehow, she reminded, they had to get the transmitter from this Warden.

Daniel was simply angry. He'd had real feelings for this woman and she'd led him on like an idiot. Amaya seemed embarrassed for him. Ico looked at him with a smirk. Only Tucker's friendship seemed unchanged: he seemed less panicked by their predicament than the others, expressing no anxiety about getting back. And Raven? She avoided him, looking pained. The damn thing was, though, that sometimes when he looked at her—the tilt of her head, the grace of her body—she still just about took his breath away. Yet how did he know she wasn't lying to him still? He brooded from hurt, telling himself to get over it, to get hold of his emotions.

When Tucker could maintain an ambulatory hobble they set out grimly for Erehwon, a place Ethan said was about three days distant at their slow pace. He led them with assurance even though there was no obvious trail or landmarks that Daniel could see.

"How do you know where you're going?" Amaya

asked Ethan, whose brittleness had softened at Raven's revelation. Now he was one of them, against her.

"We're following a songline."

"A what?"

"It's an aboriginal term. They believed the world was created when giant proto-creatures roamed an empty plain, singing into being all the rocks and plants and animals we see today. It's not such a strange idea to me—the new physics contends that matter at its most fundamental is just vibrating strings of energy, a kind of music. That *we're* made of music, fundamentally. These routes of creation are songlines, and aborigines were assigned to them. It's religious, and somewhat mysterious, but the practical aspect of it is that these lines formed a map, or a pattern, of trails. In a preliterate society you learned your way by singing the features you would encounter as you proceeded. The Warden picked up on this and had the inmates compose ditties to help them find their way when they make treks from Erehwon. *'Turn east toward kangaroo rock, the next good water is half a day's walk.'* That kind of thing."

She smiled. "Is it hard to keep in your head?"

"No harder than the telephone numbers, passwords, entry codes, and Social Security digits I held before. My brain's been emptying of one kind of memory to make room for another."

"And if you get back you'll have to switch again."

"Yes. But I'll have learned I can do both."

"Do you miss all the old numbers?"

"No. But I miss what they represented. When I came here I threw all my gear away and I've been regretting it ever since. We're tool apes. It's our only edge. So until we get out of here I'm trying to use what I can salvage.

You've got an eye for that too, like with the sulfur. The purists would let the wilderness kill them, but with balance you can survive."

He showed the group how an old hubcap could be used to collect a tiny pool of morning dew, or how a pit could be lined with salvaged plastic, tented by another piece, and collect atmospheric moisture like a still. As they hiked, he demonstrated how a length of yellowed tubing cupped with cloth could be used to filter drinkable water from a muddy wallow by sucking it like a straw.

"You could use a reed for that too," Daniel said.

"But I don't have to. That's the point."

Daniel plucked a reed. "I don't have to have tubing. And *that's* the point."

Amaya continued to explore nature. At Raven's direction, she found and unearthed buried frogs in a wash. The hibernating animals, cool to the touch and sluggish from their muddy encasement, had exterior bladders swollen to the size of footballs. "I read about these," Amaya recalled. "They store rainwater in this mouth pouch until the next storm. They haven't digested it, so it's supposed to be no different than water in an animal skin."

"You're going to drink frog vomit?" Ico asked.

"It's not vomit. It's less ingested than milk from a cow's udder." She squeezed and the frog regurgitated the water into her mouth, splashing her face. "Feels good."

"Geez, that's disgusting."

"Not if it saves your life. Raven's right about one thing: the desert is full of water, if we know where to look." Casually, Amaya tossed the torpid animal away.

The others tried it too. Raven laughed at her squirt, the first time they'd heard her do that. Daniel jerked at the sound, remembering before.

"People really did survive here, didn't they?" asked Tucker. "Outback Adventure must have briefed you to survive here a long time."

"Not really," Raven said. "I was intrigued by this idea and did my own research, just so I knew survival was possible. Outback didn't think I'd be here that long."

"Which makes me wonder why *you* bother, Amaya, if we're about to call a taxi," Ico said. She was stooped over some plants, adding to her inventory.

"Because the taxi isn't here yet."

CHAPTER EIGHTEEN

The cluster of natural stone monoliths that sheltered the convict colony called Erehwon first poked above the desert's horizon like sails on an ocean. Ethan told the group that the immense rocks sheltered a network of wetter valleys between, their creased crusts funneling water into shaded pools. That description was enough to make the party quicken its pace, despite apprehension about meeting the people who lived there. They camped that evening still eight miles distant, the setting sun making the geologic curiosity glow like coals.

"The rocks look like big loaves of bread," Amaya said.

"I'm hungry enough!" groaned Tucker.

"They'll have food," Raven promised. "They've even started irrigation. You can see how the formation is a natural place to draw people adrift in the desert. A small group of convicts huddled there first and started to hammer out a society. Others were drawn in as if by gravity. The place keeps growing despite its management."

"The Warden?" Ico asked.

"He didn't get his position by charm."

"So what kind of society? Free? Anarchic?"

"It started like that, I think, but became just the opposite. We're talking about people who hate rules but need them more than anyone. I think they fell back on the model of a prison, the community they're most familiar with."

"That just sounds dandy."

"It's harsh. But that's what seems to work."

They crossed the remaining distance the following morning, the rocks sheer as fortresses and smooth as breasts. There wasn't a cloud in the sky, but tendrils of smoke announced human habitation. With it came Daniel's realization that the challenge had shifted from coping with wilderness to coping with people. In less than three weeks he'd entered the wild, been humbled by it, and now was coming for succor to a society that sounded more restrictive than the one he'd tried to escape.

He'd tested himself, he thought gloomily, and failed.

"Welcome to Erehwon," Ethan said as they reached the edge. "Some people just call it the compound."

"Easier to spell," Ico quipped.

There was no fence or boundary that Daniel could see. The settlement's outskirts were marked by refuse: scraps of salvaged metal and glass glinting in the sun, random shreds of hoarded plastic and fabric, a pit of garbage picked at by birds, and the acrid odor of a latrine. Two women were moving slowly through this litter, bent and swaying as they picked through the debris, their features hidden by the curtain of their long hair. On a rock above a canyon entry, a squatting sentry with a spear watched the approach of the newcomers, laconically waved, and then stood to blow on what looked like a cattle horn. Its blat echoed through the canyons ahead. They'd been announced.

"He doesn't seem very surprised to see us," Ico said.

"No," said Ethan. "Most who try to escape come crawling back."

A sandy track led into a grove of trees, the shade a relief. They'd entered the labyrinth of valleys and canyons between the red loaves of rock, a hot desert breeze rustling the gum and acacia trees. When they had passed out of view of the sentry, Raven told the group to wait for a minute and left the trail, disappearing into a small side crevice. When she came out a bulge in her pack was gone.

"It's important to keep quiet about the activator," she explained.

"Just make sure you put it where we can find the damn thing again," Ico replied. "No more misplacements."

The party passed a wooden corral where two sleepy-looking camels rested, dusty and huge. "The British brought them from Afghanistan and some escaped into the wild," Ethan explained at their questioning looks. "They're still in the bush so the Warden caught a few to try to break. So far they eat more than they're worth, so we may just eat *them*. We've also got a few wild cows, a horse, and some kangaroo in the stables. We're trying to learn how to ranch them."

Ico wrinkled his nose. "It stinks," he said.

"That's a farm smell, city boy," Amaya replied. "Stables." She looked thoughtfully at the crude barns.

Farther along was a pit and scattered logs indicative of a sawing operation, and beyond that racks where meat dried in the sun, orbited by flies. Despite the primitive nature of the settlement—it reminded Daniel of a medieval village—the adventurers began to unconsciously relax. Here was the familiarity of a community. Whatever might happen, they weren't alone anymore.

The canyon opened to a broader park between the sandstone monoliths, an area several hundred yards across that was a mix of trees and trampled clearings. Water glinted at the base of one towering rock and a cordon of dry brush blocked casual access to it. Thatched huts, sheds, and simple roofs were scattered about in a seemingly haphazard plan. On a slight rise with its back to a cliff was a more substantial cabin of freshly cut logs, the wood still new and white-yellow. Smoke wafted from its chimney. Tame dingoes snoozed in the shade of the clearing and cockatoos stalked across the dirt. In the shade of a brushwood awning, someone slept in a fiber hammock. There was a pungent odor of unwashed humans, fire, cooked meat, and manure.

I'm in a time machine, Daniel thought.

They stopped at a rock-rimmed well and Ethan brought up a skin of water. Tucker slumped in the dust. It was quiet in the midday heat. Flint had told them more than two hundred people lived in this cluster of rocks but most seemed to have dispersed to one task or another.

"Well, Ethan," Ico assessed, "this Warden character sure picked the right name for this dump. Erehwon! We're right in the middle of it, no doubt."

"You can walk away at any time."

"Calling yourself a Warden implies you can't."

"He doesn't think you'd make it. That's why I don't expect him to be surprised we've come back."

Raven told them to wait and mounted the hill to the

cabin, speaking to someone in the doorway. Then she returned. "The Warden is still asleep. We'll get some food, and then you'll meet him. I'm going to try to get access to the transmitter."

"Asleep at noon?" Ico asked. "What's to stay up late for?"

They moved to the shade of a thatched lean-to and ate smoky meat, some white root, and a strange, nutty bread. "Kangaroo, bush banana root, and mulga seed bread," Ethan identified. "The bread was difficult. Appreciate it."

"After some time in the bush, bread does seem pretty marvelous," Amaya agreed. "But the roo is pretty plain. Don't you believe in seasonings?"

"We don't have any, except salt. Or what newcomers bring with them."

"So the last of our food is about to go into the community pot?" Daniel asked.

"Yes. Marx would approve."

"And who the devil is this Warden we're waiting on?" Ico asked. "Some goon sent by United Corporations? What makes him top dog?"

"He's just a convict," said Ethan. "A thief and assailant, sent here to rot like the rest of them. No one really liked chaos, so he put himself in charge."

"No vote?"

"Two men challenged him. Both disappeared."

"Disappeared?"

"The ones he just wants to punish he makes more public, like hanging them up on rocks in the sun. A day of that, and the fight goes out of them."

"And two days of that and they're like the pilot."

"Exactly. Don't anger him."

The door of the cabin opened and a young, slim blond woman came down the dusty hill to find them. She was dressed in a simple shift that looked cut from salvaged cloth—a parachute? Daniel wondered—that showed her figure to good effect. Her brown arms and calves were bare and she was shoeless, her soles apparently hardened to the hot earth. "The Warden will see you now," she said, smug as a prom queen, her eyes passing appraisingly over Raven and Amaya to calibrate any competition. "Bring your offering." Then she walked back, provocatively swaying.

"Offering?" Tucker asked.

"That's you," Raven explained. "Fresh labor."

"Great."

"At least I know what he stayed up for," Ico said, following the blonde with his eyes.

"Keep away from her," Ethan said. "Drina is Rugard's."

"Rugard?"

"That's the Warden's name. Rugard Sloan. But don't call him that. He doesn't like it."

They climbed the hill. The log cabin walls facing the compound were broken only by the stout wooden door and slit-like loophole windows. Side walls extended to the rock of the backing cliff, making the structure look more like a blockhouse than a residence. The door opening was dark, and the newcomers expected the house to be stifling inside. When they ducked through, however, they saw that a back wall was absent from the cabin and the roof extended only halfway. There was a rear open terrace of hardpan dirt against the cliff, half of it shaded by a flat roof of woven branches. A low cave in the cliff face was closed off by a stake door, and a spring at the rock's base fed a shallow pool. The backing cliff rose two hundred feet. Daniel recognized the essential elements of a well-situated fortress: high ground, thick walls, a secure water supply, and even an apparent storeroom. The place was designed to withstand a siege. No vote, indeed.

He looked around. A shadowy figure leaned in one of the dark corners, the gleam of what looked to be some kind of long knife or sword at his side. A bodyguard? Drina lounged on a crude wooden bed in a corner.

"So you didn't like the desert after all," a rough voice said from another shadow. They turned to the sound, graveled from liquor or barked commands. "I could have told you what you'd find out there." Their host was sitting, they saw as their eyes adjusted, lazing arrogantly back in a surprisingly modern chair of metal and fabric. It came from an airplane, Daniel realized: probably the one that had crashed with Ethan.

"We found more than you think," Raven said.

"Yes, four more boobs, dropped from the sky. Well, come on then. Let's have a look." They shuffled forward, the Warden evaluating them as they studied him. He was tanned a swarthy dark like his underlings, his face clean-shaven and his dark hair cropped close as a helmet. Small scars wrote a history of combat on his face. His jaw was strong, his nose slightly hooked like a Roman aristocrat's, and his eyes were a curious, empty gray: the color of lunar dust, Daniel thought. The effect was cold.

"Not much of a find, Raven. And me to care for them."

"We weren't looking for anybody's help," Daniel interrupted.

The Warden's eyes narrowed at him. "Then lucky for

you that you found it," he growled. "You'd be bones otherwise." He had an arrogant authority that dominated the room, and the corded muscle of a man used to hard company. There was a stink of menace about him, a manner as instinctively vicious as a pit bull. He also appeared unapologetic about it. No, proud.

"I'm not as bad as all that," he said, as if reading Daniel's mind. "I'm not going to bite." And then he gave a yellowed smile that suggested he just might. "My name is Rugard Sloan, but you'll call me Warden. *Only* Warden. I'm the father of this community."

"Of Nowhere-ville," Ico said.

He squinted at Ico. "You appreciate my joke. And you chose to come to Nowhere because the alternative was death in the desert, right? So. Who are you? What are your skills?"

They gave their names and, at the Warden's urging, their former occupations. Only Ico hesitated. "A systems manager," he finally said.

"Fired." It was not a question.

"An opportunities transfer," Ico said defensively.

"And before that?"

"Tax analyst."

"And fired. And before that fired. And before that fired. Am I correct?"

Ico looked at him sourly. "Only because I tell the truth."

"Don't be embarrassed. Your work history is typical of half the wanderers who come to me. Misfits, rejects, incompetents, rebels. In *that* world. But not in mine. I give them a home. In return they work for me, and work hard. We've come a long ways in a short time. I hope you give our little community a chance."

Daniel spoke up. "We came here on a kind of wilderness sabbatical. Since our arrival we've been flooded, baked, and bitten. We weren't warned of any of this. We're a little hesitant to give anything a chance right now."

Rugard nodded. "Do you think *I* created our little Purgatory? That *I* pulled the strings that put you here?" He snorted. "They told me less than they told you. But I've put it together, by gleaning information from this soul and that."

"That we're marooned with a bunch of cons," Ico said.

"I believe the phrase is 'morally impaired.'"

"But rehabilitation . . ." Amaya began.

". . . Is a fairy tale to lull dumplings like you into believing they're safe from people like me," Rugard completed. He grinned. "Oh, they tried, of course, but I was really quite wicked. I *like* to be wicked, because it's payback for a lousy, unfair world I never asked to be a part of. They made me what I am! So they don't cure us, dear, they get rid of us. It used to be drugs and costly warehouse prisons; now it's a continent full of nowheres, fit for nothings. Cheap, guiltless. We got a speech: 'No guards, no walls. You're free to starve, slit each other's throats, or live like brute savages. If you try to get back by boat we'll sink you with the help of satellite surveillance. But if by some miracle you make it through our net, no one will believe you. And even if they believe you—even just as a paranoid legend on the cyber underground—the story will never get into our corporate-controlled media. Oh, and have a nice day.'"

"So there's a lot of you?" she asked.

"Thousands, I'd guess. Most die before we ever see them. Or maybe there's other compounds like this one.

Who knows? Who cares? We're all just heinous criminals, sent Down Under to remake ourselves. Except we never get back, even when we do."

"A whole continent as a prison?" Ico asked.

"A whole continent to salve their conscience, is my guess. We all know capital punishment is abhorrent in today's politically correct world. Life imprisonment is expensive. Rehabilitation for the worst of us is a fraud. And Australia is already written off, a killing ground of plague. So my kind is dumped here while United Corporations makes up stories about our scientific rehabilitation, claiming they give us new identities to reenter society without moral stain. 'Cause any strife and you lose your old life.' We've all heard the jingle. It's just truer than we thought. It's not because we're brainsponged that we don't get in touch with our families. It's because we're down here. It saves them a fortune."

"But we're not convicts," Tucker objected.

"Yes, the puzzling mystery. Why drop urban dilettantes into Devil's Island? Certainly you prove useful for my kind to feed off: we started robbing you of your supplies from the beginning. But if they wanted to deliver manna from heaven, why include you useless knobs of flesh in the freightage? It was only after talking to enough of you self-absorbed bastards that I figured out the common linkage."

"Our challenge of authority," Ico said.

"No! Your pathetic *acceptance* of it. You didn't challenge society, you whined about it. It's not just that you're useless—God knows the world is carrying billions of chunks of human deadwood right now, dispirited and zoned out—but you were *worse* than useless. You spread dissatisfaction like a virus without proposing any cure. At least my kind had the balls to *take* what we wanted. But you weaklings! You wanted to run away! So, they put you down here with the likes of me, the criminal and disaffected in one happy family. The only difference is that you *paid* to go."

"That's not fair," Tucker protested.

"Isn't it? Don't you recognize yourselves? They make you think you're a select few. Self-selected, the fact is. They make you think hiking through a wasteland is somehow going to qualify you for the corporate elite. What delusional vanity! What are you going to bring to a board gathering—marshmallow-toasting skills? They dupe you with your own self-importance! They turn your desires against yourselves! It's diabolical, really, how well they know you—how they let you betray yourselves. Challenging? Hell, you're compliant as sheep."

The others glanced at Raven. She was expressionless.

"Are you offended by my honesty?" Rugard went on. "You're simply not used to it. I find it ironic, kind of like advertising in the United Corporations world which always emphasizes a product's weakest point. If it's cramped they call it roomy, if it hurts they call it painless, and if it's bad for you they pick an athlete to sell it. And who gets to tell you the truth? Me! A moral-impaired! The first honest man you've met!"

"And you're the smart guy, Rugard?" retorted Daniel. "Lord of a log cabin? Sultan of a sty?"

The answering movement was so swift it was like the blurred attack of a wild animal. The Warden sprang from his chair and with the same fluid movement of his leap let the back of his hand crack across Daniel's face with a sound as loud as a whip. Daniel's head snapped sideways, shocked, and the entire group fell back, stunned.

Rugard leaned toward them, breathing hard, his eyes bright, holding out a quivering finger in warning. "I *told* you not to call me by my name. I *told* you, and I only tell once. To you I am the Warden, and if I even *suspect* insubordination, I'll gut you in an instant and unwind your entrails for the dingoes to feed on." Tucker's hands had bunched into fists but the shadowy guard with the sword had taken a warning step forward, and Ethan put a hand on the big man's arm to caution him. Daniel put his hand to his jaw. His ears were ringing and he tasted the salt of blood.

The finger dropped, the point made. The Warden let his features mask into a judicious amiability and he sat back down in his chair. "Does that seem harsh? Believe me, I'm the only thing that has kept all of you from being gutted already by the animals they send here. I run Erehwon like a prison, because I'm the ruler of prisoners. I'm the one keeping you safe."

Ico looked at Rugard thoughtfully. Life stripped of bullshit.

"This can't be possible," Amaya said. "Someone back home must know . . ."

"Why should anyone know? There's never a complaint, because no one gets back to complain. People compete to come here! Only a handful at the top know, and yet they have no blood on their hands. It's the perfect murder: profitable, easy, guilt-free. I wish I'd thought of it."

"You're lying," Tucker accused. "You want us to stay here with you."

"And you want to go to Exodus Port? Go look for it if

you wish. Just remember that no account of what's *really* happening in Australia has ever surfaced in the outside world. Ask yourself why."

"We *are* going back, Warden." It was Raven.

"Really?" He was scornful. "You didn't last in the desert for a week."

"We weren't trying to get across the continent. We were trying to get a ticket home."

Rugard's face slowly revealed intrigue. "What ticket?"

"I worked in aviation electronics," she lied again, counting on her companions to back her up. "When I came here and realized we were trapped and met Ethan, I got curious about his crash. The rescue transmitter didn't work? Then I realized how ignorant you are."

He scowled.

"I realized how little you know about modern technology."

"Don't try me, bitch! What are you talking about?"

She reached in her pack and pulled out a cloth bag. Shaking it, she scattered some electronic chips and wire across Rugard's table. "Any beacon needs to be activated to penetrate the Cone of electronic jamming over Australia. They can't put normal rescue beacons in transport aircraft because convicts could signal to escape. You have to know the trick. Pilots know it, but you killed the one we had."

"He couldn't perform the trick! He was a double-talking aristocratic flyboy who led us on a wild goose chase after that moron standing next to you, and then promised money if I'd give him more time. Money! I wanted escape! His kind thinks they can buy anything. They've always thought that! He found out they can't."

"*I* can do the trick."

He looked at her suspiciously. "Yet you came back to me."

"Yes. Because I need something else."

"Which is?"

She glanced at the storeroom. "Send the others out and I'll tell you."

CHAPTER NINETEEN

I don't trust them," Ico said.

It was evening. The four original Outback Adventurers were waiting in a cluster of boulders off the main clearing, a private place Ethan had picked out earlier where Raven would meet them after her negotiations with Rugard over the transmitter. The quartet had spent the afternoon touring Erehwon, a community that struck Daniel as a cross between a prison compound and a pirate outpost, repression atop cultural anarchy. They'd been told they would work for their keep: the men digging a reservoir while Amaya toiled in the kitchens. They were to design and build their own huts, using a stockpile of brushwood, and would have to earn their way to jobs of greater interest and responsibility: Microcore all over again, he thought. While everyone in the community was a kind of refugee, united by desperation, there was also a pecking order in the Warden's world in which the strong tended to exploit the weak. Bullying was epidemic. And because men outnumbered women two to one, sexual tension was palpable. Some of the women had paired off but most preferred to sleep in their own settlement in a separate canyon from the men, some trading sexual favors and others trying to maintain a rigid celibacy. It was a place of social disorder kept from boiling over by the rule of Rugard. What linked them was a longing for home.

"Raven wouldn't have brought us here unless she wanted to help us," Tucker now reasoned.

"She wanted to help *him*." Ico pointed to Daniel. "I just don't like being cut out of the loop while she brokers a deal with this Rugard guy. He *is* honest: but only about his own lack of scruples. And now he's closeted with this female hireling of United Corporations. Who knows what they're up to?"

"It's not like we have a choice," Daniel pointed out.

"Right," said Tucker. "Until she came along we had no hope at all."

"And we still might not if we don't keep watch on what Raven's doing," Ico warned.

"I don't think she's a bad person," Amaya said. "Just wrong. And useful right now. I don't know if this is going to work, but if it does we'd better start thinking about what we're going to do once we get back."

"That one's easy," Tucker said. "Take a shower."

"Have a beer," Ico amended.

"No, what are we going to do to put an end to this place? Who do we tell?"

"The media is transfixed by entertainment, not information," Daniel said. "Rugard is right. Why hasn't anybody heard about this place? Somebody has to have escaped. But no one tells. Or no one will listen."

"We've peeked behind the curtain, man," Ico said. "We gotta tell *somebody*."

"We're going to be sneaking back, not welcomed back," Daniel pointed out. "Our story is going to have to make an end run around authority. I think we start with the gurus of the cyber underground. This isn't mere conspiracy theory, this is a verifiable monstrosity, provable to any inspector sent down here. We get this on the Internet, tell the world, and suddenly the facade crumbles. Somebody in power will seize on this to embarrass their opponents. Once the truth gets out, Australia can't be sustained."

"Damn right," Ico agreed. "If we get back we've got the atomic bomb of scandals. We fan out and scream bloody murder. Then this asylum gets closed down."

"Why would Raven help us do that?" Tucker asked. "She thinks this is good for us."

"Raven doesn't need to know. All she has to do is get us back." Ico glanced out into the dusk. "Heads up, here she comes."

Ethan came with her, the two slipping into the cluster of rocks with a furtive dart, Raven's lips slightly pursed. They sat in a circle to hear what she had to say.

"It's going to be trickier than I thought," she began. "Rugard still has the transmitter in his storeroom, and he's going to let me work on it in return for my promise to take him along. But he won't let it out of his cabin. We can't just sneak out of here."

They looked at her gloomily.

She took a breath. "So I'm going to have to fake a repair with my electronic junk until we can steal it. There's a compound meeting and autumn celebration tomorrow night, lubricated with the compound's latest innovation: moonshine. Everyone will be there. We sneak into his cabin then."

"Won't he have guards?" Daniel asked.

"Probably. But I've got another idea about how to get inside. Has anyone done any climbing?"

There was an uncomfortable silence. "A little," Daniel finally conceded. "On an adventure vacation. But . . ."

"Could you rappel down that cliff?" She pointed to the monolith by Rugard's cabin. "Lots of drunks, a moonless night, and any guards facing outward. You slip down the cliff onto his terrace, steal the transmitter, and get hoisted back up."

"That's crazy."

"That's our only chance."

"Break in!" Ico exclaimed. "Why don't we just take Rugard with us? Cut a deal?"

She winced. "Because there's something else I haven't told you."

"Ah, geez. I knew it."

"The instrument will work, but it will only call in a rescue craft, not a transport. A small hover. My superiors knew the risk of sending me into this place with the knowledge I have and so they warned me up front that the beacon response plane would only take me. I have to be recognized. Me, and . . . the missing pilot."

They all looked at her in disbelief, stunned. Hope had been slammed shut again.

"I was really sent to find *him,* or at least learn his fate. He's the nephew of a board member who was being groomed to start up the ladder of promotion, and he was proving himself with this job. His failure to return caused quite a shock: apparently a crash like that had never happened before. There's even some suspicion of sabotage, because of his political connections. In any event, Rugard killed him. So that just leaves me . . . and room for one other."

"You want to go back with Dyson," Ico accused.

She looked at Daniel, then away, her face betraying just a moment of doubt. "No. I promised the seat to Ethan after he told me the pilot was missing and probably dead. I promised so he'd help me find the wreck." Ethan's face was impassive. "It's still his, by rights. It was his transport that crashed."

"But you didn't tell us this," Ico said.

"No."

"So we'd help you."

"Yes."

He looked at Ethan. "No wonder you weren't happy to see us. We threatened your spot."

"I just didn't want to use you."

"But *she* did. Because *she* works for U.C.! Because *we're* still being screwed!"

"Ico, shut up," Daniel said.

"Why should we believe you?" Ico persisted to Raven. "Why should we believe a thing you say?"

"Because I still need your help," she said stubbornly.

"For what? A bon voyage party?"

"If you help me steal the transmitter, you'll still have a chance to get back. Here's my plan. We retrieve the activator I hid, flee into the desert, call for help, uncouple the activator from the transmitter again so it can't penetrate the jamming, and you four go on toward the coast."

"Now there's a great plan. You go, we stay. How could I have ever doubted you?"

"No, this is your ticket to get back. Listen. The authorities won't bring me back without the activator. That was my assignment. I have to take the activator with me.

But the transmitter alone—the piece that Rugard has been keeping—*will* work on the coast. It *will* work, if you get far enough east. I think. You hike there, signal, and by that time I'll have explained your cooperation to my superiors. They'll send in another hover and you'll come back heroes after doing what you set out to do: cross Australia. Such a reward has happened before."

The quartet looked at each other. If they made it back, it wouldn't be to become chums with United Corporations.

"The transmitter alone will work?" Tucker said, sounding skeptical.

"You're not supposed to know that, but yes, it will. There, not here."

"All we have to do to make Rugard's transmitter work is go to the coast?" Daniel clarified, puzzled.

"The Cone," Amaya said slowly. "The circle. That's what she's talking about. I've been wondering about that myself. If a satellite is projecting a blanket of electronic interference it should fall on Australia with a regular geometry such as a circle or oval. But the continent can't be that regular. At its edges, some pieces of land must leak out from under the Cone."

"They'd just make it bigger."

"No," said Raven. "There are too many sea and air lanes and nearby islands to overlap out onto the ocean very far. Australia is wider east to west than north to south. If you get to the east coast, the transmitter should work."

"*Should* work?" Ico asked.

"That's what they told me," she said defensively.

"And that must have been what the pilot was talking

about when he gave me the activator," Ethan said. "That if we didn't have it, we'd have to walk to the beach."

"Listen, Daniel, this is insane," Ico pleaded. "We can't let these two run off with our help and then be stranded here, taking our chances in the wild. Who cares if the transmitter will work by itself? They know we'll never make it across the remaining desert! One of us should go on that plane with Raven to make sure she'll bring somebody back for us: somebody back *here*."

"You want to wait with the morally impaired?"

"Better than dying of thirst on *her* itinerary for us. I'm sorry, but she's lied to you from the minute you met her. If she wants our help, one of us gets to go."

"Who?" Daniel asked.

"Not you. You can't be objective about her. Frankly, it should be me. I understand the system now, I'm a good talker, and I won't be taken in by a bunch of United Corporations bullshit."

"You?"

"I've seen through them from the beginning. And I'll see through them at home."

"No," said Amaya. "You're not the right person, Ico. No offense, but you rub people the wrong way."

"We need a revolutionary, not a glad-hander!"

"We need someone who will be *listened* to. You'll sound too abrasive. Too extreme. Too . . . nutty."

"I'm the only sane person here!"

"I'm sorry. I just don't trust you to do this."

He threw up his hands. "Okay, *you* then. Not just these two, who somehow find us in the desert and have been using us ever since. They're going to leave us in the lurch, I know it."

"No I'm not," said Ethan. "I came here like you, Ico.

I'm as angry about it as you are. I forced Raven to agree to take me back if she wanted to be shown that plane."

Ico ignored him. "How about it, Amaya? Women and children first."

"No! That's silly." She looked hesitant. "I . . . I want to finish trying to sort out my life here." Her look ended at Daniel as she said that. Raven would be gone again. "Ethan's one of us. He's been here longer than any of us. He's the one who was in the crash with the transmitter. United Corporations can't object to taking him back after he helped Raven. And he can talk for all of us, even the convicts. He makes the most sense by far."

"Yes," said Daniel. "Ethan's the logical one."

"Tucker, for God's sake . . ."

The big man shrugged. "I don't know if any of this is going to work, but *I* came to walk across Australia. I say Ethan too. This way the four of *us* stick together. All for one, one for all."

Ico looked around the group. "In Purgatory."

Daniel shrugged. They were set, the decision made.

"Fine, great." Ico sighed. "Let's go break into the house of Napoleon fruitcake up the hill there, and then run out into the desert."

"Ico, I'm sorry I can't take you all right now," Raven said. "It's the only way."

"That's what you say."

The four men were roused at dawn and marched to work on the reservoir. The community needed more water and was excavating a basin at the base of a cliff. Daniel would have preferred to have stayed in camp to make final plans with the women, but he knew such malingering would only arouse suspicion. All he could hope was that Raven's crazy plan to steal the transmitter could work, and that in the confusion of preparing for the night's festival, Amaya could succeed in foraging supplies for their escape.

Amaya told him at breakfast not to worry. "The women are friendly, most of them. We're a minority here, so they tell me where things are. I've also got another idea."

"What's that?"

"It's a surprise. Something Raven and I are cooking up."

There was a sullen mood to the group of men detailed to dig the sand pit, the hardest and dirtiest of Erehwon's current projects. "Welcome to the Warden's shit detail," one muttered. The digging team, equipped with crude tools of wood and hammered scrap metal, was an amalgam of freshly arrived convicts and impressed adventurers, as well as the stupid, slow, and those who'd drawn Rugard's ire. Accordingly, the pace of excavation was desultory. "I'm supposed to be excited about building my own prison?" one grizzled moral-impaired, a chronic petty thief, complained to Daniel. "It feels like I'm digging my own grave. I don't want a reservoir. I want out of here."

"So go," Daniel said.

"And die in the desert."

"So quit."

"One man tried that. The Warden made the rest of us drink his blood from the bowl of his skull. He said we needed to bond if morale was so poor."

The work on the west-facing impoundment was tolerable until mid-morning, when the sun cleared the cliffs and began beating into the pit. Then the temperature began to soar. The men took a two-hour break at midday but the enclosure was even hotter afterward, everyone coated in sweat and dust and tormented by flies. By mid-afternoon, Ico did little more than lean on his shovel, depressed and exhausted, staring blankly out at the pan of surrounding desert with his thoughts far away.

"You okay, Washington?" Tucker asked him at one point.

"No, Tucker, I'm not okay."

"Can I get you something, man? Some water?"

He waved him off. "Leave me alone. I'm trying to figure out a way to get okay."

They broke off work with the sun dipping toward the horizon, the cliff face still throwing off waves of heat. The sky remained cloudless, the air parched. It was difficult to imagine the pit and its surrounding dike collecting anything but heat.

Back at the main compound, they got a skin of water to drink and wash and then slumped tiredly, waiting for the gathering at dark. The community would party hard and sleep it off the next day. As the stars popped out, Raven found them.

"I worked on the transmitter to confirm it's in his storehouse and pleaded the need to scrounge more parts," she whispered. "A rope is hidden at the base of the monolith. We'll all go to the party to allay suspicion and then you guys will have to slip away. If you can steal it, we meet at two A.M. at the boulders. If anything goes wrong, you four pretend I tricked you into all this."

"That won't take much pretending," Ico said.

She looked at him impatiently. "Ico, I didn't put you here."

"I'm just skeptical about who's going to get me out."

"Let him be," Daniel said wearily. "He's cranky. We're exhausted. Concentrate your thinking on going."

They dozed, and ate, and after dinner Daniel went in search of Amaya. He found her down by the stables, carrying a bag of something up toward the canyon where the women had been assigned. "Need any help?"

"No, it's not heavy. Besides, it's for the surprise."

He wrinkled his nose. "A pretty fragrant one, I take it."

"You'll see. Didn't Ico call me the devil's prospector?"

"Something like that." His look became serious. "How about the supplies?"

"Enough to get us started. We'll be living off the land again."

"Can we do it?"

"We have to. Wasn't that the point from the beginning?"

He nodded and then frowned, gathering his thoughts for what he was about to say. "Amaya, before we make our move tonight I want you to think about your options. I admire your courage for being willing to stay in Australia but I want you to reconsider. I think Ethan would step aside if you wanted to leave on the rescue plane with Raven. Australia is pretty tough, and I don't know how this Rugard is going to react when we steal his means of escape. He might try to run us down in the desert."

"I know."

"It's just going to be hard. And dangerous."

She nodded. "I know. But I'm really not all that anxious to get back, Daniel, despite all the bad luck. Something is happening in my life."

"I worry about you with all these men."

She laughed. "What a ratio! I should be looking forward to all these men!"

"You know what I mean. These guys are convicts, most of them. The shrinks couldn't straighten them out. All I'm saying is . . . this may be your last chance."

"To escape, you mean, despite what Raven promises."

"Yes."

She nodded, more serious. "I know. But I've thought about it. I've been thinking about it ever since we woke up in Australia, not just since Raven told us about the transmitter. Sometimes I feel I belong, and sometimes it scares me to death. But to go back now would be to give up on myself. I'm feeling new things here, seeing new things, thinking new thoughts. Back home it's just . . . noise. So thank you, I'm staying."

"All right. I thought that's what you'd say." He looked at her with a tilt to his head. "You're what Raven pretended to be, I think."

"I think Raven pretended to be what she wants to be. She's just not there yet."

He shook his head. "I don't understand her."

"She doesn't understand herself."

He looked at her quizzically. "Are we going to stay friends?"

"I hope so."

"I mean after Raven's gone. You're a special woman, Amaya. A good woman."

"And you're a good man. But I've seen how you look at her. It's not the way you look at me."

His expression was guilty.

She smiled. "Not yet, anyway." And then his eyes followed her as she walked jauntily away.

CHAPTER TWENTY

If Rugard Sloan thought he was about to leave Australia, he gave no hint of it in his meandering harangue to the crowd of two hundred that gathered in the clearing that night. He introduced the latest arrivals, crowed about the community's achievements, and gave dire warnings about the consequences of insubordination or shirking. "The sons of bitches in the real world sent us here to *rot!*" he shouted in hoarse reminder to the assembly. "Every day we survive here, every day we prevail here, we're spitting in their faces!" They roared their approval at that, and he grinned viciously. "We spit at them! And someday we'll pay them back! But meantime I *love* you people, and what we've built here! So it's time to take a night off and . . . party!" The crowd whooped.

A makeshift band of drummers and wooden flutists started a pounding, hooting beat, and some of the assembly began to awkwardly dance in the sand. Fermented plant juice was passed out, forgivably awful because it was so fiery. A bonfire roared in the night. Daniel studied the cliff face above Rugard's cabin. It was dark, a slab against the stars.

The Warden worked the crowd and then came up to Raven. "Why isn't it working yet?" he growled quietly.

"I'm almost there."

He grasped her hand that held a cup and tipped it forcefully toward the sand. His grip was like a vise. "I don't want you drinking tonight. I want you up at the cabin later, with me, getting that transmitter to work. The compound will be hungover and half-conscious tomorrow. We can't take all of them, so it would be a good time to slip away without saying goodbye. Understand?"

"You're willing to leave these people you love?"

"I'm willing to leave my own mother to get out of this dung hole."

"I'll come to you later."

"You'd better. I'm watching you, bitch. Don't think about leaving without me."

"Relax, Warden." She smiled tightly, her wrist twisted. "We're working together, remember?"

He looked at her intently, his gray eyes like hollows. "Don't fuck with me." Then he dropped her arm and moved away.

Her group danced, to be seen. Except for Raven, they pretended to drink, to be seen. And then Daniel, Tucker, and Ethan slipped quietly away into the dark, one by one, even as the noise of the celebration grew. Sparks wafted up to dance amid the stars. Raven and Amaya drifted through the crowd, laughingly fending off advances and keeping an eye on the hill to Rugard's cabin.

Sometime after midnight the women met in the shadows, wary and tense. "I can't find Ico," Raven reported. "I haven't seen him for an hour."

"I don't think he's one for parties," Amaya said. "He told me he was getting more supplies before going to watch Rugard's door. You should have seen his pack when we started. He brought everything."

"I haven't seen the Warden, either."

"He's hanging on a new concubine. Drina looked furious."

Raven looked out into the dark, feeling her sore wrist. "Ico wants to get back very badly, doesn't he?"

"I think he's angry. He wants revenge."

"I hope he's not so angry he does something foolish. Did you move the supplies away from the boulder cluster, like I told you?"

"Yes, but I don't understand why."

"And try making what I suggested?"

"Yes. I don't know if it will work."

"Good. Hopefully none of it is necessary. I'm going to get the activator. We'll meet the men with the transmitter and slip away."

"Then why the precautions?"

"Because it may be more difficult to get out of Erehwon than I would like."

The monolith that formed the sheer cliff at the rear of Rugard's cabin was more a steep slope on its opposite side, its rock the texture of sandpaper. A watercourse that funneled periodic thundershowers down the face of the rock had made enough of a crease in the formation to give Daniel, Ethan, and Tucker a desperate chance of scaling it. They shouldered the ropes that Raven had liberated from a compound warehouse and then started their climb at a dead run, sprinting up the rock's lowest slope with a momentum that took them to a pool in a fold of rock thirty feet above the surrounding sand. They clung to its rim.

"You okay?" Daniel asked the others.

Tucker looked around at the bare stone. "No snakes so far."

"I don't think a flea could cling to this dildo," Ethan said, looking upward at the pale formation rising like a horn. "How the hell are we going to get up this, Daniel?"

"Friction."

The watercourse gave them just enough of a dent to brace themselves as they wedged upward, and the rough texture provided a tenuous grip. None dared look down. Daniel's sweat left a trail of dark droplets and Ethan breathed in short gasps, his muscles trembling from the tension. Tucker grunted with the effort to keep his bulk from sliding back downhill. There was enough slope to give them purchase, but it was like climbing a funnel, gravity trying to pull them toward a dark drain. The night was cool, the stars cold, and yet Daniel was hot from the exertion.

At least the view was extraordinary, he noticed when he glanced up. Other monoliths in the cluster of rocks gleamed gray in the dark like the domes of a religious sanctuary, their canyons and valleys lakes of shadow. The sky vaulted down and the desert horizon climbed up to tie into one vast sphere of ghostly luminescence, the rock he clung to at the center of this spectral universe. It was as if he was climbing the crest of a floating asteroid, he thought. His goal, the summit ahead, seemed to lead to space itself. The effect was dizzying.

His floating reverie was interrupted by a scrape and a muffled curse. Tucker was sliding backward down the chute. "Damn!"

Daniel tensed, praying. After several yards the big man managed to brake himself, abrading his arms and legs to keep his precarious contact with the rock. He skidded to a halt.

"You okay?" Daniel inquired quietly.

There was a long silence. "I'm okay. I can tell by the pain."

They started up again. It helped to keep eyes to the stone. There was one short stretch where the pitch was nearly vertical and they climbed by pushing against almost imperceptible undulations in the surface, straining from the exertion. Then the slope began to ease and finally to flatten. Daniel crawled shakily onto the roof of the monolith, his muscles rubbery. The surface of its crest was rough but basically level, eroded into shallow depressions that held pools of water separated by ridges of tougher rock. In the compound below figures still staggered drunkenly in the dying firelight. He felt horribly exposed, yet it was unlikely anyone could see him in the darkness. Dropping to his knees, he made his way to the far edge. Here the rock tower dropped straight down to Rugard's cabin, completely black in the night. There was no light from the house, and none from the brush nearby.

It was like dropping into the dragon's den.

"Gawd," Tucker said as he came up next to Daniel. "If my ass had puckered any more on that climb I would've collapsed on myself like a black hole. This is the craziest damn thing I've ever done, you know that?"

"A computer would never do it," Daniel agreed. "But it's not as crazy as me going down there." He peered into the darkness. "I can't see a thing, but I have to hope the transmitter is really down there and everyone is gone, drunk, or passed out. Rugard hasn't shared our secret, I'll bet, so nobody should be particularly alert. You're going to have to lower me as I rappel, and Ethan will help feed the line. Then you can both hoist me up. Can you do that?"

Tucker considered. "I can brace my legs against these little ledges up here. I won't be able to see anything though, so I'll just lower until Ethan says you're down. Ico's keeping an eye on the front door?"

"That's the plan."

Tucker began flaking the ropes loose in businesslike fashion while Ethan used knots to join them. Daniel tied an end around his waist and crotch vaguely similar to his memory of the rappeling harness he'd used on vacation. Backing down a sheer cliff was not as difficult as it looked, he reminded himself, so long as you were sure the partner feeding the end from around his waist was absolutely dependable. He hoped Tucker's snake venom had thoroughly worn off.

Daniel stood, saluted his companion, and walked backward as Tucker fed out the rope. He paused on the edge, double-checking his knots. Not exactly just another day at Microcore. Then he leaned back into space. His legs were braced against the cliff, his body straight, and the taut rope cutting into his waist was all that suspended him from eternity. The helplessness of it—the requirement for implicit trust in another human being—was exhilarating. As Tucker slowly let out rope he began to descend, walking backward down the cliff toward the pool of darkness below. He waited for a shout of alarm, but all he heard was the increasingly discordant drum of music. The band was getting drunk.

In the end it was almost too easy, far easier than the climb up had been. He dropped to the cabin's roofless ter-

race breathless but elated. He was down! Daniel waited
until slack rope pattered into a pile beside him and then
moved cautiously forward, listening. The guard, Jago,
presumably still stood on the other side of the front door.
The interior of the cabin was dark, its corners spooky, and
Daniel tried not to think of the corpse of the crucified
pilot, or convicts drinking from a skull.

He glanced toward the table. Raven's electronic junk
was still scattered across it—she must have put on a good
show. Thankfully the transmitter sat there too, a beckon-
ing machine. Or like cheese in a trap, he thought wryly.
He took a step. No sound but his own panting and the distant, dying sounds of merriment. Another step, and then
another. He felt like he was being watched. But no, the
cabin was empty, wasn't it? Then he was at the table,
groping across it to softly cradle the machine in his arms.
You might just pull this off, he told himself. You might
just walk out into the desert with the means for Raven to
call home.

With the means for her to leave you. She'd be waiting
in the starlight with the activator, waiting to go back to a
world he'd wanted to escape from, waiting to go back to
a system he wanted to condemn. Would she really come
back for them? Did he want her to? Or did he really wish
she would stay as they hiked to the coast—

He froze. There was something else on the table, he
saw dimly. A metal box the size of a shoe box. He
reached out, his fingertips brushing the familiar dented
surface of flaking paint. Tough enough to withstand an
airplane crash, to weather a flood, to . . .

What was the activator doing here?

A match flared, brilliant in the inky darkness, transfix-
ing Daniel like a deer. "See, we don't need her anymore,"

a voice said quietly. "Now we've got both units, and can signal whenever we want." The illuminated hand lit a candle.

It was Ico. He'd stolen Raven's hidden activator and gone to Rugard.

Outside Daniel could hear a rumble of feet up the hill as convicts began a charge for the front door. They'd been waiting for the light. He snatched the activator up to cradle with the transmitter, backing toward the cliff. "Don't do this!"

"It was the only way, Dyson." Ico stepped into the light, holding the tip of a crude sword against the floor like a cane, as if the idea of pointing it at someone had not yet occurred to him. "The only way to make sure one of *us* got back. Not that seductress from United Corporations! But the Warden . . . he has to have underground connections it would take us years to find. They'll harbor us, and hide us, and we'll get the cyber word out . . ."

"No! Not with convicts!"

There were men at the outside of the cabin door now, jerking it open.

Daniel stood at the cliff base, still roped in, his arms awkwardly full, looking up. "Pull!" he screamed.

"Don't be a fool," Ico hissed. "He'll kill us all! Think!" And then he jumped forward, the sword swung high to chop at the rope. At the same moment the door burst open and Rugard, Jago, and half a dozen convicts burst into the room.

"Sneaking thieves!" the Warden roared.

Daniel had only a second to consider. Which machine was more expendable?

Then he heaved the activator at Ico Washington as hard as he could. The heavy box hit his attacker full in the face and Ico went backward with a muffled cry, falling into the surging convicts. Daniel wrapped himself around the rope and was suddenly jerked up into the night. A spear skimmed past his swinging boot and clanged against the cliff wall.

"Get him!" the Warden howled.

Dancing like a puppet, Daniel was hauled by brute strength up along the dark cliff, using his feet to fend himself off as he swung. Something whizzed by him and missed. Then his ascent stopped and he dangled, helpless, the shadowy figures below taking aim. He was about to scream for his companions to pull some more when something heavy sizzled by as it fell, the wind cuffing him. It hit below with a crash, splintering, and the convicts howled. Ethan had dropped a rock! Then with a jerk Daniel was being hauled upward again.

"What if that had hit me!" he hollered upward.

"We could stop pulling!" Ethan called back.

From the confusion of shouts below he could hear the Warden's roar. "Come on, we'll get them when they come off the monolith!"

Then Daniel smelled smoke.

Ico's illumination of the slitlike windows in Rugard's cabin had signaled the waiting convicts—warned by Ico of Raven's plan—to rush the front door. It had also alerted Raven and Amaya, who had crept in behind Rugard's men. Once she found the activator missing from where she had hidden it and guessed what Ico had done, Raven had realized that his betrayal might be another kind of chance. Now it was all playing out as she had expected. With a little luck, the tables would be turned. "Let's go!"

The women seized either end of a stout wooden log and ran up the dark hill toward the cabin door. Raven had noticed a curious detail: the Warden had built his stout door to open outward so that any attackers could not easily batter it inward against its log frame. An excellent plan to keep assailants out.

Or the Warden in.

Even as they heard the shouts and cries of the men inside, the women slammed the log firmly against the door, bracing it against the dirt. Then they lit two brands and ran along the cabin wall, firing its thatched roof.

Heavy shoulders crashed against the cabin door from the inside but it didn't budge. In an instant, smelling the smoke, the Warden understood. "It's a trick! A trap! The table, the table! Get up on the roof and out of here!"

Even as they dragged furniture over to boost themselves to the inner lip of the half-covering roof, a wall of flames breathed heat on the cabin eaves. From somewhere in the dark, a woman screamed. One of the braver convicts hauled himself up on the roof and danced on its brushwood frame to try to dash through the curtain of flames. He broke through near the wall and crashed back down into the cabin, burned, smoking, and howling. Frantic, the men hurled themselves again against the stout door. It wouldn't give.

"We're going to fry!" one of them yelled.

"No we're not! Get back to the cliff!" Rugard snapped. "The fire will just bring the others to unblock the door!" He started to cough then, cursing, as smoke billowed from the underside of the thatch. His men began bailing spring water, throwing it up toward the growing conflagration, but it did little good and in any case wasn't really necessary. There was no real danger, the Warden thought: there was a sufficient gap between roof and cliff where the flames wouldn't reach. If they had to they could retreat into the stone storeroom. But Dyson was getting away, a jerking fly now against the stars high above. *That* was humiliating.

Angrily, the Warden clutched Ico's arm. The smaller man seemed in shock, hypnotized by the flames, his nose bleeding from where he'd been hit. "Why didn't he cooperate, like you promised?"

Ico shook his head. "The woman. She's bewitched him."

"Where are they going?" Rugard demanded. "Where will they signal?"

"They won't," he said, and pointed shakily.

The Warden followed his finger. The activator to penetrate the jamming was sitting on the cabin floor. He sprang forward and grabbed it, suddenly exultant. Yes! "He dropped it?"

"He clobbered me with it. I would have had him otherwise."

"They can't signal without this, right?"

Ico looked at the spreading flames, smoke boiling out. They could hear the confused shouts of the rest of the compound as it was roused by the fire.

"Not here. Not unless she's lied to us again." Why had Dyson thrown away the means of escape? Desperation at his own clumsy attack? Or something more? "But now *they* have the transmitter. So *we* can't signal without *them,* either."

CHAPTER TWENTY-ONE

The fugitives rendezvoused at a dry creek bed in a side canyon where Amaya had cached their packs. Behind them was a confused yelling and the glow of fire. The three men were scraped and bruised from hastily sliding down the rear of the rock tower, Tucker limping painfully from a sprain. The women were panting. When they'd slipped by the cluster of boulders where they'd originally planned to meet, they saw more of Rugard's men waiting there and ran. Ico had obviously told the Warden where their supplies were supposed to be stored. It was good Amaya had moved them.

"Little snitch," Raven now muttered.

"Are they going to burn?" Amaya asked worriedly, looking back at the flickering orange.

"Just held up a bit, and angry as hornets. We have to move fast if we're going to get away and signal for rescue. You've got it, right?" She turned to Daniel.

"How did you know to pen them in like that?" he asked her instead.

"When Ico disappeared I got suspicious. Then I found

the activator was gone. Amaya and I got a log to brace the door shut."

"But you let them lower me into the cabin anyway."

"Yes. Because we needed the transmitter. If I'd warned you off, our position would be hopeless. Now we can still get back."

"Don't you mean *you* can get back?"

"Ethan and I are your best hope."

"You're ruthless, you know that?"

"I'm practical. Besides, it was *your* friend who betrayed you, not mine."

Daniel was quiet at that.

"Can we just go, please?" Tucker said impatiently.

They shouldered their gear and fled into the canyon of the women's camp, brushing by a few confused occupants who'd turned out groggily at the noise and confusion. They paused at a cook hut to snatch a last few bites of food, but even as they did they heard the call of a cattle horn. One of the women was blowing an alarm to relay their direction, so they hurried on. As the fugitives reached the end of the canyon they saw the torchlight of a posse entering its head. Many of the convicts were drunk or unconscious, but not all.

"We're in a race," Tucker panted. "I'm slowing you down."

"Amaya's cooked up something to slow *them* down," Raven replied.

"If it works," the second woman said.

They entered a gorge at the upper end of the women's valley. The defile wasn't much more than a slit in a huge rock that looked like it had been split asunder, but it was a door leading to the desert east of Erehwon. Narrow as a corridor in places, the cleft's floor was sand and its lower reaches stained dark where past floodwaters had swirled through. Only a wedge of sky with a scattering of stars, hundreds of feet above, shed any light. Ethan and Raven had used the passageway to slip away before and now were using it again, but this time pursuit was only a mile behind.

"What will they do if they catch us?" Tucker asked, limping along.

"I've been through this before," Ethan said. "We get away, or we kill ourselves. Surrendering is not an option."

A fall of rock had almost plugged the slit at its midway point with a wall of boulders difficult to climb over. Floodwaters had carved a low sandy tunnel under the rocks that Raven and Ethan had earlier crawled through.

"This is the place I told you about," Raven said to Amaya.

The other woman nodded. She stooped to dig in her pack as they paused to catch their breath. They could hear the calls of pursuit behind them, like the baying of hounds.

"Why are we stopping?" Daniel asked. "We have to *move*."

"Raven and I think we might slow them down with this," Amaya said. She took out a leather skin shaped roughly like a sphere and slightly smaller than a basketball. Cord and a coating of hardened fat helped seal the outside.

"What the devil is that?"

"It's a bomb." She announced it as proudly as she would a baby.

The men looked at her in confusion.

"I got the idea when we saw the stables. If we set this

off at the right moment it should block this gorge and scare hell out of them too. It will buy us time."

"You're serious, aren't you?" said Tucker.

"Remember the sulfur spring? That was one ingredient of gunpowder. Have you ever made it?"

"Not in the last couple of days."

"It's simple, really. All you need is sulfur, charcoal, and potassium nitrate in the right proportions."

"Charcoal?" Tucker asked.

"From the fires. Nitrate from the urine deposits in the stables. Calcium nitrate, actually, which works in a pinch." She regarded her invention. "Maybe."

"Tomorrow she splits the atom," Daniel said. "How do we use it?"

"In the tunnel. The explosion should collapse it, and maybe jar more rock loose besides. I'll wait to light it."

"No," said Tucker quickly. "I'll do it."

"It's my idea, Tucker. My risk."

He shook his head. "I'm the slowest, with this bum ankle, and the strongest. They'll hesitate with me." Tucker looked up at the sky, a slim silver band high above. "This is the pass to make a stand, I think. Like Daniel's Spartans."

"What?"

He sounded excited. "The Greeks and the Persians! Remember, Daniel?"

"Tucker, you're not a damned Spartan."

"How do I know if I've never tried?"

"You have no training!"

He looked back down the defile. "It's the perfect place, the perfect time, and the perfect person."

Daniel looked at him worriedly.

"I'll back them up a bit, light the explosive, and run,"

Tucker reassured. "Or at least hobble. With any luck they'll decide we're not worth chasing."

There wasn't time for argument. "All right. Light it and crawl like hell. We'll be waiting on the other side."

"No, don't wait! Make all the distance you can! I'll catch up!"

"He's right," Ethan said, dropping to the sand to wriggle through. "We can't risk any delay."

Raven went next and Amaya ducked to follow.

Daniel put his hands on his friend's shoulders. "You be sure to come, promise?"

"I've got to see the rest of Australia." He grinned.

Amaya was through and the others were calling. Daniel hesitated a moment more and then fell on his belly to crawl, his head and back bumping against the overhanging rock. Ethan helped drag him out the other side.

"Okay, he's buying us time," Daniel said. "Let's run like hell."

"They're going to tear him to pieces if he doesn't get through that hole," Ethan said soberly.

"He knows that," Daniel said. "If his courage is going to mean anything, we have to get away."

The canyon widened slightly on the other side of the blockage and they trotted down it toward the eastern opening that showed a gray horizon. There was already a barely detectable blush in the sky. Dawn was coming.

The bomb would have to work.

The canyon walls were so steep that it would be difficult to get around him, Tucker was betting. It might take hours to circle the enclosing rocks. Precious minutes, at least. If he could hold Rugard's men here for a while, the others would have a chance.

He studied Amaya's bomb. A fuse extended from one end, and tied to it, wrapped in leaves, were two of their remaining matches. Could it really choke off the canyon? He couldn't rely on that alone. Rugard's men were already in the defile, pushing forward cautiously and clumsily by torchlight, the reflections throwing shadows well ahead of the actual pursuit.

"Let's give you something to think about," Tucker growled. He set down the explosive, picked up the spear he'd been using as a cane, and crouched at a bend of the canyon, waiting.

They came around the curve arrogant and angry, and he charged them like a cornered bear. Surprise was complete. His initial thrust only glanced off the first man, who was twisting desperately out of the way, but the wound was enough to raise a howl and throw the convicts into confusion. Their quarry had turned! The front rank stumbled back, some tripping in their haste to get away from Tucker's whirling staff.

A braver criminal plunged ahead with his own spear and Tucker knocked it aside. The man came at him again. Tucker parried, seized his opponent's shaft, and jerked forward with the glad ferocity of instinctive combat. The convict stumbled, dropped to his knees, and lost his weapon as Tucker wrenched, his own ankle pain forgotten. The man was trying to retreat on his hands and knees when Tucker speared him. The convict screamed, pinioned through the leg, and then was jerked to safety by his friends, the shaft trailing out of his thigh. Rugard's men fell back, relaying the news of danger.

Tucker got up, breathing heavily, his ankle even worse, and looked at the retreating torchlight with satisfaction. "Yeah, back off, you bastards," he muttered.

Then he studied the cliff wall and boosted himself gingerly a short distance up it, bracing himself precariously.

"You keep away from us, Rugard!" he yelled, his voice echoing. "Come up here and we'll kill you all!" No one answered him. He dropped back down to the sand and waited, considering the bomb again.

He could hear the pursuers arguing, picking up the thread of Rugard's rasping, impatient voice. Then the convicts fell ominously silent for a while. Finally someone was being pushed forward, scuffling through the sand. "Get your damn hand off me!" There was a pause and then a familiar voice called out down the canyon. "Tucker, is that you? Listen, we have to talk!"

It was Ico.

"I don't talk to the morally impaired!" Tucker shouted back.

"Come on man, listen to me. We still need each other. We can still work together! Daniel wouldn't listen, Tucker. I'll bet he didn't even tell you he can't get you back. Not without me!"

He was lying, wasn't he? Daniel said they got the transmitter.

"Listen to me! We can still cut a deal!"

"You made your deal, Ico!"

The little man fell silent for a minute. Then: "Let me talk to Daniel!"

Tucker didn't reply.

"Let me talk to Raven!"

Again he was quiet. They were trying to determine how many were ahead.

"What did they do, ditch you too? You all alone, Tucker?"

He didn't answer because he did feel suddenly alone,

terribly alone. The quiet of the convicts bothered him. What were they up to?

"Tucker, listen, I did it for your own good! That corporate bimbo was bewitching Dyson! You know that! She was going to fly off and leave us all here like a bunch of bumpkins! It was insane to let her escape! This way, *we* get to go!"

"Your Warden pal promise that?"

"Tucker, think! If we don't get the transmitter back, our party is stuck here! If you don't help us, we're *all* stuck here for the rest of our lives. Come on, listen to *reason!*"

"You come up here where I can see you!" Tucker called. "You come up here where we can talk!"

There was more wrestling, and Ico was shoved lurching ahead. He stopped, straightened, and then walked forward hesitantly.

"All we want is the transmitter, Tucker," he soothed, his arms spread wide. "We're not going to hurt you guys. We need each other now. I did it for *you,* man."

When Ico was close enough, Tucker hurled the spear. The shorter man squeaked and dodged, but not quite quickly enough. The spear head sliced across one arm and he yelped, scurrying back out of the way. The convicts roared, the sound angry and ominous, and rocks and a couple of other spears fired back. Tucker ducked behind an outcrop as the missiles rattled harmlessly by him. Then he retrieved them and ran back around the corner of the canyon. No one followed. Somewhere to the east, the others were getting away.

Yeah, come on you bastards, Tucker thought. Come and get it.

Several minutes passed. Tucker stayed pressed against

the canyon wall, looking for movement. Nothing. He was alone in a dark hole.

It was funny to feel so confined, after the big spaces of Australia.

Then there was a shattering rattle from above and Tucker looked up. Something was falling in amongst the stars. Rock fall! They were up on the rim and trying to get around him! They were throwing things at him from above!

He lurched back to the tunnel entrance and fell on the bomb. Stones banged down. He wiggled into the tunnel backward, pulling Amaya's crude device after him, the rocks bouncing harmlessly outside. Well, that was that: they'd outflanked him just like Daniel's Spartans. This damn bomb had better work.

He unwrapped the matches and put one carefully in a breast pocket.

There were already voices outside the hole. They'd tried to rush him and were baffled at his disappearance until they spied the tunnel. Now someone was scrabbling in. Tucker struck the other match, held it to the fuse, and waited. Nothing. A dud. Oh boy, Amaya. And then there was a flash, a fizz, and the bomb began burning. God be praised, the crazy woman had done it! He dropped the smoking sphere in front of him and began wriggling backward toward the eastern entrance, light from the fuse helping illuminate the way. He heard cries of alarm and a frantic crawling from the convicts.

Then the light went out with a smothering hiss. "I got it!" Someone had extinguished the thing.

"Damn!" Tucker reversed course and hurriedly crawled back, seeing the dim shape of someone backing up the tunnel. He caught up with the bomb snatcher just as the other man was about to wriggle out, and grabbed.

There was a grunt of pain and a curse. Jago, Rugard's guard! The man stank from the smoke of the burning cabin roof. The convict and Tucker grappled awkwardly in the tight space, the others clustered outside the tunnel entrance. "He's got me!" Jago shouted. "Get me the hell out of here!" Tucker was punching, clawing, butting, trying to get the bomb back. It was like a struggle for a football. Hands were reaching in, clutching at them both, and he felt the two of them being inexorably hauled out of the tunnel. Jago was cutting him, he realized—a knife, he supposed—and he chopped at the man's throat, stopping the irritation. The bomb came loose and Tucker clutched it to his own breast. Men were starting to pummel his body as they pulled him out toward the open.

The match. Broken, but he could feel the piece with the head in his pocket.

The mob was howling, yanking them like a cork from a bottle, whooping at the opportunity for revenge. Tucker felt Jago being jerked away from him and then hands dragging, punching, tearing. Their screams of frustration filled his ears, the anger hitting him harder than the pain. He lit his match and pressed it to the fuse. Please, let me succeed at something just once, he prayed.

Just once.

He felt a curious lightness as they beat him. The future had disappeared, and with it the weight of the past. Here in the eroded cluster of sculpted rock, carved by unimaginable eons of time, he was at the cumulative instant he was supposed to be at, he recognized. All his life had come down to this. So when the fuse flared and screams erupted and hands clutched frantically at the bomb, he felt a curious serenity. Tucker had found his why.

Then the bomb went off.

The quartet of fleeing adventurers heard the boom of the explosion as they ran out into the broad desert, the horizon flush with the coming sun. The thudding roar echoed and reechoed among the labyrinth of canyons, sending startled birds flying prematurely up and into the morning air.

They stopped and turned. There was a groan of collapsing rock and a following rumble, as if stones were sliding down to seal the defile more completely. "It worked," Amaya said quietly, as if she'd never really been convinced the ancient formula could be quite so simple. "It exploded."

"Did he make it?" It was Ethan, asking a question he knew couldn't be rationally answered yet. A cloud of smoke and dust rolled out of the slit they had emerged from.

The noise finally grumbled away and there was dead silence.

"No," said Daniel, knowing the answer without knowing it. "He didn't."

Amaya was silently weeping.

"Let's not make it be for nothing," Ethan finally said. "We have to be out of sight by sunrise and lay low until it's safe to trigger the beacon. Maybe tomorrow night."

"We can't," Daniel said.

"Can't what?"

"Trigger the beacon. We can't signal for rescue. We can't penetrate the Cone."

"I thought you said you got it!"

"I got the transmitter but . . . I threw the activator at Ico." He looked at Raven. "You two are going to have to hike to the coast with us."

The other three looked stunned. Amaya was looking from Daniel to Raven, crestfallen.

"It's better this way," he said. "Not some of us fly off, some of us stay."

Raven was looking at him in shock. "Oh, Daniel," she whispered.

"It will give us time to ask why we do."

Then he turned, and led the way into the rising sun.

"Lord, what a painting."

Rugard Sloan, blackened and scorched, turned a grim circle at the mouth of what had been the tunnel. Fresh rock had covered it, and the walls nearby had been sprayed with gore. One man had done this, he thought, one big man he hadn't had time to reach with reason. One man! This giant named Tucker had killed five men, wounded half a dozen more, and turned the remaining pack of pursuers into a band of drunken, sick, whipped dogs. Rugard couldn't have driven them on at gunpoint, not right now.

The snitch Ico had lived by hanging back because of his little spear cut, whimpering like a punished child. Rugard himself had been saved by the death of a man in front of him, a flesh-and-blood shield that had knocked him flat. He was spattered with offal and singed and grimy from the flames of his own roof. They'd made a fool of him, of that he was certain.

Otherwise, it was hard to think. The Warden's ears were ringing and his head ached. There was a fuzziness to his vision he suspected would take hours to go away.

And in front of him was a wall of unstable rock, sealing the fugitives' exit route. Men could climb over it or dig through it, he knew, but none had the stomach for it at the moment. Least of all him. The bastards were gone, escaped into the desert, and to follow them he'd have to organize a party with proper food and water to hunt them down. It was maddening.

Despite this fiasco, Rugard knew the others would look to him for answers. People were dung, expendable and cheap, and they'd follow a strong man as far as he'd lead them. The Warden felt not a thing for the men who had just been blown to bits by the explosion. They were fools to be in the front rank.

He limped back down the canyon past his groaning, stunned men. Explosives! How? Had that bitch Raven brought them with her? There was something odd about her, some lack of ordinary fear and confusion. He hadn't liked her arrogance from the start. She'd scorned his advances, was condescending to his authority, and was probably laughing at him right now. Clearly she knew too much. And she'd go on laughing until he hunted her down and had her in a different way. And then turned her whole being into a bloody locus of pain.

"We can't let them go."

Rugard turned. It was the weasel. He held men like that in contempt, but they were necessary. This little pissant might know where the others were going.

"We've got to get it back, so *we* can get back," Ico mumbled, as dazed by the explosion as the others. "The activator is useless until we get the transmitter to hook it to."

"Obviously," Rugard growled. "And you're going to help get it for me. You're going to help me hunt them down in the desert by telling me which way they'll go. They can't get back either, not without us. Right?"

Ico winced. "Not exactly." He looked down in wonder at his bloody arm. Welcome to real life, he thought drolly. It ached like hell. "I know where they're going, I think."

"Where?"

"The coast. Raven thinks the transmitter alone will work there."

"What!"

"If we don't catch them before they reach it, she'll be gone." Ico looked around morosely. He'd thought he'd be leaving these cretins in hours, or days. Now he might be stuck with them for weeks or months.

"We'll catch them then." They'd follow the thieves to wherever they might run, Rugard thought. Use them to assuage his own humiliation. Get the transmitter to unite with its activator. And then take proper vengeance on the whole damnable world.

PART THREE

PART THREE

CHAPTER TWENTY-TWO

The fugitives strode toward the rising sun with a grim, anxious pace, always looking backward: for a miraculous reappearance of Tucker, for pursuit, for a last glimpse of human settlement and community. They saw none of these. Just burnished domes of rock beginning to slip down the horizon as they hurried, and ahead shrub-shrouded desert and the undulating swell of red sand dunes.

There was no conversation. Their narrow escape, continued peril, and Daniel's loss of the activator had shocked them all into a tense silence. Raven's fury and fear at being trapped in Australia had left her speechless. Ethan looked at the pair with an accusatory stare, as if their tangled emotions had doomed him as well as themselves. Amaya was morose at the loss of Tucker and Ico and the continued presence of Raven. Their little family had become dysfunctional.

"We need to talk," Amaya ventured once.

There was no answer.

The fugitives would be easy enough to track if pursued

immediately, Daniel knew. Their feet left a scuffed trail in the sand like the frozen wake of a passing boat. The question was whether Rugard would bother to follow and, if he did, how quickly he could organize a posse. Given time, wind or rain would eventually erase their footsteps, and then surely the fugitives could elude pursuit in the immensity of the continent. They would pick their way slowly east to the sea, signal for a rescue craft . . . and after that? The possibility was so impossibly distant that it wasn't worth thinking about.

It was more important, Daniel knew, to think about the here and now. To stop focusing on the world of United Corporations and start focusing on Australia. It was this obsession about getting back that was causing so much trouble.

By weary agreement they didn't take a midday break but pushed on, the sand giving way to hardpan and dry, dead-looking vegetation. The land was ugly but easier to walk across. The day grew hot but not as oppressive as the punishing furnace of their first arrival. The desert winter was slowly approaching. Daniel also noticed the group's steady endurance after a sleepless night. His own body had acquired a wiry stamina far different from the calculated strengths of his health club regimen. He could push on with a dogged tirelessness that allowed him to keep going even when reason called for collapse and sleep.

They were close enough to Erehwon that Raven and Ethan knew of a dependable seep. It was a risk making for it because any pursuers could guess at their decision, but it was a greater risk to push into the unknown without as much water as possible. They threw themselves down at the puddle at mid-afternoon to drink to satiation, and then slowly, impatient at the delay, topped off every container they had.

"I still don't see him," Amaya said quietly, looking back the way they had come.

"No," Daniel said. "We won't."

And then they pushed on.

The sun set behind their backs, the monoliths black stubs in the distance now, and they marched on into dusk. There was no question of stopping. They walked as the moon came up, the desert lit like an old black-and-white movie, and held their direction by keeping the Southern Cross on their right hand. It was so quiet they could hear the squeak of sand under their feet. At midnight they came to the bank of a dry wash where ghost gums overhung the sandy channel like adults leaning over a cradle.

And there they collapsed and slept, fallen carelessly to the ground like leaves. The four of them slept in a cluster, huddling instinctively for warmth and reassurance, and were unconscious from exhaustion before anyone had a chance to comment on their geometry.

Ethan roused them shortly before dawn. They wordlessly wolfed down a few mouthfuls of cold food, drank, and pushed on. They didn't dare light a fire yet. A rhythm came into their flight. They walked hard for about an hour, rested five minutes, and then pushed hard again. They began to cross a series of flat pans of featureless clay. "Dry lakes," Raven guessed. "They probably flood in the rains." White salt glittered on the cracked mud.

At midday they crawled wordlessly into the shade of a cluster of ironwood trees to nap restlessly for two hours. Then they hiked on, walking again until midnight, their conversation mostly monosyllabic. The rocks of Erehwon had slipped permanently below the horizon. They saw no one, heard nothing. They were alone again, four adventurers in a desert wilderness, with no idea where they were or precisely where they were going, except east. It didn't matter. Walking was a substitute for talk.

When they stopped that night their weariness was so complete that it kept them from immediately falling asleep. They were brittle with tension. Ethan refused to sit after he dropped his pack and simply looked out over the dark desert, his shoulders hunched, his face gloomy, his body shivering slightly from the long hours of exertion. Raven sat slumped forward and pressed into the pack on her lap, her hair falling around her face like a cowl. Daniel's muscles were so tired that he watched his thighs tremble, tendons jumping under his skin like snakes.

It was Amaya who again broke the traumatized silence. "I think we should talk about Tucker," she said.

No one answered again.

"If we don't, we aren't going to make it."

Ethan turned, his arms around himself. "What about Tucker?"

"Our guilt."

"What guilt?"

"That we're alive and he's dead."

"We don't know for *sure* that he's dead. And it was his decision to be the rear guard."

"Not guilt," Raven interrupted. "Fear." She hadn't looked up and the voice seemed to come from deep inside her, as if issuing from a cave. "That we'll all end up like him."

"You mean dead," Ethan said.

She didn't reply.

"We know we shouldn't have let him stay behind alone," Amaya persisted. "We shouldn't . . ." She stopped, sighing hopelessly.

"Have built a bomb?" Daniel guessed.

Amaya looked away.

"If you hadn't we'd all be dead or worse," he said. "You didn't take Tucker's life, you saved ours. We were in a pretty desperate situation. We still are."

"Because we threw away our means of escape," Raven amended hollowly, still not looking up, her voice exhausted. "Used it like a rock, to hit someone."

The rebuke irritated him. "*Your* means of escape." He said it bitterly. "After you let me be lowered into a trap you knew was about to be sprung."

"That's not fair," Ethan told Daniel sullenly. "She didn't know what this little irate friend of yours would do until it was too late. We'd met as a group and agreed as a group that she and I would go. And it's no secret why you might prefer to leave the activator behind. You threw it all away because . . ." He stopped in frustration.

"Because we've *never* been a group and *never* truly agreed. Raven has been setting us up from the beginning and so have you, never telling us our true situation until the last minute and using us like game pieces to get *you* back home. You turned us against each other. You turned Ico. Tucker's almost certainly dead. You've made a goddamned mess of the whole situation and now you can just sit in the middle of it like we have to. We walk to the coast, or stay in Australia, together."

"That's unfair!" Ethan shouted. "You'd already be dead without us!"

"Daniel, I was trying to *help* you," Raven added with

a groan. "Help you get back, where you could do some good."

"Why?" he challenged her.

"Why what?" Her reply was weary.

"Why get back? Why are you trying to achieve what United Corporations obviously doesn't encourage: our return? What if your bosses are right, Raven? What if I really belong here? What if *you* belong here?"

"Don't be absurd. Rugard belongs here. Not me. Not . . . us."

"Why are you even here, Raven?"

"I had a mission. I wanted to see."

"No you didn't."

"It's for the best, Daniel. It's always for the best: I believe in them. It's all I have to believe in. I was going soft and getting confused, and so by checking the pilot's fate and getting the electronics I'd prove myself and either be confirmed in my mission or abandon it. I'm being tested, just like you. The problem is, you've turned a test into torture. We're more than a thousand miles from where we need to be."

"Are we?"

Raven looked at him with exasperation. "Yes. It's a long walk to the beach."

"What if *this* is where we need to be?"

"What do you mean?" Amaya asked.

"What if we *don't* get back, ever? Could we make a life here? Find meaning here?"

"In that lunatic's prison?" Raven scoffed.

"No, not there. Not even here, exactly. But in Australia. There have to be more habitable places than this on the continent, if people truly lived here. What if we could find one of them and start over?"

"Haven't you had enough privation and savagery yet?"

"There have to be ruins we could use for salvage. New adventurers arriving with needed skills. Maybe we could turn the tables on United Corporations and stay by choice, creating a new colony as radical as America was, or the old Australia. It could be the utopia they pretended they were sending us to. We'd start over, but we wouldn't make the mistakes they made. Lives would have more meaning. We'd always be asking why, instead of how much."

"Stay in this wilderness?"

"Stay for what I came for. To truly live life."

She looked at him in wonder. "You've gone insane, haven't you? You didn't throw the activator away, you *thrust* it away. You've burned our ships so we can't turn back, like Cortes in Mexico. You haven't learned a thing by coming here."

"I've learned to keep asking why. You're the one who taught me that."

Raven looked hopelessly out across the desert. "I don't think I see what you seem to see out here."

"Now you'll have time to."

She took that as a challenge. "No I won't. And by the time we get to the coast *you'll* be begging to come back with *me*."

"Great," Ethan muttered, watching the two of them.

"I said he'll be begging, Ethan. I didn't say I'd take him." For the first time she allowed a slight smile. "He's unreliable."

"Unpredictable." He looked at her wryly. He was mad as hell, but he still wanted her. The talking had helped, somehow.

"Co-dependent," Amaya corrected.

It was true. As frustrated as they were with each other, they were forcibly linked and shared a simple goal: to get to the coast. Everything else could be set aside, perhaps.

"Beg you to take me back?" Now Daniel grinned. "And give up this?" He gestured toward their bed of sand. "I don't think so."

They slept.

At the end of the third day they came to the road.

It was a ribbon of broken asphalt, vegetation erupting from its cracked surface like green pimples. Its course was broken entirely in places by washouts or drifting dunes. Such disrepair meant the highway was impassable to any vehicle short of a tractor, but it was still a startling piece of linear regularity, running north and south as far as they could see. The Australians had come this way! In roaring trailer trucks or whispering solar cars. There would be towns on such a road—empty and ghostly, yes, but still the ruins of communities—and maybe water. There might be faded signs, rusted wrecks, fallen ropes of copper wire and fiber optic cable sheathed in rubber: a junkyard of delights. It was funny how fabulous and yet foreign such detritus sounded after weeks in the wilderness. The technological litter of a lost world! The fugitives paused a minute, dazed by the familiar paved firmness beneath their boots, a goanna lizard lazily sunning itself on the radiant macadam a hundred yards away. Here was a path to *somewhere*.

"We'd better not use it," Raven said.

"Why not?" Ethan asked. After stone and sand, the highway looked marvelously easy. And the idea of looking for useful scraps of technology appealed to him.

"Because if they come after the transmitter this road would be the most obvious place to look."

"We'd make better time on the road."

"They'd make better time too."

"Besides, it goes the wrong way," Amaya said. "North and south. If an edge to the Cone exists, it should be east. The country is supposed to get better that way."

"It's gotten worse," Ethan said.

"Maybe that's because we haven't really come that far," she countered. "A few hundred miles, at best. It takes a while to see a difference on foot."

Ethan looked morosely out at the desert. "I hope you're right."

"At least we can use the road like a river to throw off pursuit," said Daniel. "Water erases scents a bloodhound can follow and pavement erases footprints. Let's follow it a ways until we find a rocky area and then strike east. That should discourage anyone from following."

They did as he suggested, walking north two miles until they came to a stony ridge that led east. They left the road there, taking care not to make any mark. After three miles on the ridge they dropped into an adjacent gully and dug successfully for water, then pushed on. Within hours the road had faded in memory like a mirage.

The gully petered out so they kept walking east across undulating sand. Their pace was less anxious now. Reaching the road had become some kind of psychological milestone, relaxing their fear of recapture by confirming they were getting someplace. The highway seemed likely to confuse Rugard if he ever bothered to come this far, and it was clear they'd outpaced him. It also promised that there were more remnants of civilized Australia somewhere ahead. Still, they walked into the night again to put as many miles behind them as possible before finally camping. Measurement again! Daniel thought. Because they'd met other humans. Their camp was dark and cheerless. There were no tents and no stoves now. They had no wood for a fire and dared not light one anyway. Instead they ate a few more mouthfuls of cold food and collapsed into sleep.

Daniel woke to find himself cuddled tightly against Raven. Instinctively, they'd crept together in the chill of the night. His chin was on her hair, and his cock embarrassingly hard against the small of her back. The instinct startled him. Gently, he sidled his hips away from her and she shifted, blinked, and slowly came awake.

If she'd noticed his unconscious state, she gave no sign. She glanced sleepily over her shoulder at him, as if bemused, and then got up quickly and moved away to prepare for the day's journey.

Amaya had cuddled into Ethan.

They ate quickly, chattering a bit more now, their mood still tense but improved by their distance from Erehwon. At least they were alive, and the transmitter that remained gave them purpose. Maybe the worst was behind them. Everyone was still tired, but the exhaustion of the first day of their escape had slowly been pushed back. In a few more days they would look for an oasis to stop for complete recuperation. Meanwhile they were still pushing hard due east, as near as they could judge it.

Their higher spirits didn't last long. The walking became progressively tougher. The domination of sand was mounting, and they realized they were entering utter desert: not just arid scrubland, but the edge of a sea of sandy dunes, red and sinuous. Each dune ran north and south as far as the eye could see and crest followed crest in a succession to the eastern horizon. It was like looking across an ocher ocean. Walking became increasingly laborious because level ground had disappeared. They trudged up the face of dunes that seemed twice as high as they really were because of the tendency to slip backward, gained the crest, and then slid awkwardly down the other side. Any breeze was absent in the hot hollows. Vegetation had disappeared and water seemed never to have fallen. Their boots, clothes, nostrils, and mouths were all irritated by sand.

By early afternoon, even Amaya was ready to call a halt. They stood on one of the tallest dunes yet, a fifty-foot-high drumlin, and felt like shipwrecked sailors adrift on a sea of sand. The desert looked endless.

"We can't cross this," Amaya admitted. "We don't have enough water."

"Maybe Ico was right," Daniel speculated. "It does seem to get drier, not wetter, the farther east we go. Maybe Outback Adventure lied to us about that too."

"No, it gets better near the coast," Raven said. "They told me."

"Why do you believe anything they say?"

"Because they've made a better world than this one."

"Come on, Raven. Were you really happy there?"

"Happiness is a luxury. I was . . . useful."

"Well, survival isn't a luxury," Ethan said. "The plain truth is that we really *don't* know anything. Nothing useful. That's what's going to kill us. The plain truth is that, essentially, we're lost."

"So what do we do?" Daniel asked. "Go back to the road? To go where?" He thumped the transmitter; they'd taken turns carrying it like a baby. "We need to go that way if you want to use this."

Raven was looking back westward uneasily, a growing wind from that direction blowing back the fan of her hair. The horizon was hazy, the place they'd come from losing all distinction. "Maybe our decision has been made for us."

The others turned. "Rugard?" Amaya asked anxiously.

"No." Raven pointed at the dark cloud swelling there. "Where we need to go right now is off this crest to some kind of shelter."

"Shelter? From what?"

"From that." They looked to where she was pointing and realized it was difficult to tell where the land stopped and the sky began. "I think a sandstorm is coming."

The storm rose over them like a rust-colored cliff, its edge a shadowing overhang. The highest tendrils of dust sprinted ahead of the main wall of sand like out-runners, pushed by hot winds up high. The fugitives sprinted over the dunes back the way they'd come, retracing their own footprints until they reached a rocky ledge a half kilometer away that erupted through the dunes like an exposed root. The sandstone had no cave or hollow but did offer a rib of stability among the soughing sands. Something to anchor to! They skidded down to its base, shed their packs, and crouched, waiting.

The sky got darker and darker. "And we paid to come here," Ethan said.

"I didn't," Raven replied.

The tempest curled over them like a breaking wave and then broke with dark fury. Its shriek ended all conversation, filling their ears with a kind of rasping static. The sand stung like needles and blotted out their sight. They hugged the broken rock and each other, wincing at the abrasion and struggling for breath. Their clothes snapped like flags. While their hollow offered some shelter, the fold of ground also confused the wind so that sand blasted at them from all directions, swirling and pricking. More sand sluiced off the crest of the outcrop, raining down on them like a dry shower. Periodically they struggled upward, pulling their packs with them, to avoid being drifted in by the blowing grains. The adventurers gagged for breath through rags hastily tied around their heads like makeshift bandannas. It felt like they were suffocating in an eerie red twilight. No inch of them was free of grit.

Then the worst of the onslaught was over almost as suddenly as it had come. The wind dropped abruptly as the front of the storm blew on. The sand fell out but the air remained filled with lighter dust, a swirling orange fog. Shakily they stood and untangled themselves, heaving off accumulated sand with a twist of their backs. The dark mass of the storm swept eastward, the desert behind it seeming to smoke. They were left looking like clay statues, coated from hair to boot.

Ethan spat, trying to clear his mouth of grit. "I want my money back, Raven."

The others laughed.

"I want every red cent. With interest."

"It's a small price to come alive," Amaya replied for her, shaking herself like a dog. "Though I wish it would buy me a shower."

"Don't say *that!*" Daniel warned. "You'll bring the damn floods back."

"I'd say we're about due for a forest fire," Ethan corrected, glancing about with mock trepidation. "Not to mention locusts, earthquakes, tornadoes, and a tsunami wave. Let me check the itinerary." He pretended to thumb through a brochure.

"I can't believe people really lived here," Raven said. "Heat, flies, dust. See, this is what I'm talking about, Daniel. This is the alternative. United Corporations is big and impersonal and bureaucratic and routine, but it also saves us from squalor. It's understandable to be romantic about the outdoors, sure, but *this* is the reality."

"No it isn't," he spat, trying to clear his mouth of dust. "This is no more representative of wilderness than a slum is of civilization. This desert is the reality you sent people to, but Australians didn't live *here*. They lived . . . somewhere else. So could we."

"Not comfortably!"

"Spiritually. Contentedly. Earnestly."

"We're redheads, Raven!" Amaya shouted to interrupt the arguing, swirling her hair so a plume of dust shot off it. "Outback chic!"

"Hey!" The others put their arms up against the flying grit. Amaya twirled away from them, dancing along the rock wall and narrowly dodging an unstable dribble of sand that drained downward. It was a relief to get away from those two! She came to a corner, laughing giddily as she rounded it, and then stopped as if she'd hit a glass wall.

"Okay, glamour girl!" Daniel called. "Which way now?"

Slowly, Amaya backed up and lifted her arm to point past the corner of the cliff. Her voice was quiet, but it carried clearly in the dryness of the now-still air. "Let's ask him."

* * *

The newcomer was as shrouded in dust as they were. He strode along the base of the outcrop in long, skidding strides that sent his tattered range coat flapping. The stranger had fled to the outcrop for shelter as they had, Daniel realized, and was as surprised as they were at this meeting. But not intimidated. Their huddled manner reassured him and he marched ahead, his cracked lips widening in gritty welcome.

"Now look what the wind blew in!" He looked at them with bright dark eyes from beneath a greasy bush hat. "Some of the good ones, I'd venture. G'day to the mud people, then!"

"Do you recognize him?" Daniel asked Ethan quietly.

"No. I don't think he's with the Warden."

The man squinted at Ethan. "I'm not with anybody, mate! Though I'm wondering where the likes of you are coming from, that always wants to be with *me!* For a long time, nothing. Then people here, people there. I spies on more than ever spy on me. Christ! Bloody crowded, it's getting. I come out here to get away from them all, and still I meet you!"

"We drop out of the sky," Ethan said dryly.

"Well, you brought a lot of dirt with you this time, didn't you!" the man replied, squinting up at an atmosphere still brown from dust.

"Who are you?" Raven asked.

He considered. "Why Oliver, I think. Who are you?"

"My name is Raven."

"Oliver is what I *remember.* Though to a pretty lady like yourself, just Ollie, I suppose. *I'm* the proprietor."

"The what?"

"The owner! The inheritor! This land is mine, by right

of first possession! So don't get any ideas, now! I don't care how damn many of you there are!"

Daniel glanced at Ethan. This one had been in the sun too long.

Amaya was looking thoughtful. "You didn't come with Outback Adventure, did you . . . Ollie?"

"Outback what?"

"And you're not a convict, either. Not a moral-impaired."

He straightened himself up. "As straight as a ruler, missy. *I* believe in the *law*."

"So, where *did* you come from?"

He looked impatient. "Now that's what your kind never understands. I didn't come from nowhere. I'm just here. On walkabout, you see."

"Walkabout?"

"The aborigines did it," Raven said quietly. "Sort of like a native American spirit quest. Go out alone into the wilderness to wander and survive and find a spirit. Magic."

"Like the old prophets," said Daniel.

"Like us," said Ethan.

"No, not like you," Oliver objected. "You're no abo, I can tell. Me, I've got some of the blood. I can hear the old ones when the wind blows. Heard 'em just now."

"How long have you been on walkabout, Oliver?" Raven asked.

He shrugged. "All my life."

"Do you remember the time before the Dying? Before the plague? When there were cars? Buildings? Other people?"

He looked troubled. "I dream it, sometimes. That's what I look for, missy. Not that I've ever found it."

"Great God," Ethan whispered. "He's a damned survivor. Somehow, he's immune."

Raven nodded at Oliver encouragingly. "And have you ever looked to the east? Ever looked where the sun comes up?"

He turned to look in that direction, his eyes bright in dark hollows under the dust like the mask of a raccoon, his stubble beard gritty, his body overclothed in the vagrant manner of someone who had no other way of carrying his belongings. "A bit. No different than here."

Their spirits sank.

"Unless you go to the wet part. Hard walking, some of that. Too many trees."

Raven brightened. "You've been there?"

"Oh yes. I've been everywhere. Have to, when you're the only one."

"Could you take us there?" She pointed.

"What? Across the sand? Are you crazy, missy?"

She looked confused.

"This is the bloody desert, right? No water here. We'd die, we go out there." He looked at them as if they were daft.

"Where then?" she asked in despair.

"Up to the mountains, the way I was going," he said impatiently. "*Then* east. You can find water up there along the ranges."

Their smiles cracked their dust-covered faces in an eruption of hope. "Ollie, we're lost," Raven said carefully. "Can you show us the way to the mountains? Show us how to get east?"

"East!" He considered a moment, scratching his beard. "Why east? Of course, then again, why not? I could go that way I suppose. What's east, I wonder?" He squinted at them. "Eh? What in the devil makes it so important to go that way?"

"Our home, Ollie. We're lost, and we want to get home."

"Home! Ah, well. That's what I'm looking for too."

CHAPTER TWENTY-THREE

They turned north, following the sinuous line of the dunes. The walking was easier now that they could march along the sandy crests, and their guide, however strange, boosted their spirits. Oliver pointed out the occasional track of an insect or lizard across the sand that suggested the dunes were not quite as sterile as they seemed. Still, when the sand gave way to a more familiar hard and arid plain, rocky and thorny and spotted with stunted trees and shrubs, the adventurers greeted the transition with relief. Here, at least, was something green.

A day later they began to cross stony ridges running east to west, a change in topography that broke the Outback's monotonous flatness. They could visually measure progress! As Oliver had promised, springs were easier to find at the base of these outcrops. Finally they came to a more imposing ridge about a thousand feet high. The range was the worn, polished nub of once-great mountains, the surviving sedimentary layers sculpted into battlements so shiny that they seemed to sweat. Touch confirmed the rock was as dry as old enamel, however.

The adventurers began following the base of the range, camping in gaps where intermittent floods had cut passageways as direct and level as a highway. These canyons were shaded by gum and acacia trees.

Without quite realizing it, the group fell into a new rhythm. During the first couple of weeks in Australia, Daniel's whole body had been sore from unfamiliar exertion. The ground had been hard and lumpy, his neck had bent at unfamiliar angles in sleep, his feet constantly ached and his muscles had stiffened. Now the miles seemed routine to a body that had become leaner and harder. The adventurers had far less gear than when they'd arrived in Australia and were more comfortable despite that, or perhaps because of it. Their load was lighter and their tasks simpler. The ground had become a familiar bed, and the open sky a familiar roof. Bird calls, a fold of land, the march of insects, or a change in vegetation could all, they'd learned, direct them to water.

Alert and more familiar in their surroundings, they found the daily search for food to be easier as well. Fruit-bearing plants had become recognizable, and their skill as hunters was growing. Oliver proved an apt teacher. Sometimes he would disappear for a day or two and reappear with game, but at other times he would take one of the party with him and patiently point out animal sign, demonstrate a quiet stalking, or bring down prey with a well-aimed throwing stick or rock. He taught his new companions to follow the tracks of the sluggish blue-tongued lizard—an easy kill—and to recognize wild onion, bush cucumber, and pigweed seed. Oliver carried nothing but what he wore, picking up and discarding sticks, rocks, or scrap to use as tools when he needed. He seemed not only to understand animals but to be half animal himself, and his wild, casual freedom struck the others as both enviable and disturbing. Is this what they could become?

With the absence of seasonings, their mouths were becoming sensitive to a more subtle palate. They found they could take more pleasure in the dribble of a fruit's juice, the smoky energy of cooked meat, or the chewy nuttiness of roasted seeds. They never had enough to feast—they'd gotten used to, in fact, a daily rhythm of hunger pangs before the evening meal, something almost entirely unfamiliar in their lives back home—but they were finding enough food to live on and keep moving. After a rain they hunted for yalka bulbs, roasting them to release their nutty flavor. They dreamed of richer foods, of course—sugar!—but subsisted on what they had.

Raven, who had expected to escape this experience and who instead had been forced to share it, remained stiff with the others. She was both the potential means to escape and a representative of the system that had stuck them in Australia, and their feelings toward her were confused. She was angry at Daniel for making a hard situation more difficult by losing the activator, worrying aloud that Rugard could still hunt them down before they could get back. Yet she also seemed to adapt to the wild with relative ease, suggesting her attitude in the tunnels had not been entirely an act. She was not squeamish about killing and cleaning game, displayed endurance, and had an emotional resiliency that warded off despair. Daniel tried to joke about their plight one evening.

"I've had to check into hell, throw away the activator, and walk a thousand miles to get another date with you, Raven. You seem to be doing quite well." He was watching her skin and cook a rabbit, the smoke and roasting meat mingling with the scent of eucalyptus. He felt strangely content. The convicts had been left behind, tomorrow was simply tomorrow, and life was no longer a set of deadlines and meetings and pressures. Did she feel what he felt?

She looked at him skeptically. "When I told you I was a cheap date, this isn't exactly what I had in mind."

"It isn't so bad though, is it? Isn't this the kind of freedom we talked about in the tunnels?"

She sat back on her haunches, using a forearm to brush her hair out of her eyes. "I never said it was bad. That's why I wasn't very guilty about sending people here. But this is a fantasy land, Daniel. This is recess. Our little party has hundreds of square miles to live on because we're the only people here, but Australia can't work for the rest of the planet. The only thing that can work for so many billions of people is obedience. The only thing that can work is United Corporations." She looked out across the dusky desert. "It's best that most people never see this. It would only confuse them."

"But don't you feel the *rightness* of this? For the first time I feel like I'm in a place where I belong. Humans were born in country like this. The savanna."

"Exactly. You do, and I don't. Normal people don't. I miss my machines. I miss my security."

"Even if it deadens the spirit?"

"Poverty and strife and fear are even more deadening. I told you, we came from different experiences. The companies took me in as a child, after my father died and my mother broke down. They schooled me, trained me, and finally convinced me I had to help sustain what they stood for. And I wanted to! I'm not blind, Daniel. I'm not immune to the beauty of this place. I'm not unconscious of the fate of some of the exiles. I just don't see this as a realistic option. And I don't appreciate your sticking me here by throwing the activator at Ico."

"As we didn't appreciate being sent here without the full truth."

She shrugged. "Okay. We're even. So don't try to get me to endorse what you volunteered for and I didn't. Camping is fun only if you get to go home at the end."

She wouldn't look at him as they ate their rabbit. He glanced at Amaya and she looked away from him too. Well, he couldn't blame her for that.

Still, his optimistic mood wouldn't leave him.

"I like this," Daniel tried again with Ethan the next day as they trudged along.

The other man glanced around, wondering what he was talking about.

"I like being here and just going," Daniel continued. "The simplicity of it."

"Mindless?"

"Fulfilling. I'm just doing what I'm supposed to do but not trying to do any more. Like an animal. I'm content, I mean."

"You're going someplace. Animals don't do that."

"Migratory ones do. Humans must have started like this, wandering out of Africa until we wandered all over the earth. Nomads. Drifters. It's why this seems right, I think."

"Except eventually humans settled down," said Ethan. "They got hungry, and had kids, and invented agriculture. Then came civilization."

"With tyranny and war."

"And medicine and art."

Daniel smiled. "That's why men are torn, I think. Between settling down and moving on. There's this yin and yang in our brain that comes from all of human history. The nomad versus the farmer. But what if farming was a wrong turn? What if that's the underlying story of Genesis: how people turned away from the Garden of the natural world to the temptation of our artificial one? The Tree of Knowledge?"

"If we hadn't bitten the apple there'd be no Genesis, no Bible, and no Gutenberg press to tell us about Eden," Ethan countered. "This isn't us, not really, Daniel. Civilization is. I've changed my mind about being out here. I was a gadget freak, and quite frankly I miss my gadgets. They were my toys. I like logic, regularity, and predictability, and all those things seem in short supply out here. So to me, the challenge isn't surviving without civilization. It's learning from the wild and bringing that experience back to make civilization better."

"You sound like Outback Adventure."

"First we believed everything they told us and then we believed nothing. I'm just wondering if some of what they said is really true, in a deeper sense than they intended."

"So what are you going to do if we get back?"

Ethan sighed. "I don't know. My worry is I'll end up not feeling I fit in either place, or will be on the run as an underground outlaw. Maybe I could make a life here, but not like Oliver. Not like an animal. I'd want to build back some of what I had, and strike a compromise." He looked at Amaya, walking ahead. "Find someone to build with."

The dusty, ragged, and unkempt members of Rugard Sloan's Expedition of Recovery, as he'd grandly decided to call it (although it was more like a lynch mob in mood and moral development), almost tiptoed along the black-top road in wonder. Pavement! A small thing, but as fervently appreciated in this trackless wilderness as an exercise yard in a prison compound. Here was evidence of past civilization! Of destination! Possibility! Somewhere over the horizon were ruined cities and salvageable luxuries. Somewhere over the horizon was Raven's electronic key to getting out of this whole sorry mess. And because of that, the hardened, bitter inmates of Erehwon ran up and down the skin of asphalt like excited children, clucking over the road as if it were an open gate in a coop of fenced chickens.

The reaction made Rugard slightly uneasy. His followers were angry, yes, for the slaughter in the canyon. They were set on getting back what the bitch had stolen if it meant even the slightest chance of escape from this continental hell: and he'd told them that Raven held the key to getting back. But at Erehwon his rule was the only possibility. In leading them out into the desert, Rugard had made possible the danger that some of them might actually begin to think. He'd have to drive hard to discourage that.

What drove *him* was not just the desire to break out of this unwalled prison but to revenge himself on the urban smart-asses who had run away. Rugard hated their type, these wealthy urbanites who came here—hated their manner, their unconscious superiority, their naïveté, their indignant outrage, their privilege, their whining, and their clumsy helplessness. How well he knew their kind! It mattered little to him that they were stuck in Australia as he was: they were of the same class of arrogant bastards who had imprisoned him. The same class that had held him down all his life: quietly sneering at him, ignoring him, jailing him, always trying to crush him. He was better than they were! Smarter, tougher. Now they'd done it again, humiliating him in his own home, and the possibility they might escape was so maddening he couldn't rest until he hunted them down. Yet Raven and her accomplices had a long head start because of the time it had taken Rugard to assemble supplies, saddle the camels pressed into service to help carry them, sharpen the weapons, and muster resolve. Some of his inmates had balked at following the fugitives at all! The Warden had reacted swiftly, making clear the necessity of fearing him more than they feared the desert. "You can stay with the ants then," he'd growled, burying one of those who hesitated to his scrawny neck and squeezing fruit pulp over his screaming head. Rugard had waited until the insects had eaten out the man's eyes and he'd begged for death, and then ordered him dug up, alive, his head pitted and bleeding with bites. A bandage had been wrapped around the victim's empty sockets and he'd been brought stumbling along, a reminder of the consequences of disobedience or hesitation, infection swelling the man's face like a balloon. The lesson had been salutary, the Warden judged. Still, the thieves were far ahead and the Expedition of Recovery needed help if it was to catch up. They needed an advantage.

Rugard looked with dislike at Ico Washington, kneeling on the pavement with a battered map spread before him. The weasel was oily and obsequious and slyly mocking. No wonder his former superiors had encouraged the little toad to run off to this wasteland! The Warden couldn't wait to get rid of Ico himself. Still, the man was convinced his piece of paper might give them a chance, even though to Rugard it looked like the kind of fantasy chart that fools bought from liars.

"Well? Did they come this way?"

Ico squinted upward. "Obviously we don't know. If I were them I'd stay off the roads to avoid contact with groups like us. But this highway could be the break we need. If we follow it we might be able to get ahead of them."

"The road goes north and south, not east. You said they'd go east."

Ico nodded. "They must, to use the transmitter. But look here. If this map is correct, this road must join an east-running one a few hundred miles north of here. We can make twice the time on graded pavement that they can cross-country, I'll bet. We follow these highways, get ahead of them, and throw out a net near the coast. They'll be lulled into complacency by then. We find them, get the transmitter back, and escape."

"That will take months!"

"The alternative is to rot like savages. And that could take years."

Almost imperceptibly, the country began to change as the quintet of adventurers hiked eastward. It rained a couple times, hard but not torrential, and that eased both their minds and the search for water. So did the ecology. The vegetation was getting denser as they traveled, changing from dead-looking desert scrub to savanna bush. The trees were fuller and grew closer together. The grass clumps were less separated. It was still dry country, with empty rivers and starched sky and conical red clay termite mounds that jutted from the soil like dented dunce caps, but for the first time since they'd landed in Australia the continent seemed to be getting greener. There was no hint of the sea, but their spirits improved with the health of the landscape.

Oliver half led and half tagged along, both guide and pet. It was difficult to get any kind of clear history out of him. He must have been a child when the sickness hit, and probably lost a piece of his mind when he watched a whole nation dying around him. Yet he'd survived from some inexplicable immunity and been wandering ever since. He was skittish, as if he might take it into his head to drift off at any minute, but he wasn't difficult to travel with. Content to mostly walk by himself, muttering at rocks and whistling at birds, he'd periodically demonstrate some bush skill or disappear to come back with fresh meat. Occasionally he'd hang on them like a dog, as if he took periodic comfort from human company. The next day he'd walk and sit and sleep apart. He displayed little curiosity about the modern world they'd come from and ate by himself, squatting on his haunches. He smelled rank but efforts to get him to wash were rebuffed, and perhaps he had a point. Even the insects kept their distance.

Among the other four, awkwardness persisted. Raven sulked, Daniel felt alternately fulfilled and at a loss, and Amaya seemed wounded. She reacted to Ethan's attempts at quiet conversation with gratitude but seemed cautious about striking up a real relationship. She'd obviously had a crush on Dyson. And Daniel still seemed smitten with Raven, who'd led him on. Only the journey held them all together.

So they walked, and talked of day-to-day things, but their feelings were temporarily corraled lest they threaten survival. Until one evening when Ethan approached Amaya as she took a turn gathering firewood.

"What's with Daniel and Raven?" he groused.

She sighed. "What do you mean?"

"They sidle around each other like gunfighters. I feel like I'm at a bad dinner party of a dissolving marriage."

"They're just in love." She said it morosely.

He looked at the two cooking silently by the fire already started, Raven unhappily avoiding eye contact. "One of them, maybe."

"It's both, Ethan. They're also mad at each other."

"For a while they were sleeping like spoons."

"Until they weren't so exhausted that they could start thinking about it. Now they're like repelling magnets. Serves them right to shiver."

"I like sleeping next to you."

She didn't reply. She knew he wanted more.

"But you're edgy around me in the daytime. Don't you like me, Amaya?"

She straightened at that, a forearm full of firewood, and looked levelly at him. She didn't answer.

"I like you. I like how you're smart. I like talking about building things with you."

She frowned.

"I like being with you."

"Here." She handed him the firewood and marched back to the campfire. Ethan followed. Oliver looked up with interest, sensing she intended to make an announcement. Indeed, Amaya now stopped and drew herself up.

"I think that now we need to talk about Ico."

Raven and Daniel looked at her curiously. Behind her, Ethan looked confused. "What?" he said in surprise.

"I think there are a lot of things being unsaid here that

we should talk out," Amaya went on. "To help the group."

"What things?" Daniel asked warily.

"Well." Amaya looked at them each in turn. "Ico betrayed us, but we have to decide whether we're willing to forgive him. If we don't, there's going to be this poison."

There was a moment's uneasy silence.

"I don't forgive the little bastard," Ethan said, dumping the firewood onto the ground. "If he hadn't run to Rugard I wouldn't be fleeing here through the bush."

"Yeah," Daniel agreed. "Screw Ico."

"Who's Ico?" Oliver inquired.

"A former friend," Amaya told the Australian. "We didn't trust him." She turned to the others. "So why should he have trusted us?"

"What are you talking about?"

"You didn't trust him to take the pack and come back for us when we were dying of thirst, Daniel. Remember? We didn't trust him to represent us back home. He was the one who most wanted to go, and we all said no."

"That's because he's this weird little blowhard," Ethan scoffed, sitting down on a rock disgustedly. Amaya looked at him reprovingly but he just returned her stare.

"And what difference does it make if we do forgive him?" Daniel added. "He's not even here."

She looked at the men impatiently, as if they were particularly dense. "Because I think there's a lot of anger people are bottling up that's getting in the way of . . . other things."

"Jesus Christ." Feelings. Women wouldn't let them lie.

Raven said nothing.

"For example," Amaya persisted, "your anger toward Raven."

He glanced at her. "It's not *me* who is angry with *her*."

"Isn't it? You blame her for putting you here, Daniel. You don't really trust her. But she's right. We came here ourselves."

"Amaya . . ." Ethan objected.

"And Raven's angry with you. If you hadn't been so damned . . . *attractive*"—she said it with exasperation— "she'd never have gotten confused about what she was doing, and never been assigned to Australia. And then you throw away her means of escape! I think you were trying to punish her."

"I was trying to get away from this Ico you want me to forgive and who was coming at me with a sword!" His look was stubborn. "I'm just trying to let Raven experience what she sends other people to."

"No. You're in love with her and couldn't stand to have her leave you."

"You don't know that!"

"And she was so guilty about sending you here that she came herself."

"Amaya," Raven groaned.

"We're not going to get comfortable until everyone sorts their feelings out."

"Well, *you're* certainly getting *your* feelings out," Daniel grumped. He turned to Raven. "Is that true?"

She looked embarrassed. "I'm here on a mission. Don't flatter yourself."

"Why didn't you tell me things from the beginning?"

Her look was sullen. "Because you wouldn't understand. You couldn't handle the truth of things. You still can't."

"What does that mean?"

She looked away. He knew what it meant.

"You're just so damn difficult to talk to half the time . . ."

Raven was suddenly furious. "Only because you won't *listen!*" She glared at the group. "Did it ever occur to any of you that maybe I tried to save him when he wouldn't save himself—that he didn't listen to me—and that I never expected to have to *deal* with all of you when I came out here? I'm just trying to get back!"

Daniel scoffed. "*Save* me? How about making a damn fool out of me?"

She glared at him, wounded and in pain. Then she sprang up and bolted into the bush.

The men were uncomfortably silent for a moment.

"Go after her, you dolt," Amaya finally advised, quietly, sadly. He looked up at her and, for just a moment, a look of longing flickered in her eyes. "Forgive her. Forgive yourself. And move on to what you're meant to do."

Dusk was falling as Daniel followed Raven as he'd once followed her running down an urban street. It was easy to track her now: a sandy footprint here, a broken twig there. She was climbing up the ridge they'd been following, making for a rocky outcrop that would provide a view in every direction. He half trotted to catch up with her, breathing anxiously, the oily perfume of Australia beguiling as he sucked it into his lungs.

He saw her form ahead like a slim phantom, disappearing in the shadow of an overhang and then rematerializing as a silhouette along the crest of the ridge. Rocks skittered out from the feet of both of them and she heard him once and turned. But she didn't stop and didn't call, just kept moving upward, as elusive as hope.

The sky was a vast blue bowl, its color deepening with approaching night. Australia lay around them in a shadowy panorama, its reds having faded to cobalt. There were no lights, no roads, no memory of civilization. It was the dawn of time. The crest of the ridge was a dragon's back, a series of short pinnacles like the plates of a dinosaur. For a moment he thought he'd missed her in the shadow of one, or that to avoid him she'd doubled back and slipped down to camp. But then he saw her ahead at the uppermost peak, alone under the first stars.

She was sitting hunched, knees pulled up to her chest, on a shelf of time-smoothed rock that was slick but dry and still radiating heat from the day's sun. A full moon was cresting the horizon. It was orange and huge, an autumn lantern, and it threw enough warm light to illuminate the profile of her body and the architecture of her face. Her features had the same polished fineness of the rock, immaculate and tan, her eyes large and dark as she looked sorrowfully out across the grass and scrub plain. Her back was bent, the pattern of her spine visible against the tightness of her tattered cotton shirt, and her breasts swelled where they were pushed against her thighs, her slim arms holding her knees. Her black hair was tied with the scrap of a leather shoelace to fall toward her waist. A withered flower she'd picked earlier in the day was still tucked into the knot. She was the most beautiful creature Daniel had ever seen, a nemesis who was vulnerable, lonely.

She heard his footsteps behind her. "Go away."

He ignored that, kneeling at her back.

"Please, just leave me alone," she said wearily. "It's too hard."

He touched her shoulders.

She stiffened. "Daniel, just let it be!"

He ignored her protests. He held her by her shoulders and bent to kiss her rigid cheek, wet with tears. Then her neck, and then he let his lips drift up to her ear. "Amaya's right. I think I do love you, Raven," he whispered.

"Daniel . . ." she groaned.

"I'm sorry I haven't said it. I was angry, because it's true I came to Australia because of you. But not because you tricked me. That's what I've been thinking about, and what I've had to admit to myself. It was because you were the one thing in life I could decide I wanted, after a lifetime of not knowing *what* to want. So I came to the Outback on a million to one shot that I'd find you and somehow break through to you—that I could somehow convince you to love me like I love you."

He kissed her cheek and then her neck, again, and again, descending to her shoulder.

She remained rigid. "You can't. You can't convince me."

He stopped, and took a breath, determined now. "I came because there was something in you that hit me with instant recognition when I met you, some part of you that I recognized in myself. I *knew* you, Raven. Or I'm going to know you. In some past life or some future one. That's what I thought way back in the city. I couldn't forget you. The only reason I haven't been able to forgive you is because I couldn't forgive myself. I couldn't forgive wasting so much of my life, going after the wrong things. I blamed you for me. But when I climb up these rocks and look out at the wilderness in all its timeless size and beauty, I realize how conceited such unforgiveness is. We're both so microscopic. We counted for nothing at United Corporations and we count for nothing here. We're *nothing*—except to each other. To each other, we count for everything."

He reached up to touch her face and turn her to him, her eyes wet, bending to kiss her fully on the lips.

And then she thrust him away. "No. Don't do this to me."

"Raven . . ."

"*I* count for something, Daniel. I count in that world because *I* believe in it. You're a dangerous man, Daniel Dyson, dangerous to them and dangerous to me. So I'm going to leave you here, abandon you in Australia, while I go back and let *them* decide what your fate should be."

"*They* put you here. They don't deserve your loyalty!"

"And I don't deserve yours. Please don't complicate things with this love of yours. Because I don't need it. I don't need it from anyone."

"You know you do . . ."

She rolled away from him and kneeled, looking at him intently. "Look. I need you to help get me out from under the Cone. Do that first. Do that for me. And *then* I'll decide where to go, or what to do, or how to live my life. Then, and only then, when I have a true choice, am I going to decide my why."

CHAPTER TWENTY-FOUR

As the land grew more hospitable, the fugitives began to encounter ruins that seemed both reassuring and disturbing. The decaying structures proved that humans had lived here, and presumably could again. They also warned of the impermanence of existence. People had not just lived here, but lived in comfort, with machines and full pantries and regular mail. Now they were gone, their memories weeded over.

The dented and holed aluminum blades of a windmill came first, peeping from the brush near the crumbling remains of its wooden tower. The steel water tank it had once fed was ruptured and sinking into dirt that was the same red color as its corrosion. When Raven touched the metal, it flaked like scorched paper. Five miles farther on they came across the shell of a cattle station, the roof of the ranch house long since ripped off by clawing winds and its walls sagging inward with the graceful weariness of old wood. The weathered gray of the wreck was spotted by scraps of plastic and metal and glass: a disintegrating metal wash tub, a faded plastic shampoo bottle, a broken frame with no picture. There was rusting metal machinery, a garden long dead, and brush-snarled lengths of old plastic pipe, purchased for an irrigation project the plague had not allowed to be completed.

"It's funny how fast things go in a bit more than a quarter century," Daniel remarked. "People still lived here when I was born, and now everything they did has sunk into the desert."

"It's interesting how much stuff remains," countered Ethan. "Metal that doesn't have to be mined, plastic that doesn't have to be refined. It's like a rummage sale. There must be huge amounts of salvage in the old cities."

"You're thinking of treasure hunting?"

"I'm thinking how fast a group of people could rebuild things, given the kind of junk that's in a place like this. I mean if we had to stay here. Here we are at one farm and we've got enough to make better hunting weapons, containers—even lumber to make a cabin if we wanted it."

"Yes, lots to take," Oliver said. "Old things everywhere. But so are the spirits of the old ones. The Australians! Everywhere, even here. Can't you hear them?" He cocked his head to listen to the wind. "This is their place, not ours. So it's bad luck to take anything from a place like this, mate. Bad, bad luck. We shouldn't camp here either. They'd come to us, in the night. We have to walk farther on, into the bush."

"You believe in ghosts, Oliver?" Daniel asked.

"I don't have to *believe*. I see them all the time. The dead people, killed by new things. Killed by this stuff here." He kicked at the machinery. "I sleep away. I sleep where they don't come."

"See them?"

"They're here, if you know how to look."

"I agree," Amaya said, as she looked around. "This old station gives me the creeps. I feel like it's infectious."

"It's just a ranch," Raven said.

"It's a bunch of sad memories," Amaya said. "United Corporations should document and memorialize this, not hide it by sealing off the continent. This was genetic tinkering gone too far. Ordinary people should see this."

"Ordinary people can't handle this," Raven said. "They wouldn't understand."

"Understand that their system is run by blunderers?"

"Understand that sometimes mistakes are made, or sacrifices ordered, for society's greater good." She was talking about them, they knew.

"And sometimes lives are wasted because of venal stupidity and greed," Daniel countered. He'd been sour since the previous night.

Ethan was tired of the arguing. "Let's take what we can use on the trek and leave."

"No, don't take!" Oliver warned anxiously.

"I think he must have seen people pick up the plague from sifting through stuff, early on," Amaya speculated. She put her arms on Oliver's shoulders and looked him in the eye. "It's all right," she said to the Australian. "I've seen the ghosts too, and they want to help the living. They want the Australians to come back."

His look was puzzled. "They're coming back?"

"Us, Oliver. You, Daniel, Ethan, me. The new Australians." She did not include Raven.

He looked doubtful, but didn't interfere as they took some metal to try to fashion spearheads, two glass bottles to carry water, and a handful of rusty nails. The fact was, they couldn't travel with much more. The weight wasn't worth the benefit. No wonder nomadic warriors used to destroy more than they acquired, Daniel thought. How much could they steal? So they walked on, heeding Oliver's advice to camp well away in the bush. They joked about it, but they were all secretly relieved in the morning that no ghosts had come at night.

Dirt station tracks sometimes led east now. When they were encountered the party followed them, making good if monotonous time. When the crude roads turned a different direction the five of them continued east by striking cross-country, the idea of finding their own way no longer foreign. On and on, by compass and by sun, a ceaseless rhythm. The days blurred into weeks and the land became thick with grass, the trees taller. They realized they'd left the worst desert behind. Australia was getting greener.

The first river with actual water in it was like a deliverance. The water was brown and the current limpid, but by God it flowed—a real river! They plunged in, clothes and all, even dragging a reluctant Oliver in with them, and then shed their clothes and splashed each other like savages, the sand cool and yielding between their toes. There was no self-consciousness; they'd been together too long. Besides, Ethan and Amaya sometimes slept away from the others at night and were assumed to be making love. Raven, however, stayed on her own side of the fire, aloof and unhappy. Daniel dourly watched her.

They camped by the river for two days to wash, play, and recuperate. Ethan didn't want to leave.

"This is the first time I've really been happy since I crashed in this nightmare," he confided to Daniel. "Maybe we should just stay here for a while."

"And not get back?"

"Just take a break. What's our hurry? I'm finally having a good time."

"With Amaya."

"With the wilderness. What I came here for."

"The batteries on those boxes won't last forever. Raven says maybe a year. We have to signal before then if we're ever going to warn the world."

"So I have to walk again *tomorrow?*" The complaint was a deliberate imitation of a childish whine.

"Afraid so, mate. I'd rather stay in bed too."

"I hope we're getting close to that beach."

"We've found the sand. It's the ocean we're lacking."

Their first hamlet was a place called Urandangie, according to a weathered sign still hanging by a nail from the one standing corrugated steel wall of a collapsed building. It was a desolate portal to civilization. Most of the tiny town had burned down, either in a riot or subsequent brush fire, and what remained looked like it had been pillaged. Broken glass crunched amid the weeds that filled abandoned gravel streets. The loneliness was sad testimony to the chaos that must have descended on the continent when its inhabitants realized they'd been abandoned to plague. Oliver didn't want to pause. "Best to walk on," he said.

They initially agreed with him, but at the far edge of the town there was an old garage that looked inhabited. There were new boards on its sagging roof. Inside they saw heaps of collated junk: old fabric, rusting tools, salvaged bottles. Outside, a fire pit smoldered. Someone lived here, but had fled.

They looked uneasily at the curtain of dusty trees

around the building. There was a clear sense of being watched.

"Do you think it could be the Warden's men?" Amaya asked.

"They wouldn't be hiding from *us*," Daniel said. "Maybe it's others like Oliver."

"Maybe we should help ourselves to their belongings," Ethan suggested practically. "They'll come out then."

"No," said Raven. "Maybe they're like us, and if we leave it alone they'll know we're not stealing." She raised her voice. "Come on out! We're peaceful! Maybe we can help you!"

There was no answer.

"Let's just go," Ethan said. "Oliver's right. This place is gloomy."

"No," Amaya said. "Raven's right. We need to help each other. I think we should camp here, away from their things, and wait for them."

The men looked around the bleak little town and then at Oliver.

"They're here," the Australian said. "I can feel them."

"What about the transmitter?" Daniel asked the others.

"We don't say anything about it until we've sized them up," Raven replied. "But we might want to invite them along. There's safety in numbers."

There was a small creek nearby and a stack of firewood. They built a fire, set up camp, and settled down to wait. The smell of their dinner drifted into the trees.

Their neighbors emerged at dusk. It was a man and a woman, both holding wooden staffs sharpened like spears. They approached cautiously, as if Daniel's group might spring on them at any moment, and they looked like the adventurers did, dressed in the dusty and faded synthetics they must have been wearing when dropped in the Outback. Their skin was clean and the man's beard neatly trimmed. The woman's hair was tied back. They were making an attempt at normality, but strain showed in their faces.

"Hungry?" Raven asked.

There was no reply.

"Quiet," Ethan observed.

"Why don't you eat with us?" Daniel offered.

The couple stood far enough away to bolt. "Who are you?" the man finally asked warily.

"Outback Adventurers, like you."

They started at that.

"We're just passing through," Raven added.

"You're the first women I've seen in a long time," the female said. "That's why we came out. Because you're women, but free."

"I'm Raven and this is Amaya. We're going east."

"To Exodus Port?"

"Sort of."

"We were told it doesn't exist," the man warned.

"And you are?" Daniel inquired.

"Peter. Peter Knowles, and this is Jessica Polarski. We've had a rough time and learned to be wary of strangers."

"I understand." He made introductions of his group. "And this is Oliver. He was born here."

The two newcomers looked in surprise at the tattered Australian companion. "I was *always* here," Oliver said proudly. "This place is *mine*."

"Somehow he survived the plague," Daniel explained. "Is he your guide?"

"Sort of. He knows a lot of bush craft and we persuaded him to tag along. He's a little . . . eccentric, but I suppose we are too. What's your story?"

Peter sighed. "There were four of us, originally. We got lost, and then in trouble, and fell in with a nomad group. We thought they were hikers but then they said there's no way to get back and we had to join them. Except they were convicts! Thieves, murderers. It became this bizarre nightmare. They said there were morally impaired people being dumped all over Australia. They killed my friend for his gear and started raping his girlfriend."

"We ran away," Jessica confessed. "It was horrible."

"We had to," Peter added guiltily. "We hid from everyone we saw."

Raven looked down.

"How long have you been here?" Daniel asked.

"I don't know. A few months, maybe. We wandered for weeks and then this place had water and some shelter. It's not that we planned to be here. We just stopped and haven't been able to get started again. We don't know where to go. How many people are out there, anyway?"

"We don't know. Maybe more than we thought."

"We're just so confused," Jessica said.

Daniel nodded. "So are we. Come have some dinner."

The group ate, trading brief life histories, and then when Peter and Jessica returned to their garage, Daniel's group talked late into the night. In the morning, the decision was obvious. They asked the couple to join them.

"We're told there's no Exodus Port either," Daniel explained. "But we do have a transmitter salvaged from a crashed aircraft that might—might—be able to call for help if we can reach the ocean. It will only work on the coast because of electronic jamming inland. The only one they'll take back for sure is Raven, here."

"Why her?"

"She was sent by United Corporations to bring the instrument back."

"She's one of them?"

Daniel looked at her. "She was. Now she's one of us." He waited to see if she'd correct him, but she didn't. "There might be room for Ethan too. I don't think United Corporations will save us, but if we can get word out, maybe someone in power will want to exploit this scandal back home. Then somebody might shut Australia down and rescue us."

"That's your plan?" Peter sounded skeptical.

"Do you have another one?"

He sighed. "No. I'm just not sure anyone will listen."

"They certainly won't if we don't do our best to bring back word," Daniel said.

In the end, the couple's decision was simple. To go with these newcomers offered hope. To stay put offered none. "If helping get this machine to the coast could put a stop to all this, it's worth whatever it takes to get it there," Jessica said. "Then we'll wait for . . . whatever." The possibility of getting back still seemed too remote to dare voice.

Amaya smiled encouragingly. "I don't think we should have to wait for anything," she replied. "When we get there I think we should start building the kind of lives we always wanted to lead. By the time we really get back home, we'll have learned what to live for."

Australia continued to unfold ahead of them, vast, seemingly endless, but also steadily changing and ever more intriguingly beautiful. The season had pleasantly cooled and they felt more acclimated to living outside than in. They came through a region of artfully interspersed rocky knolls and forested valleys and then encountered flatter grasslands and scrub savanna again. The continent was becoming a mosaic of landscapes. As they traveled their party began to swell. Adventurers were wandering or camped in this wetter country, dazed and fearful, and the appearance of a large, safe, increasingly well armed group with a purpose and destination proved irresistible. Within two months after fleeing Erehwon they numbered eighteen in all, seven women and eleven men, including a second native Australian named Angus. Oliver seemed briefly stunned by this aboriginal competition for ownership, and then embraced his countryman like a long-lost brother. The two continued to share their survival skills and the others pooled information. It was beginning to feel like a pilgrimage, or a migration. The original quartet enjoyed the company of these newcomers but also privately talked nostalgically of the "old days" of a few weeks before, when they'd been on their own.

Angus claimed to recognize some of where they were. "We're nearing the great range that runs north to south," he told them. "And beyond that: the sea." His promise brought a murmur of excitement. The east coast had been everyone's goal since departure from civilization. It *would* be something to actually get there.

The growing group had developed an intense camaraderie. It came partly from their nightly sharing of tales of danger and trauma, confusion and shame. It also came because the group walked, ate, slept, and bathed together, and within days newcomers would seem more familiar in camp than had office mates who'd occupied an adjacent desk for years in the corporations of home. Soldiers and pioneers must bond the same way, Daniel thought. The sense of human community was novel: strangely missing in the far bigger society of United Corporations.

But while the new recruits were encouraging, the logistics of the trek were becoming more complicated. There were more people to feed, and the noise of their approach drove game animals farther away. Hunters had to be sent ahead or on the flanks to help bring in food and spot edible plants. People were beginning to instinctively specialize: hunters to get meat and scout, armorers to make weapons and tools, and then gatherers, cooks, menders, fire wardens. An easygoing youth named Rupert volunteered, despite inevitable ribbing, to each night mark out—and dig—a latrine. "Lack of sanitation will kill us faster than a wild bull or poisonous snake will," he said. A flag was fixed to indicate whether the facility was occupied, giving some measure of privacy.

With the added numbers their pace had slowed. Sometimes the group would camp two or three days to give time to hunt, treat skins, cook more ambitious meals, sleep, heal blisters, repair clothes, and socialize. The delay worried Raven, who feared the Warden might still be doggedly following, but Daniel believed they'd left the convicts far behind. How could they be found again in this immensity? The party did encounter a small gang of other wandering convicts one afternoon, but the predators fled from the sight of their greater numbers. The experience boosted their confidence. Surely they were safe! And they needed the rest from the relentless walking. It gave people time to bond. The dire nature of their predicament seemed to push people instinctively to friendship, flirtation, commitment, and experimentation. As a result the group bubbled, sparked, and occasionally boiled over with sexual chemistry as partners tried each other and then split back apart.

"It's like a cross between a soap opera and the Oregon Trail," Daniel concluded one night to Ethan. "This is so different than what I expected Australia would be, back when I planned to trek with just three friends."

"If we find many more companions we're going to have to start calling you the Warden," Ethan replied. There was no formal leader but the new recruits deferred to the direction of the initial group and its promise of having the magic to call for help. Unexpectedly, Daniel found himself making more and more of the decisions. There was something about him people responded to, even Ethan. As if he *knew* what to do. Even Raven noticed it. She said he was becoming more like her.

"God, I hope not," Daniel now said of the Warden jibe. "But that's a problem with bigger numbers, isn't it? Rules."

"We've got enough people now to make a real community on the coast while we wait for whatever." Ethan let his finger wave vaguely at the sky. "But it does pose organizational problems. I told you we were naturals for civilization."

"Can't we do better this time?"

"That's the test, isn't it?" Ethan stirred the coals of the fire, his voice low. "What will we do different when we do settle down to wait? How will we make decisions?"

"I don't know," Daniel said. "I just want to let people keep a sense of identity, instead of only identifying with their company or agency—or our new tribe."

"Maybe there's room here to do that."

"At least we seem to have eluded the convicts. I can't believe Rugard would still be following. Maybe he never left Erehwon."

"Or, if he did, we're going to break clear of the Cone so soon that his pursuit will become academic." Ethan glanced around. "I hope." They hadn't told the newcomers about the Warden, and didn't want to. They didn't want Rugard to become a new bogeyman, seeming to hide behind every tree.

"We've been meandering for months. I don't think *we* could find *ourselves*."

"Not unless he knows something we don't."

The convict had been nicknamed Wrench for the things he did to people's arms and legs when they didn't meet their obligations on time. Here in the Outback, his size had won him leadership of one of Rugard's scouting parties. As such he was drowsing in the shade of a ridge-crest eucalyptus, lazy but mentally restless. He'd thought it lunacy when the Warden had ordered them to chase the Outback marks across the desert, and greater lunacy when that smart-mouthed toad called Ico had led the Expedition of Recovery off on highways that seemed to go in the wrong direction. Even assuming the fugitives weren't already dead—birds pecking out their eyes five hundred kilometers back—what chance did they have of intercepting them on the other side of Australia? But Ico the Psycho, a nickname he'd inevitably been tagged with (his shrill protests assuring it would stick) had insisted that he could lead the Warden's men to a point *ahead* of the fugitives. Ico had predicted that terrain and old roadways might push them in *this* direction, toward a pass in what his dog-eared, oft-ridiculed map called the Great

Dividing Range of Australia. The convicts believed the little bastard not because they thought he was really right, but because there was nothing else to believe.

Actually the journey hadn't been too bad. They'd found some wanderers to rob, shortening their own necessary search for food, and some women to forcibly enlist into what Rugard had jokingly dubbed their Cohort of Joy. They'd found wild cows and pigs and goats to hunt as they went east, whole rivers of clean water, and plague-emptied buildings to sleep in. The truth was, Ico the Psycho had brought them to a far nicer place than they'd come from, and whether they found the transmitter or not, Wrench wasn't about to go back to Rugard's desert dungeon. Screw that! Life was better here.

But unless he wanted to run off on his *own*, Wrench still had to humor the Warden by keeping watch for the fugitives. It was an easy, brainless job, but so far it had also been a futile one. The convict wished his boss would just give it up and enjoy this greener paradise, but Rugard had become steadily more obsessed with the transmitter, not less, turning ever more irritable and vicious. So Wrench had been posted here for a week, waiting for the bitch and her boyfriends to show up. He was bored beyond belief.

Except that Ico's suggestion did have a core of sense. There *was* a pass through the mountains that led down to a big lake, with a river canyon below the lake. The only easy way across the water was on the crest of the old dam that had created the reservoir. Anyone passing through came here, to the dam, and here Wrench would wait. And wait. And wait. Until the Warden tired of the game and called them in.

"Wrench! Somebody coming!"

He groaned. "If they're not carrying a damned communications satellite on their back, let them pass." The convicts had already robbed and killed two nitwits who'd stumbled this way. He was tired of it. Let the next ones go by.

"No, this is a big group! A regular army!"

Rivals? Cursing, he rolled upright to look, squinting at a group switchbacking down a hillside toward the dam. No army, but quite a few traveling together. Why? It was peculiar, and didn't match the four they were looking for. Then he looked harder.

"That one there," he muttered, pointing. "That's the woman, isn't it?" A slim, dark-haired woman strode steadily in the midst of the group. Raven, her name was.

"Where'd they get all those other people?"

"Or where did they get her?"

"She doesn't look like a captive. And I think I recognize some of the others."

Wrench wondered if the scouts on the other side of the canyon wall had stayed awake. "Didn't expect this many, but damn! Signal the others! It looks like Ico the Psycho was right after all." He grinned, wondering if he'd get some kind of reward. "We got 'em."

CHAPTER TWENTY-FIVE

The dam was the most substantive relic of Australian civilization that Daniel's group had seen yet, and it was intact. The reservoir it had created was full, water lapping near the lip of the dam, and a small falls poured over the spillway gates at its middle. The wedge of concrete was of moderate size, its crest two hundred yards long and its downstream face thirty feet high. At its middle was a notch thirty yards long where the dam elevation dropped half the height of a man to a set of rusted spillway gates. It was here the reservoir water slid to the river below.

Before the plague the spillway gates were routinely opened and closed to control reservoir depth, electricity generation, and the flow of the river downstream. Disuse and rust had frozen them shut, corrosion eating into the steel to allow a spray of leakage around the gate edges. The reservoir had risen enough to top the old gates, the outlet water looking orange where it ran down the old steel. Bridging this sheet of water was an old wooden catwalk, connecting one end of the dam's concrete crest to the other. The dam and its catwalk made a bridge across the waterway, its top wide enough for Daniel's group to begin filing over two by two.

"Well, this is convenient," he remarked to himself, leading the way. Almost too convenient.

There was a small concrete blockhouse on the western dam crest, adjacent to the spillway gates. Its door had rotted to paper. Out of curiosity, Ethan kicked it down and went in. Wet concrete steps led down in the gloom to a cluster of gigantic gears and levers that had once controlled the spillway gates. The electric motors to do so were powerless, their electrical cables withered like dead vines. Amaya poked around the machinery curiously, fingering the levers.

"This must be a manual override," she said, pointing to a large wheel.

A short flight of wooden steps led up to the catwalk over the spillway. Daniel told the others to wait, mounted the steps, and stepped out onto the wooden bridge. It creaked and rocked slightly because its posts were slowly rotting, but it still looked capable of bearing human weight. He looked down at the river below the dam, flat and brown, flowing north through a thickly forested valley. At some point it must turn east through the mountains to the sea. Maybe they could follow the river to the coast.

But first to the other bank. "One at a time!" he called. "It's pretty wobbly!"

He went across gingerly. So far, so good. One by one the others began to follow, those having crossed the creaking catwalk waiting on the eastern half of the dam for the others to catch up.

The group was evenly split, half on either side of the spillway, when a rock suddenly sizzled out of the trees on the far bank and hit a recent recruit named Ned Putnam.

He grunted in surprise, spun, and almost went over the lip of the dam before the others caught him. Everyone crouched in stunned surprise. The attack was so unexpected they had difficulty grasping what had happened.

The trees on the eastern shore hid their attackers. Ned was down on the concrete, cursing. "It might be broken," he hissed, holding his shoulder.

Daniel and some others quickly picked up a few random chunks of concrete that had eroded on the crest, and others anxiously pointed their spears. They felt exposed and vulnerable. Then three men stepped into sight, one letting a sling dangle menacingly from his right hand. It was the most ancient of weapons, the simple killer that had allowed David to topple Goliath. A stone was fitted into a long loop of leather, twirled around the head to gain momentum, and then released with a snap of the wrist. If it hit the head it could kill. The other two convicts had steel-tipped spears, crude swords, and the same kind of curved throwing sticks the aborigines had once hurled. It was a war party. The trio were tall, bearded, ragged, streaked with menacing daubs of white mud, and confident-looking. Not to mention familiar.

"Who the hell is *that?*" their first recruit, Peter, asked in bewilderment.

"I recognize them from Erehwon," Ethan muttered. "Rugard's clan."

"Who?"

"There's some convicts who know we have the transmitter," Daniel reluctantly explained. "We thought we'd left them far behind, but obviously we didn't."

Peter looked at the trio with alarm. "We've got the morally impaired after us?" he asked in disbelief. "We have to fight for it?"

"If we want to get back," Daniel replied grimly.

"You didn't tell us about this!"

"No, I hoped we wouldn't have to. Now we have to decide what to do."

The three convicts stood shoulder to shoulder at the end of the dam like an impassable wall. "You left without saying goodbye!" one of the ominous trio called. Gallo, Daniel thought his name was. Extortionist, if memory served. Bullying or sniveling, depending on who he was with. The man pointed toward the groaning Ned with the tip of his spear. "So we dispensed with hello, as well! That's just a warning!"

"A warning of what?" Daniel said, trying to think as he stalled.

"There's a toll for crossing this particular waterway! One stolen transmitter!"

"Daniel, let's rush those bastards," Ethan growled. "We outnumber them."

"No, we're not ready for that." He glanced back. "We haven't talked this over, and there are a lot of women. I don't want to get anyone killed. Maybe we can find another way around them." His group quickly filed back across the catwalk in retreat. Yet even as they did so, four more of Rugard's men appeared at the other end of the dam. The tallest one was easily recognizable, his scarred face memorable. Wrench, Daniel remembered. A brutal enforcer before he came to Australia.

"The toll is the same this way too!" Wrench called.

They were trapped, and without cover or room to maneuver on the crest of the dam.

"How the devil did they get ahead of us?" Ethan wondered. "And behind us? And where's Rugard?"

"We haven't been moving that fast," Daniel said.

"Somehow they guessed where we're going: maybe Ico helped them. Who knows? I was foolish not to hurry, but I thought they'd have given up by now."

"Why would they give up? We've got the only way back." Ethan's tone was gloomy.

"What are we going to do?" a woman named Iris asked plaintively. She was looking from one end of the dam to the other.

Daniel was silent, thinking.

Raven came up out of the gearhouse.

"Rugard's goons are here," he told her quietly. "It's your transmitter. Your ticket home. And these people's lives. Do you want to fight for it, or not?"

She glanced around quickly, taking in the situation.

"Better hurry before the Warden gets here!" Gallo shouted. "The toll goes up then!"

"If we give it up and Rugard uses it, he'll simply disappear," Amaya warned. "The world will never know what's happening here. Or believe him, even if he tells."

"But we didn't tell these people about this danger," Daniel added. The others had clustered around. "It's a terrible place for a battle."

Raven shook her head. "I can't ask you to fight so I can get back."

"Damn right," the injured Ned said. "It wasn't right not to tell us about this."

"I didn't want to worry anyone," Daniel said. "You've had worries enough."

No one said anything.

"Well, it's a group choice," he went on. "We can give up the transmitter."

They considered that.

Finally Ned sighed and spoke up again, his voice

strained from the pain in his shoulder. "Daniel, you weren't right for not trusting us with the full story, but I'm also tired of being picked on by men like these. These are the kind of bastards who killed my best friend. Their force is divided and we outnumber both groups combined."

"Yes," Ethan said. "Let's fight."

Raven had been looking about. "There's a better way," she said quickly. "Let's just jump into the river."

The others looked down the face of the dam, as high as a three-story building. "That's a good drop," Iris objected.

"And the river's sluggish," Daniel said. "We can't swim faster than they can run. They'll just follow us down the valley and we'll lose all our supplies too." He glanced around, trying to summon some of the tactics he'd once studied on dry, dead pages. They outnumbered their antagonists, yes, but the narrowness of the dam crest made it impossible to flank Rugard's watchdogs and bring their superiority to bear. It was like the narrow defile at Erehwon except here the situation was reversed: it wasn't Tucker holding Rugard off, it was Rugard's men holding them in place until the Warden could arrive with reinforcements. "Maybe a few of the men could swim downstream and circle back around," he thought aloud. "Take them from behind."

"We don't have time for that," Raven said. "Who knows when Rugard might show up? And we didn't come all this way to give away everything, either. Amaya, do you think we could get those spillway gears working?"

"Maybe with that old wheel and the levers. They're rusted, but with enough men pulling . . ."

"What good will that do?" Ethan asked.

"The catwalk supports are half rotted," Raven explained hurriedly. "We lash our supplies onto the decking, use the tools we've picked up to hack at its base, and send the platform over the dam. With any luck it becomes a raft that people can cling to on their way downstream."

"Meanwhile," Amaya added excitedly, grasping her idea, "we open these gates for an instant flood. That pushes us downstream and leaves Rugard's men stranded on either side of the dam. Maybe it buys us enough time to get to the coast and try the transmitter!"

Daniel looked at his two female strategists with wonder. "Let me get this straight. You want to start our own torrent and jump into it? With our supplies lashed to a rotting catwalk?"

They nodded.

He shrugged. "Makes sense to me. Ethan?"

He looked down the gearhouse steps. "We'll have to hold them off while we work. There's some deck gratings down there. Maybe we can pry them up for temporary shields."

Daniel smiled. "Okay. Two men behind each shield. Women to chop down the catwalk. The rest of the men down here on those levers." He began snapping out names, the authority coming naturally to him now, glancing at the blocking convicts at either end of the dam. "It's time to leave again without saying goodbye."

The fugitives pried up two of the steel floor gratings on one side of the gearhouse and carried them up the stairs, putting one on each side of the central catwalk. Two men took position behind each grating, spears pointed out. Meanwhile the old tools salvaged from the ruins were rapidly distributed. Some of the women dropped down into the shallow water running over the spillway and cautiously felt their way under the catwalk, holding on to its posts as they moved. Other women carried their packs to the decking of the catwalk overhead, hastily lashing their belongings in place even as their sisters began hacking at the posts beneath them. With each blow, the wooden bridge trembled. Meanwhile the remaining men descended into the gearhouse to pry at the frozen workings of the dam spillway gates.

Rugard's men watched uncertainly. Belatedly, Wrench and Gallo realized that the entire party they were hunting had disappeared as easy targets: some men were crouched behind some kind of metal mesh, others had hidden in the gearhouse, and the last of the women were dropping down to muck about in the spillway underneath the catwalk, almost entirely hidden as they bent over. Something was going on, and it wasn't surrender. The men glanced nervously at each other: none had forgotten the shocking roar and concussion of the bewildering explosion back at Erehwon. Did the transmitter thieves have more witchery up their sleeve? While the convicts had the fugitives pinned, their quarry outnumbered them. Gallo wished Rugard were here, but it would take a couple of days to find and bring him. Maybe they should just back off and trail these troublemakers.

"Send some rocks at them," he instructed his slingman uncertainly.

The man whirled his weapon over his head and let fly. The stone rocketed along the crest of the dam and banged off the metal grate harmlessly. He flung again, and again. One rock ricocheted into the adjacent reservoir and a third bounced up in the air and fell down on the dam crest behind the bastards crouched with the grate. One of them scampered back, scooped it up, and hurled it back, forcing Gallo's men to duck out of the way.

"You dropped something, you clumsy cretins!" the pitcher yelled. It looked like the bastard they'd already hit with a rock.

"Maybe we should just rush them," one of the convicts ventured.

"There's too many," Gallo snapped. "You want to get pushed off the face of this dam? I say we keep them pinned here until help comes. They're trapped."

Wrench had arrived at the same conclusion. He'd actually loped forward along the other end of the dam with the intention of jabbing tentatively at the metal grating with his spear, but as soon as he started the fugitives hurled chunks of concrete, the blows sending him scampering back out of the way. If he tried to climb over the gratings they'd stick him like a pig. Well, if he couldn't advance on the dam's crest, neither could they, right? It was a standoff. He hoped.

Still, he was worried about doing nothing and getting the Warden mad at him. He stood watching the frenetic activity at the center of the dam with foul confusion. What the hell were they trying to do?

Suddenly there was a shrill, wailing shriek, so loud and unearthly that the convicts on either side of the structure instinctively jumped. What the devil was *that?* Excited shouts were coming from the gearhouse. Then there was another shriek, and encouraging yells from the women. The flow of water down the face of the dam began to quicken. The catwalk was beginning to lean out over the dropoff, increasingly precarious.

"Are they trying to commit suicide?" Wrench muttered, his chest sore from a thrown missile. If they lost the transmitter in the river Rugard would hang them all. Damn! He began to realize that things were going horribly wrong.

There was another metallic squeal, the complaint of corroded metal, and then a sudden bang. One of the spillway gates snapped open and a plume of water shot out from the crest of the spillway, carrying two women with it. Screaming, they hit the river below. The catwalk shuddered and, with a creak of its own and a snapping of timbers, it followed the two women off the top of the dam, toppling into the river with a titanic splash. The wood went under for a moment and then floated in a boil of foam, rocking away downstream. Shrieking with a combination of triumph and fear, more women jumped into the growing waterfall and slid down the face of the dam to follow their makeshift raft.

Behind them there were more snaps of metal, a chain reaction of failure, and the spillway gates pried open wider, pushed by the force of the reservoir behind them. The roar of the unleashed flood was growing. Men boiled out of the gearhouse, shouting and waving their arms at their comrades behind the shields. Abruptly the gratings clanged down and the two defenders behind each one ran to the lip of the spillway. "Jump, jump!" Daniel cried. One by one, they obeyed him.

Wrench and Gallo started to lead their men across the top of the dam.

Raven hesitated at the edge of the spillway, eyes wide with excitement at the growing flood, the transmitter strapped to her belly.

"These are your people, now," Daniel shouted to her

above the growing roar of the water. "They've decided to put their trust in *you*. Don't let them down!"

She looked at the heads bobbing downstream, thrashing after the makeshift raft. "I won't." Then she leaped.

"Ayyyyyy!" Daniel glanced around. Wrench was charging at him with a wild cry, sword swinging over his head.

It cut empty air where Daniel had been. He'd jumped too.

There was the terrifying erruption of foam below, the endless seconds of free fall, and then the plunge into cold water and the buffeting of current until he could force his way back upward, gasping for air. All he could see was water. He began swimming downstream.

Gallo and Wrench wavered to a stop at the two edges of the spillway, separated from each other by ninety feet of roaring flood. "Fire, fire!" the two squad leaders screamed. The convicts hurled spears and sticks but the fusillade was a pointless mistake: they were simply throwing away their best weapons. All they had to aim at was mist, and white water, and beyond it a series of heads swirling downstream like corks. One by one the fugitives were reaching the floating catwalk, accelerated by the growing flood.

"Jump in after them!" Wrench roared in frustration. But his companions hesitated. The pounding of the unleashed water was getting more violent as the corroded gates were pried aside, the reservoir swirling toward the dam's open mouth with an ominous suck. And how would they fight in the water? Rugard's scouts began backing warily away from the spillway lip.

The fugitives were already out of sight.

Wrench and Gallo looked at each other across the gap,

as impassable as an ocean. The lake behind was big and might take hours, even days, to drain itself back down to the level of the new opening. They howled in frustration. And then turned to try to follow as best they could along the steep, brushy banks on either side of the river, falling farther and farther behind.

The energy that swept Daniel's party downstream was frightening in its power, and a narrower river canyon with more rocks might have resulted in serious injury to the members of his party. The reservoir water was cold, deep, and turbulent. But the valley below the dam was wide enough so that the pouring water had room to spread and run smoothly as it rushed downstream. The fugitives were mostly young, immensely fit after months in the wilderness, and good swimmers: none had come to Australia without that skill. So instead of being caught in a white-water death trap, Daniel's group was instead sped by a brownish current that was tidelike in its steady power. The wreckage of the catwalk became a life raft that supported most of the fugitives, though a few clung to random logs that had been picked up and carried downstream as well. The water moved so fast that the frustrated cries of Rugard's men were soon left behind. Then the pulse of the current began to slow, and by concerted effort the group clinging to the catwalk eventually managed to kick the structure to the eastern side of the stream so that it grounded on a sandbar. By that time they'd been washed down several miles.

The shaken trekkers staggered ashore to collapse and steam in the sun, panting, and then roused themselves to unlash their belongings and sort themselves out. Surprisingly, few of their supplies had been lost: Raven's plan had worked. And besides cuts and bruises, there were no serious injuries. Even Ned had decided his shoulder was only hurt, not broken, by the slung rock.

"Well, we crossed the river," Ethan spat. "Not quite the way we intended."

The other fugitives were looking at Daniel with a mixture of triumph and stunned uncertainty. What now? He stood stiffly, took a deep breath, and faced them. Everyone was a bit dazed by the sudden confrontation but also exhilarated to have escaped: thrilled to have beaten this sudden foe, thrilled to still be alive. Come alive! Outback Adventure had promised. They had this day.

Now they had a choice to make, and a hard one. If they were going to help him, he had to play to their desire for escape.

"We've told you all that we think we have a way to get a couple of us back to where we came from," he began quietly. "And if the transmitter works they might just be able to expose this scandal for what it is and get the rest of us back as well. But to use the transmitter we were forced to flee with it from a convict community hundreds of miles to the west of here. After so much distance and time, we thought the convicts had given up any hope of pursuit, but obviously we were wrong."

The others were watching him grimly. His vague promises of journeying to a point to seek help had seemed like deliverance, and now his admission that a rival group was still on their heels smacked of betrayal. It was like the misleading half-truths of Outback Adventure all over again, he knew. By now, they trusted no one.

"We can't let this destroy us," he continued. "One of my original friends betrayed us in his desperation to escape. We can't let that happen again."

"So what do we do?" Peter asked.

"We've escaped for now. But they may find us again soon. That leaves all of you with a choice. You can stick with us in hopes we can elude our pursuers and try to call in some kind of rescue craft, once we get out from under this electronic cloud of jamming. That's always been a long shot, but it's our *only* shot. But if you come with us, we may end up in a bad fight—a desperate fight—trying to do it. Or, you can bail out now. If we split up you don't have any chance of getting back, but the group that is chasing us will probably leave you alone. Maybe." He stopped.

"Risk death with you or stay marooned by ourselves," Peter summed up. "That's it, isn't it?"

He nodded. "A bad choice, but we've never had very good ones, have we? I wasn't trying to keep anything from you, Peter. I just didn't want to worry you needlessly. If we can just signal for rescue, the convict pursuit becomes pointless. I hope."

There was a gloomy silence.

"And the only one guaranteed to have a ride out of here is her?" Iris clarified, pointing to Raven. "Why her?"

He took a breath. "Because she's the one who told us about this chance. We're going to send her and Ethan to try to bring help. That was our original plan and we're not changing it now. Any fight over who gets to go would be fruitless."

His followers digested all this. "Wish you were here—and I wasn't," Ned tried to joke.

Jessica stepped forward to stand next to Peter. "Well, I'm not giving up my only chance of getting out of here to a bunch of damned convicts," she announced. "I'm sticking with Daniel."

"Me too." Peter sighed. "If I'm going to die in Australia, it might as well be for a reason. At least with you guys there's a hope."

"Be realistic, everybody," Daniel warned. "If it comes down to a fight it will be with people United Corporations deemed beyond rehabilitation."

"In that case, we'd better start thinking about some serious weapons," Ethan said. "Amaya, could you work on a flamethrower, please?"

The others laughed, breaking the tension. Her ingenuity had become well known. There was a new fierceness to them since the dam, Daniel realized, a new confidence and resolve. They had a goal, and now they had the unity from sharing danger. One by one they began to stand. Unity like . . . United Corporations. No! Not like that!

"Which way, mate?" Oliver asked, a little unsteady now.

"Ollie, this really isn't your fight," Daniel said. "Or Angus's. I'll understand if you Australians want to bug out and leave it to us immigrants. Really."

Angus shook his head. "You said we're all Australians now."

Daniel glanced away, trying to hide the surge of emotion welling up in him. They were following! For desperate reasons, perhaps, but behind *him,* of all people. What would harridan Lundeen think?

"This river eventually leads to the sea, of course, but because of that it's a little too obvious," Daniel judged. "They'll expect us to go that way." He pointed east, over a range of mountains. "So we'll climb. Do it the hard way."

"Sounds like a bloody Outback Adventure!" Ned quipped, shouldering a pack.

"I'd pay a year's salary for this experience any day!" Ethan chirped.

"For people who ask why they do!" Jessica warbled.

"And need their bleedin' heads examined," Peter amended.

They headed east again.

CHAPTER TWENTY-SIX

Australia had changed. The taut harshness of the Outback had given way to the soft contours of rounded hills and thick forest, cut by streams and interspersed by meadows and abandoned pasture. Old farmsteads had become frequent, the rotting and rusting houses half swallowed by eruptions of brambles. Wild cows, horses, pigs, and goats were frequently encountered. Sheep had disappeared, destroyed perhaps by roving packs of wild dogs. And now the first city was glinting on the horizon.

Ethan sat next to Daniel as they rested in the grass of an east-facing slope, studying the abandoned towers. Ragged remnants of the building windows still caught the light of the sun. Somewhere, not too far beyond, must be the sea.

"Daniel, I've decided not to go back," Ethan announced quietly as they let their eyes skip across the overgrown cityscape, searching for any sign of life in the distant ruins.

"What?"

"I've decided it would be better if you returned with Raven. Not me."

"Why?"

"I think you make a better fit."

"It's your seat, Ethan. Your crash, your transmitter, yours by length of exile. We already decided this."

"I don't *want* to go back." He shook his head, as if puzzled himself. "Not yet, anyway. I miss things, sure, but not enough that I need to get back right now. There's things I'd miss even more here."

"Amaya."

"Yes. And another thing."

"What?"

"This country. I'm falling in love with it too."

They looked out across the rolling hills, blue with haze. Even in the underpopulated areas of the United Corporations world, roads curved, power lines strutted across the contours, and the invisible matrix of property lines and survey markers reminded how the planet had been parceled out. Here, everything was at the beginning again. No one owned anything. Everything still seemed possible.

Daniel sighed. "I'd rather have *you* go and *want* to come back. Amaya would be a pretty good guarantee you wouldn't forget us here."

"No, I'm beginning to think I could make a better life here, once we get past the convicts. Not out in the desert, no. But here we have wood and water and livestock and the remnants of a lot of technology. Not to mention land, and room, and freedom. It's beautiful here. In fact, it's the most beautiful place I've ever seen. The new Australians, like Raven said."

"I've been thinking the same thing."

"There you go then."

"So now we're going to argue about who has to go instead of who has to stay?"

He laughed. "We'd get plenty of volunteers, still. I'm just saying you make the most sense of any of us."

"I can't go back, Ethan. I can't lead this group in a race to the coast and then abandon them."

"You wouldn't be abandoning them, you'd be saving them, or at least giving them a choice of which world they want to live in. And you'd have far more influence over Raven than I would: you two together could get to people in power, maybe. She'd *listen* to you."

"No she wouldn't. She doesn't want anything to do with me."

"Nonsense. She's haunted by you. You haunt each other."

"Now you sound like Amaya."

"Amaya is smarter than any of us. You know, she'd take you over me, if she could."

"That's crazy."

"No it isn't. And it doesn't worry me. Because this connection between you and Raven is as obvious as gravity and as weird as . . . love. Not simple attraction so much as entwined destiny, I think. Everyone can see it. And somebody has to go, Daniel. Somebody has to take the story back. If Raven has to be one of them, the next most obvious choice is you. Start thinking about it, please."

"She keeps defending United Corporations."

"She keeps defending herself. Trying to live with herself. She'd love you for accepting her for what she is. And helping her to become what she wants to be."

* * *

The city was called Gleneden, and it was one of the New Towns that United Corporations had erected around the globe to rationalize the distribution of its workforce and maximize the efficiency of resource extraction: in this case, minerals in the foothills of the Great Dividing Range. They approached the town on the raised deck of an expressway, the pavement littered and cracked but the underlying structure sturdy enough to last for centuries. A few abandoned vehicles sat on the roadway shoulder, their shells rusting through and their glass imploded, the fragments clustered on rotting seats like drifts of diamonds. Trees had grown up to embrace the causeway railings so the bridge deck seemed to float on the forest canopy, and birds sounded an alarm and glided ahead of them in a startled weave, announcing this unexpected reappearance of humans. More flocks exploded off the derelict towers, wheeling in consternation. Then the avian inhabitants settled down and Gleneden was quiet again. In the distance down an empty avenue, a wild dog loped away.

"What if we see bodies?" Iris worried. "I don't want to see bodies."

"I don't think there'll be anything left by this time," Daniel reassured. In truth he was unsure, and uneasy at the thought himself. He didn't want to find buildings of bones.

"I don't think we should go in at all," Raven said.

They ignored her. It was curiosity more than need. They were in too much of a hurry to thoroughly explore or salvage anything in Gleneden, but the roads they were using to get ahead of Rugard led them to the New Town and they'd all quietly wondered how much remained. Or how much had been lost.

As they entered they saw that many stores had been looted and a few buildings had been torched. Yet taken as a whole, very little had been destroyed in the panic that accompanied the plague, and it was only the obvious hollowness of the towers and emptiness of the streets that proved disquieting. Everyone was subdued, morbidly wondering what it must have been like to have a civilization—in all its complexity and anxious energy and optimistic enthusiasm—suddenly snuffed out. Careers, romances, dreams, and regrets: all suddenly gone, rendered insignificant, by the breath of bioengineered plague.

The planned and hastily erected community was a snapshot of early twenty-first-century architecture, its retro style tempered by cost-conscious design and its warmth compromised by the demands of transportation. Human-scale pedestrian malls were backed by cardictated parking lots, and tower villages were separated from each other by a moat of expressways and empty, overgrown lawns. Faded and streaked billboards and powerless neon announced sales of products that no longer existed. Directional signs pointed with names that were now obsolete. The architecture and layout were as precise as the geometrical design of a computer chip, and just as inhuman. Without people, it was just a collection of boxes. Instead of human skeletons they found automotive ones, the metallic carcasses of cars scattered now like corroding bones. The pavement had cracked and plants had rooted, spreading across the detritus of leaf litter and dust that had accumulated atop the impervious layer. There were vines and scrubby weeds and the buzz of insects, all announcing that the inhabitants of Gleneden were dead.

Daniel realized the desolation was slowly making him angry. "These people were abandoned just like we were," he said. The group had stopped at an intersection, instinctively huddling together.

"Left with no hope at all," Amaya added.

The quiet was gloomy.

Raven looked irritated, as if this journey through a dead city was designed as an affront. "They weren't abandoned, they were quarantined," she corrected. "There was no cure, so it was imperative the plague not jump to another land mass. It wasn't ruthless, it was . . . necessary." She looked around grimly at the empty office and condominium towers.

The trekkers regarded her with distaste. "And that pragmatism is what you worked to protect," Daniel said.

She bit her lip. "It's cruel to individuals. I don't deny that."

"And now you're one of those individuals. Outcast like we are."

"Yes."

"Think of the souls that were lost here, Raven. The individuals. How long would it take you to write down their names? This place is a sin. A crime."

"Don't you think I see that! But think of the souls that were saved elsewhere by this abandonment, or are saved every day by an economic and political system you think is so heartless." She wasn't going to back down. "Think of the billions that have tolerable lives because of the United Corporations order you call stultifying. This tragedy is an embarrassment, but it doesn't discredit that system, Daniel. It underlines its necessity. This shows how fragile all of human society is, how thin the civilized and technological veneer is that keeps out the darkness. *That's* what I've worked to protect."

"This wasn't caused by a breakdown of civilization! It was caused by its culmination! How can you defend the scientific arrogance that led to all these deaths?"

"How can you not admit the worth of the scientific and political expertise that has allowed more humans to live today than ever before in history?"

"Raven, this is a mausoleum," Ethan objected. "I mean, come on."

"Because of *one* accident," she amended with exasperation. "Before that it was a city, with life and laughter, created as part of a system I still feel an allegiance to. Of *course* this is wrong. All of it. All of Australia. If I get back, I'll be working to expose that. But not the rest. I can't not believe in the rest. I can't give up on the rest. I have to believe in something."

Daniel looked at her sadly.

She wouldn't tolerate his pity. "What do *you* believe in besides your wilderness nihilism, Daniel? What do *you* believe in besides running away?"

"I believe in what *feels* right," he said quietly. "I believe in what we are, instead of what we build." He glanced around. "I believe that United Corporations lost something along the way—not their soul, but *our* soul, and that we've come to a place like this to get it back. Not this city, but this continent."

"Even if that were true, not everyone can come here."

"Maybe everyone doesn't have to. Maybe it's enough to have the wild for the few who truly need it, and who bring back its spirit to the rest. None of this would be so wrong if they allowed us to get back. It's the keeping us here that's so wrong."

"Now you're going in circles, contradicting yourself, just like in the tunnels. It's your determination to get away from here that makes the lesson of Outback Adventure so *right*."

Her dogged certainty irritated him. "I'm not—"

"Enough!" Ethan held up his hand. "This is the debate we'll get to have if any of us can get past Rugard and back home. For now we have to keep moving."

"I think we should look around a bit," said Amaya. "Raven and Daniel both have a point, and here in this city we've got both worlds: the technological and the wild. Let's see if there's anything worth taking."

"Don't take!" Oliver exclaimed. "It's bad luck!"

"Just for an hour or two," Amaya said. "It won't hurt."

Some of the trekkers nodded. They were looking speculatively at the stores, wondering what might still be worn or acquired after more than three decades.

"It would be fun to go shopping again," Iris said.

"Fun not to have to pay for anything," Ned added.

"No!" Oliver said. "This is a bad place, a dangerous place. We need to move on! Too many died here, I can hear them."

"We're just looking around a bit," Amaya said. The others nodded. "Why don't you and Angus go ahead and wait for us at the end of town?"

The native Australians reluctantly agreed.

"All right, we meet back here in two hours," Daniel told them. "Be careful in these old buildings!" He looked at one of the towers. "I'm going to go up to one of these rooftops and try to see the ocean."

The office tower was fifteen stories high, modest by the standards of the city they'd come from, boxy and plain. Still, it was imposing after months in the wilderness. Daniel recognized the name at its base from the corporate subsidiaries and institutional advertising elsewhere: Coraco. Industrial mining and development. The security pod in the central lobby was deserted, of course, and its news kiosk was frozen in time. Many of the periodicals had been shredded by rodents for nests, but a few pages of the *Gleneden Paradise* revealed a yellowed November 19, 2023.

"Illness Spreads," one headline stated. "Massive Relief Effort Promised." Had that been the day of panic? The day of realization that no relief was actually coming, that there was no escape, and that the only alternative was blind flight that became as hopeless as staying? What about the few who'd survived, like Oliver and Angus? He remembered from his college days the dire prediction of what would occur if the bizarre arms races of the twentieth century had ever resulted in nuclear war: "The living would envy the dead."

He heard her bootsteps on the broken glass behind him and ignored her. He was tired of trying.

The elevator wouldn't work, of course, so he took the stairs.

Daniel climbed steadily. She followed, two or three flights behind, their echoes a kind of lonely conversation. The paint was flaking and water stains from the failing roof ran down the walls. The structure itself was solid, a web of concrete and steel. How many centuries would it last before sharing the fate of Australia's eroded mountains? Or would someone come back, implode it, and start over?

On a whim he left the stairs on the fourteenth floor. There was no thirteenth, but superstition hadn't saved them. There was a dark hallway, and then a brighter, windowed expanse of office cubicles lit by broken windows. The carpet was rotting, mold grew on the walls, and bird droppings spotted the desks, and yet nothing had really changed. Dark computer screens—this was before the cheaper opti-glasses—were the central shrine on desktops that still bore yellowed or wadded memos, cracked cups, dried pens, and posted corporate guidelines. Everything had been abandoned abruptly. Chest-high beige dividers formed a succession of cubicles. As familiar as Microcore.

This was my life, he thought.

He could hear the light breathing of Raven, resting after their climb of the stairs. She'd come in behind him. "Look familiar?"

"Too much so."

"What we're tying to get back to."

"What I came here to escape from."

"These people were happy, Daniel. They had lives."

"Yes. They did."

He walked past a supervisory desk to a window and looked out over the city. Its rational grid reminded him of the sole of Ethan's boots, a street plan that dated back to the Roman military camp. What do the animals call us, he wondered, we of the right angle and straight line? The rulers, of course. We rule, with rules, from streets and towers of ruled calibration. Until it all goes wrong. Until we bet everything on our own cleverness, and disappear so fast we leave no explanation of the fatal mistake. How many other lost civilizations had succumbed like this one?

"So do you feel nostalgic at all?" she persisted. "Do you feel the pull of society?"

"Of course. My society."

"You mean the pull of your tribe. The pull of the primitive."

He looked down. Some of his followers were coming out from stores, chortling over improbable finds of small appliances and decaying clothing. They'd try on something, or punch the buttons of a powerless machine, and then abandon them in the street. In truth, little that was useful remained.

"The pull of my new friends, Raven. Of people who need people. Not some gigantic institution like this company. Not like United Corporations."

"Daniel, an institution *is* people. That's *all* it is."

"No. When it gets too big something happens to it. Like getting too much money, or eating too much food. It can make you sick, mentally and physically. That's what's wrong with United Corporations. The more they envelop, the less they become. Until finally they start decaying and destroying, like this place."

"It was an *accident.*"

"Was it? When it grew out of the total domination they try to achieve, of both man and nature? When does an accident become inevitable?"

She closed her eyes. "When is a mistake just a mistake?"

He looked out across the city. "You could defend a tower like this, I suppose," he mused absently. "From people like Rugard, I mean. But a castle also becomes a trap. When you lock the door you have to have a way back out."

"You're speaking of us in Australia."

"Yes. Like Australia." He turned then and smiled at her, suddenly feeling lightened at this encounter with the ruins. He hadn't been sure of his own reaction and now realized he missed none of this old world. His past held no allure for him, despite all the hardships in this one. "I said I don't blame you for putting me here, Raven."

"And I forgive you for throwing away the activator. The trip has been good for me. I admit it. So why is this so difficult?"

"Why is what so difficult?"

"Us."

"Because . . . I'm in love with you without even being sure I like you. Because you won't love me."

She sighed, saying nothing.

He watched her carefully. "Ethan wants me to come back with you, you know."

"He does?"

"He wants to give up his place on the rescue plane. He's falling in love with Amaya, and falling in love with Australia. It's beautiful here, far more beautiful than home. He wants to stay and send me in his place. Send *me,* to tell the world."

"Would you?" She said it cautiously.

"I don't know." He cocked his head, as if this were the first time he'd truly considered it. "I don't know if anyone would listen, or care, even if they knew the truth. I don't know if they'd let me live to tell anyone."

"I wouldn't let them hurt you, Daniel."

"You already did, remember?"

She flushed, and he instantly regretted the retort.

"But that's not why I'm hesitating. I'm unsure because I've come to believe the planet does need a place for misfits like me. It always has."

"You understand that?"

He moved away from the window, walking back into

the cubicles. "Not in the way you do. Come here. I want to show you something."

She followed warily as if he were going to shock her with a pile of bones. But there was nothing like that, just a sheet of faded paper pinned to a cubicle wall. He pulled it off and gave it to her. "Your institution."

The paper was so aged it was hard to see. At first she thought it was something abstract, or a painted copy of the aboriginal designs they'd seen on rock walls. Then she realized it was a child's drawing. She squinted, looking closer. There were faint pencil lines on the drawing, forming two words.

For Daddy.

"It's not about economic systems, Raven. It's about the human heart."

She blinked, flustered at this offering from a little girl long dead. The child would have been a woman now, with children of her own, looking ahead to grandchildren. Except she wouldn't.

"It's about letting people be themselves. Letting people be. This child didn't deserve her fate."

"That's not fair." There was a tremble in her voice that she hated. "This city—this girl—might never have even existed without—"

"We have to go *outside* in order to get into our *inside*. Because if we don't then all that United Corporations stands for doesn't mean anything. It's just stuff, and disastrous mistakes, and little girls that end up killed by our own plagues in our mania to control our environment. We don't need an Australia as a dumping ground. We need wilderness to save us from ourselves, to remind us what's basic and simple and true."

She squeezed her eyes shut again, the drawing fluttering to the floor. "You have to look at the big picture . . ."

"That's why I don't know if I can go back with you, Raven. Because my heart doesn't know where it belongs."

She was quiet for a while and then she spoke. Her voice was small. "I'm sorry I can't say I love you. I don't know what I *am* supposed to say, to make you come back with me. I just want you to."

"Why? I challenge everything you stand for."

"To save the others."

"That's not why."

"I do care for them, you know. I do like them."

"That's not why."

She lowered her eyes. "So I'm not alone."

He stepped close, reaching out to grasp her arms. His grip was firm, his eyes intense as he looked into hers. "Then say *you'll* stay here with *me*, Raven. Say you'll give it all up, for me. Say you'll stay in Australia. Say that and maybe it won't matter where *I* am, so long as I'm with you." And then he bent to kiss her.

She stiffened again, but only for a moment. Then she was kissing him back this time, her lips open, her arms coming around him, her body pressing and then moving against his. He held her roughly, hungrily, his hands roaming to caress.

"I *do* love you, dammit," she admitted fiercely when she broke briefly away. "You know I do! I love all the mixed-up craziness that's in you, all the longing, all the desire. That's been the problem from the beginning!"

"Then it shouldn't matter where we are, should it?"

"No." She sighed and kissed him again. "It shouldn't."

He took her hand and led her back to the musty stairs.

Instead of descending, they climbed upward. It took two kicks to break open the door to the roof. Birds flew up, crying, but the couple found a corner away from their nests that was clean and warm, bleached deck boards providing a platform above the vinyl roofing. She knelt with him beside her, looking east. "I wonder when we'll see the ocean."

He reached over her shoulders from behind and began undressing her, watching the garments slide off her brown shoulders and mounding around the swell of her hips. Her nipples were hard, her belly trembling, and he caressed her torso as he kissed her, pulling the luxuriant fall of her dark hair aside to bare her neck. "Say you'll live with me in Australia," he murmured. "Say you'll trade that world for this one."

And with a moan she pulled him down on top of her, making a bed of their clothes on the wooden slats of the deck and promising nothing—except, that for this moment, they were one.

CHAPTER TWENTY-SEVEN

Ico Washington believed he knew what Exodus Port really was.

He hadn't found a *geographic* Exodus, of course. There was no bay on Australia's eastern coast that harbored an exit from this continental hell, of that he was sure. But there *was* a way to get back, Ico thought, a way that depended on exercising the mind more than the legs. You had to find a key to the lock, the answer to the riddle: that was the test of Outback Adventure. A test of wits! And in his case the answer was the transmitter. Whoever successfully signaled *deserved* to get back, and whoever did not *deserved* permanent exile. Every man for himself! Survival of the fittest! The orange-speckled cube that he'd safeguarded across half of Australia, and the battered transmitter that Raven had stolen, were—in combination—Exodus Port! With them he could not just escape, but return to the world of United Corporations a designated winner. Unless Raven got out from under the Cone and signaled first.

Right now Ico was in a world of losers. A dust-shrouded column of the crude, stupid, stinking, and dull. Rugard's Expedition of Recovery seemed to have developed some kind of perverse gravity, drawing in the desperate and cruel to make a small army, despite periodic desertions from its less-than-reliable ranks. People liked to belong to a group, Ico supposed. They liked being led. Plus, the vaguely understood promise of possible escape fired the growing mob like a promise of treasure. None knew, of course, that there was no room on a rescue craft for anyone but Rugard and himself. They'd realize that when the pair were gone.

Ico's conscience was not bothered by this planned abandonment because he'd come to loathe his allies. Familiarity had given him time to despise their tasteless jokes and vile nicknames and adolescent gang mentality. They *deserved* to be forgotten! They'd called him Psycho! And yet *he* was the only one who had brought them this far, he and the map that everyone had laughed at from the beginning.

Well, he'd leave them soon. Ico would win, he told himself, because unlike the others who were marooned, he'd been thinking from the beginning. *That,* he was convinced, was what United Corporations was secretly looking for. While the others had been drugged to sleep, he'd fought to stay awake. While the others had sheepishly agreed to geographic ignorance, he'd been out buying a black market map. Admittedly the map was crude and somewhat inaccurate. It showed highways that didn't exist, and omitted some that did. In main, however, it was a decent redraw—maybe from memory—of an Australia that had been real. Ico was convinced of this now because the map had been right too many times. Now, after the report of the confusion at the dam, the main army should meet the transmitter thieves on the road. Maybe in this abandoned city ahead in the foothills. The Expedition could see its towers.

Information was the edge, always the edge. Ico had it.

He looked back along the line of trudging men, swaying camels, and captured horses, the Warden riding commandingly on one steed liberated from an owner whose foolish resistance had gotten him killed. There were clusters of women too, some as heavily armed and nasty as the males and others the terrified and subdued inductees to Rugard's Cohort of Joy. A mob united by greed and fear. But they were following *him.* And if his guess was right, they'd already outflanked the fugitives and now, heading back west, they would shortly intercept them. It was *possible* he was wrong, of course, but Ico trusted his own instincts. Dyson had been bullheaded about direction from the very beginning: east, east, east. Dyson would think he could still outrun Rugard's big group. But then Dyson thought the map was useless, that Ico would tolerate being left behind, and that the bitch he was smitten with could be trusted. Dyson was a smug, immature, naive nitwit who deserved to be left behind. He *belonged* here.

Ico couldn't wait, from the door of an aircraft, to wave goodbye.

It was a scream which jerked Daniel awake, a wail of fear that penetrated the afternoon slumber he'd fallen into after satiation with Raven. He jerked up guiltily, momentarily disoriented. There were shouts of alarm in the plaza below.

He crawled to the edge of the parapet surrounding the flat roof. There was a confused knot of people and two horsemen galloping wildly away, one swaying unsteadily.

as if injured. There'd been some kind of brief fight, Iris weeping. He watched the mounted scouts retreat toward a stream of people coming into the outskirts of the city just two miles away down the main avenue, a swarm of convicts trotting toward them with excited purpose, yipping and crowing like animals. His heart sank. They'd been found, and not just found, but likely trapped.

He woke Raven and they hastily began to dress.

"Daniel! Where are you!" Amaya's voice.

"Just a minute!"

They both were half covered when Amaya stepped out onto the tower roof, jerking to an abrupt halt when she saw them. Then she blinked and composed herself.

"Thank God I found you. They surprised Iris and the men just barely saved her. Everyone's coming into the lobby."

"Rugard?"

"I think so, with a small army. A hundred people or more. Should we run?"

"Too late for that, especially if they have horses." Daniel thought about the tower. "Better to fight them here, perhaps, than in the open." He looked down to the plaza, one hundred and fifty feet below. "Keep everyone out of sight. I'll be right down."

She disappeared.

Raven touched his sleeve. "Daniel, if it doesn't matter where we are—you and me, I mean—maybe I should just give it up. Surrender the transmitter to Rugard."

He smiled at that, leaning to kiss her. "We can't make that decision by ourselves. Because it's more than just us now." He stood. "You'd better go get the machine and see if it works yet. This may be our last chance to get back."

She looked over the parapet at the approaching convicts and nodded gloomily.

Down in the lobby, Daniel assessed his group. Their look was of defiance. They were tired of being marooned, tricked, tracked, and preyed upon. Tired of being pushed around. That was good. There was a hard core to these people now, a determination to hang on to the hope they'd earned. He could rely on that.

"Okay," he began. "Is everyone here?"

"Even Iris," Ned said. His shoulder had almost healed but now his forehead had a new raw cut. From the horse scouts, Daniel assumed. "Our shopper."

She'd calmed from her fright. "The best prices I'd ever seen and I dropped it all."

The others laughed.

"It was bad luck to linger here," Angus reminded. He'd come back when he saw Rugard's army, and now he was trapped with them.

That made them quiet.

"Where's Oliver?"

"Staying away."

Daniel took a breath. "Okay. What's done is done. We tried to outrun them but that didn't work. It doesn't look like we can run through them, either; there's too many. What they want is the transmitter. What they *want* is to take away our chance to get back. So, we give up. Or, we fight so hard that *they* give up."

"You've seen this Warden," Peter said quietly. "What are our chances?"

"As bankable as a lottery ticket. As unanswerable as a prayer. They're tough, wild, nasty people." He grinned fiercely. "But so are we, now."

"Damn straight," Ethan said.

"The only ones who can decide if it's time to fight, however, are you. It depends on how badly you want to get back. How badly you want the outside world to know what happened to you. How willing you are to stay here."

"We decided this at the river, Daniel," Jessica replied. "It's not just getting back. It's what's *right*, not just for us but everyone. It's about contacting the cyber underground and the opposition and exposing this place in order to shut it down. It's about not just our little group, but every person they put in Australia. We ran away to come here. We've all run away our whole lives. We're *still* running. But Outback Adventure suggested we'd find our why if we came here. This is mine, I think. Not to get back, but to make a stand for something. It's not right for those convicts to steal our hope. To steal *everyone's* hope. I say we fight for that. For hope."

The others nodded. There was a grim resolve in their eyes. A quickening of pulse. A tensing of muscle.

"Can we beat them?" asked Peter.

Daniel stuck his hands in his pockets and glanced upward at the lobby ceiling. "Well, we've got the high ground. We can barricade the lobby and throw things down from above. This building will work as a fort, or a castle. If we hurt them enough, maybe they'll go away. If we can talk to them, we can tell them the truth: that Raven is the one allowed to get back."

"But can we do that?" Peter persisted.

He pulled out a figure from his pocket. "My good luck charm tells me we can."

"What the devil is that?"

"Gordo Firecracker, nemesis of evil," Amaya recalled dryly. "The worst charm you've ever seen. He's been carrying that doll all the way across Australia."

"Gordo is *not* a doll," Daniel said with mock tartness, holding it up so others could see. "He's an *action figure*. Not to mention my field marshal and chief strategist."

They laughed again.

"Great," Peter said. "And what does Gordo suggest we do?"

"Fortify for attack. Prepare for negotiation. And . . ." He looked thoughtful.

"Pray for a miracle?" Peter suggested.

"Build a catapult."

So the fugitives had run to ground in the first city they came to! After all the fancy talk of wilderness nirvana, they'd taken instinctive refuge in a damn skyscraper!

Ico snickered at the irony of it.

The Expedition of Recovery might have missed the fugitives entirely if they'd had the sense to hide in this civic labyrinth, but instead they'd gone looting for all the goods they professed to disdain. One of their fool women had been spotted scurrying down a side street, her arms loaded with useless jewelry. When the scouts had tried to ride her down the fugitives had boiled out of the Coraco Building like a disturbed hive, Rugard's men barely galloping off with their lives. But the incident had revealed the thieves' location and number, allowing the convicts to swiftly surround the base of the tower. Ico could see the baubles now, scattered on the plaza as uselessly as coins in a fountain.

The fugitives, visible through the broken windows, were working desperately to prepare. The lobby had been barricaded and it wouldn't be easy to get to them, the convicts knew. The Warden circuited the office tower thoughtfully and then walked out into the plaza, alone. Arrogant, weaponless.

Both sides watched him, the fugitives crouched by the windows.

He took a breath. "I . . . want . . . *Raven!*" he suddenly roared. His voice echoed away among the old towers. "Where *is* the bitch? She *has* something of mine!" The demand seemed to float, hanging in the air.

Daniel stood up in full view. "She can't come to the door right now!"

Men on both sides laughed. Rugard jerked around and his side quieted.

He turned back. "Your run is over, Dyson! You're surrounded, outnumbered, and out of options! You can't get back now without us!"

"And your men can't get back at all! Have you told your rabble there's no *room* on the rescue craft for anyone but you, Rugard? Have you told them that you've led them a thousand miles and are risking their lives to save only your own skin?"

He wheeled around to face his troops. "That's a lie!"

"No it isn't!" Daniel shouted.

"It's a lie like the lies United Corporations has told us all our lives!" Rugard roared. "Look at him! He's built a whole gang out of his promise to get people back, and they're laughing at us right now! He's sucked in followers with the promise that *they* can have the seats that by rights go to you!"

The convicts growled like the thunder from an approaching storm.

"No! That's not true . . ."

"He's a thief who's trying to keep you here like the others of his kind back home!"

The convicts roared, angry now, and a drumming started. They beat on pavement, they beat on stone, and they beat on rotting benches, rusting siding, and corrugated doors. Rugard strode back and forth in front of them, jerking his arms up in rhythm. Boom. Boom. Boom. As regular as a machine, as ominous as an approaching footfall. There was no complexity to it. Just a steady, solemn, ceaseless pounding to drive home their menace. It was a music of warning, a drumming to summon courage and infect a prey with fear. They'd found it! The key, perhaps, to getting back.

The sound rolled up to the windows where Daniel's followers worked more furiously, stockpiling anything they could pry loose to hurl down on their besiegers. It looked like a battle.

"The one advantage we have is height," Daniel kept lecturing, climbing from one floor to another. "I want them to think this tower is coming down on them if they try to rush us. I want an avalanche of furniture. A blizzard of debris."

I sound like a demented Napoleon, he thought wryly. He stopped to see what Amaya was doing. "You couldn't whip up another batch of gunpowder, could you?"

"Probably something worse if I'd time to thoroughly explore," she replied. "There might even be modern explosives somewhere, if we looked: this was a mining town. But we didn't get time for that so all we can do is strip this building." She began to point. "The rubber bumpers on some of the table furniture are being stripped off and fashioned into slingshots. For ammunition we can pull nails and screws out of the walls. There's metal trim with enough flex to pull back for makeshift bows, rods from shades already notched for scraps of glass to make arrows, and sprinkler pipe to use as spears. Not to mention tons of stuff to simply heave out of the windows."

"Your talents are wasted, Amaya. You belong in an arms race."

"I want to get rid of these people so we don't have to have arms races." She looked past him through the window to the green hills beyond the city's buildings. "It's so beautiful here, Daniel. Why infest it with criminals?"

"It must have seemed like an easy solution."

"If they ever came here—if they ever got out of their boardrooms and visited this place they've made—they'd see their mistake." She meant the executives of United Corporations.

"They won't. And I'm not sure they didn't intend this. Everyone at each other's throats. As a lesson for us, and a solution for them."

She looked at him softly. "It's good then that you and Raven . . ."

"Yes." He smiled sheepishly. "Things might have been different between us, you know, if she'd gone."

"If you'd let her go."

He nodded. "Right. You know, I love her, but I still don't know about her, Amaya. I still don't know her heart."

"I do. She's changed."

The drumming went on for an hour. The sound was enough to unnerve, if you let it, but they wouldn't.

"Christ, they're out of tune," Ethan complained, covering his ears.

"Musically impaired," Amaya added.

The convicts drummed and shook and reached inside themselves for the savagery the modern world had tried to cram beneath their surface, bringing it out again in snarls and wild howls so that they'd have the courage to charge for what they wanted. The coordination of the drumming brought them together, focused on the building and transmitter within. Then Rugard lifted his arm and the convicts fell raggedly into silence.

"Listen to me!" he shouted to his followers. "You want to get back? The way back is in that building! You want to get out of prison! It's through those people up there, the kind of people who put you *into* prison in the first place! Up there is the only way!"

"Don't listen to him!" Daniel tried again from the third story. "You can't get—"

"The way back is through *him!*"

The convicts roared. And as the Warden swung his arm the ragged army surged forward in the afternoon sunshine, a Stone Age charge of spear and club and sling and rock as timeless as humanity. Clan against tribe. Ego against ego. Pounding blood and dry-mouthed excitement.

Instinct had come to Eden.

CHAPTER TWENTY-EIGHT

Rugard had a mob, not an army. He had a goal, not a strategy. His aim was simply the transmitter. The men and women who surged toward the base of the office tower came in a ragged yelling line like a noose being tightened on a condemned neck, but it was a garrote that was frayed. Some assailants lagged back, hoping their comrades would do the hard fighting. Others, faced mostly with blank concrete on three sides of the first two floors, ran around to congregate at the lobby door.

The windows above erupted.

The defenders threw everything they had at their attackers. Desks came hurtling down like meteors. Lengths of pipe whistled down like spears. Light fixtures plummeted, porcelain sinks that had been ripped loose from abandoned lavatories exploded on the pavement, and bits of metal were fired from Amaya's makeshift slingshots and bows. Screams and panic erupted among the convicts. Some were struck down, many fell back in confusion, and a few of the boldest ran the gauntlet to hack their way through the initial barricade and into the lobby.

Ethan met them with half a dozen adventurers in a wild counterattack, swinging staves, makeshift swords, and hardened wooden spears. Cut off from reinforcement by the rain of debris from above, the convicts recoiled. Beyond their opponents was the stairwell with yet another barricade. Who knew how many defenders were behind that?

Wrench dodged a spear thrust, clubbed one of the adventurers aside, and then saw the convict on his right howl and go down with an arrow. Hellfire! It was like the dam, a space so narrow that numbers didn't count.

"We've seen enough!" he shouted, turning to retreat. The others followed him out while dragging their wounded, two staggering as they were hit by still more hurled pieces from the building. Fired bolts and nails whizzed around their ears, bouncing off the pavement and then skittering away. One retreating attacker slipped on the debris littering the plaza and sprawled, giving those above enough time to hit him with a rain of junk. He scrabbled away.

It was the same quick dumb rush they'd tried in the canyon at Erehwon, Wrench thought. Four attackers were left behind, either unconscious or dead. A dozen were hurt.

Back across the plaza, the leaders clustered under a nearby overhang.

"Well, that didn't work," Ico observed.

"Shut up." Rugard looked at the offending office tower with fury. They could hear defiant, derisive cheers from the transmitter thieves within.

"To get at them we've got to go through a bottleneck,"

Wrench described. "We'll win eventually, but not without a lot of blood."

"How many are there?" Rugard asked.

"Not that many, I think, judging from what we saw at the dam. Less than twenty. But if we fight them in the stairwells, going uphill, they have all the advantage."

"So if we could spread them out . . ."

"But how?"

"I've got an idea," Ico said.

There was a new hammering, but not rhythmic this time. Rugard's troops were building something, and it didn't take long to figure out what it was. Daniel hastened to build his own weapon in defense.

The torsion catapult of the ancient world was a sophisticated device, relying on twisted rope or sinew for the energy to repeatedly fling a projectile at an enemy. While such a machine was quick to aim and fire, Daniel's beleaguered fugitives didn't have the time to build artillery so complex. Simpler was a catapult that relied on a simple counterweight: a trebuchet. It actually had two buckets, one on either end of a beam of wood that pivoted on an axle. One bucket held the missile, and the other a counterweight that was hoisted into the sky. When fired, the counterweight dropped, the other end of the beam snapped up, and the payload was launched skyward. Gravity provided the energy.

Daniel's trebuchet was mounted on the roof. Two tripods that had supported radio masts, unbolted from their bases so they could be moved to allow the machine to pivot, held the pipe used as the catapult axle four meters above the ground. This axle threaded through an unbolted steel beam that became the trebuchet arm. A hole was hacked in the roof to a central shaft where a dusty, powerless elevator was tied to one end of the trebuchet arm with its rusting cables. This box could be dropped as the counterweight. Amaya and Ethan contributed ideas about some simple gearing rigged to ratchet the elevator up a floor for each firing. Upon release it would plummet the same distance before automatically braking, hurtling the bucketed missile.

"You could throw an electric car with this thing," Ethan promised, black from grease he had collected from frozen machinery and redistributed on their new one. With a throwing beam six meters long, the trebuchet looked formidable.

"Or a year's supply of Microcore company directives," Daniel added. "But we've got to throw what we have. Are they bringing up some desks?"

"Cursing your name in vain even as we speak." Metal desks from the floor below were being laboriously carried up to the roof and dumped there as ammunition: gigantic catapult balls. "Even if it doesn't hit anyone, it should scare the hell out of them."

"Amaya's shotgun payload might prove more effective," Daniel said. She'd heaped a small mountain of mugs and bottles, dismounted pencil sharpeners, dead modems, frayed manuals, and broken lamps to spray at any attackers.

"Well, they're going to try to spread us, to bring their superior numbers to bear. We'll have four on the roof here to fire this thing, and the rest down below again to guard the entrance. If they get a foothold in the building, it's over."

"Which they will if this doesn't work," Ethan said.

"I built another one once," Daniel said. "It sort of

worked." Centuries ago, he thought, when his only task was winning the attentions of Mona Pietri.

"Sort of?"

"The only thing wrong was that it missed."

The convicts came again at night, their advance marked by torchlight and bonfires lit in the corners of the plaza. The drumming now marked time to the stately advance of what Ico had suggested and Rugard had ordered his army to build: a siege tower.

Inspired by the towers used to assault castle walls, this one used as its foundation the bottom frame of four automobiles, two side by side in the front and two in the rear to create a square platform with sixteen rusting steel wheels, stripped of their flattened rubber. An aluminum electrical transmission tower, shorn of its arms, had been lashed to this foundation using some dead electrical cable, producing a tower one hundred feet high. Car hoods and trunk lids had been bolted to it like scales, giving it a protective covering of light armor on three sides. At the top was the flatbed of a light truck, mounted on rails, that could be slid forward when the tower reached Daniel's office building. If the tower worked as planned, attacking convicts would swarm up ladders to its summit and charge across the flatbed, smashing through the windows of the ninth floor at the same time another group stormed the lobby. The creaking contraption would give the convicts attacking on the ground some cover by blocking fire from the plaza wall of windows.

"We've advanced from the Stone Age to the Medieval in half a day," Ethan marveled. "What happens in the next round? A nuclear exchange?"

"Let's get through this round first," said Daniel. "Can you hold the lobby again?"

"If you can keep that moving junkyard away."

A skirmishing fire from the office tower windows and the surrounding streets began immediately, the convicts trying to provide cover for their approaching siege engine with sling-launched rocks. The women under Amaya replied with slingshots and bows. It was impossible to be accurate in the darkness but the whiz and swap of stone and bolt and arrow created a weird pinging music, some of the shots bouncing off the armor of the approaching siege tower with a punctuating clang. Those on both sides jerked in apprehension at the sound. One of the convicts howled as an arrow struck home, and a woman in the offices screamed as a rock broke her hand.

"Fire!" Daniel shouted. With no powder to ignite the word didn't really fit a catapult, he found himself thinking randomly: ancient artillery captains must have yelled something more appropriate to their technology such as "shoot," or "throw." No matter, his trebuchet operators knew exactly what he meant. A ratchet gear was released, the old, now powerless elevator made a brief plunge down its shaft, and the steel beam sprang forward. With ponderous grace a metal desk was launched into flight with a whoosh, arcing toward the approaching siege tower.

It missed to the right by twenty feet, plunging down to explode into shrapnel, its panels clattering as they bounced in all directions. The impact got the convicts to jerk to a startled halt but otherwise didn't hurt a thing.

"What the hell was *that?*" one of them cried.

"They're trying to hit us!" Rugard's voice roared. "Hurry, hurry! Get against the building and they can't reach us!" The convicts leaned against the rear of the tower platform again and it began lumbering forward once more, groaning and swaying. Some convicts darted forward to pull debris out of its way. At the tower's top, a couple of the Warden's men began trying to lob stones at Daniel's trebuchet squad on the roof of the office tower.

The trebuchet had been reloaded. "Release!" Daniel cried this time.

"What?" his befuddled crew asked.

"I mean fire. Fire, fire!"

"Oh."

Another desk was hurled into the night, again arcing down at the approaching tower. This time it clipped the contraption with a loud bang, jerking the top so violently that the convicts there were nearly thrown off. One of the protective auto hoods was torn away and came down with the desk. The tower stopped again.

"No, no!" Rugard shouted. "Go faster! Get in under their reach!"

His men were hesitating. The source of these meteoric desks was unknown and the escalating war was beginning to rattle them. They wanted the transmitter, but not at the cost of their lives.

"Move! Move if you want to live! If you don't move, by God *I'll* kill you!"

The tower had just started trundling forward again when it was hit broadside, a desk hitting it like a gong and making the entire structure reverberate. Then the missile slid harmlessly down the steel scales, crashing onto the pavement below. Two men ran forward and dragged it out of the way before the defenders could hit them with missiles.

"They can't break it!" Rugard roared. "It's stronger than their fire! Now, now, move across and let's end this thing!"

Up on the roof of the office tower, Daniel's men were desperate. "That was our best shot," Peter said grimly. "The thing hardly even rocked. What are we going to do?"

Daniel looked wildly around. "We need something heavier." He pointed. "That rusted-out air-conditioning unit, maybe!"

Peter looked dubious. "That elephant? I don't know if the elevator is heavy enough to counterweight it."

"It might be if we climb onto the elevator!"

"Are you crazy! The cable might snap!"

"Then we'll use the automatic brakes! Come on, help me pry this sucker loose!"

The air conditioner was not much bigger than a hurled desk, but twice as heavy. They rolled it on the trebuchet arm and balanced it between holding prongs. It seemed too ponderous to throw. Daniel ran to the lip of the building. The siege tower was rolling closer.

What other chance did they have?

"Okay, we've got one shot at this thing!" He jumped onto the top of the elevator. "Peter, you aim and fire!"

The others looked down the elevator well dubiously at where he was standing, eight feet below them. A loose steel cable led from the elevator to the trebuchet arm. "Come on, get down here with me! We need your weight!"

They jumped aboard. Peter had disappeared. Then they heard his voice: "Launch!" With the jerk of a lever the elevator began to fall. The cable went taut, the counterweight arm came down, and the ponderously heavy air-conditioning unit soared up.

Then there was a jerk, a bang, and the counterweight elevator cable snapped. Instead of stopping after a one-floor drop, the box with three men on top started plunging toward the basement of the building.

"Brakes!" one of them screeched.

The emergency brakes had been pried open with a steel bar. Now Daniel lunged at it. "I can't get the damn bar out!" he shouted.

The elevator was accelerating. Angus lurched over, grabbed, and jerked. Suddenly the bar was out, whipping so violently that it slapped them against the concrete of the elevator shaft and scraping them as they tumbled, falling with the box. Then the brakes designed to halt such falls snapped outward in a shower of sparks. There was a long howl of metal. Then the elevator abruptly stopped, rocking slightly.

The three men were in a stunned heap on the elevator roof. "I hear cheering," Angus grunted.

"Which side?" Daniel gasped.

"We stopped near a door." The third man, named Royce, pointed. They used the brake bar to lever it open and crawled onto the sixth floor, then ran to the window.

The siege tower was gone.

No, not gone, but toppled, broken, its transmission tower framework crumpled and the hurled air-conditioning unit wedged where it had creased the tower in two. The women, three floors below, were cheering.

The men ran down to them. "What happened?"

"You hit them dead center and it went over like a tree," Amaya reported excitedly. "They ran like cockroaches from light. Some are pretty badly hurt and I think the fight went out of them. They'd started to rush the lobby but ran back out!"

"Casualties?"

"Henry's dead and three more are seriously wounded. Almost everyone is a little banged up, and everyone's shaken. The convicts are hurting even worse."

Peter came down. "The trebuchet arm broke when we fired," he reported. "Maybe we can repair it but we've lost our counterweight, and we have to drag up more ammunition."

"We're also running low on things to throw or shoot," Amaya added quietly.

Daniel nodded. "Where's Raven?"

"Here." She came out of the shadows. She was bruised, and a hand was wrapped in a bloody bandage. "I keep trying the transmitter, but it's still jammed. We're awfully close to the ocean, Daniel. Maybe the Cone doesn't have an edge, at least not here. Maybe the coastline extends farther east elsewhere. I'm sorry, but I'm afraid the only way it's going to work is to get back the activator."

"You mean make a deal?"

"I mean we may be fighting to save something I can't promise will work."

He regarded them somberly. "Do we give up?"

Then they heard Rugard's voice, calling ftom the plaza.

"Dyson! You in there? You still alive, you son of a bitch?"

What a balls-up, blood-spattered, rubble-strewn, humiliating nightmare of a mess! Damnation! Rugard Sloan had felt like a goddamn Genghis Khan when he came up with his siege tower idea, straight out of old movies—

well, it was the weasel's idea, but same thing—and then
that bitch and her thief companion had started spitting
furniture at him like they'd packed an atomic cannon!
Where the hell had *that* come from? Stuff flying off the
roof like it was being put into orbit! The hastily erected
tower had toppled, he had a dozen people dead or seriously wounded, two dozen more crying about minor injuries, and a whole army that was thoroughly spooked.
Rugard wasn't certain a single convict would follow him
if he led another charge across the plaza. The Warden was
desperate, as desperate as he'd ever been in his life. He
just hoped the fugitives he'd trapped were desperate too.

"Dyson! You too hurt to answer?" He kept edging farther out into the plaza, keeping a wary eye for a sudden
rock or bolt.

If *he* couldn't get in, Rugard reasoned, *they* still
couldn't get out. That was his key. He could starve them,
or maybe smoke them: start a fire at the base that might
choke them where they stood. But maybe there was an
easier way: a way he should have tried from the beginning.

"Dyson, you come out where I can see you! You come
out and talk like a man!"

"You coming to surrender?"

Rugard looked up. The voice had floated defiantly
again from that third-floor window and he could see
Dyson's head up there now, a pale balloon in the firelight
from the rim of the plaza. He'd love to put an arrow or a
rock in the middle of it, but that wouldn't do what he
wanted to do.

"I'm coming to gut you all like pigs!" the Warden
replied, hoping his bluster masked his frustration. "I'm
coming to put your heads on poles! I'm coming to set a

fire that'll roast you all like hamburger! Unless you listen to reason!"

It was quiet for a moment as they digested this. Then, "We're not giving you the transmitter, Rugard! We've beaten the best you can do and we'll beat you again! Let us go! Someday, maybe *all* of us will get back."

Rugard hesitated. The problem was, Dyson didn't sound scared enough. Not that he doubted he could beat him if they came to grips with each other, but he wanted more *fear*. That's when he knew he had his opponents, when they mentally gave up. There was a disquieting chance that this guy had a martyr complex, and that gave Rugard pause. The truth was, *any* man could be dangerous if he was unafraid to die. Yet what choice did the Warden have? The others wouldn't follow him much longer.

"I'm not a man of violence, Dyson!" he now yelled. "I'm just a man of order. Of organization! I didn't want it to come to this! I just want what's rightfully mine! So I say we end this before any others get hurt. You and me! One on one!"

"What?" Dyson's voice was quieter now.

"You heard me! You got the guts to back up your big mouth? You willing to fight for all these people you led into a trap? I'll fight you for the transmitter alone. At dawn! I win, I take it back! You win, we let you go!"

The face disappeared from the window. Somebody had pulled at him. Raven, it looked like. She knew what a mean sonofabitch the Warden could be. And Dyson was weak for her. He was afraid she'd talk him out of it.

"You and me, Dyson, to the death!" he called. "Your choice of weapons! Then it's over for everyone! You man enough to face me alone? You man enough to come away from that woman of yours?"

Nothing. Silence. If nothing else his challenge was winning his own followers back, he felt. Rugard wasn't asking them to do what he wouldn't do. Rugard was going to fight for it himself.

"Dyson!" He was getting impatient. "You willing to end this thing?"

Then the head came back. "No!" Daniel shouted. It echoed over the plaza. "You win, you get the transmitter. *I* win, we get the activator and free passage. That way, *somebody* gets back. And the bloodshed stops."

Rugard was taken aback a bit. Give the fugitives the activator? Gamble everything? He didn't like the strength of Dyson's voice.

"You and me at dawn, Rugard!" Daniel continued, the challenge coming down defiantly, almost mocking. "Spears! Winner gets the other's machine, and free passage! Winner takes all!"

Damn him. The Warden was quiet, absorbing his surprise at the acceptance. They must be desperate because the transmitter still didn't work. And yet that just drew them into his trap, didn't it? The fight was still his way out, his key to escape. Because Rugard Sloan could take a pissant like Dyson any day. He could chew up little men like that with hardly a breath, his domination complete. And then leave all these cretins behind.

"All right then." He said it absently, almost to himself. Then he raised his voice. "All *right* then! You be ready, boy! Dawn! To the death!" He swaggered as he left the plaza, a swagger for both Dyson and his own men. He knew he could take him, take him easily.

But he'd have to be careful. Rugard glanced back. Men without hope were dangerous.

Ethan shook Daniel awake. Light was filtering through the broken windows of the battered tower. Dawn was near.

Surprising himself, Daniel hadn't brooded on his decision but slept. Slept well: the battle had left him exhausted. He'd pushed aside Raven's fear before it became his own. Now it was almost morning. His last day in Australia if he won the activator, signaled for help, and left with Raven.

Or his last morning ever.

"It's time, mate." Ethan stood back to let him get up.

"You're starting to sound like Oliver, you damn Australian."

Ethan smiled. "Oliver came back last night you know, after you were asleep. Through some tunnel under the city, like a little mole. Pretty shaken when he got here. I don't think he's used to what big groups of people do to each other."

"I'm not used to it either."

"Do you want some breakfast?" It was Amaya.

"No, I'm not hungry." The statement made him chuckle at a memory.

"What?" she asked, looking at him strangely.

"Outback Adventure's screening lady. She asked me what I'd want for my last meal."

She looked sad. "And what did you say?"

"That I wouldn't have an appetite."

He walked to the window. It was light enough that he could see the tired convicts sleeping around the edges of the plaza, keeping them penned. He didn't see Rugard.

It will all be over in fifteen seconds, one way or another, a trainer had said. He turned back. "I need a good spear."

"I'll find one," said Ethan.

"And I'd like to say goodbye to Raven."

"I'll find her," Amaya said.

He sat by the window, still waking up, enjoying the growing pink splendor of the dawn in the direction of the sea. Such a lovely place, Australia. He should be concentrating on tactics—*It wouldn't hurt to know how to run,* the instructor had told him—but his mind was so crowded with memories it was impossible to think about the fight. Microcore, the tunnels, the clearing where he'd awakened in Australia, the wrecked transport, the climb up the monolith. It seemed like a dream.

That was the way to go, he thought. In a dream.

Ethan came back with a spear and Daniel hefted it for balance. They'd fitted an old knife on the end and it was dark with blood, which was good. Give Rugard something to think about.

"You okay?" Ethan asked.

"I'm okay."

There were steps on the concrete stairs and he turned to greet Raven. Instead it was Amaya, looking worried.

"Raven's gone," she said.

"What?"

"I looked all through the tower and she isn't here. Neither is Oliver. She's gone, with all her gear."

"With her gear?" he looked at her dumbly, not comprehending. "Gone?"

She nodded. "Gone. With the transmitter."

CHAPTER TWENTY-NINE

Ico Washington felt vindicated as he clung awkwardly to a pony and rode hastily eastward away from Gleneden with Rugard and Raven. He'd been right! Right about the enigmatic double-talk of Outback Adventure. Right about his map. And right about Raven DeCarlo. In the end she'd deserted her friends and betrayed her lover in her desperation to get back to civilization. She'd cut a deal with the enemy! Ico didn't despise her for it, he respected her. It was the logical thing to do. But it also confirmed his view of human nature. People are what they are, not what they pretend to be.

Now they were trying to put as much distance between themselves and the derelict city as possible, before signaling for rescue and escape.

Raven had come to Ico out of some sewer in the city, accompanied by a strange, smelly Australian who'd delivered her and then melted away in that deepest darkness before dawn. "The bad people need to stop," the man she'd called Oliver had kept muttering. Raven had come whispering that she was going to take him, Ico Washington, home. Then she had him quietly summon Rugard and they met in the empty showroom of an abandoned auto dealership. There she professed that she'd come to save the life of the suicidal Dyson because of his lunatic agreement to a duel. Too vain, still, to admit she wanted to save her own skin like anyone else. "If you and I and Ico run with the transmitter, there's nothing and nobody for them to fight about any longer," she explained.

Rugard was suspicious. "What's to prevent me from slitting your throat and taking that transmitter right now?"

"The hover won't put down unless they see me. They won't wait unless I walk to the door. They'd *shoot* at you as soon as rescue you. Ask Ico if you don't believe me."

Rugard looked at Ico.

"That's the story she's been telling from the first," Ico conceded. "Who knows if it's the truth?"

"So let's cut a deal," Raven said fiercely. "I need your activator. We're almost to the coast and the transmitter still doesn't work."

"We were wrong about the Cone?" Ico asked.

"I don't know. I don't think so, if your pilot talked about walking here. But maybe we'd have to find a point where the coast extends farther eastward. So right now I need the activator, and you need me to call in the aircraft."

Rugard scowled. "You promise to get me on board?"

"I promise."

"Wait a minute," Ico protested. "Back at Erehwon you said there was only room for two on a rescue craft. I count three of us."

"I can count," she replied impatiently. "Rugard can overpower the co-pilot. We leave that aviator here, take his place, and have the two rear seats as well. Then the pilot flies us to wherever you two want to go."

"But why take the runt along?" Rugard asked dubiously.

"Because I *got* you here!"

Raven ignored him. "We both need him to help us watch each other," she told Rugard. "I don't trust you."

The Warden spat. "I don't trust you, either."

"And neither of us trust him. This keeps us all honest."

The Warden smiled. "Hey. I'm the first honest man you ever met."

So now they rode, awkwardly trotting on their unaccustomed transport, taking three horses Rugard's army had gathered along the way. The Warden had distributed the few horses to reward whichever men held his favor at the moment, like parceling out women or sharing the best food or intervening in a quarrel. It maintained his hold over the convicts. The man had a base political craftiness to him, Ico admitted. When he vanished his mob would disintegrate like an unstable star.

Raven was crafty as well, or at least had a core of hard practicality. Ico looked over at her beauty, cold and remote when directed at him. He didn't like her, never had. But he admired her realism. He saw now what she'd been trying to protect: order, against anarchy. She'd always done what she had to do, just as his own alliance with Rugard had been necessary: both had acted in order to get back. They were no different, morally speaking. *Somebody* had to get back, if there was to be any hope for the others. Not everybody *could* get back. So it came down to the most logical people. Her, the United Corporations minion. He, the only one who had really seen things clearly. And Rugard . . . Rugard to cow the pilot into taking them where they needed to go.

It should have been this way from the very beginning.

Ico didn't feel pity for the ones being left behind. After spending so much enforced time with them, he wasn't at all sure United Corporations didn't have the right idea about Australia. There was an advantage to stability, after all, to having a society safe from disruption from cretins like these. An advantage to a pressure-relief valve. When you had unruly children, you sent them to a time-out corner. Was this continent any different? Even sending *him* here, he realized, had opened his eyes. There was a method to their madness.

But it rankled Ico that Raven didn't trust him. Like Dyson hadn't trusted him. When they stopped at a stream to water their horses he approached her.

"Raven, I didn't want to go to Rugard," he tried to justify. "I didn't want to leave *you* behind. I just wanted to go too. I *needed* to go, as the one best able to understand the political situation back home. If the rest of you hadn't run away from the compound we could have worked something out, I know it. I tried to reason with Tucker, but he wouldn't listen either. None of this violence was necessary."

"Yes it was," she replied.

He looked at her in frustration.

"Because I was going to leave *you* behind. I'm not your friend, Ico. You're just a means to an end."

"To get away."

"To save Daniel. Rugard would have killed him easily and he would have died for nothing."

"You did it to get away."

She didn't answer. Didn't want to. Because in the end

her loyalty was stronger to United Corporations than to the man who'd fallen for her. Dyson was a fool. She wasn't *that* beautiful.

The disappearance of Raven and Rugard hit the warring groups hard. All that blood and then they'd been abandoned in Australia after all! Daniel had been prepared to die to end the fighting, but in the cool ruins of the morning's dawn he found he'd been condemned to a worse fate: abandonment by the woman he loved.

"She's trying to save you," Amaya reasoned. "That's the only way she would've gone with Rugard and Ico. You *know* that."

"I don't know it." His reply was hollow. He didn't know anything anymore. "That's what's so hard to accept. Why would she steal off like that without a word? I mean I felt I'd finally broken through to her. To leave me with no way to know . . ."

Amaya looked at him sadly. She didn't know why either. To slip away without a word or a message seemed a betrayal worse than taking the transmitter. Didn't Raven love at all? In the tumult of the last few months, Amaya's own life had changed profoundly. She'd found herself— a confidence in herself as a resourceful, valuable human being—and once she'd done that she'd found a man named Ethan she was beginning to love deeply. Would she leave *him* with no explanation? It would kill her if he left that way.

As for the transmitter, she was relieved it was finally gone, and with it all the trouble it had caused. She didn't need to get back. Not anymore.

* * *

Daniel's group came out of the office tower at mid-morning, their hands empty. Rugard's demoralized army met them the same way. With the transmitter gone, there was nothing to fight about. They gathered in the plaza.

"We're not getting back, are we?" one of the convicts asked plaintively.

"You've gotten back as far as you're going to go."

"Maybe we can catch them," Wrench said darkly. "Together."

"No," Daniel said. "They took horses, right? And I told you the truth. Only two can go on any rescue plane. Rugard misled you. You'd never have gotten out of Australia anyway."

The convict studied the office tower gloomily. "We've been fighting over nothing?"

"It always seems like something at the time. Now listen. We're marooned here, unless a miracle happens, but this is good country. My group is going to keep heading east until we reach the ocean. That's what we trekkers set out to do, and it's a kind of closure for us. It won't get us back anymore, but we'll have gotten . . . someplace."

They looked pained and confused.

"Or we've always been there," said Amaya. "From the very beginning."

He nodded. "So now you have to decide. I don't care what your past was. I don't care what we did to each other last night. You can join us, if you care to. If you behave. I expect we'll try to settle down somewhere and make a new community better than the ones we came from. We don't want anything from you, and we don't have anything *for* you. But if you're done fighting, so are we."

In the end about a dozen of Rugard's followers joined

Daniel, as well as the frightened women of the Cohort of Joy. The others drifted off, many of them dazed by their sudden freedom. Possibility! It was the most frightening thing about the wilderness.

Wrench took him aside. "Look," he confessed, "I don't know much except fighting. Can I come with you anyway?"

Daniel looked him up and down. "To do what?"

"I'm strong. I can work."

Daniel sighed, debating. This man looked like an animal, and he remembered him from the dam. "If you come with us, Wrench, you have to be civilized. You have to follow the rules. Can you do that?"

"What rules?"

"I don't know. We'll have to make some." He winced at his own words.

The trio stopped at a grassy ridge about thirty miles east of Gleneden. In the distance was the glimmer of the sea.

Rugard pointed at Raven. "Can you make it work from here?"

"I hope."

"Then get to it. I'm late for my appointment with a soaking tub, two Asian whores, and a bottle of scotch."

"You're quite the man of refinement, Warden," Ico remarked.

"I'm quite the man of fucking appetites." Lord, he was tired of having to be polite to these two! Just a few more hours. If the bitch thought he'd forgotten her treachery then she had quite the education coming. She'd be getting off the hover with *him*, at a place of *his* choosing. And then he'd begin to teach her how to beg.

The weasel he'd simply destroy.

It was late afternoon by now, the light golden. She took the two pieces of the transmitter and united them swiftly this time, using the electronic supplies that Ico had safeguarded across the breadth of Australia. Then they sat regarding it for a moment, all their hopes on two linked boxes of battered metal. Would the batteries still work? Would anyone even listen?

She switched it on.

It pulsed as before, but this time its digital readout displayed their geographic coordinates. It could read the Global Positioning System satellites overhead. The electronic fog had lifted!

"It's penetrating the Cone," she reported. "It can send and receive. If I had the right equipment I could phone my parents. I could receive some news. We're back, in a way."

Rugard looked sourly out from the ridge to the hills along the coast. In the distance were the ruins of another town, glimmering and decayed. "Not yet. We're still in a fucking graveyard."

"What do we do now?" Ico said.

"We wait," she said. "We're a thousand miles from where they expected to get this signal. I have no idea how they'll react to it. Or how long it will take."

"What if it doesn't come?"

Rugard snorted. "Then I cut out your little weasel heart. Before our ex-friends catch up with us and cut out ours."

It took eleven hours. The rescue craft came in at the end of a long night, lightless and with a low whine, dropping from the heavens like a spaceship or angel. They were only certain it was there when a stabbing spotlight painted the ridge with illumination.

Raven stood in the glare. "Get ready!" Ico and Rugard began circling around, outside the cone of light.

The craft slipped in closer, the grass flattening down beneath its blowers and shuddering from the exhaust. How many other hovers were also dropping down across Australia this night, depositing fresh groups of eager Outback Adventurers and sullen, frightened convicts?

The rear cockpit door swung open and she ran for it.

"What the hell are you doing *here?*" the pilot barked at her.

"I had some problems. It's quite a story."

"The beacon—you have both parts?" A light was in her eyes as he scanned her identity picture. She wondered how close to it she still looked. More like a wild woman now, she supposed. A wilderness woman.

She nodded and pointed. "Back there, in the grass."

"You know we can't leave that crap here! Go get it! Now, now, move!" He glanced around nervously. They hated to touch down in this place.

She sprinted back, trusting their eyes would hold on her form as she did so. That gave enough time. Rugard and Ico rushed the hover from the other side, and before the pilots could react the convict was on top of them, his knife at the co-pilot's throat.

"They held the gate for us," Rugard cooed. "Aren't you going to say 'welcome aboard'?"

Ico crawled past him and began hunting for a seat belt to snap himself in.

Raven came running back and threw the transmitter and activator on board.

"Who are these guys?" the pilot asked.

"The ones you're taking back."

"There's not *room* for three. Can't you see that?"

"Indeed I can," Rugard agreed. "You friend here is getting off." He pulled the knife tighter to the co-pilot's throat and began to half haul him out of the aircraft. The man's hand drifted and the knife cut into flesh. "You reach for that gun again," Rugard hissed to his victim, "and you'll deplane dead."

"Let him go," Raven said.

"He's in your spot, bitch."

"No he isn't. I'm staying here."

The men turned to look at her.

"You two go on. Ico, do what you think best when you get back."

"Are you crazy?" Ico protested. "This is the only ticket home!"

"I don't want to go back. And I don't want the transmitter, either. It's caused nothing but trouble. I'm staying in Australia."

"But *why?*"

She smiled then, a secret smile to herself. "When I went outside, I found my inside," she explained softly. "I'm in love. With a man. With a place. And maybe, someday, with myself."

There was a dead silence. Rugard stared at her in disbelief. She'd give up the world to stay with a loser like Dyson? He broke into a harsh laugh. "You're choosing squalor?"

"I sent people here, and I've sent enough. It's time to see what it was I was trying to send them to."

"To hell!" Ico cried.

She just smiled at him. "Goodbye, Ico."

The men looked at each other, then shrugged. Rugard

confiscated the co-pilot's gun, took his knife away from the man's throat, and shoved him back into place. Then he settled into the seat behind him. "Fine. What do I care?" The bitch was getting away again, but so what? Staying in the wilderness was a worse fate than anything he could devise for her. She'd suffer a lifetime. "You're welcome to it."

"This man," Raven told the pilots, pointing to Ico, "is my designated successor and replacement. He can tell my superiors everything I can about conditions here. Probably more. He's earned the right to get back. Do you understand?"

Slowly, they nodded.

"Be careful of the other one," she said. "He has a temper."

"Damn right I do."

Then, before anyone could change their mind, she ran from the rescue craft and vanished in the bush like an extinguished spark. The hover lights switched off and the craft began rising into the sky.

"Stay off the com," Rugard told the pilots. "If you need to talk, you can chat with me."

Raven looked up at the hover's shadow wheeling away across the stars, and gulped. *I'm trying to lose my way,* she'd once told Daniel. It had seemed like a clever line at the time. Now it was simply true.

Then she walked back down the ridge to find her way with the man she loved.

The hover swung out over a glittering sea and followed a road of moonlight. The illumination was so bright they could see the dark pattern of huge reefs below, the water sparkling with luminescence.

"Where are we going?" Ico asked.

"To a recovery ship offshore," the pilot replied.

"No we're not," said Rugard. He tapped the pilot's shoulder with the gun. "Set a course for Jakarta. There's a lot of islands in Indonesia a man can get lost in."

"They'll be suspicious if we turn off course," the pilot warned.

"Then go down to wave level and get off their fucking radar, you moron." He grinned. "This is your captain speaking."

They descended to skim the sea surface as they flew north, spray speckling the hover canopy. Rugard sat back more easily, the knife in one hand and the gun in the other. He'd done it! He was getting back! He'd slipped out of the toughest cage they'd devised for him yet, and he had a lot of plans to make up for lost time. "See how easy life is when you just *take* what you want?" he told Ico. "And after that little spell of Purgatory, I've got a lot of taking to do. A *lot* of taking, indeed!"

"You're a moral-impaired, aren't you?" the pilot accused.

"I am the fucking face of pure evil, my friend! Your worst nightmare, sitting just one row behind you! That's why I *say*, and you *do!*"

"You got that right." The pilot's hand had drifted to an armrest console. Now a finger extended, and before Ico could open his mouth to ask why, there was a bang, a howling hiss, and Rugard was gone.

Ico was stunned, slammed aside so hard that the wind had been knocked out of him. Rugard Sloan and his flight chair had been shot out of the aircraft with a small explosion, moist tropic air now roaring into the emptiness where the convict had sat a moment before. Later, much later, Ico would remember he'd heard a trailing scream. But maybe that was just his imagination.

Certainly there was an impressive splash where the convict hit the ocean, twenty miles from the Australian coast.

The hover canopy snapped back down and the shriek of wind was shut out. They banked. "Some of the biggest sharks in the world down there," the pilot commented. "Of course he might never come conscious enough to notice, since his chute didn't have time to deploy."

Ico sat as if made of stone, his arm bruised from where the adjacent chair had erupted upward. The emptiness of the space it had occupied felt like an abyss.

"These Q-180s all have ejection seats," the co-pilot added. "Of course, a smart boy like you probably knew that, didn't you?"

Ico opened his mouth but could say nothing. His bowels felt like water. He was waiting to be fired out into space. Had Raven known?

"Now," the pilot continued in a drawl, "where was it *you* wanted to go?"

"Where . . . wherever you take me," Ico stammered.

"That's what I thought." And the craft set a steady course to the east.

CHAPTER THIRTY

"What do you miss most?" Daniel asked his wife.

Raven was showing now, swelling like a ripe melon, but they still came for daily walks. They followed a grassy ridge above the watered valley where the group had finally settled. To the east the sea glittered, to the west blue mountains loomed. It was such soft land after the desert. A place kissed by rain.

"Who says I miss anything?" She sat on a rock, sighing contentedly and feeling her unfamiliar roundness. She wasn't really tired but she stopped more frequently now for the baby, making sure the new Australian inside her had time to absorb the country as she was doing. She could see the new wood of their cabin in the glade below, and a wisp of smoke from the forge where Wrench, improbably content, was developing a new skill refashioning salvaged metal. She was alive and in love, if a little breathless. The climate was good and the potential of this place boundless. "I don't," she replied simply.

"Come on, you know you do. We all do."

"All right, what do *you* miss?"

He considered, looking down at their new village. Domestic animals gone wild had been captured to start new herds, and overgrown fields had been recleared for new crops. They'd been unanimous in agreeing to not settle in the sad ruins of an abandoned city, choosing this new site instead. But they made frequent trips "to town" to salvage the fundamentals of survival. Windmills turned lazily and a waterwheel spun with tireless regularity. They had a crude dynamo and lights now. The pooling of skills had lifted them out of the Stone Age rather rapidly, and they lived better than most people of just a couple centuries ago. They were already planning a school, and children to fill it.

"I miss knowing," he reflected. In the months since Ico and Rugard had disappeared there'd been no sign that anyone knew of their exile. Sometimes they spied flashes of light high in the sky and wondered if there were aircraft or surveillance drones far overhead. If so, they were as remote as heaven. Periodically another exhausted adventurer would stagger in from the west, a refugee from Outback Adventure, recounting a familiar struggle for survival. Nothing seemed to have changed. Their isolation continued.

"I like the work I do now," Daniel went on. "Build this, grow that. The payoff is tangible and it seems honest. And I don't miss the entertainment of the old world. It's like a blinding noise has fallen away that's allowed me to see. I like our *new* stories, told around the fire, and our walks, and our long, slow meals. I like knowing people again, knowing them deeply—even their faults. My friendships are deeper here. I like belonging to this place."

"Me too, Daniel."

"I miss the obvious things," he admitted. "The lack of medical expertise, for instance. We're young and healthy now, but what if we really stay here all our lives? I worry about the pregnancy."

She shrugged. "Women had babies without doctors for a long time. I'm not afraid."

"I should miss the art and science, I suppose, but I don't. It didn't mean anything to me in the life before. I should miss the stores, but I like making things for myself. It's more satisfying than buying. I should miss ideas, but we're finding old books and now I have time to read them. I feel healthier than I ever have, since we walk everywhere. It would be nice to flip a switch once in a while, but since there are no switches—no one else has them either—I don't even really miss that. All that I've lost has been filled up with other things: the land, the animals, the friends. You."

"So why did you even ask the question?"

He sat on the grass beside her. "I still feel guilty, I suppose, that you didn't go."

"Guilty! You weren't even there!"

"Guilty that I was so irresistible that you couldn't bear to leave me."

She laughed. "Oh, please!"

"Guilty that I couldn't give you a proper ring. Find us a proper church. See you in a proper dress."

She shook her head. "I don't miss any of those things. I miss . . ." She pondered for a minute. "Chocolate."

He nodded. "Okay. There's one."

"Coffee," she went on.

"Ouch. I remember that."

"Perfume. Ice cream. Toilet paper. Aspirin. Magazines. Music—symphonic music. Refrigeration. A laundry. Immunizations. New underwear. A flush toilet." She looked at him mischievously.

"Okay, enough already! We're working on some of those things," he added defensively.

"I know. And I don't *really* miss them, Daniel. I mean, if I had to choose between them and this place, or maybe I should say that time and this time . . . I thought I'd desperately miss them when I was back in that world, and even when I first came to this one. I *did* miss them. But they were just things, not happiness, and somehow the need for them has subsided. I'd miss my old sense of belonging to my company but instead I belong here: people have been very kind, after what I've done. I'm astonished at what I don't miss."

"Sometimes I miss the trek," he said. "When it was just the four of us. It's easier now and more secure but when you add all these people . . . that meeting last night!"

She laughed. There'd been an argument about sanitation. More rules. Daniel had been trying to back away from his role as de facto mayor, but Ethan wanted a charter.

"Sometimes I miss *you*," she said. "When the others demand so much of your time."

"I don't want to be sucked in by that. I want a balance."

"And sometimes I miss not knowing, like you."

"I wonder how we'd react if we did know? If we still had a choice?"

They sat there, soaking up the sun. And then a black-clothed figure emerged from the edge of a wood and walked slowly toward them, his palms upraised and empty, his eyes cautiously watching. He stopped a few feet from them.

"I've been listening," said Elliott Coyle.

He was stylishly dressed as before, his kangaroo pin a point of contrasting brightness. There was a directional cone at his belt to eavesdrop on conversations but otherwise he carried nothing. Coyle regarded them with calm purpose, a half smile on his lips. Like a creature from a dream. Or the end of one.

"Hello, Daniel. Raven. It's been a long time."

They stared at the Outback Adventure counselor in shock. Coyle stood without apology or surprise, as if this reunion should, after all, have been expected. He studied them curiously as if they were the oddity, not him. "You're looking well, I see."

They were speechless.

"It's true what they say. About motherhood making you glow."

Daniel felt irritated at that, feeling the observation from this man who'd helped put them here was presumptuous. He opened his mouth to retort but Raven put her hand on his arm. "What are you *doing* here?" she asked instead.

"We've been watching you. Monitoring your progress. Even logging your daily walks. I had a hover set down last night and I've been waiting for you. I'm sorry about the spying, but I wanted to approach at a proper time. You're in a reflective mood today, so my timing is impeccable."

"Timing for what?" she asked.

"I've come to bring you back." As if the answer was obvious.

"What?"

"Your adventure is over. You've passed."

They looked at him as if he was crazy.

"We didn't lie to you. Exodus Port exists but just not in the way you expected. When you're ready we come get you. When we judge it's time."

"Is this some kind of joke?"

"It's no joke, Daniel. We told you it would be the toughest test on the face of the earth. Very few pass it. You two have. It's time to come back to United Corporations with me." He nodded reassuringly. "Ico is waiting."

"You're taking us all back?" Raven tried to clarify.

"Not all of you, not yet. Just you two for now. A few more, maybe, when they're ready. When they've developed the skills needed to contribute to the United Corporations world."

They looked at him blankly, awash in so many conflicting emotions that they didn't know how to respond. "How did you first find us?" Daniel finally asked.

"Ico, of course. He told us where to look."

"So he made it."

"Yes, he made it." He waited for the next question.

"And Rugard Sloan . . . ?" Raven asked.

"Did not."

"And now we're to trust you?"

Coyle glanced up at the sky. "Surveillance data helped pin your position and progress. It's quite impressive, frankly. Your little group is outside all theoretical parameters for this point in time. You two have exceeded all projections. You've become a leader, Daniel! An organization man after all! So it's time to leave the land of the losers and come back to modern life. Time to abandon the past for the future."

"Like you," Daniel said.

Coyle nodded. "Yes. Like me."

"Come back to the companies that cooked up this monstrous hoax. That marooned us here. That let people die like flies. Come back with *you*."

"Come back like I came back," Coyle replied softly. "Angry. Smart. Transformed. Don't you think I felt the same way as you do now? I was building a boat to float off when they finally offered me Exodus. I was furious. I wanted to expose everything. But when I thought about it, when I talked it over with them and let all my frustration pour out, I realized I was really angry at *myself*. For being blind so long about me, this place, and what was best for the wider world. Outback Adventure didn't lie to you two. Not really. We told you which way to go. We told you it would be hard, and dangerous. We told you what you needed to survive, and told you *only* enough to make you appreciate the value of civilized society. The only trick was that you didn't escape *to* a refuge, you *left* it. Eden is back there, with me! With United Corporations! Where all your needs are taken care of by machines! Where life is the easiest it's ever been! *That's* the lesson of this nightmare. That United Corporations doesn't just work—that it's *vital*. It needs to be protected. Australia protects it. *I* protect it. Just like the centurions once protected Rome."

"No," Daniel said slowly. "What you do is murder."

"What we *do* is give people what they *want*. We make clear the danger in that. The wilderness is a hard lesson. So the few with a knack for survival and organization are taken back. Always."

"What if they don't want to come?"

"That's not really an option. If we left you here, you'd

corrupt the wilderness. Australia is a home for social misfits, not a breeding ground for would-be pioneers. You've come through the plagues of disorder, Daniel. It's time for Exodus."

"And the price home?"

"There's a few confidentiality forms to sign. Ico did. A discussion of how your new talents might best be used. In return, you win an important, prestigious life. More money than you dreamed, and as much responsibility as you can handle. We're really quite a remarkable fraternity. Let me be the first to congratulate you." He waited.

Daniel glanced at Raven, the gentle swelling of her breasts and abdomen. It would be easier to go back. Boring, perhaps, but safer and more comfortable. Their child nursed and schooled. Their child raised to be—

"No," Raven said. "We're not coming back with you, Elliott."

He shrugged. "That's a common early reaction."

"We're not coming back with you because you're not from some kind of technological heaven, you're from an oppressive social hell," she went on calmly. "It was a place I believed in with all my heart but it *required* my heart. It devoured and froze it. It left me wedded to stability instead of possibility, and tore me in half. You're a demon, Elliott, on a devil's mission. You've got the blood of a thousand people on your hands. Ten thousand! I've seen them. I've seen the *bones.* You're a corporate monster, a robot with no soul, and I want my baby as far away from you, and your kind, as he or she can be. I *despise* United Corporations!"

Coyle had taken a step back at this assault. "That's not fair," he objected, raising his hands. "Do you think that campground of yours over the hill is in any way realistic? Do you think twelve billion people can live like—"

"We can live like this," Daniel interrupted quietly. "We earned the right, by coming here and surviving here. You gave us that right by sending us here. We want to make a new society. And already it's more real, more satisfying, than anything *your* world has to offer."

"No." Coyle shook his head. "No, no, no. I'm sure your hamlet is . . . quaint," he conceded, the condescension plain. "But can't you see the irony here? You're not wandering. You're not nomads. You're not some kind of new human, reborn into some kind of grace. You're settling. You're becoming *us*. By building your new civilization—by doing what comes naturally to our species—you're setting out to destroy the very wilderness you came here for! You can't escape human nature, Daniel. You can't escape your own instincts. By building your village you're just starting down the road to another United Corporations world, except with more dirt and disease along the way. History will simply repeat itself. It's inevitable! Cut the pain short, and come with me."

"It's not inevitable. We're going to strike a balance and make a better world. We've learned from your mistakes."

"That's not what history teaches. It's an endless wheel of mistakes. Until now."

"Until here. The other thing our species does is *learn*."

Their counselor's look grew impatient. "If we have to, we can destroy you," he warned.

"No you can't," Raven replied. "If you come we'll go back into the bush until you go away. If you try to hunt us down your secret can't be kept from the thousands of soldiers it would take to prosecute such a war. And even if you did destroy us it would only prove how phony and bankrupt all your pretensions about this place are. Come after *us*, Elliott, and the truth about this place will pull your pyramids down around your ears. It's *your* society that's fragile, that can't tolerate questions or challenge, that has to fear its own best people and turn its back on its worst. So if you try to harm us it will ultimately be *we* who destroy *you*. Leave us alone: as a secret, a rumor, a myth. We want nothing from your world."

"You can't survive in the long run! It's impossible!"

"People survived here for fifty thousand years."

"I don't want you wasted!"

"Then stop sacrificing people here! Cultivate your so-called misfits before your civilization fossilizes! Because if you don't use them, we will, in our new society. And because of that, we're your only hope." She looked at him evenly.

Coyle's mouth was a line. "United Corporations has no need for your hope."

"Goodbye, Elliott." Raven took Daniel's hand, squeezed it, and, turning, began walking away.

Their counselor stood rigid, looking after them.

"Are you okay?" Daniel asked her, glancing back at the man in black.

She nodded, glancing up at the sunlight filtered by the trees. "Very okay."

"It's the opportunity of a lifetime!"

Ico Washington shook the candidate's hand reassuringly, smiled confidently, and saw himself, what he had once been, in the Outback Adventure client's eyes. Unhappy, suspicious, anxious, hopeful, vain. They were all like that, the young men and women who came through his door. Walking time bombs of dissatisfaction. They would go, and learn, and come back.

Or not.

There was always doubt, of course. These were people filled with doubt. So if you could never decide for them—that was against the rules, to push too hard—it was necessary to reassure. "It's the perfect experience for a dynamic, independent individual like you," he recited. "A win-win opportunity for everyone. It changed my life. I'm sure it will yours."

It was so easy. Just tell the truth.

The recruit left, liberated as always by the drastic decision and the vacuuming of his savings. Ico stood from his desk and stretched, looking out the tinted glass window. The city ran to the horizon, a chessboard of light as dusk fell, the office towers the board's strategic pieces. Ten millennia of human thought had created this. It was the apex of civilized achievement, and he its unsung defender.

Finally, he had a job he succeeded in.

Ico looked at the glow of corporate names, the tracery of lasers, the streams of homeward traffic. The city throbbed with the reassurance of ten million human hearts. He saw it differently since he'd come back. Saw what it all was for.

So strange, then, that Daniel and Raven had stayed.

Their decision troubled him. He'd thought of contacting the cyber underground, of course, but on reflection thought better of it. It would become another rumor of losers, and people wouldn't understand. It would change nothing, or ruin everything. So he'd done for Daniel and Raven what he could: more than they'd ever done for him! Told of their progress, urged their rescue. Coyle had gone himself and come back moody and irritable. The pair had sent him away!

He thought he'd known them better than that. What had the whole trip been about, if not getting back?

As he looked out he saw his own reflection in the glass. His tan fading now, his body a little softer. But a different confidence, surely. He'd done the right thing, hadn't he?

For a moment he saw in the glow of the city lights the red dust of Australia, and he recalled the snow-white trunks of the twisting ghost gums. The unreal clarity of it. A strange, strange place. His nightmares of it were of hot sand and relentless pursuit, so sometimes, after jerking awake in his vast, soft bed—the shadows of his condominium looming and the drumming of the city a mutter beyond his thick walls—he'd try to remember the sound of the birds. So many birds! But they wouldn't come to him.

Just as well.

He wondered, for the thousandth time, if Virus 03.1 had really been an accident.

Then Ico sat at his console, clicked up his schedule, and glanced at his watch. The one he'd worn to the wilderness.

"Your next appointment is here, Mr. Washington."

More
William Dietrich!

Please turn this page
for a
bonus excerpt
from

DARK WINTER

a new
Warner Book
available wherever
books are sold.

Sometimes you have to go into nothing to get what you want.

That was the Jed Lewis theory, anyway. West Texas oil patch, Saudi, the North Slope. Hadn't worked for him yet, but one kind of extreme had led to another, one kind of quest to its polar opposite. Sometimes life patterns like that, when you keep changing your mind about what it is you *do* want. So now he'd come to the very end of the world and was peering over its edge, too late to turn back, hoping that in the farthest place on Earth he'd finally fit in. Atone to himself for his own confusion of purpose. Belong.

Maybe.

"The Pole!" Jim Sparco had seduced him. "Feels closer to the stars than anyplace on Earth. It's high desert, a desert of ice, and the air's so dry that it feels like you can eat the stars. Bites of candy." The climatologist had gripped his arm. "The South Pole, Lewis. It's there you realize how cold the Universe really is."

The money had almost been secondary. They'd understood each other, Sparco and he, this longing for the desolate places. A place uncomplicated. Pure.

Except for their rock, of course. That raised questions. It was their pebble, their tumor, their apple.

The world is round but it has an edge. A cold crustal wrinkle called the Trans-Antarctic Range runs for more than a thousand miles and divides Antarctica in two. On the north side of the mountains is a haunting but recognizable landscape of glacier and mountain and frozen ocean: an ice age world, yes, but still a world—our world. To its south, toward the Pole, is an ice cap so deep and vast and empty as to seem unformed and unimagined. A vacuum, a blank. The white clay of God.

Lewis crossed in the sinking light of Antarctic autumn. He was exhausted from thirty hours of flying, constricted by thirty-five pounds of polar clothing, and weary of the noisy dimness of the LC- 130 military transport plane, its webbed seats pinching circulation and its schizophrenic ventilation blowing hot and cold.

He was also entranced by beauty. The sun was slowly dipping toward a six-month night, and the aqua crevasses and sugared crags below were melodramatic with blaze and shadow. Golden photons, bouncing off virginal snow, created a hazed fire. Frozen seas looked like cracked porcelain. Unnamed peaks reared out of fogs thick as frosting, and glaciers grinned with splintery teeth attached to blue gums. It was all quite primeval, untrodden and unspoiled, a white board to redraw yourself. The kind of place where he could be whatever he made himself, whatever he announced himself, to be.

The Trans-Antarctic Range is like a dam, however, holding behind it a plateau of two-mile-thick polar ice like a police line braced against a pressing crowd. A hundred thousand years of accumulated snowfall! A few peaks at the edge of the ice plateau bravely poke their snouts up as if to tread water, but then, farther south, relief disappears altogether. The glaciers vanish. So do ridges, crevasses, and theatrical light. What follows is utter flatness, a frozen mesa as big as the contiguous United States. When the airplane crossed the mountains it entered something fundamentally different, Lewis realized. It was then that his excitement began to turn to disquiet.

Imagine an infinite sheet of paper. No, not infinite, because the curve of the Earth provides a kind of boundary. Except that the horizon itself is foggy and indistinct with floating ice crystals, suspended like diamond dust, so that the snow merges without definition into pale sky. There was nothing to see from the tiny scratched windows of the National Guard transport: no relief, no reference point, no imperfection. When he thought he saw undulations in the snow the load master informed him he was merely looking at the shadow of cirrus clouds far overhead. When he thought he saw a track across the snow— left by a tractor or snowmobile, perhaps—the load master pointed to a contrail being left by an outgoing transport. His track was the shadow across the sky of that dissipating streak.

Lewis moved among the pallets of cargo from window to window, waiting for something to happen. Nothing did. The plane lumbered on, cold slithering along its fuselage.

He checked his watch, as if it still meant anything in a place where the sun went haywire, and looked out again.

Nothing.

He looked out a different window. No movie would start on the blank screen below. No progress could be discerned. He searched a sky and plateau that seemed blank mirrors of each other, vainly searching for some rip, some imperfection, some reassurance that he was *someplace*.

Nothing.

He sat on his web seat and chewed a cold lunch.

After a drag of time the Guardsman cuffed his shoulder and Lewis stood again, looking where the sergeant pointed. Far away there was a pimple on the vastness. A tiny bug, a freckle, a period with a white runway attached to make a kind of exclamation mark. Amundsen-Scott Base! Named by Americans for the Norwegian who got there first in 1912, and the hard-luck Brit who froze to death weeks later after seconding at point zero. Lewis made out a bottle cap of a dome that sheltered the South Pole's central buildings and an orbit of smaller structures like specks of sand.

From the air the human settlement was remarkable only for its insignificance.

"The buildings fit in a circle about a mile wide, altogether!" the load master shouted to him over the roar of the engines. "Doesn't look like much, does it?"

Lewis didn't reply.

"You staying the winter?"

He shrugged.

"Glad it's you and not me!"

They buckled in, the snow seeming to swell up to meet them, his heart accelerating during that disquieting gap between air and ground, and then with a thump and a bang they were down, swerving slightly as the skis skidded on the ice. The plane shuddered as it taxied, continuing to vibrate when it stopped because the pilots didn't dare shut down the engines.

Lewis stood, stiff and apprehensive. He was the only passenger, the last arrival of the season. An antimigrant, swimming against the tide of humans fleeing north. Well, his timing had never been the best. The cargo ramp opened to a shriek of white, and the cold hit him like a slap. It was palpable, like a force you waded into.

"We had a fly stowaway from New Zealand one time!" the load master shouted, his military mustache almost brushing Lewis's ear. The propellers were still whirling so the hubs wouldn't freeze, and the National Guard sergeant needed this intimacy to be heard. "Buzzed like a bastard for three thousand miles! When we opened the doors it flew to the light and made it three feet! Three feet! Then the fucker dropped like a stone!" The man laughed.

Dizzy, Lewis walked out. He couldn't get a proper breath. There was a crowd of orange-parka people at the edge of the runway, waving but fidgety, anxious to get away. The last of the summer crew, going home. Snow from the prop wash blew over them, hazing them as if they were already being erased. Awkward from his duffel and enormous white-plastic polar boots, Lewis staggered toward the group in seeming supplication. A figure detached from the crowd to meet him. The man's hood was up and all Jed could see were goggles and frosted beard, framed by a ruff of fur. Lewis had been supplied the same government-issue parka. He'd been told it cost seven hundred dollars and a sacrificial fox.

"Jed Lewis?" It was a shout, above the noise.

A nod, his own goggles giving the Pole a piss-yellow tint.

The man reached, not to shake hands but to shoulder the duffel. He turned to the others. "Let's move, people! Let's get this cargo off so you can all go home!" His goggles rotated across their rank, taking mental roll. "Where's Tyson?"

There was a long moment of silence, goggled heads turning, a few smiles of unease and amusement. In their cold-weather gear everyone looked alike except for strips on their coats with block-letter name tags.

"Sulking!" someone finally called.

Jed's greeter stiffened. There was another silence beneath the drum of the engines, someone shrugging, his guide sucking in an unhappy breath. "Well, someone go the hell and find him and tell him to get the damn sled up here so we can get this plane off! He's got eight long months to sulk!"

The others shifted uncomfortably.

The man turned back to Lewis, not waiting to see if anyone followed his command. "This way!" They set off toward the central aluminum geodesic dome, half-buried by drifting snow, their pace briskly impatient. Lewis looked back, parts of the orange-clad group now breaking off to troop to the plane. Then ahead to the dome, an upended silver saucer, dramatic and odd, like surplused flotsam from a World's Fair. He'd read the dimensions: fifty-five feet high, a hundred and sixty-four feet in diameter. An American flag snapped at the top, its edge ragged, its gunshot stutter audible now above the idle of the plane. Streaks of snow dust curved across the top of the dome in neatly drawn parabolas.

Jed's nose hairs had already frozen. The cold ached in his lungs. His goggles were fogging up, and his cheeks felt numb. He'd only been outside a few minutes. It was worse than he expected.

They descended a snowy ramp to a dark, garage-sized entrance at the base of the dome, Lewis mincing in his Frankenstein-sized boots so he wouldn't fall and slide on his butt. His guide paused to wait for him and let their eyes adjust to the dimness inside the door.

Two cavelike corrugated-steel arches extended into gloom to his left and right. "BioMed and the fuel arch that way, generators and garage over here." Jed had a shadowy impression of walls and doors of plywood and steel, unpainted and utilitarian. Before he could peek into the arched tunnels he was led straight ahead. "The dome where we're quartered is this way."

The overturned bowl shielded the core of the South Pole base like a military helmet, keeping warmth-sucking wind and blowing snow off the metal boxes where people lived. Three of these boxcar-shaped structures, colored orange, sat on short stilts under its shelter. Since the base was built on snow, the powder didn't stop at the entrance but formed the dome floor, drifting over wooden crates and mounding against the orange housing units. Dirt and grease had colored the snow tan, like sand.

"It never melts," his guide said, scuffing at it. "The ambient temperature in here is fifty-one below."

Lewis tilted his head back. There was a hole at the top of the dome that let in pale light from a remote sky. The entire underside of the uninsulated structure was covered with steel gray icicles, pointing downward like a roof of nails. It was beautiful and forbidding at the same time.

"You didn't finish the roof."

"Ventilation."

Someone bumped Lewis, and he staggered to one side. It was another winter-over, rushing a crate of fresh fruit to the galley before it could harden in the cold. "Sorry! Freshies are like gold!" They followed the hurrying man to a freezerlike door and opened it for him. To get inside you pulled a metal rod sideways and tugged at a slab like a wall. Jed realized that the freezer wasn't *inside* here, it was the Outside: Anything not carried into the orange housing modules would turn hard as a brick. They followed the fruit bearer. There was a vestibule hung with parkas and beyond it a galley of bright fluorescent light, warmth, and the excited chatter of more people saying good-bye. Their duffels were heaped like sandbags. People were packed to go.

His guide let Jed's gear drop with a thud and pushed back his goggles and hood. "Rod Cameron. Station manager."

"Hi." Lewis tried to fix the face, but the men in their parkas looked alike. He had an impression of beard, chapped skin, and red raccoon lines where the goggles cut. Lewis was wondering about the absentee at the plane. "Someone not show up for work?"

Cameron frowned. He had a look of rugged self-confidence that came from coping with cold and administration, and a hint of strain for the same reason. The Pole wore on you. "Egos in kindergarten." He shook his head. "My job is to herd cats. And I'm having a bad day. We had a little alarm last night."

"Alarm?"

"The heat went off."

"Oh."

"We got it back on."

"Oh."

The station manager studied the newcomer. Jed still looked smooth, sandy-haired, and tanned, with the easy tautness of the recreational athlete.

It would pass.

"You got your file?"

Lewis dug in his duffel and fished out a worn manila envelope with employment forms, medical records, dental X rays and a list of the personal belongings he'd shipped to the Pole in advance of his own arrival. His new boss glanced inside, as if to confirm Jed's presence with paper, then put the folder under his arm. "I've got to go back outside to see this last plane off," Cameron said. "I'll show you around later, but right now it's best to just sit and drink."

Jed looked around the galley in confusion.

"I mean drink water. The altitude. You feel lousy, right? It's okay. Fingies are supposed to."

"Fingie?"

"F-N-G-I. Fucking New Guy on the Ice. That's you."

Lewis failed at a grin. "Latecomer."

"Just new. Everybody's a fingie at first. We know we're lucky to get you last minute like this. Jim Sparco e-mailed about you like the Second Coming."

"I needed a job."

"Yeah, he explained that. I think it's cool that you quit Big Oil." Cameron gave a nod of approval.

"That's me, man of principle." Lewis had a headache from the altitude.

"Course we need their shit to keep from freezing down here."

"Not from a wildlife refuge, you don't."

"And you just walked out."

"They weren't about to give me a helicopter ride."

"That took some guts."

"It had to be done."

Cameron tried to assess the new man. Lewis looked tired, disoriented, chest rising and falling, half-excited and half-afraid. They all started like that. The station manager turned back to the door, impatient to get away, and considered whether to say anything else. "I've got to go get the plane off," he finally said again. "You know what that means, don't you?"

"What?"

"That you can't quit, down here."

A stream of people followed Cameron out, some looking at Lewis curiously and others ignoring him: the winter-overs going to off-load the supplies and the last from summer flying home. The Pole had a brief four-month window when weather permitted incoming flights, then in February the last plane left, fleeing north like a migrating bird. In winter it was too dark to see, too windy to keep the ice runway clear, and too cold to risk a landing: Struts could snap, hydraulics fail, doors fail to open or close. The sun set on March 21, the equinox, and wouldn't rise again until September 21. From February to October the base was as remote as the moon. There were twenty-six winter-overs who retreated under the dome to maintain its functions and take astronomical and weather readings: eight women and eighteen men this year. It was like being on a submarine or space station. You had to commit.

The galley had emptied, and Lewis took a place at a Formica table. The room was low-ceilinged, bright, and warm. A bulletin board was thick with paper, a juice dispenser burbled, and in the corner a television monitor displayed outside temperatures. It was fifty-eight below zero near the runway, the breeze lowering the windchill to minus eighty-one. The reading was an abstraction except for the freezer door he'd come through. That was old, and cold leaked around its edges to rime its inner face with frost. The frost reached all the way across it in stripes, like fingers. The pattern reminded Lewis of a giant hand, trying to yank the door away.

"Drink as much as you can. Best cure for the altitude."

Lewis looked up. It was the cook, bald except for a topknot that hung from the back of his head. His skull looked knobby, as if knocked around more than once, and he had a gray mustache and forearms tattooed with a bear and eagle. Here was somebody easy to remember.

"It doesn't look high."

"That's because it's flat. You're sitting on ice almost two miles thick. Our elevation is ninety-three hundred, and the thinning of the atmosphere at the Poles makes the effective altitude closer to eleven thousand. Walking out of that transport is like being dumped on the crest of the Rockies. Your body will adjust in a few days."

"I feel hammered." The short walk from the plane had made him ill.

"You'll be racing around the world before you know it."

"Around the world?"

"Around the stake that marks the Pole." He sat down. "Wade Pulaski. Chief cook and bottle washer. Best chef for nine hundred miles. I can't claim any farther because Cathy Costello back at McMurdo is pretty good, too." McMurdo was the main American base in Antarctica, located on the coast.

"Jedediah Lewis, polar weatherman." He shook.

"Jedediah? Your parents religious?"

"More like hippies, I think. When it was a fad."

"But it's biblical, right? You're a prophet?"

"Oracle of climate change by temporary opportunity. Rock hound by training. And it's actually just another name for Solomon. 'Beloved of the Lord.'"

"So you're wise."

His head was pounding. "I take my name as God's little joke."

"What do you mean by 'rock hound'?"

"Geologist. That's my real job."

"So you come to the one place on earth where there aren't any rocks? Doctor Bob will have a field day with that one."

"Who's Doctor Bob?"

"Our new shrink. NASA sent him down to do a head job on us before they plant too many people on the space station. He's wintering over to write us up while we fuck with each other's minds. He thinks we're all escapists."

Lewis smiled. "Rod Cameron just told me we can't quit."

"That's what I told Doctor Bob! It's like being paid to go to prison!"

"And yet we volunteered."

"I'm on my third season." Pulaski stretched out his arms in mock enthusiasm, as if to claim ownership. "I can't stay away. If the generators stop like they did last night, we've got maybe a few hours, but we always get them running again."

"Why'd they stop?"

"Some moron turned the wrong valve. Rod went ballistic, which meant nobody was in a mood to confess this morning. But it was a stupid annoyance, not a threat. And you're going to learn that as long as you don't freeze to death things are really good down here, especially now that the last of summer camp is leaving and the bureaucrats are ten thousand miles away. I give you better food than you'd get back home and there's no bullshit at the Pole. There's no clock to punch, no bills, no taxes, no traffic, no newspapers, no nothing. After today everything calms down, and this becomes the sanest place on earth. Cozier than most families. And after eight toasty months you come out with your head straight and your money saved. It's paradise, man."

Lewis reserved agreement. "You got any aspirin?"

"Sure." The cook got a bottle from the kitchen and brought it back. "You feel like shit right now, but you'll get better."

"I know."

"You even acclimate to the cold. A little."

"I know."

Pulaski went to the counter where food was passed. He bent under it to get a commissary-sized soup can, its label stripped and its inside cleaned to a bright copper. "Here, your arrival present."

"What's this for?" Lewis realized he felt stupid from the altitude.

"You'll drink all day and pee all night, this first night. It's your body adjusting to the cold and altitude. This can saves you about three hundred trips to the real can."

"A chamber pot?"

"Welcome to Planet Cueball, Fingie."

To read more, look for *Dark Winter* by William Dietrich